CW00456460

AN ASPEN COVE ROMANCE COLLECTION

BOOKS 2-3

KELLY COLLINS

BOOK NOOK PRESS

FOREWORD

You might be asking why didn't I include book one in this set, and that's an excellent question. I would have loved to put it in here, but I don't own the publishing rights to it. It was a Kindle Scout Winning book and Amazon currently owns the publishing rights which means I can't include it in the first boxset. I hope this helps clarify things. Enjoy Aspen Cove, where big things happen to normal people.

Live for love,

Kelly

KELLY COLLINS

ONE HUNDRED
Heartbeats

AN ASPEN COVE ROMANCE

Copyright © 2018 by Kelley Maestas
All rights reserved.
No part of this book may be reproduced in any form or by any electronic or
mechanical means, including information storage and retrieval systems, without
written permission from the author, except for the use of brief quotations in a book
review.

Cover design by Victoria Cooper Art

DEDICATION

To Jim, Nik, Alec, and Gabby. My heart beats for you.

CHAPTER ONE

There were three things Katie Middleton knew with absolute certainty:

Hope appeared in a pink envelope.

Prince charming rode a Harley.

Some secrets were better left unspoken.

Katie relaxed at her favorite table in the bakery—the one directly under the Wishing Wall—and checked items off her bucket list. It was unlike the list most people had with dreams like climbing Mount Kilimanjaro, running a marathon, or writing a book. Her list had the simple things she had never done, like flying a kite, rowing a boat, and baking a muffin.

Katie's life had been full of wishes for as long as she could remember, most of which had never materialized, so when she got a pink envelope with the deed to a bakery inside, she packed up her stuff and moved from Dallas, Texas, to Aspen Cove, Colorado.

It came as a shock to her family and friends when she disappeared without a word to a location she hadn't shared. She refused to allow anyone else to have control over her life. Illness had been her jailer—her parents, her parole officers. She scribbled the word "independence" at the bottom of her list. Katie knew her happiness would come from within. Family was great. Friends were fabulous. But to feel truly independent, she needed to be the helper, not the helped. Wasn't it ironic that the most generous help she had received came from a stranger? It was a gift that allowed her to bury her past and become her future.

"Why me, Bea?"

Her voice echoed off the walls of the empty bakery. It was a question she'd asked herself countless times over the last seven weeks. Why would a woman whom she'd never met give her a bakery in a town she'd never been to?

Katie flipped to the back of her journal, where a piece of worn pink stationery sat tucked close to the binding. The tri-folded paper had been opened and closed hundreds of times. She'd read every line, looking for clues. There was a list of one hundred reasons Bea gave the bakery to Katie, but not one made sense.

You have a good heart, it began, but how did she know? That might have been the biggest clue because it sat at the number one position, but it didn't lead Katie to anything conclusive. *You're a good person* was the second entry. Although Katie tried to give more than she took, she didn't consider herself any more deserving than the next person. She'd logged hundreds of volunteer hours in the pediatric cardiac unit in Dallas, but it never felt like work, and she didn't do it for any reason other than to bring a smile to those around her. Was that what Bea meant when she wrote reason number one?

Katie scrolled down the list:

Joyful to be around.

Pretty smile.

Resilient.

"How do you know?" she asked.

Part of her glowed under the positive accolades. The other part couldn't grasp how this woman knew her. Had Bea stalked her or had her followed? For what purpose? That was the million-dollar question.

Katie looked around the bakery. It wasn't a million-dollar property, but it was something special. Where the pinstriped wallpaper once hung, there was a fresh coat of paint the exact color of soft butter. On the walls were pictures of the muffins she had baked. Photos of the seven daily specials hung in a row.

Behind the counter was the new coffeepot she'd purchased. It wasn't the espresso machine her friend Sage had suggested, but it was better than the percolator that once sat spitting and sputtering on the Formica surface.

No, this place wasn't worth a million dollars. It was worth more because it had changed Katie's life.

In the end, it didn't matter why the older woman had given her the gift. All that mattered was what Katie did with it.

She tucked the pink page back into her notebook, then flipped back to her bucket list and wrote things that came to mind:

Ride a roller coaster.

Meet a celebrity.

Cut down my own Christmas tree.

Fall in love.

Her number one priority was never to overlook an opportunity to try something new.

While Katie continued to jot down notes, she saw a flash of red out of the corner of her eye. Her friend Sage had hopped out of her SUV near Bishop's Brewhouse and headed her way. Her corkscrew red curls bounced with every step.

The bell above the bakery door rang as Sage skipped inside. From her bright smile to her rosy cheeks, she glowed from her happy life with Cannon. Katie couldn't believe only seven weeks ago, Sage had a black eye and an unquenchable desire to flee Aspen Cove, but no one knew better than she did how life could turn on a dime. Good could become bad, and awful could become amazing in the time it took to take a breath.

"What's up?"

Katie rose from her seat to give Sage a hug. At five foot six, she looked like a giant compared to her pint-sized friend.

"Sheriff Cooper's friends are back at the bed and breakfast tomorrow, and the last time they were around, they ate everything but the furniture. Can I take what you have, or do you want to make me two dozen muffins?"

"I'll make them fresh and bring them to the bar tonight." Katie looked at what she had left in the display case. There were just over two dozen muffins remaining. She'd have to whip up another batch for the afternoon crowd anyway. "Is Cannon's brother still coming home tonight?"

"It's a go, as far as I know." Sage plucked a sample off the tray that sat on the glass counter and popped it into her mouth.

"That's great. I hope he follows through this time."

Cannon had been expecting his brother, Bowie for the last two weeks. Bowie had told him twice he was on his way then canceled the day he was due to arrive.

Katie imagined how difficult it would be to come back to the town where both his mother and fiancée had died. According to Doc Parker, it had been a decade since Bowie had been home. Wasn't it time to bury the past like Katie did when she left Dallas?

Sage's bright-green eyes lit up. "Hey, I know cakes aren't your thing ... yet, but maybe you can bake a welcome home cake for Bowie."

When Katie showed up in Aspen Cove, she barely knew how to boil water. Now she made the best muffins in town. They were the *only* muffins in town, but still ...

"I've never made a cake."

Sage cocked her head to the side. "Never? Not even from a mix out of a box?"

"I lived a very sheltered life. Ovens were hot and dangerous."

From the age of thirteen on, Katie had been sickly. Her mother stuck to her like lint on fabric, hovering over her like an aseptic balloon, warding off everything that could set Katie's health back or place her in danger.

"Unbelievable. Even *I've* made a cake. Although I'm most famous for my reheating skills."

"'Famous' isn't the word I'd reach for. That makes it sound pleasant. 'Notorious' is more like it."

Sage laughed as she rounded the corner to get herself a cup of coffee.

Katie had a rule with her friends. If she'd served them a cup at least once, then they were family and could help themselves. However, if a stranger walked behind the display case, she would have nudged them out with a rolling pin. She'd consider a baking pan to the side of the head if they caused her trouble.

"We can't all be Betty Crocker," Sage said.

She followed her friend to the other side of the counter and prepped her new coffeemaker for a cup of decaf. Sage liked her coffee laced with electricity, whereas Katie chose the heart-healthy option of decaffeinated.

Sage looked at the coffee dripping into the cup. "I don't know why you bother drinking that. It's dirty water." She lifted her own octane-filled cup to her lips.

"It makes me feel grown-up without hurting my organs." Katie placed her hand on her chest. Under the cotton, she felt the raised scar tissue from her surgery.

"I'm a nurse, and I don't take care of myself as well as you do."

"You have to take care of the body you've got."

Katie had told no one about her medical history. She'd kept it a secret because she didn't want people hovering over her. For once, she wanted to live her life like everyone else. Her anonymity in Aspen Cove had given her that. What no one knew couldn't hurt her or influence how they perceived or treated her.

"What about the cake? Are you up for the challenge?"

Katie looked over the counter at her journal, which was sitting open on the table. This instance fit the bill as a new opportunity. How hard could making a cake from scratch be?

"I'll do it. What flavor?"

"Let's keep it simple. White cake and white frosting."

"You want frosting, too?" she teased.

Sage shook her head. Katie had seen that incredulous look before on Sage's face. It was the one that screamed, *You're kidding, right?*

"Without frosting, cake is just flavored bread."

"Fine, frosting, too." She pulled her cup from the coffeemaker and took a sip. "What are Ben and Cannon doing today?"

The two women leaned against the counter and looked out the window. What once was a ghost town had new life. It experienced a rebirth every year in May when the tourists and fishermen showed up. The once whitewashed windows of the closed dry goods store across the street were cleaned and now sparkled under the afternoon sun. It turned out that from May to October, the women of Aspen Cove brought their wares to town to sell to the visitors. They offered everything from soy candles to beeswax soap.

"They're at the cemetery. The new grave marker for the Bennett's is being set up today. It has Bill's, Bea's, and Brandy's names carved in granite. Bowie will eventually visit to say goodbye to Brandy, so Cannon wanted it to be perfect."

Katie had been to the gravesite that had only a temporary marker with Bennett painted in block letters. It broke her heart that this little town had lost so much.

"At least Bowie's not coming home to a drunk father," Katie said. Ben had sobered up and stepped back into the roles of father

9

and friend. "He's been a lifesaver here. Without him, I'd be working seven days a week." Katie kept him busy at the bakery. She'd taught him how to make the weekend muffins, which gave her some much-needed time off.

"That's a blessing, for sure." Sage snatched another muffin bite from the sample plate. "I'm not sure how Bowie will acclimate to being back in town. He never wanted to return after Brandy died. He's been tight-lipped about what happened to him in Afghanistan, but he was medically retired from the United States Army, so it can't be good. It's one thing to come back home because he wants to, another if he's back because he has no choice."

"That's so sad, an injury added to a broken heart." Katie imagined both would require recovery time, but she never considered it would take so long to adjust. "You'd think all those years would be plenty of time to get past the grief and move on. Ben did, so I hope his son can, too."

Katie had no earthly idea how long it took to get over losing the love of one's life. She'd never been in love, but she'd added it to her bucket list.

Sage drank the rest of her coffee and tossed the paper cup in the nearby garbage can. "Who knows how long that takes? Everyone works at a different pace."

"Speaking of pace." Katie needed time to figure out how to make a cake. She looked at the muffins in the case. With Ben gone for the day, she was on her own. "You know what? If I'm going to make that cake, I better get to it." She opened the display case and boxed up the remaining muffins. "On second thought, why don't you take these? I think I'll close up early so I can do justice to Bowie's welcome-home cake." The least she could do was provide something sweet for a man, no doubt, filled with bitterness.

Sage gave her a sideways glance. "Are you sure? I've never known you to close early."

"You've known me for seven weeks."

"I think I've got a good handle on you."

What Katie wanted to say was, "You don't know me at all," but she didn't because that would open an entirely different dialogue. She wasn't ready to give up her secrets.

"Sometimes I don't think I know myself." She knew who she wanted to be, but there was a part of her that was a mystery. A part of her that had belonged to another—her heart.

Donors were kept anonymous, so Katie had been in the dark. Records were sealed. She'd thought Bea's daughter's heart might sit in her chest. The April day of her death fell eerily close to Katie's new chance at life, but the rest of the timeline didn't fit. Katie's second chance came years after Brandy's death.

Sage picked up the bakery box and gave Katie a one-armed hug. "The party starts at seven. Everyone will be there."

As soon as Sage left, Katie locked the doors and turned out the lights. There was only one thing left to do. She'd make the best cake she could for Bowie by adding a dash of courage, a pinch of resilience, and the love and compassion she had in her borrowed heart.

CHAPTER TWO

At thirty-four years old, Bowie Bishop didn't think he'd ever come back to live at home. It was never his plan to return to Aspen Cove, but then again, he didn't expect to get shot again while in Afghanistan. When those bullets hit his femur and shattered the bone, everything changed.

He sat at the end of the dock and let his legs hang over the side. The soles of his boots skimmed the water, creating ripples that danced across the smooth surface.

He'd forgotten how high the lake could get after the snow melted; well, not exactly forgotten, more like banished from his memory. He looked across the water to where the tree line split—it was the only place where the side of the mountain dropped off into the lake. He hated that patch of road. In fact, he hated just about everything.

At night, in his dreams, he still saw her—eyes the color of amber, chestnut hair, and a laugh that could warm even the coldest heart. Brandy was his everything, and when he lost her, he knew he'd never be happy again.

The familiar sound of a can popping open and the hiss of

carbonation escaping meant he wasn't alone with his thoughts any longer.

"I thought you might like one before we go to the bar." Cannon sat down next to him and handed over the beer.

"I don't feel much like celebrating my return. I think I'll stay here."

"No can do, bro. You've got a lot of people looking forward to seeing you. If you don't show up, they'll come here. There's no way to avoid it."

Bowie lifted the can to his lips and took several big gulps. It would take a lot more than a can of beer to get him through the night.

"Why did you tell them I was coming back?" This trip wasn't a social visit. It was a place to land until the VA assessed his disability rating, and then he was gone.

"Because seeing you back in town would be like seeing a ghost."

Cannon had described it accurately. He'd been a ghost. Most of him died when Brandy did.

"I don't want the attention."

"Fine, show up, stay awhile. Paste on a fake smile. Then come back here and hide in the house until tomorrow morning, when you get up to run the bait and tackle shop. I've been taking it all on by myself for years. You're back, so you can help."

Bowie never knew his brother to be so stern, but then he figured years of dealing with their drunk father had taken the softness out of him. He'd always felt bad that he left his brother to pick up the pieces, but Bowie couldn't bear to spend another second in the town that reminded him of his loss.

"I'm not staying. Besides, Dad looks like he's got a handle on things. He can run the bait and tackle store." Cannon had told Bowie how bad his father had gotten, but to look at him now, he couldn't believe it. He knew his brother wasn't one to exaggerate, but Ben looked fine.

"No, he's helping Katie at the bakery. It's where he found his sobriety. It's best if things don't change too drastically for him."

Cannon picked up a few pebbles from the dock and tossed them into the water. Rings formed around the disturbance and spread out wide. That's how life was. One thing created a ripple, and an entire life changed.

"Change isn't good for Dad, but it's okay if *I'm* propelled into a nightmare?"

He pushed the boot of his good leg beneath the surface of the water and kicked forward, sending a splash outward. Ten feet in front of him, a fish leaped from the water to catch a bug.

"It's not my intent to pick at your wounds, but I want a life, too. I gave up everything—my life, my career. I gave it all up to come back here and try to save what we had. When will it be my turn to have something?" He emptied his beer and crushed the can in his fist. "Sage entered my life and changed everything. I'm in love with her, but I need time with her. I won't get that if I'm running two businesses and watching out for Dad."

Cannon was right. Bowie had bailed on his brother, but at the time, he had nothing left to give. As he sat on the dock and looked around, he worried he had even less now than he did then.

"I'm not staying," he repeated.

"I hear you. Just remember, I stepped up when you couldn't. I'm asking you to step up while you're here. I'm rarely selfish, but dammit, Bowie, you owe me."

That was another fact he couldn't deny. He owed Cannon. He'd given up his dream job to come home and be responsible for the family. He was only twenty-four years old when everything went to hell. Too young to be a full-fledged adult, but too old to be a kid.

"You're right. I owe you more than I could ever repay."

He turned to his left and took a really good look at his brother. He'd grown into a man while Bowie was gone. They'd been close as kids but drifted apart when Bowie fell in love with Brandy. He'd spent all his time with her. The hardest part about losing her was he didn't know how to live without her. He'd made a promise to himself the day they buried her: he'd never allow another woman to enter his heart.

"I'm not asking for blood. I'm only asking you to stay around for a bit. I've missed my brother." Cannon reached over with one arm and bro-hugged him.

"Let's take it a day at a time. Now tell me about this girl of yours."

Footsteps sounded behind them. They turned to see who approached.

Cannon's stoic expression softened, and a smile took over his face. "How about you meet her?"

He stood and walked halfway down the dock to meet the tiny redhead. He picked her up and twirled her around. The only piece of Bowie's heart that remained squeezed so hard it was almost painful. He watched the two kiss.

It wasn't that Bowie hadn't had female companionship since Brandy died. He'd seen plenty of action, but he was always clear about where those relationships would go. Bowie was like a boat full of holes, and you couldn't fill up a leaky vessel. He was a sinking ship and refused to take anyone else down with him.

He struggled to his feet and limped his way down the dock to meet Sage. She stood in front of him and rose up onto her toes to kiss him on the cheek. It was an odd greeting from a complete stranger, but he liked her forwardness.

"Finally, I get to meet the infamous Bowie."

He looked down at the runt in front of him. "*Infamous*, huh?"

She smiled, and Bowie could see why his brother had fallen so hard. With a smile like that, it was like the sun radiated from her pores.

"Oh, yes. I've heard everything from how you terrorized him as a kid to how you protected him at school."

Cannon looked at her and shook his head. "Sweetheart, that was bedroom talk and should have stayed in the bedroom."

Sage rolled her eyes. "That would mean we couldn't talk about anything. You work so much, I only get to talk to you in bed."

Cannon looked at his brother with a see-I-told-you-so look. Although Bowie knew he'd never fall in love again, there wasn't any reason Cannon shouldn't. Someone in their family deserved to be happy.

"Let's see if we can change that. I'll be around for a bit so Cannon will have more time to spend outside the bedroom."

"Dude, I don't want to reduce my bedroom time; I only want to increase my other time. Who knows, I might want to spend that time in the bedroom, too."

Sage wound up and punched Cannon in the chest. "I'm not invisible here. Don't be talking about our bedroom activities with your brother."

It was hard not to laugh. Here was a woman who, on her tallest day, reached Cannon's neck, and yet she was in control. God, he missed those days.

"Although due to your height, you're easy to overlook, now that I've seen you punch, you're hard to ignore." Bowie threw his arm around Sage and began the walk to the house. "One thing you should know, none of the Bishops kiss and tell. Your nocturnal secrets are safe. Nothing else is sacred, though, so give me some dirt on my brother. It's been a long time."

Sage told him about Cannon's one-eyed cat. She laughed at the fact that such a tough man could have such a soft spot for a special-needs pet, but she had no place to talk because when they walked into the house, lying at Ben's feet was her three-legged dog, Otis.

"Aren't you the pot calling the kettle black?"

While Bowie walked over to his dad, Sage and Cannon disappeared into the kitchen, saying something about microwaving dinner.

"Hey, Dad. You're looking good." Dad had a nice scar on his forehead from where he fell at the cemetery.

"I'm alive. That's a start." Ben pivoted on the old leather couch to face him. "I was wondering when you'd come in to say hello."

"You could have come outside."

Ben looked down at the beer in Bowie's hand. "I try to stay far away from alcohol."

"Shit, Dad. I'm sorry. I wasn't thinking." Bowie rocked forward to stand, but his dad pulled him back down.

"It's my problem, not yours. I can't expect the world to change because I have an issue with something. I'm learning."

Bowie took his beer and reached over the arm of the chair to put it out of sight. "You're right, but I don't have to flaunt your weakness in front of your face."

Ben did something unexpected. He leaned in, pulled his son against his body, and hugged him tightly. "I'm glad you're here. I hope you'll stay awhile."

His plans were short-term, but before he could tell his dad, Cannon and Sage called them for dinner.

Just like the old days, Bowie sat in his place at the family dinner table next to the window. While they ate microwaved stroganoff, Cannon and Ben filled him in on all the things that had happened over the years.

Louise Smith had married Bobby Williams, and they recently had their seventh kid. Doc still ran the clinic, although he was older than dirt. Dalton had done time for murder. The town finally got a sheriff, Aiden Cooper, and Mark Bancroft was the deputy. Zachariah Thomas lit himself on fire when one of his stills blew up. While some things had changed, others remained the same. He'd missed having a place where he belonged. He'd missed his family. As much as he hated to admit it, no matter where he ended up, Aspen Cove would always be home.

CHAPTER THREE

Would anyone notice how lopsided the cake was? Katie tried to camouflage the error with extra frosting. Whereas one half of the cake had a mere quarter-inch layer of frosting, the other side had over an inch.

Even after watching a dozen YouTube videos and an episode of *Cake Boss*, it looked like an amateur baked it. In reality, that was exactly what happened. Her consolation was that it tasted good, and hopefully everyone could look past the imperfections and enjoy the cake.

If the party started at seven, then Katie would wait until ten after to show up. That would give enough time for everyone to say hello to Bowie, or so she hoped.

The only reason she was going, she told herself, was Sage had asked her, but she was curious about the man who had left town a decade ago and never returned.

In some ways, they were alike. She'd packed up and left Dallas. Although her departure happened abruptly, she had considered it for years.

There were lots of reasons people ran away, but it always came down to either running from or running to something. In her case, she was racing to have an authentic life. One she couldn't have in Dallas.

Katie looked at the clock; it was time to go. Dressed in blue jeans and a flowered thermal shirt, she entered the chill of the May night and walked across the street to Bishop's Brewhouse. She'd never seen the bar so full, except for the day they buried Bea. It seemed like the town came out for deaths and births. Bowie coming back to town was a sort of rebirth.

Katie knew his presence was important to Ben. She could only imagine what it meant to Cannon. With the sheet cake in her hands, she twisted and turned her body through the crowd until she was at the bar.

Sage stood behind the taps, pulling a pitcher of beer. "You came."

"Did you think I wouldn't? From the sound of the chitchat around town, this man coming home is like the second coming of Christ—a miracle." She set the cake on the worn wooden surface and looked around at the crowd. "I'm a true believer in miracles." Katie never put much faith in anything until the day her heart quit. From that point on, faith was all she had.

"The cake looks amazing." Sage took it and put it on the back counter. "Was it hard?"

"Hard" was a matter of perspective. It was hard to get the courage to try something new, easy to do it once she decided. Hard to take the reality it wasn't perfect, but easy to hide her mistake.

"Not hard at all," she said with a roll of her eyes. "I imagine it's like anything you do the first time—scary but worth it."

She looked to the end of the bar toward the man everyone crowded around. Baking the cake wasn't nearly as hard as what Bowie had experienced. Even though she didn't know him, the telltale signs of stress were written on his handsome face. Hard eyes. Creased brow. The strained twitch from a fake smile. Katie knew all too well the look of being present for everyone else when all you wanted to do was be alone. *Poor Bowie.*

"You want to meet him?"

Sage poured her second pitcher of beer. She looked comfortable behind the bar. Katie was envious that Sage had settled into Aspen Cove so easily, especially when she was the one who didn't want to stay. All this time, Katie had wanted to stay. She'd found lots of things in Aspen Cove she'd been searching for. She'd found friends, a sense of belonging, a purpose. The one thing that remained elusive was love. It was unlikely she'd find it here, where most men were seasonal visitors and the ones who weren't were like brothers or a father. Besides, finding love wasn't her number one priority. Independence took precedence.

"I'll wait. He looks overwhelmed."

She looked back at Bowie, who talked to Cannon. All she could see was his profile. Strong nose. Chiseled jaw. Tan skin. Brown hair. Sitting on a barstool, he was taller than most men who stood around him. His fake smile was heartwarming; she could imagine his real smile would be heart-stopping.

She climbed onto the barstool at the opposite end of the room.

"I'm sure he is." Sage delivered the pitcher to Bowie and Cannon and came back to stand near Katie. "He didn't want to come."

Katie watched the man smile and chat with the town folk. It reminded her of all the visitors she got in the hospital. She'd smile and nod and make nice conversation, but all she wanted was to be alone.

"It's got to be overwhelming."

The crowd split, giving her a chance to get a look at the rest of him. When Sage had said he was medically retired from the service, Katie thought maybe he'd lost a limb, but he appeared fully intact.

A tight, olive-colored T-shirt stretched across his chest, leaving little for her active imagination. His biceps bulged, expanding the band of cotton to its limit. Her eyes followed the line of his body. He was half on and half off the stool. One leg extended, as if ready to bolt at the first opportunity. His jeans, though worn, looked like they were custom made for him. He was perfect all the way from his cropped hair to his black boots. The only thing missing was a Harley. He had that bad-boy look about him. She'd considered him almost too perfect, but then he turned his head toward her, and her heart skipped a beat. A jagged scar ran from his temple to his chin, bisecting his cheek along the way.

Magazine men weren't her thing. Men who sought perfection in themselves often sought it in others, and Katie was far from perfect. She'd learned long ago that the true test of a man was in how he lived with his flaws. Bowie's scar was the sexiest thing about him. He wore it like a badge of honor. She was intrigued to find out how he got it.

"Can I have a soda?" Katie would have loved to imbibe with the rest, but she rarely drank. Given her health condition, it wasn't recommended.

Sage poured her a soda. "Let's give your cake to Bowie."

"You give it to him. I'm happy here."

Sage gave her a growl. "Suit yourself. He's much sweeter than he looks. Then again, wasn't it you who told me you like them to look like murderers?"

Sage picked up the cake and brought it over to Bowie. She said something that made the entire group look Katie's way. She gave them all a weak smile and a wave but stayed put.

Katie liked sitting in the corner, taking everything in. She seldomly had the opportunity to be an observer. A girl could learn a lot about the people of Aspen Cove if she watched long enough. For example, it was obvious which men in town had grown up with Bowie. Mark Bancroft, Bobby Williams, and Dalton Black had that easy look about them. The one that said, "I've got your back." They talked and laughed like they hadn't lost a day together.

The men who hung back, like Sheriff Aiden Cooper and resident lawyer Frank Arden, were taking it all in, just like Katie. Sitting back and observing. In the corner was a group that included Zachariah Thomas and Tilden Cool, who lived up in the mountains and made moonshine. The only reason for their appearance was the free beer.

Then there were the women. Abby, the beekeeper, was too old for Bowie, but it didn't stop her from hanging on to his every word. Lloyd Dawson, a cattle rancher, had come to town with his family in tow. He and his wife, Maggie, had five daughters, ranging in age from eight to twenty-eight. Poor man. It was his oldest daughter, Poppy, who showed the most interest in Bowie. Katie couldn't blame her. Living with her parents at twenty-eight was no fun. Katie figured marriage was Poppy's easiest way out of the house. Her sisters lined the walls like wallflowers, with names like Rose, Lily, Daisy, and Violet. Their only brother, Basil, hung back and drank beer with the sheriff.

Sage waved Katie over. It was a battle lost if Katie thought she'd get away without an introduction. That was until her phone rang. She knew who it was. Few people had her new cell phone number, and ninety percent of them were in the bar, so when she pulled her phone from her pocket, it was no surprise it was her mother.

She pressed answer. "Hey, Mama. Hold on, okay?"

Her mom continued to talk, but Katie pulled the phone away from her ear. She looked at Sage and pointed to her phone, mouthed the word "Mom," and disappeared out the door to take the call. People were overflowing onto the sidewalk, so she rounded the building and walked to the back of the bar.

"Are you there?" her mother asked.

"Yes, I told you to hold on. I had to get somewhere quiet so I could hear you."

"It sounds like a party."

"It's a welcome-home party for a friend's brother." Katie counted to five because she knew it wouldn't take longer than that to get to the next question.

She only got to three when her mom asked, "Where are you?"

"You know I'm not telling. You have the ability to get in touch with me."

"About that, why did you change your phone number? Daddy and I were happy to pay for your service."

Katie inhaled deeply and let the breath out slowly. She'd always considered herself a patient person, but her mom could try a saint on Sunday.

"You were happy to pay for my phone when you could track it. I'm a grown woman, Mama. What's the point in living if I don't have a life?"

This was where her mom would spring a tear. "We only want what's best for you."

Katie heard people behind her, like someone had opened a door to the bar, but the sound muted right away, so she ignored it and replied to her mother, "You want what's safest, but safest isn't always what's best. I had to run away from you and Daddy just to breathe. Mama, I love you, but I can't live if I can't breathe."

"And I can't breathe not knowing if you're okay."

There was no one to see her roll her eyes, but Katie did it anyway. She stood there, staring at the woods behind the bar, and rolled them in every direction she could.

"You're talking to me. I'm okay. In fact, I'm finer than frog hair split seven ways."

"Are you taking your medicine?"

"Yes, ma'am. I'm eating healthy. I'm making friends. I even baked a cake today for the party. I'm happy for the first time in a long time. Please be happy for me." Katie heard a sound behind her and turned to find Bowie tucked into the shadows of the building. He lifted his beer like he was toasting her. She nodded back. "I've got to go. Please trust me to know what's right for me, okay?"

Her mother's exhale was a sign of surrender. Katie would have loved to tell her parents where she'd run off to, but she knew the minute she did, they would be on her doorstep, ready to drag her back to Dallas. She would eventually tell them, but on her terms.

"I love you, sweetheart. I trust you. It's just that I'm as lonely as a pine tree in a parking lot." Katie grew up on southernisms, but her mother never ceased to come up with a new one regularly.

"I'll call soon," Katie told her. She dialed them at least once a week. There was no sense in making them worry, but there was also no sense in talking to them daily. If she did, she might as well move back home.

"Come home soon," her mother replied.

That didn't deserve a response because if Katie said anything but *I will*, the conversation would go full circle back to the beginning.

"Love you, and tell Daddy I love him, too." She waited for her mom's *I love you, too*, before hanging up.

Katie walked over to where Bowie stood in the darkness. His back leaned against the brick building, one leg anchored to the ground, the other knee bent with the sole of his boot against the wall. The moon glinted off his skin, making it look almost gold and godlike.

"Welcome home, Bowie." She pressed her hand in his direction for a shake. "I'm Katie Middleton."

He smiled.

Help me, Jesus. She was right; there was a difference between his forced smile and the one that came naturally. This smile came from his eyes instead of his lips.

"Nice to meet you, Duchess."

His hand was so large, it wrapped around hers when he shook it. He had hard-working hands. They weren't soft and fleshy like the account managers at the insurance office where she used to work. No, Bowie's hands were calloused and manly and warm and strong.

"Duchess, huh? I can live with that." She liked that he didn't call her "Princess" the way everyone else did. He was the first person to call her "Duchess." "I'm sure you're trying to get some peace and quiet, so I'll let you be."

She turned to walk away, but he stopped her with a question. "You made the cake?"

"I did." She laughed, remembering the condition of the kitchen when she finished. She swore there was more flour on the floor than in the cake. "If it was terrible, just tell me you're a diabetic and couldn't have any. That way, I won't feel awful."

"I liked it … a lot. How did you know I like extra frosting?"

"I'm intuitive, or … I made a lopsided cake and straightened it out with the sweet stuff. You choose."

He gifted her with another heart-heating smile. "I'll go with intuitive." He offered her his beer. "You want a drink?"

Katie didn't want to appear rude. "Thank you."

She took the mug from his hand. It was no longer frosted, but the beer remained cold. She lifted it to her mouth and let the suds touch her upper lip.

"Has Aspen Cove been good to you?" he asked.

His eyes left her and stared out into the blackness of the night. Up in the mountains, it turned dark the minute the sun set. Tonight, the moon was only a sliver and offered no light.

"I love it here. The people are good. It was a true blessing to come here."

"I hear Bea gave you the bakery." He reached for his beer and took a long swallow. "What's your connection to Bea?"

A moment of awkwardness hung in the air between them.

They didn't know each other, but they had something in common. They both had a connection to Bea, only Katie's was still a mystery.

"My inner sleuth is still trying to figure it out."

"You will. The one thing I've always known about Bea was she did nothing without a solid reason."

Katie laughed. "She gave me a list of a hundred, but none of them make sense. The only thing I can think of is she found out I did a lot of volunteer hours at a children's hospital."

Bowie kicked off the wall. "That would make sense. Bea loved kids, and she was always quick to reward good behavior." He turned and headed to the bar's back door. "I suppose I should attend my own party. Are you coming, Duchess?"

Katie noticed a slight limp to his walk but ignored it. They entered the bar, where the crowd had diminished. All who were left fell under the categories of close friends and relatives. It made Katie sad that Bowie's father, Ben, had to stay away, but she gave him credit for knowing his limitations.

"Everything all right with your mom?" Sage asked as Katie took the barstool beside her.

"She's still hovering like a true helicopter parent, but hey, she loves me."

"Can't fault her for that." Sage looked down the bar, where the men had congregated. They each had a plate of cake in their hands. Bowie was on his second piece. "Bowie seems to like it. I saw you two walk inside together. Did you get a chance to meet?"

"Briefly. He seems nice."

"He is nice. I'd love it if you two hit it off. Wouldn't that be awesome?"

So awesome, but the timing is wrong. She needed to establish herself first. In the five minutes they'd talked, Katie got a feel for Bowie. She'd always known that when she met *the one*, she'd know it, and something inside her told her he was it. It was more than his

27

looks. His wounds attracted her. She knew what it felt like to hurt
—to watch her life slipping away from her and get a second chance
to embrace it. Maybe that's what Aspen Cove would be for Bowie.
Maybe coming home was his second chance.

"Still on for fishing tomorrow?" When Sage said the word
"fishing," she turned up her nose like she could already smell their
catch.

"Yes."

Katie bounced with excitement in her seat. Fishing was on her
bucket list, and after tomorrow, she'd be able to cross it off. If she
were lucky, she'd get *rowing a boat* completed soon, too. She
looked at Bowie and wondered if he had a list; if so, would his
include silly things like hers? Things like falling in love?

CHAPTER FOUR

The fish flopped onto the dock while Katie hopped around it, making sure the slimy thing didn't touch her.

Sage had been the first one to pull in a catch. She got it off the hook, but it slipped from her fingers and fell to the wooden surface. At first, the two women thought it was dead. Poised over it, they looked at its lifeless body and squealed when the poor thing came out of shock and flopped around their feet.

"Save it," Sage pleaded to Cannon, who stood at the rail and laughed.

"What's the point? You're only going to barbecue it later." He picked the fish up and held it out to her. "If you don't want to eat it, then you should save it."

Sage shuddered before she palmed the fish and brought it to her face. Katie watched from a distance as her friend looked at its mouth open and close. "I'm so sorry, little guppy. Back you go." Sage tossed it into the lake and watched it swim off. "Visit when you get a chance," she called after it.

"Why did you throw it back?" Cannon asked. "The point was to catch it and eat it."

"No," Sage said. "The point was to catch a fish. I've done that. My life is complete."

Cannon pulled Sage into his arms and kissed her. "I'll complete your life."

Katie watched the two interact. A thread of envy wound up her spine and twisted around her heart. Watching them was like watching soul mates connect. There was an energy that crackled under the surface when those two were together. She was so happy her friend had found love and sad she had never experienced anything so wonderful.

"Get a room," came a deep voice from the end of the dock.

Katie turned to find Bowie walking toward them, his limp less noticeable today.

"Don't mind if we do." Cannon looked toward Katie. "She's still zero-for-zero. Care to take over the fishing lesson?"

Bowie scowled at his brother. "I came home for lunch, not to give lessons."

He looked at Katie. His eyes skimmed her body, from her long-sleeved T-shirt to her tennis shoes. She felt a blush rise to her cheeks when his eyes stalled on her bare legs. She'd always considered them her best feature, and now that the sun was out and the temperature in Aspen Cove had risen to about sixty degrees, she was happy to wear shorts and show them off.

"I don't need a babysitter," Katie said. She turned toward the water and prepared to cast her line.

Sage's and Cannon's voices faded as they walked into the house. She didn't need to turn around to see if Bowie was still there; she felt his presence. He was like heat that wrapped around her. She recognized the tightening in her stomach and the uptick in the pace of her heartbeat. Ever since her surgery, certain feelings were heightened. Any kind of excitement or arousal felt ten times more acute. She wasn't sure if it was because her donor heart beat faster than her original heart or because she was more in tune with what her body told her. All she knew was that her attraction to Bowie was undeniable. He fit her type—tall, broad, and brooding. She liked her men damaged. Not that she had much experience with men. With parents more diligent than prison guards, she had never had much interaction with the opposite sex. But with damaged men, her problems didn't seem so problematic. His problems and her problems put them on even ground from the beginning.

Pole gripped in her hand, she ran through the steps Cannon taught her: *Hold the rod at waist level with the reel above the rod. Press your finger to the line, so when you push the doohickey button, the weight doesn't drop to the ground. Pull the rod back and swing it forward, swiftly pointing the tip of the pole at your target. Let your finger off the line so it can fly.*

Katie smiled as the weight hit the water. She let it sink for a count of three and then wound the reel like Cannon had shown her.

Feeling accomplished, she turned around to face Bowie. His hand cupped his mouth to suppress his laughter. His shoulders shook like he was suffering a seizure.

"What?" She narrowed her eyes at him. "That was a perfect cast."

He walked up next to her and gripped the wooden rail of the dock. "You're right. It was a perfect cast."

She turned to face him. At five feet, six inches tall, she was average height, but Bowie towered over her, which made her feel small. "Why are you laughing?" She tried to sound stern, but it was hard because the smile on Bowie's face made her insides turn to goo. She'd never seen anything so beautiful.

"What are you trying to catch?" He walked around to her other side and leaned against the rail. She wondered if he changed positions so she couldn't see his scar.

"Anything. I'm not leaving until I catch something."

He looked down at her legs, which now had goose bumps rising on her thighs. "You'll catch a cold before you catch a fish."

Little did he know, the gooseflesh was simply a condition of his proximity.

"Sage caught a fish. Why would you think I'm incapable?"

His chuckle came from deep inside him. It moved through his body like a tremor. "I'm pretty sure she used bait."

If there were ever a moment Katie wanted the ground to open and swallow her, it was now. Bowie was right; she'd cast an empty hook.

She turned toward the water and spooled in the line. Swinging in the slight breeze was her barren hook. "I can't believe I did that." It was hard to feel embarrassment for too long because it was so funny. She reached into the open tackle box and pulled out the neon yellow PowerBait.

"That's cheating."

"I don't understand." She set the container on the edge of the rail. "It's what Sage used."

Bowie opened the jar and pulled out a pellet, then held it in front of her. "Using this isn't really fishing." He flicked the glowing ball into the water. "It's like walking naked down the street and not expecting men to look at you."

Katie frowned and leaned against the rail. She didn't understand what he was getting at. "Can you clarify?"

Bowie turned his back to the lake and leaned on the rail next to her. "All I'm saying is, it's not really fishing. There's a skill to fishing. It doesn't really count if you drop the meal in front of the prey and turn on a flashing neon sign that reads 'eat me.'"

"What does it matter if, in the end, I catch a fish?"

"Stay here." Bowie left for a few minutes while Katie looked out at the water. When he returned, he was dangling a worm between his fingers. "Use this."

She took a step back. Katie didn't do bugs or snakes; a worm, in her opinion, was an amalgamation of both. "I'm not touching that."

He stepped forward. "Oh, come on. It's only a worm. If you want to one-up Sage, you'll use it."

"I'm not interested in one-upping Sage. I want to catch a fish."

"Compromise? I'll put it on the hook. You cast the line. You get the bragging rights when you catch your fish."

Katie looked at the neon container sitting on the rail. There was something unnatural to use bait with the texture of a marshmallow and the glow of the sun.

"Fine, but if I don't catch a fish, it's your fault. You'll have to live with denying me the ability to cross this off my bucket list."

"You don't have a very ambitious list." He pierced the worm and watched it dangle from the hook.

She imagined his list, if he had one, would include things like running through fire, hang gliding, or swimming with sharks. There was a dangerous vibe attached to him. Not that he looked dangerous, but he didn't seem the type to avoid it.

"I want to experience more common things before I try jumping out of an airplane."

She gripped the handle of the pole and went through the motions of a perfect cast. This time when the hook hit the water, she knew she was set up for success. How could she go wrong fishing with the man who ran the bait and tackle shop?

"I've done that hundreds of times. The jump is always exciting. The flight invigorating. The landing terrifying. At least for me."

She reeled in the excess line and waited. "Haven't perfected the landing?" She knew from Cannon that Bowie had been a Ranger. No doubt he had jumped out of many things, including airplanes.

"The landing can be a real bitch when you're dodging bullets."

"I can't imagine, but I thank you for your service. I'm sorry it was cut short by injury." She looked down at his leg. A red scar ran from the bottom of his knee until it disappeared under the frayed edge of his cut-off cargo pants. "Does it cause you a lot of pain?"

"Some, mostly stiffness, but I cope."

"Sometimes coping is all we can do."

Katie understood that concept too well. She'd never experienced a crushing pain as profound as when they cut through her breastplate to remove her heart. It took months to heal. Occasionally, she felt the phantom pains of healing—the sharp stabbing of bones stitching themselves together. It had been years, but some things she never forgot.

A ripple in the water and the bobbing of her line caught her attention. "I've got a bite."

"It's just a nibble. Wait for a second." He stood behind her, wrapped his arms around her body, and showed her how to hold the pole. "On the next nibble, let's give it a firm tug."

His chin sat on her shoulder, and a ripple of awareness coursed through her body. Katie didn't know what made her heart beat faster. Was it that Bowie was pressed against her or that she had a fish on her line?

The end of her pole bent, and with his help, she gave the line a yank. Within seconds, she was in a battle against the fish. By the way the thing fought, she was certain it weighed a hundred pounds. To her surprise, when she finally got it reeled in, it was no bigger than her size eight shoe.

"It's a good size. You want to keep it?" Bowie gripped the slimy fish and finessed the hook from its mouth. The poor thing didn't even get to keep the worm that came out with the hook.

Her head shook before the words were out. "Nope. I'm happy just knowing I caught it." She was so giddy with her accomplishment that as soon as Bowie tossed the fish back into the water, she threw her arms around his neck and kissed his scarred cheek. "Thanks so much for your help."

He stood back and stared at her. "You're easy, Duchess."

"Yes, but I'm told I'm not cheap." She giggled as she took a knee on the dock and packed up the tackle box.

"You're funny, too." He stood above her, throwing a shadow across the dock as she put everything away.

"Only on Saturdays." She closed the container and stood. "I should get back to the bakery so your dad can have lunch, too." She picked up the pole and box and started toward the house.

"How did you get him to work there?" Bowie followed her to the porch, where she dropped off the pole and tackle box, then continued on her way to her SUV.

"That was Sage. She got him started. He only stays because he gets free muffins."

That wasn't the truth. He stayed because, contrary to Katie's desire to be independent, she needed him. One thing she'd learned about Ben was he needed a purpose. Although things might change down the road, Katie provided him with one.

"Will you stay?"

Bowie looked around. His focus landed on the bed and breakfast. "There are just too many memories here for me." He opened her car door. "I'll stay for the summer. Cannon needs the help." His eyes lit on her legs as she climbed into her car.

He's a leg man. "You could make new memories," she said in a hopeful tone. Even though she'd just met Bowie, there was a vulnerability that pulled her to him.

"There's nothing left here for me." He waited for her to put on her seat belt before shutting the door.

She backed out of the driveway. When she turned her car down Main Street, the only thought in her mind was, *I'll prove you wrong.*

She couldn't wait to get home and jot a new item on her list. Somehow, she'd make Bowie see Aspen Cove in a different light.

CHAPTER FIVE

"You want to help in the bar tonight?" Cannon asked. Both brothers were in the kitchen, raiding the refrigerator. Bowie pulled out the rotisserie chicken while Cannon grabbed for the jelly.

"You need help at the bar?" He ripped a leg off the chicken and took a bite. He was a leg man through and through.

"It's Saturday. I could use all the help I can get."

After Katie left, Bowie had grabbed a piece of fruit and returned to the bait and tackle shop. He'd been busy with the influx of tourists. It started in the spring and didn't die down until the first snow.

The smell of baked goods seeped through the walls from the bakery next door. It was a constant reminder of his past. He remembered how the smell of sweets meant Brandy was next door whipping up something delicious. It was a bittersweet reminder to inhale the perfect scent of his past and know she would never be in his future.

Over the years, he'd grown accustomed to the idea that his life would be a string of one-night stands. The best way to avoid a broken heart was not to expose his. Hell, after Brandy died, his heart had dried up and shriveled. It was a wasteland. Many a woman had tried to plant the seed of love in his heart, but it never took hold. Nothing could grow in barren land.

"Let me shower and clean up. I'll meet you there."

Cannon slathered peanut butter on bread and plopped a glob of jelly in the center before he pressed the two halves together. He took a bite. Muffled through the food in his mouth, he asked, "Did Katie catch a fish?"

Bowie smiled at the memory. How proud she looked when he held up the fish. "Yep, she caught a decent-sized trout the right way—with a worm." He tossed the bone from his chicken leg into the trash can. "I can't believe you let her use that crap bait."

That mischievous look took over Cannon's features again. When Cannon's eyes grew wide and that glint lit him up, he was either doing something, hiding something, or guilty of something. Bowie had missed that look.

"I had other plans, and fishing wasn't one of them."

"You really love her, don't you?"

It was a stupid question. Cannon couldn't keep his hands off Sage. When he wasn't with her, he talked about her nonstop. It reminded Bowie of what it felt like to be in love.

Better him than me.

"What do you think about Katie?" Cannon lifted a brow.

"Don't go there. The Duchess seems like a nice enough girl, but I'm not interested."

What he meant was, he wasn't interested in her long term. There was plenty to be interested in for fun. She had legs that would wrap around his waist just right. He couldn't help noticing she was toned and curvy in all the right places. Despite her neck-high T-shirts, it was hard for her to hide her breasts. Breasts Bowie was certain would be the perfect size to fill his large hands.

"It wouldn't hurt you to let someone in."

"Advice coming from the guy who lost less and waited years to do the same. I'll pass."

"Whatever." Cannon grabbed his keys and walked to the door. "Kind of a coward move if you ask me. You're willing to dodge bullets but not risk the razor's edge of a relationship." Cannon walked out.

Bowie couldn't argue with him. Bullets were easy unless they ended a career. He looked down at his knee. The scar started there and ran to his hip. He hated that his brother considered him a coward, but he had no idea how to change Cannon's mind. He wasn't about to fall in love again.

He entered his old bedroom. Nothing had changed; it was like he'd walked out yesterday. On his dresser was his collection of model planes—an obsession since he was a kid. Next to the B-1 Bomber was a ticket stub to a movie he'd seen the week before the accident. He and Brandy went to see *Witch Mountain* because she had a love for all things Disney.

He made his way into the shower and stood under the stream of hot water, trying to wash the memories away. As the water sluiced over his body, he closed his eyes and didn't see Brandy; he saw Katie. He relived the moment when she said she was easy but not cheap.

His body reacted in the only way a man thinking about those long legs wrapped around his waist could. He grew and hardened until he had no choice but to relieve himself. Bowie had done a lot of self-gratification over the years but never had a release held so much power and deliver so much pleasure.

After that experience, he really wanted to crawl into bed and sleep, but his father was home, so he dressed and joined him in the living room.

"Hey, Pops." Bowie took a seat on the sofa next to his dad.

Ben lowered the volume on the television and turned toward his son. "You made it past your first twenty-four hours. I'd say that's the hardest." He reached out and patted Bowie on the shoulder. "It won't be easy, son."

"You're right, but you have to know now, I'm only staying long enough to figure out my next move."

Whatever light Ben held in his eyes dimmed. He lowered his head. "I'm not a great role model for dealing with grief. We all have our own way. Mine was the numbness alcohol provided. I imagine yours is the shot of adrenaline that comes from running for your life." He shook his head. "Neither are healthy options. Mine could have killed my liver. Yours could have flat out killed you. Haven't we had enough death?"

"Yes, we have."

Dad was right. Bowie's life had been surrounded by death that started with his mom and Brandy. Then he joined the United States Army, became a Ranger, and experienced a regular dose of death. He'd become anesthetized to it. Bowie had felt little in years —until her. Something about Katie made him feel. The attraction was palpable, but more than that, something about her got under his skin. He wasn't sure if he liked it or hated it. All he knew was, he had nothing to offer her but a good time. If she was okay with that, then his short stay in Aspen Cove would be tolerable.

"You helping in the bar tonight?" Dad reached for his cup of coffee.

"Unless you need me to stay."

Bowie prayed his dad would ask him to stay, but he knew he wouldn't. The only time he'd known of his father being selfish was every day for the last several years, and he hadn't even seen it firsthand. But the selfish man in him was gone, and back in his place was the father he'd always loved.

"You go help your brother. I wish I could help, but it's not smart to put an alcoholic in a bar. The bakery closes early tomorrow. How about I help you out at the store?"

Bowie laughed. "Still can't believe you're a baker."

"I had to put my energy somewhere else." He patted his stomach. "Can't say eating all those sweets is a better addiction, but at least I'm not waking up in strange places. Besides, that Katie ... she's a special one. Can't put my finger on exactly why, but I think she needs help. Although she'll be the last one to ask for it. What do you think of her?"

"Too early to tell. She seems all right."

He wouldn't tell his dad his thoughts turned carnal each time he saw her. First, that would give him hope there was a chance for Bowie to love again, and that wasn't an option. Second, something told him his father would warn him away if his intentions weren't honorable.

Bowie had no desire to be dishonorable. He'd honor every inch of her body. He'd share every inch of his except for his heart.

"You better get going. There's a crowd in town this weekend. Besides, I'm babysitting tonight."

Bowie's brows lifted. "First a baker, and now a babysitter. I can't believe it."

"It's not what you think. I'm watching Sage's dog, Otis. She should be bringing him over any minute."

As soon as the last word was out, the door opened, and Sage stuck her head in. "Ben, I'm here with Otis. Are you ready?"

Bowie wasn't expecting to get attacked, but as soon as the furry beast cleared the door, he ran directly for the couch. When the dog leaped into the air, Bowie took a good look at his missing hind leg.

So Cannon isn't the only stray she's collected.

He moved his head from side to side, trying to avoid the dog's wet tongue, but it was no use. Otis was intent on giving Bowie a kiss.

"Otis," Sage scolded. "Stop."

The dog looked back at her for a second, then went back to licking Bowie's face. He laughed because no matter how forceful

Sage tried to make her voice, she could never instill the feeling of fear in others. The woman was like a tiny leprechaun, red hair and all.

Bowie lifted the dog and placed him in Ben's lap. "You're next." Otis didn't miss a beat. He wasn't particular about whom he loved as long as he licked someone. He looked past the ball of fur to his father. "See you later, Pops."

Outside, he pulled his Harley out of the garage. He'd towed it behind his truck to Aspen Cove and had been dying to ride it. Tonight, the weather was perfect.

"Is that a Harley?" Sage said with a giggle from behind him.

He looked at her with curiosity. He didn't understand what was funny. "You want a ride?"

"Oh, no. You've got the wrong girl. That would be Katie. She loves the bad boys on bikes." Sage walked to her SUV and opened her door while Bowie put on his helmet. "You don't have an arrest record, do you?" She didn't wait for him to respond. She laughed and closed her door.

Bowie had no idea what to think of that conversation. He didn't have a prison record. He might look like a murderer, but he wasn't that guy. He started his bike and throttled it until it growled. He could do bad boy. He could do Katie.

He took the short drive down Main Street and parked in front of the bar. The sun set low in the sky, and within minutes it would hide behind the peak, cloaking the town in darkness. He looked to the bakery's dimly lit windows and wondered what Katie did with her evenings. It wasn't like Aspen Cove was a mecca for entertainment. There was the bar, and that was about it.

He turned from the darkness and entered the light of the brewhouse. His question was answered when he glanced around and saw Katie playing pool with Dalton and his friends. Maybe he was too late to the game. Had Sage dropped a hint?

Staring at the curvaceous blonde, she looked more beauty

queen than biker chick. If she liked the bad boys, Dalton wasn't exactly dangerous; he was protective. If the rumors were true, he'd acted more like a protector than a predator when he killed that man. Bowie would have done the same. There were things a man should never tolerate, and abusing women, children, and animals fell into that category.

He walked by the group playing pool, but he knew Duchess's eyes were on him. The heat of her gaze burned through his leather jacket. She may have been physically standing with Dalton, but her sights were on him.

"It's about time," Cannon said. "I was thinking you bailed on me." He nodded down toward the end of the bar where the group of fishermen he'd sold poles to that morning were huddled. "Take their orders and then change the keg to the lager."

Bowie's first instinct was to tell his brother to piss off. He'd never taken orders from Cannon. The brother he remembered wasn't the man who stood in front of him. He'd grown up from a twenty-four-year-old kid into a man.

As soon as the front door opened again, he knew Sage had arrived because Cannon got that goofy, lovestruck look in his eyes. He also knew he'd be watching the bar solo.

As soon as they got the bar stocked, Cannon and Sage disappeared down the hallway to the storage room.

"Can I get a refill?" Katie put her glass on the counter.

"Jack and Coke?" Given the dark liquid at the bottom, it was his best guess.

"Yes, but I'll take mine without the Jack. Never liked that man."

She smiled, and his knees weakened. It was ridiculous how her mere presence had him feeling like a kid. He was far beyond adolescence.

"Coke, it is." He looked past her to Dalton. "You and Dalton a thing?"

Her perfume rose to his nose when she turned to look at the man everyone described as a human oak tree. At six foot four, Bowie was big, but Dalton was even bigger. They grew them large in Aspen Cove.

"Me and Dalton?" She giggled. "No." She shook her head. "He's the older brother I wish I had."

Bowie felt awful for him. Nothing shrank a man's junk faster than a girl who played the brother card. It was as bad as the friend card.

"I heard you liked bad boys." He set her soda on the counter.

She lifted the glass to her lips and took a sip. "I do, but Dalton's no bad boy. He's like Bambi with testosterone. What about you? Are you a bad boy?"

Bowie would like to show her how bad he could be. "I am *the* bad boy."

"Braggart." She turned and walked away.

Cannon showed back up an hour later. For the rest of the night, the brothers pulled beers and poured shots.

No matter where Katie was in the bar, Bowie knew her exact location. He couldn't take his eyes off her. When she got ready to leave, Cannon asked him to walk her home.

"I don't want her walking around the back of the building alone. There are too many strangers in town to risk it."

It was a good argument, but Cannon had seen Bowie watch her all night. He'd commented on it a few times. Bowie knew his brother's intentions were somewhere else.

"Matchmaking is not a hat that looks good on you," Bowie said.

"If I left it up to you, nothing would happen. All talk, no action. Or as they say from Katie's home state of Texas, all hat, no cattle."

"Screw you." Bowie grabbed his jacket and ran out the door after Katie. "Wait up." He reached her in three long strides. "You shouldn't be walking out here alone. It's dangerous."

She looked up and down the deserted street. "I'm not seeing any danger."

They walked around the back to the bakery. When he got her to the door that led to her upstairs apartment, he turned her around, leaned against the wall, and caged her in between his arms.

"Danger is standing right in front of you, Duchess, and you don't even recognize it." He leaned in and brushed his lips against hers. "I want to kiss you, but you need to know we'll never be more than a good time."

She ran her hands up his chest. "That's all a girl can hope for."

Bowie needed no other encouragement. He pressed his mouth against hers until she opened those beautiful lips and gave him access. When his tongue danced across the velvety softness of hers, a calm blanketed him. If he thought she'd gotten under his skin, the kiss firmly planted her in his system. Each cell he believed dead came to life. Katie Middleton would be a problem for him. Hell, how could she not? She felt like heaven, smelled like flowers, and tasted like trouble.

CHAPTER SIX

The damn man kissed Katie like his life depended on it, and then he walked away. That was Saturday. He'd been missing in action since. Sure, she'd seen him in the bait and tackle shop. She passed by him in the bar, but now it was Wednesday. She hadn't talked to him, much less kissed him again since that night.

It scared the heck out of her that she wanted to do both so badly. Was it because his kisses were superior to any she'd had? Or was it that she felt a connection to him that confirmed what she knew at first glance—he was the one? She felt the tug between them, an invisible string that pulled them together. Although impossible, she knew him somehow, like they were connected by something powerful.

Every time she stood at the bottom of the stairs to her apartment, she closed her eyes and relived that brief but perfect moment.

"We're out of muffins," Ben called from the front.

Katie had been in the back, perfecting her cake-making skills. With the influx of tourists in town, she had to bake a wider variety of goodies. In the corner on a shelf, she'd found several tiny loaf pans. Yesterday, she'd made miniature pound cakes. Today, she was trying out carrot cake.

"I'm on it."

Droplets of sweat built on her brow. With both ovens running and Katie working hard to catch up, she was hot. She opened the back door and returned to dump ingredients for chocolate chip muffins into the mixer.

A shadow fell across the floor. Her eyes followed the elongated gray outline of a body until she reached the man standing in the doorway—Bowie. His hands gripped the doorjamb. He leaned in and pulled back several times. His eyes looked at her and then to the stairs that led to her apartment.

He hid his conflicted look with a smile. "Whatcha making?"

Her heart triple-timed in her chest. It was as if her thinking about him had conjured him. "Chocolate chip muffins."

Although she was super excited to see him, she didn't show it; at least she hoped she didn't show it. Over the last few days, she'd told herself to stay the course. Her desire to be independent had no room for a man who made her heart squeeze with his presence.

"I love them. Are you putting orange in them, too?" He looked around the prep area of the bakery, but he didn't step in.

"You can come in," she said.

He took a tentative step and then backed out the door. "I really can't. It doesn't feel right."

Katie shrugged. "It's okay, I understand. Would you like me to send your dad over with some muffins when they're finished?"

Bowie looked at the ingredients churning in the mixer. "Only if you put orange in the mix. Bea used to add it, and no one could figure out what made the muffins so special. Brandy once told me orange essence was the secret ingredient."

"I'll try it." When Katie had cleaned out the supplies, she'd found a lot of flavored oils. She had no idea what they were used for, but now she knew.

He stood there and stared at her. There was something else he wanted to say; it showed in his expression, but he kept quiet.

She stopped the mixer and walked over to where he gripped the doorway. "That kiss the other night?"

She knew she was playing with fire. He told her he wasn't looking for anything but a good time. She'd thought long and hard about Bowie's place in her life. He'd made it clear she'd only be a distraction.

He leaned in. "About that." He looked to the ceiling as if the words he needed were printed there.

No matter how much she tried to talk herself out of time with Bowie, she was powerless. She justified her actions by telling herself he'd be the same for her. Bowie Bishop was nothing but a good time. If there was something she needed in her life right now, it was a good time.

"Yes, about the kiss." She lifted to her tiptoes and brushed her lips across his before pulling away. "I'm pretty sure you could do better." One thing she knew was, a man like Bowie wouldn't take kindly to a girl pointing out his faults. Although the kiss he'd given was perfect, it was too short. So ... he could do better.

"Is that right?" He pulled her to him and stepped into the sunshine. "You didn't like my kiss?"

He pushed her against the brick building and pressed his body against hers. His hard chest pushed into her supple breasts. His leg took up real estate between her thighs.

She was good and trapped, but she liked it. "I liked the kiss, but it lacked length." She'd chosen her words with care, knowing he'd read more into it than the kiss.

"Duchess, I can't give you much, but length I've got." He rocked his hips into her.

He definitely isn't lacking length.

She couldn't ignore his repeated warnings. He had nothing to give but his body. That was a lie he told himself, but it wasn't her

47

job to point it out to him. Her only job was to figure out if what he offered was enough.

Could she accept only a part of him—the long, hard part? She'd never had a one-night stand. Maybe that belonged on her list as well. Then again, it was in her nature to give her all. What if she gave him everything, and he gave her nothing but a good time? She'd told him Saturday night a good time was all a girl could hope for, but that was a lie. She wanted more—needed more. She had no right to ask for more. She'd been given so much already, including a second chance at life she refused to waste. She'd learned life was fleeting, and she had to live for the moments.

"I'll take what you've got." Her fingers skimmed up his chest until they wrapped around his neck. Katie pulled him down for a kiss.

"I'll take what you're offering." He took her mouth in a rough, lust-fueled kiss. His mouth was scorching hot against hers. His tongue did a slow sweep along the curve of her lip, making her clench her thighs around his leg.

When he pulled back, his eyes danced with dangerous intent.

"Is the batter ready?" Ben called from the bakery.

Bowie traced her lower lip with his tongue, then nipped roughly at it with his teeth before turning and heading into the shop next door.

She licked where he'd bitten her and savored the taste of him. It took several gulps of air to get her heart rate to slow down. When she walked back inside, she ran smack dab into Ben, knocking them both off-kilter. She fell to her bottom, whereas Ben was lucky enough to grab the counter for balance.

"I'm so sorry, Katie. I saw the door open and thought I'd check on you." He offered her a hand and pulled her to her feet. "Did you get too hot?"

"Hot" wasn't quite the word for it. She was about two degrees from internal combustion. If Bowie could make her feel like that with a kiss, she couldn't wait to see his other talents.

"Yes, I got a little heated."

"It will only get worse as summer approaches. There's a fan in the storage closet. I'll set it up."

Ben turned and left her to the muffin batter. She searched through the flavor bottles and found the orange. After she added a splash to the mix and blended it in, she scooped batter into muffin cups and put them in the oven. It didn't take long for the smell of oranges to mix with chocolate.

"Is that orange I smell?" Ben walked behind the counter carrying a small fan. He looked through the oven glass and sighed. "You know orange chocolate chip muffins are Bowie's favorite."

Katie smiled. "I had no idea. Chocolate and orange seemed like a logical pairing." Her little fib would never be known. The speed with which Bowie moved as soon as Ben called out made it obvious he wanted no one to know what was happening between them. "When they're done, you can take some to him."

Ben frowned. "Oh, I don't know. It might not be a good idea. Could bring up too many memories." Ben plugged in the fan and watched it oscillate.

Katie stepped in front of the flow of air. She was still overheated, but it had little to do with the temperature in the kitchen.

Twenty minutes later, the timer rang, and Katie pulled out three dozen perfect muffins. People off the street must have smelled them, too, because, within minutes, two dozen of them walked out with happy patrons. She boxed up four and handed them to Ben. "Take these to your son. He'll like them."

Skepticism was written all over Ben's face. "I don't know."

She put the box in his hand and walked him to the door. "Trust me." Katie knew Bowie would like the muffins. He'd told her, but that wasn't something she'd share with Ben.

Ten minutes later, he came back with a smile on his face. "You were right. He loved them. He also said they needed more orange, but what does he know?" Ben reached for a bite from the sample tray and popped it into his mouth. "I think they're fine."

Katie picked up the oven mitt and playfully hit Ben on the shoulder. "We don't serve muffins that are *fine*, Ben. We want them to be *fabulous*. If Bowie says they need more orange, then maybe they do."

"They're good." Ben took another bite and swallowed. "He also said everyone is meeting at Maisey's at five for dinner."

"Is that so? Who is everyone?" A warm feeling oozed through her insides. It was sweet and comforting, like warm syrup on pancakes. Was that Bowie's way of asking her out?

Ben turned off the ovens. It was close to quitting time. "You, Cannon, Sage, Bowie, and me."

"Sounds great."

She condensed what was left in the display case down to a single tray of cookies and the muffins she had left. At the end of the day, whatever didn't sell, she brought to Sage. The poor girl couldn't cook a meal—a real problem because she owned an inn that served breakfast. Thank goodness for leftover muffins and Cannon's Crock-Pot casserole skills. If not for that and the cartons of yogurt she bought, her guests would starve.

"You coming, then?" Ben looked hopeful.

"Is Dalton cooking?"

"No idea. All I know is, it's meatloaf night."

Ben had come so far in such a short time. He no longer drank his sorrow away. He faced it head-on with a cup of coffee and a muffin. "One day at a time" was his mantra, and today was a good day because Ben liked meatloaf.

"I'll be there. Now get out of here and help your son close the bait shop." Katie shuffled him out the door and closed up the bakery.

Mini carrot cakes could wait. She packed up Sage's goodies

and raced upstairs to make herself presentable. Any girl worth her salt didn't show up to dinner dressed in jeans and a T-shirt.

She pulled a pink dress from her closet. It was perfect, with its sweetheart neckline and mid-thigh hem. Above the waist, it screamed, *innocence*. Below the waist, it whispered, *ready*.

At her age, she'd had plenty of experience flirting. In fact, she'd get an A in seduction—and an F in everything else. With a hovering mother and a dad who had a collection of guns that could rival Rambo, follow-through was near impossible.

She fluffed her hair, gave a spritz of perfume, and slicked on some lip gloss. Tonight, Bowie wouldn't know what hit him.

She slipped on a pair of wedge heels and walked across the street. She was the last to arrive because it was important to make an entrance. Any respectable girl knew *be there at five* really meant show up tastefully late to attract attention.

By the look on Bowie's face, her plan worked. He wasn't the only one who could dangle the bait.

Up ahead stood Dalton by the swinging kitchen door. He looked at her and smiled. She waved to her group on the way to greet him. He was an important part of her plan. She didn't know Bowie well, but she tasted desperation in his kiss. She felt the strength of his steel rod against her hip. He was ready, but one of the best pieces of advice Katie ever heard was from her Grandma Pearl. She told Katie a girl who showed the good china too early never got to enjoy the tea.

"Hey, Dalton. What are you doing tonight?"

She looked over her shoulder. Sage and Cannon and Ben were deep in conversation. Bowie paid no attention to anyone close to him. His eyes were on her, and she liked the attention.

"Going to the bar."

"Can you skip it tonight?"

Dalton leaned against the counter. "What do you need, sweetheart?"

She leaned in and whispered in his ear, "I need a distraction." She looked over her shoulder at Bowie. "Thought we could go to Copper Creek. I could use a trip to Target."

He looked past her to Bowie. "Do you know what you're doing?"

She shook her head. "Nope. I'm on the learn-as-you-go plan."

"You know he's broken, right?"

She kissed Dalton on the cheek. "We're all broken."

"I suppose you're right."

She walked to the table and took the only open seat—the one next to Bowie.

"The muffins were great," Bowie said. All eyes at the table went to him the second he spoke.

She scooted in until his jean-clad thighs rubbed against her bare leg. "I'm told they needed more orange."

Bowie gave his father a dark look. "Did you have to tell her I said that?"

Ben shrugged. "I gave up booze. I gave up sleeping on strangers' porches. I gave up lying." He waved Dalton over and ordered five blue-plate specials. "I'm not giving up good food."

As Ben spoke, Bowie slid his hand across her bare knee. No one noticed but Katie. Her entire body responded to the light touch of his calloused finger. The riot of emotions she felt made her heart race. Her body sing. Her core clench.

Dalton returned quickly with the blue-plate specials. It was as easy as plating up what he'd already made. Katie listened to everyone talk about their day. If it weren't for Bowie's hand skimming across her knee throughout the meal, she would have felt like she was at a family dinner with siblings, but no sibling would ever touch her so intimately.

"You ready?" Dalton stood by the edge of the table with his keys in his hand.

"Where are you going?" Bowie asked. "I thought you'd come to the bar tonight."

Katie smiled. She pulled out her lip gloss and touched up her lips. "Dalton and I have plans."

Bowie looked at her like she'd spoken in tongues. "Plans? What plans?"

Katie didn't answer his question. She scooted from the booth, and his hand fell from her knee to the seat. Bowie had been told she and Dalton weren't a thing, but by the look of confusion in his eyes, it appeared he was no longer convinced.

"Katie and I have a date with Copper Creek."

"A date?" Bowie repeated.

Katie put a ten-dollar bill on the table for her share of the meal and gave Ben and Sage a hug before leaning into Dalton and saying, "He goes to great lengths for me." She wrapped her arm around his and walked to the door.

Dalton reached above her to open it and whispered, "Did you see the look he gave me?"

"No, what look?"

"Like he wanted to murder me."

She laughed. Katie had seen the look but pretended she hadn't. There was so much tied up in Bowie's expression. Confusion. Agitation. Loneliness. Jealousy. Bowie Bishop was in phase one of Katie Middleton's plan. She was the hunter, and Bowie was her game.

CHAPTER SEVEN

It wasn't until a hand waved in front of his face that he paid attention.

"Earth to Bowie. Are you there, man?" Cannon said.

Bowie shook his head and turned his eyes from the door to where his father, brother, and Sage sat staring at him.

"I'm here." It wasn't where he wanted to be, but he didn't dare run after Katie. That would give everyone the wrong impression.

"She looked great tonight, don't you think?" Sage asked.

She had a knowing smile on her face, and Bowie wondered if it came from intuition or if Katie had told her about them kissing. Katie didn't seem like the kiss-and-tell sort of person, but then again, he didn't really know her.

"I didn't notice."

The hell he didn't. That little dress of hers gave all kinds of mixed messages. With its short skirt, he couldn't keep his hands from traveling across her skin. Soft skin that felt like velvet under his fingertips. Though the top of her dress came nearly to her neck, it hugged what he knew would be perfect breasts.

"Right," his father said. "Not noticing Katie is like not feeling a nine-point-three earthquake on the Richter scale."

"Seriously, who could notice what she wore when she smelled like oranges and chocolate?"

He took a quick glance out the front door and swallowed his disappointment. He'd been all set to make his move tonight. They could have had a glass of wine or a beer. He'd never seen her drink, so he wasn't sure what she liked. Maybe they would have played pool. He'd even considered a dance or two to whatever played on the jukebox if it got his body pressed closer to hers. Now the only affection he had to look forward to was Sage's three-legged dog or Cannon's one-eyed cat, both of which had taken to him. Whenever Bowie was in the bar with both animals present, they stuck to him like gum to a shoe. He seemed to attract the special ones.

Dalton's mom, Maisey, sauntered over to the table. "You want pie?" Although the question was for everyone at the table, she looked only at Ben. "I made that cherry pie you like so much."

It was an odd feeling sitting in front of his father, watching a woman he'd known all his life get sweet on him. He'd never known his father to be with anyone but his mother. Then again, he'd never known himself to be with anyone but Brandy.

He sat back and watched the two talk about pie and adding ice cream to make it sweeter. There was something comforting about seeing his father move on. He didn't want him to remain single and lonely for the rest of his life. Ben deserved to find joy and love after all these years.

Bowie glanced at his brother with Sage. It was also good to see Cannon find love. Feeling like a fifth wheel, he pulled cash from his wallet and set it on top of Katie's ten-dollar bill.

"I've got inventory to take care of. I'll stop by the bar later."

Bowie left the diner and walked back to the bait and tackle shop. When he was a teen, he volunteered to run the shop because it was located next to the bakery, where the cookies and muffins weren't the only tasty things. Back then, he and Brandy would steal kisses behind the store, much like the kisses he coaxed from Katie.

Times had changed. Life had hardened his heart, wounded his soul, and scarred his body. It struck him as funny to realize that once again, there was something sweeter than baked goods at B's Bakery. Maybe things hadn't changed so much after all.

Katie Middleton had cast her line. This time it was baited with her enticing smile, soft lips, and kisses that made him crave her deliciousness. She'd reeled him in. For almost a decade, he'd avoided being caught, but something told him he wouldn't mind so much taking a bite at Katie. He knew he'd never be hooked for good. Even if he wanted to be, he didn't deserve someone as sweet and kind as the little blonde next door. Eventually, she'd see him for the man he was—a man incapable of much more than a few hours of fun. She'd eventually cut him loose, but until then …

He was halfway finished with inventorying the bait when his phone rang. The screen flashed with the name "Trigger."

"Trig. Where are you?"

Bowie had served two tours in Afghanistan with Trig Whatley. He left the service a year ago. The same IED that sent shrapnel slicing through Bowie's gut had completely removed Trig's leg. It had been a long recovery for his friend, but they'd stayed in touch.

"I heard you got out. You could have come to California, where the weather's warm and the girls wear Band-Aids and string to the beach."

The only people who knew Bowie had been released were the men from his unit and his family. It wasn't something he broadcasted around. The shame of being considered unfit for duty chewed at his insides and ate up his self-esteem. If he wasn't good enough to be dropped in the desert, what was he good for?

"I came back home for a visit. Haven't seen my father or brother in years."

"You staying there?"

Bowie looked around the bait shop. The inside resembled a cabin, with its knotty pine paneling, and stuffed fish hanging from plaques on one wall. He still held the record for the biggest lake trout, which hung in the center of the smaller trophies.

"Nope. Just hanging out for a bit."

"Any hot chicks?"

He thought about the town and the female population. There were quite a few single women in town, most of whom he'd known in high school, but when Trig asked about hot chicks, only one came to mind. That was Katie. Blonde hair. Blue eyes. Nice rack. Small waist. Perfect heart-shaped ass.

"No, man. There's nothing worth getting excited about over here in Aspen Cove. No Band-Aids or string bikinis." There was Katie, but he wanted to keep her his little secret. Besides, he wasn't sure how he felt about her, but he wasn't interested in sharing.

"That sucks. Have you heard about Sledge?"

Bowie laughed. Sledge had been the newest guy in the platoon. Got his nickname from hammering every girl he could talk into his tent.

"No. What about him?" He hoped he didn't fall by way of injury, like himself and Trig.

"He knocked someone up, and now he's a baby daddy, but the kicker is, she had the baby, handed it over to him, and then left. He's asses to elbows in diapers and formula."

"You're shitting me!" Bowie took a seat on the stool behind the counter. He dumped out a collection of flies that needed sorting. "Sledge is raising a kid?"

"Sure as shit, man. No help either. He blames it on the sand."

"Blames what on the sand?"

"The pregnancy."

What an idiot. "We both know sand mixed with an egg doesn't produce a kid."

"True enough. That's not it. He says the heat mixed with the constant blowing sand undermined the effectiveness of his condom supply. Something about the foil packages getting blasted in the field."

Bowie continued to separate the flies by type. "I used plenty of condoms in the field and never had a failure."

"She's a beautiful little girl. Named her Sandra."

Bowie shook his head. "Perfect. And I bet he'll call her Sandy as a reminder of his lame excuse." He pulled out the plastic bin that held the flies and put the sorted ones in their corresponding sections. "What about you? How's the leg?"

"Gone," Trig said with his deadpan demeanor.

"No shit, Sherlock. I'm the one who tied the tourniquet."

Bowie would never forget that day. It was on his list of the two worst days of his life. The first being the day Brandy and his mom died. The second being that day when the Humvee was cut in half by an IED. He'd been in the front passenger seat. Trig had been in the back. Two of their squad died that day. While Bowie's gut bled like a fountain, he'd been more concerned with keeping Trig tied to Earth. Field training had him acting fast. He'd stopped the flow of blood before his buddy was emptied out, then took care of himself and waited for the medic, who was several hundred feet away in their caravan.

"Thank you for that. I wouldn't be here without you." There was a long pause. "As it turns out, I've got a slick new leg. Two, actually. One that looks more or less like my old leg down to the hair, and I've got a blade runner."

"Are you running again?" Trig had been the fitness king of the platoon. He was always on the go. When he lost his leg, Bowie wasn't sure if the man would recover. When you lose a limb, everything changes. He knew that to be certain.

"I am. I'm thinking about giving the Rock 'n' Roll Marathon a go this year."

"Damn, that's awesome." He'd seen a lot of soldiers bounce back from horrific injuries. In fact, the men who suffered physical injury fared better than those with emotional scarring. Bowie had both.

Although Brandy wasn't one of his appendages, she was a part of him. They had been connected at the hip their whole lives, so when she was gone, he felt incomplete. How did he move on from someone he loved so much? The memory of her remained chained around his heart. Losing her love pulled at him so tightly, he couldn't breathe at times. How could he pretend that love hadn't existed? It was near impossible, but he tried.

"What about you? Are you healing?"

That was a tough question. He would recover from his physical injuries, but his leg would always act up, and his joints would hurt. By the time he was fifty, who knew what his back would be like? But he was certain Trig wasn't talking about those. He had been the only one Bowie had confided to about his losses.

"I'm still here." It wasn't saying much, but it was all he could say.

"That's something, for sure. One thing I learned when my life was hanging in the balance was there weren't an infinite number of minutes. Use yours wisely, my friend."

They said their goodbyes, and Bowie sat in the silence of the closed shop. He pulled out the faded picture of Brandy and wondered what she'd look like today. Where would their life have taken them? She wanted to stay in Aspen Cove, close to her mother and the people she had chosen as a family since hers had been so small. Bowie had wanted to explore the world. Now that he'd done that, he'd come back to the place they'd both called home, but it had changed. He had changed. Everything had changed. But somehow, it was still home. He hated it and loved it all the same. There was comfort in knowing a person could leave for years and never truly be forgotten.

Rather than tuck the picture back into his wallet, he pinned it to the corkboard that had been hanging in the shop since he could remember. At the top it read, "All Stars." That seemed the perfect place to memorialize Brandy. He knew he had to let her go. Trig was right. There were only so many minutes gifted to a lifetime. What would he do with his?

Once the inventory was complete, he stood by the door and looked over his shoulder at the picture of Brandy tacked to the wall. She would have loved more minutes in her life. She would have traded anything for them, and here he was wasting his. That had to change. He flipped off the lights and walked out—tomorrow was a new day.

CHAPTER EIGHT

Katie supposed she could have asked Bowie to go rowing with her. It was another item she wanted to mark off her list. Fishing—check. Rowing—almost check. Roller blading—next. She had a list of low-risk activities she'd never tried. The problem was, doing them by herself wasn't much fun. New experiences were better shared.

Now that Sage was with Cannon, they spent a lot of their time doing couples' stuff. On the off chance Sage wasn't with Cannon, she was at the clinic or taking care of her bed and breakfast guests. Much of the time, Katie was on her own.

The smell of muffins lifted through the floorboards. Ben was busy baking for the Sunday crowd. Who would have thought taking him in as a favor to Sage would turn him into the best employee she ever had? The only employee she ever had, but he was still top-notch.

It was banana nut muffin day. Maybe she'd box up a few and bring them to Bowie. He was open until noon. That was part of the problem with small-town businesses. They were too small to hire people and too dependent on the seasonal business to close down, so most of the business owners worked seven days a week. At least she had Ben.

Bowie had been hanging around for the last two days. He'd stick his head in the bakery and say hello, but he wouldn't step inside. She understood how painful that might be. The bakery had to remind him of his loss.

She stayed clear of the alley behind the shops. Not because she didn't want his kisses; she wanted to kiss him more than anything, but she wrestled with her desire for Bowie. She wanted him, but would her desire make her dependent on him? Could she have him and not need him? She'd go after Bowie on her terms.

The trick was to get him to want her. Need her. Her decision on how to proceed was based on the laws of supply and demand. If her kisses were rare, then they would be sought. Who wanted a kiss they could get anytime they pleased?

With her mind made up, she dressed to attract in cut-off shorts she paired with a white tee and plaid shirt tied around her waist. On her feet were her favorite red cowboy boots. You could take the girl out of Texas, but you couldn't take Texas out of the girl. She pulled her hair into a high ponytail and slicked on some pink gloss before she headed downstairs.

"Hey, Ben."

She walked over to him and gave him a smooch on the cheek. A month ago, she thought he was close to seventy. He'd been gaunt and sickly looking with yellowed skin. Now that he'd plumped up, his skin pinked, and his eyes held a healthy glow, he looked more like his fifty-two years.

"Good morning, Katie. How did you sleep?"

"Like a baby."

She slept well. Her cardiologist worried about the high altitude affecting her, but it hadn't. The opposite was true. She found the crisp mountain air invigorating. To Katie, it was a calculated risk. She traded the smog and pollution for clean air and less oxygen. Over the years, she'd learned to listen to her body—she ate well, exercised, and got plenty of rest.

Ben pulled a tray of muffins out of the oven and set them on the counter. "I've got an order for two dozen from Sage. I'm sure a dozen are for her and the rest for the guys coming in later this afternoon. She's got a houseful of city slickers arriving soon. Pretty boys from Denver who think they can fish."

"Pretty boys, huh?" She picked up a four-pack box and gently placed the warm muffins inside. "I'm not much for pretty boys, but it will be nice to have some new faces in town."

"It's a madhouse out there today." Where no cars were parked last month was now a full lot.

They both looked out the window at a full and bustling Main Street. Katie thought it was a beautiful day: The sun was out. The sky was blue. A perfect day to be on the water.

"What are you doing today?" Ben asked.

"Rowing this afternoon."

She watched a woman lead her smiling child into the candy shop across the street. A resident of Gold Gulch set up the sweet shop where the tailor's had once been. It was funny how sweet Aspen Cove had become with the bakery and candy shop and Maisey's pies. Katie loved to watch the eyes of a child when they saw the lollipop as big as a dinner plate in the window or the taffy pulling machine working all day long making saltwater taffy in a rainbow of colors.

"But first I'm delivering muffins to your son, and then I'm going shopping. I saw Abby bringing in a box of goodies last night. I'm certain something in it was meant for me." The reality was, Katie rarely bought anything for herself. Most of the trinkets she purchased, she sent to her family and friends.

The dry goods store across the street was one of her favorite stops. New things got delivered every day. Yesterday, she bought deer jerky. She couldn't say she was a fan, but she got to cross *eat wild game* off her list, and Ben finished it, so nothing got wasted.

Anything Abby Garrett made with her honey was a favorite—especially the soaps and lotions that seemed to turn Katie's dry skin into silk.

Even Cannon had a few things in the country store. He'd started whittling again. Although Christmas was far away, the ornaments he carved were sold as fast as he made them. Katie would never tell him she was the one who bought them up like they were underpriced diamonds. They were her guilty pleasure. She hoped he carved enough of them to fill her Christmas tree. She loved the animals the best, but the Santas and angels were nice, too.

Katie turned to Ben. "Close up at noon. You need time off, too."

"Thanks, Boss." It was funny to have Ben call her "Boss," but she supposed the weekly paycheck she'd given him made it true. "I've got a date with Maisey tonight."

Katie almost dropped the muffin box. "Maisey?" She didn't see that one coming. "That's great. Where are you two going?"

Ben smiled. "We're going to Copper Creek to watch that new Liam Neeson movie."

"Ooh, I hear it's a real nail-biter. Have fun, Ben."

She left the bakery with pep in her step. Miracles happened every day around her, and for the first time in a long time, she was happy. She could only be happier if a grumpy ex-soldier decided she was worth more than a good time.

She entered Bishop's Bait and Tackle for the first time ever. It reminded her of a miniature Bass Pro Shops. The only thing missing was a jumbo fish tank and a bunch of taxidermy wildlife.

She figured it would smell like salmon eggs or the dirt the night crawlers lived in, but it didn't. It smelled like Bowie, which was a combination of amber and pine and pure male.

"Duchess," he said in that slow, lazy way he'd perfected. The sound left a tingle tripping down her spine, as if Bowie had slid his tongue from that sensitive part of her neck all the way to her earlobe. "What brings you in here? Going fishing again?"

She stood about ten feet from the counter and lifted the muffin box like it was a sacrificial offering. "No. I came bearing gifts— banana nut muffins."

He leaned forward and smelled the air. "All I smell is you."

She shifted her head to the side. "What do I smell like?"

"Trouble." He patted the counter in front of him. "Come closer. I won't bite, and if I do ... you'll like it."

That kind of talk made her knees buckle. She liked a man who was confident enough to say what was on his mind. She'd like him better if he could deliver on his words.

"I've been bitten by you." She thought about the day he bit her lower lip. "I liked it." She approached the counter and set the muffins on the glass case that held the most expensive reels.

"Is that right?" He leaned forward until their mouths were a whisper apart. "You must not have liked it too much since you've avoided a repeat." He was so close that when his tongue swept across his lips, it touched hers, too.

She flicked her tongue out to taste peppermint. He smelled like sex appeal and tasted like mint. "I've been busy."

"How was Target?" Inside, she laughed because although he asked about Target, he really wanted to know about Dalton.

"Good. I picked up more orange essence."

"You went to Target for that? I'm pretty sure they have it at the corner store. If not, Marge from the corner store could order it for you."

She opened the box. The smell of bananas lifted from the warm muffins. "You said the chocolate chip muffins needed more orange." She pulled one of them free and separated the top from the base. Breaking a small bite off, she lifted it to his mouth. "Why don't you tell me what's right or wrong with this one." She brushed the bread against his lip, but when he opened his mouth, he didn't only take in the treat; he pulled in her finger as well. If she weren't already leaning on the counter, she would have puddled into a heap on the floor.

He pulled her finger from his mouth but didn't let it go. When he swallowed the bite of muffin, he licked the crumbs from her wet finger. "Delicious."

Katie didn't know if he was talking about the muffin or her. "Your dad made them."

Bowie chuckled. "Oh, you thought I was referring to the muffin. That tasted fine, but you taste better." As quick as lightning, his hand wrapped around her neck and pulled her to him. He whispered against her lips, "Can I taste you, Duchess?" It wasn't a question because his mouth covered hers before she could answer. They were doing a thorough taste test of each other when the bell above the door rang, and a group of men walked in. Katie pulled away, and Bowie gave a low, throaty growl.

"Stick around," Bowie said. "We're not even close to finished." He walked around the counter to the men who stood under the mounted jumbo-sized fish. "Can I help you?"

Katie moved to the side and watched the three men who stood next to Bowie. No doubt they were trust fund babies. Probably the pretty boys from Denver Ben mentioned. Each one was at least a head shorter than him. They were dressed in polo shirts, khaki shorts, and boat shoes, while Bowie wore a threadbare cotton T-shirt and a pair of jeans. On his feet were heavy black boots. Despite his dressed-down appearance, he was a hundred times sexier than the playboys.

Whereas the trio's hair was precision cut, their brows waxed, and their skin spa nourished, Bowie had a rugged look about him. One that said he didn't need an eighty-dollar haircut to make him a man.

One man pointed to the big trophy fish in the center of the wall. "That fish come out of the lake?"

Bowie nodded. "Caught it myself ten years ago. Took me two hours to pull it in." The sound of pride lifted his voice.

"Give me what I need to catch something like that."

Bowie turned to Katie and shook his head. Even she knew it wasn't wise to enter a shop and give the guy behind the counter carte blanche when it came to picking out your purchases.

His two friends chimed in and asked for the same.

Katie would enjoy this. Bowie would either give them what they needed or what they asked for—two very different things. The next few minutes would tell Katie a lot about Bowie. Was he an honest man? Part of her wanted him to be a stand-up guy. The other part of her wanted him to be a big fat liar, because if he lied, then there might be a chance for more, despite his warnings.

Bowie moved around the shop like he'd worked there his entire life; then again, prior to his exodus, he probably did.

Fifteen minutes later, Katie was squeezed into the corner while the three men paid for their rods and reels and worms.

"Anything else you need?" Bowie asked as he rang up their supplies.

To Katie's surprise, he hadn't taken them to the cleaners. He'd even talked them out of expensive, unnecessary equipment.

The blond turned and pointed at Katie. "I'll take one of those." He moved forward and offered his hand to introduce himself.

"Don't touch what's not yours." Bowie's voice became dark and direct.

The brown-haired man next to the blond grinned. "Are you his, doll?"

Katie placed her hands on the blond man's chest and pushed. "I'm not anyone's." Her voice held no fear, but inside, her stomach twisted into knots.

"Not yet." The cocky man leaned in. "We've got time."

She marched past him and walked behind the counter to stand behind Bowie. Her mom always told her when danger came at her to hide behind a solid structure. She was pretty sure it was referenced to a natural disaster when she made that statement, but Bowie was built like a cement wall. He'd work well as a solid structure in this case.

"You can leave in one piece, or I can reduce you to chum and bait. Your choice." Bowie pushed the bag of equipment into the blond's chest. His solid structure grew before her eyes—his stance got wider, and his chest got broader. The surrounding air seemed charged with danger. "Leave."

Her hands ran across the broad scope of his back, tracing the hills and valleys of a body built for war. Under her fingertips, the stone-hard muscles softened.

As soon as the three men walked out of the shop, Bowie turned to face her. Desperation and need filled his eyes. He pushed her back against the wall and looked deep into hers.

"Now, Duchess, where were we?"

CHAPTER NINE

Lush. That was the only way to describe her body. Pressed up against her, she was soft in all the right places. Oh ... and the way she smelled so sweet was comforting. Cinnamon and sugar. Like walking inside the house on a winter's day and smelling freshly baked cookies. Somehow, what Katie baked soaked into her pores. Even her kisses tasted like treats.

The way she kissed him left no doubt she was as hungry for him as he was for her. A few nibbles at her lips weren't enough. He wanted to consume her. Thinking about her was so much easier than thinking about everything he'd lost in this town.

"I'm going to kiss you until you're drunk on me." He covered her mouth with his and savored her sweetness. The kiss began soft and gentle, but something needy and primal took over.

She gripped the front of his shirt, pulling him closer.

His tongue ran along her lips, coaxing them open. He was certain if he could have a taste of her, he'd feel less empty. Being in Aspen Cove had hollowed him out. The only way to survive was to fill the void with Katie.

She shifted her body. For a second, Bowie thought she'd break the kiss and move aside, but that wasn't her intent. He'd pushed her against the All-Stars board. She'd adjusted herself and in doing so, he'd moved enough that Brandy's picture smiled back at him.

"Shit." He broke the kiss and stepped back. "I'm sorry." In his mind, he wasn't sure if he apologized to Brandy or Katie.

Her eyes followed his to the wallet-sized picture. "Oh … is that her?"

He didn't need to explain; she intuitively knew. "Yes, I'm sorry. It's not right."

Katie licked her lips. "Tasted right. Felt right." She looked at him. "Someday, Bowie, you will learn to live again." She raised her hand and touched the picture of Brandy. "I didn't know her, but my heart tells me she'd want you to be happy."

"It's hard knowing she'll never get the chance to be happy here again." He took a few steps in reverse until his back hit the glass counter. "Have you ever been in love?"

Katie's smile lit the room. Even the dark wood paneling appeared lighter. "No, but I plan to give it a try. It's on my list."

He laughed. Her list was unconventional. "You can't plan love; it just happens. Sometimes it's gradual, like it was with Brandy and me."

He turned and walked around the glass case, putting a barrier between them. Lord knew, when he got close to Katie, all he wanted to do was touch her and kiss her, but he didn't want Brandy looking on. It felt wrong, like he was being unfaithful.

She tugged to tighten her ponytail. "Sometimes you know the minute you meet someone that they're the one … or so I've heard." She took another look at the picture. "She was beautiful."

"Inside and out." He picked up the glass cleaner and sprayed the counter. At least cleaning kept his hands busy. "You should be careful around those guys while they're in town. I didn't like the way they were looking at you like you were some kind of morsel to eat."

Her laugh was as sweet as her smile. "Oh, you mean you didn't like that they looked at me in the same way you do." She lifted the muffin box, so it didn't get hit with the cleaner.

"I'm different." The words made sense in his head but sounded ridiculous when he spoke them.

Once he'd dried the counter, she put the muffin box back. "What makes you different?"

"They'll take what they want and leave."

"So will you." She pulled out her phone and glanced at the screen. "I've got to go."

Something about her expression made everything tighten inside his chest. He was a hypocrite and knew it. Each time he'd kissed her, he'd told her it meant nothing, but his need to be near her sure meant something. It was something he wasn't ready to admit to himself.

"Where are you off to?"

She pulled out a journal from her bag. "Bucket list. Today, I'm rowing a boat."

Something about that made Bowie laugh. Not the chuckle kind of laugh, but the kind that made his belly ache. "You're going to row a boat? That's like me saying I'm going to get a pedicure."

She lifted her shoulders and stood tall. "Not the same at all. I'll look good in a boat. You'd look silly in Sex on Fire nail polish."

"Can't argue with that."

Once, in high school, Brandy had painted one of his fingernails pink. It wasn't a good look for him. He'd forgotten about it until someone pointed it out. He had to beat two kids down to reestablish his manhood and stop the teasing.

"Where are you getting a boat?"

"Seth O'Grady is saving me one."

"O'Grady's is overpriced. Besides, Seth is a perv." That was

71

his memory anyway. When they were kids, Seth hid under the bleachers to look up girls' skirts. Although he hadn't seen the guy in years, that was how he'd always remember him. "I'm not sure you'd be safe around him."

She closed her eyes and sighed. "Too late, I've already reserved the boat. If you're worried about me, maybe you should come along."

"Maybe I should." He told himself he'd go to make sure she was all right, but he lied. He simply wanted to bask in the warmth of her presence.

"It's a non-date, then." She spun around and walked to the door. "You want to drive, or do you want me to drive?"

He followed the line of her body, from the top of her ponytail to her red boots. "I'll give you a ride you won't forget." That sentence could be interpreted in so many ways. Bowie didn't care how she took it. He'd deliver regardless.

"I'll be outside at noon ... waiting." She walked out the door.

He watched that heart-shaped ass of hers sway back and forth as she crossed the street and disappeared into the dry goods store.

What the hell am I going to do with her?

He looked at the photo of Brandy. For the first time in years, he heard her voice in his head.

Be happy, she said.

BOWIE CLOSED UP THE SHOP AND RACED HOME TO CHANGE. He didn't do board shorts and boat shoes like most of the tourists. Hell no, he wore cut-off camouflage BDUs and biker boots. Those who didn't like it could piss off. He wasn't posing for *GQ* magazine.

His stomach growled. He was hungry. Had Katie eaten? She'd brought him muffins, which he'd finished in short order. The least he could do was bring her lunch. Sadly, the options were limited to peanut butter and jelly or bologna sandwiches. He made one of each and snatched two bottles of water from the refrigerator before he left the house.

He tucked the provisions in his saddlebag and hopped on his bike. He'd promised her a ride she'd never forget, and he'd start with the bike.

The throaty growl of the engine was a sexy sound and came second only to a woman screaming *yes, yes, yes*. He put on his helmet and took off toward town.

Katie grabbed a piece of shade near the bakery. Gone were her boots, and in their place were white tennis shoes. Not as sexy as the red boots, but with those long legs, she'd be gorgeous in anything.

She looked at her phone and glanced down the road. She was looking for him.

He pulled up in front of her and revved the engine before he pulled off his helmet. He thought she'd smiled widely before, but her normal smile was nothing compared to the grin that nearly split her pretty face. The woman hopped up and down like she'd won the lottery.

"You've got to be kidding me. This is yours?" She ran to where he sat and extended her hand to touch the black gas tank. His Harley was solid black, with hints of chrome. She skimmed her fingertips around him and his bike as she made a full circle. "You're perfect."

He killed the engine. "Only if you like damaged goods." He took her bag and put it in the other saddlebag.

"That's my type. Tormented and twisted."

"Good to know." He unhooked the spare helmet he had strapped to the back and placed it over her head. "Have you ever ridden?"

"No."

"Another thing to check off your list." He pushed the helmet down on her head, and she winced. Her hair was in the way of it fitting properly. "Sorry." He removed it and pulled the tie from her ponytail. Long and blonde, her hair fell over her shoulders. The scent of her shampoo lifted in the air. "Strawberry?" He leaned in and breathed deeply.

"Yes, Abby makes it. She makes the best stuff for hair and body." She took the helmet out of his hands and placed it back on her head. "Is this right?"

He pulled the strap tight, then climbed back on the bike. "Hop on, Duchess. Hold me tight. I don't want you falling off."

When she climbed on, she scooted in close, pressing her breasts against his back. He was cradled between her thighs, and it felt nice—more than nice.

He pulled onto the road and gunned it while she held on tight, her whole body glued to his. That was nice, too.

Twenty minutes later, he drove into the parking lot of O'Grady's Equipment Rentals, which sat on the east side of the lake. In the summer, they rented everything from kayaks to fishing poles. In winter, it was snowshoes and snowmobiles.

Bowie parked and helped Katie off the bike.

"That was the best," she said in a Christmas morning voice.

Her cheeks were pink from the wind. When he pulled the helmet from her head, it gave that just-got-laid look to her hair. Or at least that's what he imagined she'd look like after they slept together—all pink and flushed and sexy.

An uncomfortable ache in his groin told him to keep his thoughts on simpler things like lunch and boating. "You ready to row?"

She took her purse from Bowie and looked down at the bike. "I want to do that again."

Adorable was the only way to describe her exuberance. "You'll have to unless you want to walk home."

"Can we take the long way home?"

Bowie wasn't sure he was ready to drive the circle around the lake yet. "Let's see how you feel after an afternoon of rowing." He grabbed the sandwiches and water. "I brought lunch. You have a choice of peanut butter and jelly or bologna. What's your poison?"

"Is that bologna with mayo or mustard?"

He gave her an incredulous look. The kind that said, *duh*. "Mustard is the only way to go."

"Can we share both?"

He gave her an exaggerated eye roll. "You want everything." It was easy being with Katie. She had a go-with-the-flow personality.

"I'll take what I can get with you."

Was that a message? Was she willing to settle for so little? "You should set your standards higher."

She hugged his arm and walked him toward the entrance. "'Low standards' aren't words that come to mind when I think of you."

"What comes to mind?"

He pulled the door open, and she walked in front of him. God, he loved those shorts. They ended just at the curve of her ass. Nothing showed, but hell, his imagination ran away with what was under that frayed edge.

"Tempting." She walked at a quicker pace to the register where Seth stood smiling at her.

"Katie, right?" The man took too much time looking her over.

"And me," Bowie said in a less than friendly voice. The tension strung wire tight through his body. He walked up behind Katie and rested his chin on the top of her head and relaxed.

Seth appeared to take in the situation. "Didn't you just get back?"

Bowie narrowed his eyes at him and Katie. He hoped it looked like a sign of possession. Katie didn't belong to him, but Seth didn't know that. The one thing he'd make sure of was Katie would never belong to Seth. She was far too good for that scumbag.

"Not too long ago." He placed his hands on Katie's hips and tugged her back against his front. She leaned against him like it was a natural move.

"You work fast." Seth handed the bill to Katie. "It's fourteen an hour or thirty for the day."

Bowie pulled out a ten and a twenty and set them on the counter. "We'll take it for the day."

Katie twisted her head to look up at him. He knew an argument was coming, so he kissed her into silence. "Ready?"

Seth pointed to the front door. "Grab the oars on your way out. The boat is in slip number three."

Bowie turned Katie around and guided her out the door.

"Caveman much?" She walked next to him. "What was that all about?"

"I don't like him. I don't like the way he looked at you. Like he had a chance. He's not good for you."

"I didn't realize when I invited you along, I'd get dating advice. What else does this package contain?" She lifted her hands in question. "My car can use a tune-up. The plumbing in the bakery still sucks. My bed creaks when I turn over. Care to fix those things, too?"

The lift of her lips told him she wasn't angry; she was yanking his chain. He already knew there was no way Katie would pass up a chance to twist his balls.

"Bobby Williams is who you call for car service. Mark MacPherson is the all-around handyman. When it comes to your bed … I'll be happy to assist."

"I'll keep that in mind if I ever get you past the doorjamb."

She was right; he hadn't set foot inside the bakery since he returned. He tried to mask his frown with motion. After he helped her into the rowboat, he untied it, pushed off the dock, and jumped into the boat himself. Then he handed her the oars. "You wanted to row. Knock yourself out."

How such a little thing like gliding across the lake could give her such a thrill, he didn't understand. She was beautiful, intelligent, and kind. How did the simple joys of life pass her by?

CHAPTER TEN

Who would have thought rowing could be so hard? Katie gripped the handles and pulled the paddles through the water. She'd read about rowing last night, and it seemed simple enough. She had to scoop water and put it behind her. To turn, she simply put the brakes on one side by stalling one oar in the water.

Easy peasy.

"Give me those." Bowie reached for the oars. "You're going to wear yourself out."

Katie gripped tighter. There was no way she'd relinquish her power. "Sit back and enjoy. I'm in charge of these." She raised the handles to prove a point, only to have one of them slip from her hand and slide into the water. "Oh. My. God." She laughed so hard, her stomach ached.

He pointed to the lone paddle in her hand. "Give me that for a minute." The air between them stilled while she contemplated his request. "I'll give it back with the other one once I have them both," he said to reassure her.

She reluctantly handed it to him and watched as he maneuvered the boat close enough to grab the rogue oar floating away from them. True to his word, he handed them back to her.

"Here you go, Duchess. Row until your heart's content."

Katie was certain it was hard for Bowie to surrender power. He seemed like the kind of man who controlled everything he could. She imagined the reason he hadn't been back to Aspen Cove since his fiancée died was that he couldn't control the situation then, and he couldn't control how he felt about it now.

"Sit back and relax. I'm going to give you the ride of your life." She teased him with his own words.

"Don't tease." He stretched out on the wooden bench. His legs were so long, they extended and tucked under her seat.

"I can't believe rowing is on your bucket list. What happened to things like meet a movie star or drive a Maserati?"

Katie made sure the oars were firmly in the ring thingy, then leaned forward and dipped them into the water. It took more strength and energy than she expected to pull them forward, but she wasn't a quitter.

"I've driven a Maserati. It belonged to one of my doctors."

"You've mentioned doctors more than once. Care to elaborate?"

"Not really. I was a sickly kid and spent a lot of time in the hospital." She let go of one oar for a second to touch her chest. "I had a little heart issue, but it's all good now." She was certain most people wouldn't call heart failure a "little issue." She didn't want to focus on the past. She wanted to live her future. She looked down at the angry scar that sliced through his knee and disappeared under the camouflage print of his cut-off shorts. "What about you?"

"I've seen a few doctors, too." He rubbed his knee and pulled the fabric higher to reveal the wound. "I'm still here. You're still here." He looked around them. The lake was dotted with fishing boats. "Stay clear of everyone else. You don't want to piss off a bunch of old fishermen. They won't think anything of 'acciden-tally' hooking you with their next cast."

"I got this."

Once the boat moved, she had it. They glided across the water. The still glasslike surface broke and rippled with their movement. Several birds swooped down to see if the couple had anything interesting to offer, and when they found nothing but two people and a plastic bag, they moved on. As she neared a boat ahead, she braked and turned right.

Bowie reached for the bag he'd packed. "Hungry?" He raised a brow. "We can free float while we eat the gourmet sandwiches I prepared."

"Gourmet, huh?" She pulled in the oars and tucked them under the bench. "What makes them gourmet?"

Bowie laughed. "I have no idea, but it sounded good."

"Pony up the goods, mister. I've been rowing, and I'm starved."

"You've been rowing for five minutes." He opened the bag and pulled out two bagged sandwiches and two bottles of water. "So, you still want to share both?"

She rose from her seat. The boat rocked from side to side as she made her way to the space beside him. "I like sharing with you." She for sure liked sharing his kisses. "Most people would share a meal before they shared a kiss. We've done it backward."

"I don't know. Who doesn't like a little appetizer first?"

She took the baggie with the bologna sandwich inside. She reached in, pulled out the two halves, and offered him one. "So I'm your amuse-bouche?"

"My what?" He took a bite of his half of the sandwich—a blob of mustard caught on the corner of his lip.

Katie couldn't help herself. She rose up and licked it away and savored the tangy taste it left on her tongue. "An amuse-bouche is something you eat to whet your appetite. Something to amuse your taste buds until you get to the main course."

"I'm hoping to get to the main course with you soon." He looked at her with heat in his eyes.

"So now I'm the appetizer *and* the main course."

She took a bite of her sandwich. How a bologna and mustard sandwich tasted so good, she had no idea. Maybe sharing it with Bowie made it better. Maybe the way he teased her made a simple sandwich decadent. Who was she kidding? There was no maybe. Everything about Bowie spoke to her.

He nuzzled his face into her neck. The scruff of a few unshaven days rubbed her skin to create a nice, warm burn. The wet of his tongue traced from her collarbone to the shell of her ear.

"You're dessert, too."

A slow trickle of desire oozed like warmed honey through her veins. There wasn't a place on her body that didn't want to be dessert for Bowie Bishop.

"We'll see. Maybe your appetite will fade at peanut butter and jelly." She picked up the other baggie and pulled out her half of the sandwich. "The jelly is sweet and satisfying."

Bowie turned to face her. "I'm sure you're sweet, too, and I guarantee when I'm done with you, you'll be satisfied."

Every word he said made her shiver, but one word made her heart sink to the worn wooden bottom of the boat. He said the word "done." Which made it sound like once he had her, that would be it.

Though Katie wanted to find love, she had to be realistic. Life was fleeting. Uncertain. Unyielding. Wasn't it better to have the thing she wanted once than never at all? No one knew better than her how life could change. She looked at Bowie, who had turned to glance at the water. He also knew a person could be here today and not tomorrow.

"I'd love to be your dessert." It was a bold statement. One she'd embrace because deep inside, she knew a day with Bowie was better than any day without.

He grabbed the oars and situated them into the rings. "My turn to row. I don't want you worn out before I get you into bed."

"I love how you think."

She took her seat across from him and finished her sandwich. With each pull of the oars, his muscles grew until the cotton shirt stretched tight over his arms and chest—parts of his body certain to be exposed later.

When he turned to look toward the shore, the sunlight glinted off the faded white line that bisected his cheek.

"Where did you get that scar?" She lifted her hand to her unblemished cheek.

His eyes narrowed, and his jaw tightened. The tick of a tense muscle twitched. "Car accident."

Her heart skipped a beat. By the sternness of his reply, it had to be associated with his biggest loss. "I'm sorry. It's none of my business."

They sat in silence for a long minute. He turned the boat so they faced the west side of the lake.

"We'd been together for over ten years when she died." His voice was low and far away. "I've never talked about it with anyone, but I got this scar trying to save her and my mother. I saved neither."

The air surrounding them turned heavy with regret. She wasn't certain how to respond. "You don't have to tell me."

He pulled his eyes from the mountainside to look at her. "I feel like you need to know. You need to understand why I can never love you. Not because you're not lovable, but because I'm not capable of love any longer."

When she swallowed, it was as if a boulder stuck in her throat. "I doubt you're incapable. It's that you're resistant. Why wouldn't you be? Love is risky."

He pointed from her to him. "And you're okay with this, knowing it'll never be more?"

Inside, she wanted to cry for herself and for him. Was she okay with never having the option of more with Bowie? Not really, but she had to be. She knew she deserved more, and so did he, but something told her he was worth the gamble. "You and I both know how fragile life is. Let's not worry about tomorrow. Let's live for today."

He rowed harder until they were cutting through the water like a hot knife through butter. "You make being here better."

"Being here isn't so bad. You might find you like it after all. Heck, you might even stay." *A girl could hope.*

She watched the scenery pass as Bowie propelled them forward.

"My mom used to say, 'Never cross the same bridge twice.' I've crossed this bridge before. I'm not staying."

She tilted her head to the side and made a face. "Really? Neverisms? I hate them."

He pulled in the oars. They coasted across the water. "What are you talking about?" He put his elbows on his knees and leaned forward with his hands clasped between his legs. "Neverisms?"

"You know. All the stuff people spout off like it's sage advice. Things like 'Never look a gift horse in the mouth' or 'Never moon a werewolf.' What the heck is a gift horse? And do werewolves exist? Wasted words packaged like wisdom."

"Some of them are good."

"Tell me one that's been beneficial to you."

He sat there. She could see the gears turning in his head, and she knew by the way his lips rose in the corners and the light in his eyes sparkled, he'd thought of one.

"Never say never." He gave her a look that said, *beat that.*

"You just said never." She shook her head, exasperated that he'd contradicted himself. "I'll give you this; that's the wisest one of them all because it leaves your options open. The one about the bridge ... what if what you wanted or needed was on the other side of that bridge? Would you cross it then? If you didn't ... you'd never know."

A breeze picked up. A man in a nearby boat hooted and hollered in celebration of his latest catch. The sun had fallen on the horizon and sat above the peak. The last remnants of snow had melted away. Bright green Aspen leaves colored the mountainside. It was spring, a time for new beginnings.

"You're right. Neverisms are stupid," Bowie said.

"I hate to make a blanket statement on anything, which is why 'never say never' is good. There are a few others worth mentioning, like 'Never pass up a chance to say I love you' or 'Never lose a chance to say a kind word' or 'Never let a man rowing your boat get away without a kiss.'" She launched herself at him, knocking him over.

For the next twenty minutes, they lay on the floor of the boat and made out like teenagers. It wasn't until a brave bird landed and pecked at the empty sandwich bags they came up for air.

The sun barely peeked above the mountain, which meant in no time it would be dark. "We should get back." He turned the boat around and moved toward shore. "Let's go home and get changed and meet back at the bar for a drink tonight."

"Is that all you want? A drink?"

"I never said that was *all* I wanted."

She licked his taste from her lips. "You sure like that word 'never.'"

"I do," he said with confidence. "Here's one more for you to think about. I'm going to do things to you tonight that will make certain you never forget me."

Playfulness looked good on him. It was nice to see him relax and enjoy the moment. So when he flashed his white teeth in an open-mouthed smile, something inside her melted like chocolate on a sun-warmed sidewalk. She thought of a "never" of her own. Never had she wanted a man as much as she wanted Bowie.

CHAPTER ELEVEN

The twenty minutes it took to get to the bakery were glorious. Her arms wrapped around his waist. Her head pressed against his back with him cradled between her open thighs. He hated dropping her off.

Once she walked inside, he took off for home with a promise of later. Her last words to him were, "Don't shave."

A girl like Katie should be with a banker or businessman. What she wanted with someone like him was beyond imagination. He had nothing to offer her. Seeing as she was a grown-up, he decided not to question it.

They'd talked about a lot of things on the boat when they weren't kissing. How she'd worked as a data entry clerk for her dad's insurance company. How her parents didn't give her much space to make choices, and why coming to Aspen Cove had been the scariest and best decision of her life.

He'd shared some things about himself. Never before had he offered information about *that day*. His heart and lungs seized when he looked across the lake to where it all happened, then he looked at Katie, and everything loosened up. She was human Xanax.

Just as he arrived at home, his father walked out the door. The smell of aftershave hit Bowie head-on. "Got another date?" He couldn't fault him for wanting to share his life with someone.

Ben shrugged his shoulders. "I don't know what's wrong with Maisey, but she's good to me." He pulled out his wallet and looked through his bills.

"You got enough money?" It was funny how the tables had turned. Once upon a time, it was Bowie standing in front of his father penniless.

"I do. Enough for dinner and a movie." His dad put his wallet away. His head dropped to look at the ground. "I may not be home tonight. Will that bother you?"

Bowie stood a foot taller than his dad and leaned down to look him in the eye. "I want you to be happy. Does Maisey make you happy?"

Ben's head rose. "I'm happier than I've been in a while. You're home. Your brother's got a good woman. I've got a job I like. Katie is special." He looked at the motorcycle sitting in the driveway. "Was that her I saw on the back of your bike?"

His dad didn't miss a thing. "I took her for a ride to the lake. She wanted to row a boat."

Ben laughed. "'Special' might not be the right word. She's quirky, but she's cute. Don't hurt her, Bowie. I have a feeling she's been through a lot already."

Bowie looked past his dad to B's Bed and Breakfast. "Haven't we all?"

Ben pulled his son in for a hug. He'd been uncharacteristically touchy-feely since Bowie had come home. "I love you, son. It's time for you to be happy, too."

Bowie nodded and walked backward toward the house. "Have a good time. Glove it before you love it."

"Get in the house," his father said with mock sternness.

Bowie headed straight for the shower. When he emerged smelling like soap instead of sweat, he ran into Cannon.

"Coming to the bar tonight?" his brother asked.

"I'll be there. I'm meeting Katie for a drink."

"Is that right? You got the hots for her?"

"She's hot, but it's not like that." It was exactly like that, but he wasn't fessing up. "We're friends. That's all."

Cannon stood in his doorway, buttoning his shirt. "Don't mess with her. I don't want Sage mad at me because you screwed with her best friend."

Bowie threw his hands in the air. "Why does everyone think I'm going to hurt her?"

Cannon shrugged. "Because you might. But don't. I'll kick your ass if you do." He brushed past Bowie. "I'm running late. I'll see you there."

He heard the front door close before he entered his room. While everyone around him had changed, his space had remained the same. Stuck in a time warp. The dresser was covered with memories, from the wheat back pennies Brandy gave him to movie stubs and brochures for wedding venues.

He picked up the advertisement for a place called The Chateau. It sat on the edge of Silver Springs. A cross between a dude ranch and a spa, and it had been Brandy's top choice.

He picked up the trash can and, with one swipe, threw it all away. There was no use holding on to the past. It never made him feel good about the future. There was another "never" for him to consider.

Could he have a future? Would his heart ever soften enough to let someone in? He couldn't see a time when that would happen. His future didn't hold a place for love, but it had a slice of time where he could hold Katie.

HE WATCHED THE DOOR FOR OVER THIRTY MINUTES, BUT SHE didn't show.

"Got a date?" Doc asked from the stool next to him. "You're watching that door like you're waiting for someone."

"No, not a date, but Katie's coming by to have a drink with me."

Doc folded his napkin into a grid of nine. He was on his second beer, which meant he'd be playing tic-tac-toe with Cannon to see who paid.

"Back in my day, if a girl said she'd meet you for a drink, that was considered a date. You youngsters are confusing."

"I'm not the dating type." He pulled the beer to his lips and took a drink. The cold carbonation helped tamp down the fire he'd built inside. Just thinking about Katie made him smolder.

"She's a good girl, that Katie. She's—"

Having heard it before, Bowie finished the sentence. "I know, she's special, and if I hurt her, you're going to kick my ass." He tipped back his frosted mug and took another drink.

Doc looked at him, perplexed. "I was going to say she's a blessing to Aspen Cove, but you're right, she is special. I'm too old to kick your ass, but there's a dozen people around her who will if you hurt her." He laughed and finished his beer.

Cannon walked over and started with an O in the center of the grid. Bowie ignored the rest of the game and kept his eyes on the door. A few minutes later, she walked inside. Dressed in tight blue jeans and those damn red boots, every eye in the place was on her.

For a Sunday, the bar was full, but it was tourist season, and the people of Aspen Cove financed their entire year in the months of May through October.

He hadn't noticed before, but the idiots from earlier were

playing pool. The stupid blond guy whispered to his friends until they all turned to stare at Katie.

She paid no attention to them. Her eyes were on him, and he'd be damned if that didn't feel good. He was broken and damaged and scarred and ugly, but she looked at him like he was a prince.

"Hey," she said. She climbed onto the seat next to him and smiled. "You beat me here."

He turned to her. She was stunning. Her hair was the lightest blonde, and it looked white under the lights. Her skin, flawless. Her lips plump and kissable. She smelled like strawberries and honey. He wanted to pull her into his arms and taste that sweet mouth of hers, but that would be like claiming her as his own. She wasn't his. He wasn't hers.

"You want the usual?" Cannon asked.

It bit at him that his brother knew what her usual was. Bowie knew very little about this woman, except she was beautiful and kind. She had been sickly as a child. Had overprotective parents and few life experiences. He knew her skin felt like satin, and her mouth tasted like honey. Her desire for him was as strong as his for her. She had curves that fit against him like a laser-cut puzzle piece. Her touch calmed him. That southern twang in her voice was like music to his ears.

Cannon placed a soda on the counter in front of her.

"Soda?" Bowie asked. She looked more like a wine girl; then again, who knew? He didn't really know her.

"I love the bubbly water."

She was a puzzle. "So let's play a game."

She clapped her hands. "I love games." She looked past him to where Cannon stood, losing a game of tic-tac-toe. "You want to play that?"

"Hell no. I want to get to know you," Bowie moved closer and whispered in her ear. "Before I get to know you." He pulled back.

An appealing blush highlighted her cheekbones. He liked knowing he put it there.

"What do you want to know?"

He reached up and brushed a piece of hair away from her eyes —those beautiful, soulful blue eyes. "I want to know everything, so let's play a game I call truth or lie."

"I know this game. You want to go first?"

"Ladies first, Duchess."

Katie sipped her soda water. "I'm turning eighteen next month."

Bowie choked on his beer. "I pray that's a lie because if it isn't, I'm going to jail tomorrow."

She laughed. "I'm twenty-eight, but my birthday is next month. Your turn."

"I've been shot seven times."

She chewed her cheek and stared at him. "I'd say that's the truth. Do I get to kiss your scars?" Her voice was soft and low and seductive.

"I'd love to feel your lips on me."

Doc rose from his stool and gave a wave goodbye. Cannon brought another pitcher of beer to the jerks at the pool table.

"I recorded a record when I was fifteen." She sat there with a straight face.

Bowie wasn't fooled because even though her face was solid and serious, her hands tapped nervously on her knee. That was her tell. She was a terrible liar.

"Lie."

"How did you know?"

He leaned back against the counter. "I'm intuitive." He fed her the same words she'd given him the day they met.

Over the course of the next hour, they learned a lot about each other.

She ran three times a week.

He spent three months in a hospital after his last injury.

She had a younger brother and sister.

He had Cannon.

She loved sweet potatoes.

He loved eggplant.

She'd always wanted a dog.

He wanted a new Harley.

She loved lip gloss.

So did he when he tasted it on her lips.

She loved reading about romance.

He loved *Penthouse*.

She liked bad boys like him.

He liked her.

When the jukebox played, she pulled him to his feet. "Dance with me. I love this song."

He didn't recognize it, but she told him an artist named Indigo sang it. They found an empty piece of floor, and she fell into his arms while the moving voice of the artist sang about unfulfilled wishes and dreams.

Moments later, the blond idiot poked him in the shoulder. "Mind if I cut in?"

Bowie laughed. "You really have a death wish, don't you?"

"I'm just asking you for a minute with a pretty girl." He looked at Bowie's scarred face.

"I don't mind stepping aside as long as you don't mind castration." Bowie looked down on the man. He was stupid but brave. "You come near her again—in fact, if you even look at her, I'll rip your gonads free and feed them to you. Got it?" He pulled Katie into his arms. He loved the way she naturally curled into his side. "Let me give you some advice. Here in Aspen Cove, there are rules. You don't jump on someone else's ride. You don't fish in another man's pond. You don't touch another man's woman. This one is mine."

He nodded toward his brother, who was watching from behind the bar, then led Katie out the door.

What the hell did I just do?

He'd claimed her.

CHAPTER TWELVE

"Would you have really fed him his ... what did you call them ... gonads?" Katie walked close enough to Bowie to be considered a piece of him. Every one of her curves slipped into the notches of his body. He nestled perfectly beside her.

He stopped in the center of the street and looked down at her with a lazy smile. "I would have ripped them out through his throat as a warning to others. You are not the girl to mess with." He leaned down and pressed his mouth to her forehead. Lighting-laced lips sent a jolt through her that made every nerve ending tingle.

Although he was easily eight inches taller than her, they seemed to be perfectly matched.

"For a guy who wants nothing more than a good time, you sure put out the possessive vibe." She tilted her head to look at him. "When you're done with me, I'm never likely to get another date in this town."

The hard line of his jaw twitched. "Tonight, you're mine. I'm a selfish bastard, and I refuse to share." His big palms cradled the back of her neck as he leaned down to kiss her.

The man fried her brain with his touch. "Tomorrow, I'm free game?"

He wrapped his arm around her waist and led her to his truck. "We'll see." When they got to the passenger side, he opened the door and helped her into her seat. "Let's live it a minute at a time." He covered her mouth and stole a kiss.

Her heart galloped at a pace that left her dizzy. She'd been kissed by plenty of men but never had her heart want to leap out of her chest and live inside theirs until now.

She pulled away. "Who knows? By tomorrow I might be done with you."

She doubted every word that came out, but it felt good to say it. He'd been telling her since they met that all they'd be together was a good time. There was no questioning that fact. If Bowie could turn her insides to goo and her brain to stone with a kiss, who knew what he could do to the real estate between her legs? But part of being independent meant she got to decide, too, so she reminded him he wasn't in control of her or how this moment would turn out.

"That's a possibility, not a probability." He closed the door and walked around the truck to his side.

She liked the easy confidence of his walk. Bowie wasn't out to prove a point. She doubted very much he'd fret over her pleasure. He held an air about him that said he knew he could please her. That kind of confidence was sexy as hell.

"Your place or mine?" Katie buckled her seat belt.

"Mine. No one will be home tonight. Dad's at Maisey's, and Cannon basically lives at B's."

She turned her body to face him. "Won't that be hard for you?"

He made that warm, soft sound that wasn't quite a laugh but something closer to a growl. It sent shivers racing down her spine.

"No, but give me a few minutes, and I'll be hard for you."

She reached over and playfully punched him in the chest. "You know what I mean."

A moment of silence stretched between them as they drove the few blocks to his house. He pulled into the gravel driveway and killed the engine. He unbuckled his seat belt and shifted his body to face her. The uneasy expression in his baby-blue eyes showed the turmoil he must have felt inside.

"I won't lie to you and say it'll be easy, but we've got this place or your place, and I'm not ready for the bakery."

Katie felt a deep need to comfort the man she knew was hurting inside. She slid to his side of the bench seat and crawled into his lap. "I want to help you through this. I want you, Bowie. I want this moment with no expectations of more. Let's forget about the world and get lost in each other. Surely, the universe can grant us a few minutes of pleasure." She rested her hands on his tense shoulders. Her fingers kneaded the taut muscles.

"A few minutes?" His shoulders shook with his laugh. "You don't have much confidence in me, do you?" He swung the door open and slid out of the seat with her wrapped around his waist. She loved the way his hands cradled her bottom and pulled her body close to his. The ease with which he held her made her feel light as a snowflake. "I've learned not to expect much."

With a bump of his hip, he shut the door. Three long strides got them to the front porch, two strides up the steps, skipping several as he went. A quick stop to unlock the door. Several steps down the hallway to a room that smelled like him.

She looked around at the walls covered with classic rock posters. A lava lamp sat on his dresser, with the blob of blue oil drowning at the bottom.

"Welcome to the nineties." He lowered her to the edge of the bed. "Just pretend we're in one of those joints that rent themed rooms." He glanced around the space and shook his head. "I was never one for decorating."

Katie rose from the bed and walked to the poster of No Doubt. "I don't know ... Gwen Stefani knows how to make a room pretty."

Bowie snuck up on her and buried his head in the crook of her neck. The scruff of his unshaven face roughed up her tender skin in the most delicious way.

"You make my room look pretty."

"Flattery will get you ... everywhere." She turned around and pressed her hands against his hard chest. Her fingers traced his muscles from his pecs to the start of his beard. "Glad you didn't shave." Once her hands were wrapped around his neck, she pulled him down for a kiss. She wasn't usually so bold, but this was the new Katie, the one who went after what she wanted, and right now, she wanted Bowie.

He turned them around and walked her back to the edge of the bed. The mattress hit the back of her knees and folded her back on top of the soft blue comforter.

"Everything comes off but these boots. They're sexy as hell."

She pulled her lower lip between her teeth and chewed. She hadn't given this much thought. Sure, she'd fantasized about Bowie and her in bed since the day they met, but to actually be here with him looking at her with eyes filled with liquid lust was a different story. She felt completely unprepared for the emotions and sensations he stirred within her.

The last time she dated a guy, they made it to the fifth date. She thought being honest about her condition was prudent, but when she told Samuel she was a heart transplant recipient over dinner, he folded his napkin and stood. She thought he was going to the bathroom, but fifteen minutes later, he hadn't returned. When she asked for the bill, the waitress said the gentleman had paid and left.

He took two days to text her. "I can't be with someone so

broken." That was the first time she realized she viewed herself differently than the rest of the world. Whereas her ten-inch scar spoke of weakness to others, it spoke of strength to her.

She never considered herself broken; she thought of herself as fixed. Broken was when, at twenty, she lay in the hospital without the energy to press the nurse call button; today, she could run for miles at a stretch. The only thing broken was Samuel. Right then, she decided that telling someone about her illness weakened her position in the relationship. Then again, she didn't want to strip her shirt off and shock the hell out of Bowie.

"I'll take everything off but my shirt and boots."

He shook his head back and forth. "No way, Duchess. I've been dying to see those breasts of yours."

"Fine, but I'm scarred." Like ripping off a Band-Aid, she said the words quickly, hoping it would take the sting out.

"We're all scarred."

He reached for the hem of her shirt and pulled it over her head. She watched as he took in every bare inch of her body. His eyes lingered on the black lace that barely contained her breasts. Sitting perfectly between the two lace cups was a long, thin, silver scar that ran from the top of her breastbone to the bottom of her ribs. He took her all in, but not once did he look disgusted, or worse, filled with pity.

"You're perfect."

Those were words she hadn't expected or prepared for. If she didn't fall more in love with him, then nothing would pull her heartstrings. "Glad you're blind."

"Oh, sweetheart, I see what's important." He traced her scar with the tip of his calloused finger. "This doesn't tell me what you aren't. It shows me what you are. You're one badass, sexy woman." His thick fingers unhinged the front clasp of her bra. When it fell open, his eyes, once the color of a spring sky, turned night blue. "I can't believe you've been hiding these from me." He cupped her full breasts with his palms. "I knew it."

Katie lay back while Bowie moved up her body, knees on both sides, straddling her hips. "Knew what?"

"That these were made for my hands."

She reached up to cup the roundness of his chest muscles. "You overflow mine." For the first time, she didn't focus on her scar because he didn't. It was like he didn't see it. "Take your shirt off." She didn't recognize the throaty growl to her voice.

He sat back with his firm butt pressed to her thighs and crossed his arms, gripped the hem of his shirt, and slowly pulled the cotton up his chest and over his head. Katie sucked in a breath at his beauty. Sure, he was scarred like her, but every one of his scars represented a battle with life and death. A battle from which he came out the victor.

Her fingertips skimmed over his battle scars. A long gash across the right side of his chest. An indent to the left of his happy trail. A jagged line that ran the length of his right side.

He placed his hands over hers and moved them down his body. "Knife fight." He left the gash and lowered their hands to his side. "Shrapnel from an IED." He unbuttoned and unzipped his pants, leaving the two sides to fall open. The indent bled into another scar that disappeared beneath the denim. "Bullet wound and surgery." He let her hands go and leaned over her, his lips a breath away from hers. "They don't define me." He adjusted his body. The hot stroke of his wet tongue ran down her scar. "This doesn't define you. You are beautiful."

His lips and tongue continued their path until the denim of her jeans stopped his progress. Her entire body vibrated with need. On her elbows, she lifted and watched him tug her button open with his teeth, then quickly move the zipper down. She drew in a ragged breath and willed her heart to slow its pace. She couldn't think with the whoosh of blood sounding in her ears.

While he tugged the tight jeans over her hips, she heeled off her boots. If he wanted her in them, he could put them back on her. Distracted by her pants, her red boots were forgotten.

What started off as a languid taste of her skin turned into a frenzy of clothes flying in all directions. She pulled at his pants until they bunched around his ankles. He hopped up and out of his jeans.

God, he was magnificent. A body carved in stone. Her eyes took him in from the top of his cropped hair to the rigid length of him curved up toward his stomach. For a woman who was practically virginal for her age, he didn't frighten her. With only two solid experiences under her belt, she could have been struck by nerves. Instead, she was consumed by need.

He blanketed her body with his. The coarse hairs on his chest tickled the sensitive buds of her nipples. The scruff was back at her neck, moving against her skin in what could only be described as practiced seduction.

"You like this?" He jutted out his chin and rubbed back and forth across her chest.

"Oh, yes." A sexy sigh escaped her lips. She loved it. She wanted to feel that texture on her skin until he left her chafed and burning. "Kiss me."

"Gladly." He moved up her body, the length of him sitting heavy between her thighs. "I love your lips and your taste and that little moan that sounds each time I kiss you."

He covered her mouth with his. His tongue probed at the seam of her lips until she opened to him. The kiss was deep and moving. He wasn't simply kissing her. He explored everything about her, from her taste to her texture. That little moan he spoke of filled the air.

When his hands reached for her breasts, she inhaled sharply. With her shirt-on rule, they rarely saw action; so, when he rolled the puckered skin between his fingers, she arched up to meet his touch.

It didn't take him long to leave her mouth so he could run his hot tongue to the same buds that begged for attention. Searing, he sucked and pulled at them until she was a quivering mess.

She ignored his chuckle as he lowered himself to the cradle of her thighs. "Is this where you wanted to feel my five o'clock shadow?" The heat of his words blew across the sensitive flesh between her legs.

"Yes." She'd experienced the hunger of a man once before and could only say she was a fan. "I want to feel you everywhere."

And she did. Bowie did things to her body she only imagined could happen. He took her from shaking between the subtle strokes of his tongue to the screaming of his name several times. When she lay like a wet noodle in the center of his bed, he hovered over her. The proof of his desire twitched between her legs.

He lifted his head. "What about birth control?" His voice hung low in the air. A bit of gravel and a lot of need made four words sound like continued foreplay.

"We need to use a condom. I'm not on anything." With her condition, barrier methods were less risky.

He rose from her body, leaving goose bumps on every inch of her skin. "Lucky for us, I've got two condoms in my wallet. These suckers have been to several countries." He pulled his wallet from his pants and took out the two foil-wrapped packages.

"How old are they?" Katie knew latex had a shelf life. She had no idea what it was, but she wasn't willing to take chances.

"Less than a year." He lifted the corner of one packet to his mouth and tore the foil open. He held it up to the light. "It looks all right to me."

"Glad you came prepared."

She was glad because she couldn't imagine having to turn back now. She looked at the green condom pinched between his fingers.

100

Why condoms had to come in crazy colors, Katie didn't know. She'd never had a longing desire to be filled with green until that moment. Hell, Bowie's condom could have been any color, and that would have been her favorite.

He rolled it onto his impressive length and climbed between her legs. "You ready?"

She gripped his hips and pulled him to her entrance. "If I said no?" She shifted her hips, pressing him inside of her a fraction of an inch. She watched his eyes narrow as he rode the razor's edge of self-control.

"I'd ask you why. If I couldn't get you ready, then I'd lie beside you and hold you. I'd never force you into anything."

She hiked up her hips more. "I'm ready."

He heaved a sigh of relief. "Oh, thank Christ." With firm control, he pressed inside her.

White-hot lightning raced through her veins the minute he was fully seated inside. She reached around and gripped his firm globes and pulled him deeper. This wasn't about the sex. It was about the connection between them. She already knew the sex would be phenomenal. What she didn't expect was to have her heart sing when they were fused as closely together as possible. If this was all she would get—this one moment in time—she wanted to feel him as deeply as a person could. If she only got this one night, the memory would have to last her forever.

"So good," she whispered into the crook of his neck.

While his body stroked hers, she thought about how he'd told her he wanted to make sure she'd never forget him. There wasn't a chance of that. This moment would go down in history as the best sexual experience of her life.

"You're made for me, Katie. So damn perfect." His pace increased, and so did her passion.

Heat rose from her core to her heart, then slammed back to her core in what only could be described as implosion. She shattered beneath him while he continued to take her places she'd never been. When she whispered his name, he stilled. Time stilled. Everything stilled. In that second, she knew that, despite his warnings and her lies to herself, she would fall in love with Bowie Bishop.

CHAPTER THIRTEEN

Bowie turned and reached for Katie, but the spot where she had been curled up beside him was empty and cold.

"Katie?" he called. "Where are you?" He stilled and listened, hoping to hear movement from somewhere in the house, but it was silent.

He lifted his leg into the air and flexed it. Mornings were the worst. After the time he'd spent on his knees cradled between her thighs, he expected his body to scream at him, but the opposite was true. Rather than feel like his leg was cast in stone, he had the range of motion he'd only dreamed about. Sure, the muscle was sore, but in a good way.

He rolled out of bed, and into yesterday's jeans, tugging them up his legs. After a glorious night of passion and pleasure, he should have felt buoyant, but heaviness weighed him down—she was gone.

He checked the house for her, hoping maybe she was in the shower or on the back deck, but nope, she was nowhere in sight.

He plodded to the kitchen and popped a K-cup in the coffeemaker. While it filled the room with a comforting smell,

Bowie was anything but comforted. He thought about the woman who had called out his name all night long. Each time she said *"Yes"* or *"More"* or *"So good"* or *"Bowie,"* the wall he'd erected to protect his heart had cracked and then crumbled. By the time they fell asleep, his emotions were raw and bared. Everyone around him said Katie was special.

He couldn't pinpoint why that was true, but it was. There was an odd mix of strength and vulnerability to her.

He picked up his coffee and held it to his lips. The clock on the stove read six in the morning. He thought of the bakery. Not in the sad way he'd always remembered it, but in a utilitarian sense. She hadn't left him in bed because she wanted to. She left him because she had to. That made the sting of waking up alone less painful. He only wished she'd woken him to give her a ride.

The front door opened, and in walked Cannon. His hair stuck up in every direction.

"Why are you up so early?" Bowie asked.

"Hans is in town, and we're going fishing." He swept past him and started a cup of coffee. "Do you remember him?"

Bowie laughed. "Exchange student that knocked up the Paisley girl so he could stay in the country? I remember him. He's still around?"

"Yep. He planted a lot of seeds around town. He's almost as bad as Bobby for breeding, except Bobby plants his seeds into the same garden plot, whereas Hans likes a lot of different plots of land."

"What's wrong with these guys? I've got one word—condom."

Cannon's coffee sputtered to a finish before he brought the steaming cup up to his lips for a drink. After a satisfied sigh, he said, "Speaking of condoms ... was that Katie I saw leaving this morning?"

Bowie would not feed his brother any information that could be used against him. "Don't know what you're talking about." He turned and looked out the kitchen window. A slight breeze moved the pine needles back and forth.

"All right. If that's how you want to play this, it's fine." Cannon walked over to Bowie. Side by side, their shoulders touched while both men looked forward. "Just wanted you to know I approve. She's perfect for you."

Bowie's throat tightened. His body went rigid. "You got it wrong." Although he said the words out loud, each one tasted like the lie it was. Katie was perfect for him, but was he perfect for her? How could she settle for so little when she deserved so much more?

"Maybe, but I saw you last night. I've only seen you that way with one girl."

"Those guys were assholes."

"They are assholes. The same assholes that just extended their trip for two more days. Why do you think I'm staying with Sage?"

Bowie laughed. "Because you get laid? Because she feels good in your arms at night? Because you're in love with her?"

Cannon gave him a you've-got-me-there look. "Guilty of everything."

"Just marry the girl and get it over with. You and I both know time waits for no man." Bowie walked away from his brother and took a seat at the table. "If she's the one, seal the deal."

Cannon walked over and leaned against the wall of windows that looked out at the lake. "Do you think there's only one for each of us?"

There was a time Bowie knew that to be the truth, but it was before he kissed Katie Middleton. "I think you know when it's right in your heart. If you can't imagine a life without her or her life without you, then I'd say she's the one. If your life would be less without her in it, then she's the one. If seeing her again after just leaving her is the most important thing in your day—"

"I know, she's the one." Cannon kicked off the wall. "The

assholes are getting ready to go hiking and said something about picking up a muffin on their way."

Bowie flew from his chair and raced to his room to get fully dressed. In the background, he heard his brother's laughter.

All he thought about as he drove down Main Street was if one of those idiots was anywhere near Katie, he'd be wearing a fist to go with his polo shirt. He parked right in front of the bakery. There were a half-dozen people in line, and he scanned the men but came up empty. They were all locals stopping by on their way to work.

Bowie remembered a time when Aspen Cove bustled with business. Back when the paper mill was open. The air always smelled like fresh-cut wood, no matter what time of year you came to visit. Main Street was always busy, and there wasn't an empty house in sight. When the Guilds abandoned the mill and that Victorian Mansion on Daisy Lane, everything changed. Both buildings were like ghosts of the past.

He sat in his truck and watched Katie. She had a smile for everyone. He couldn't hear what she was saying, but he watched those lush lips move. Lips that had given him so much pleasure the night before. He was stupid to think he'd be able to get her out of his system with one night. Hell, the first time he kissed her, all he thought about was the next kiss he'd get. He contemplated the words he'd told his brother. Could she be the one? Brandy was the one. She'd always been the one, but now, here was this girl who charmed everyone in her presence, including him. Did he dare consider the possibility he'd been given a second chance at love?

Out of the corner of his eye, he saw the three douchebags stumble from their Porsche Cayenne. Before he could exit his truck, they were already in the bakery.

Bowie was torn between leaving the past behind, which meant not stepping back into it, or protecting his chance of a future, which meant steamrolling into the front door.

He stood on the sidewalk, one foot pointed in the direction of the bakery, one foot pointed toward his truck. What he did right here would decide everything.

When the bakery emptied except for the three men and Katie, there was no choice. She belonged to him.

He marched inside the building and came around the back counter to stand beside her. "You should have woken me up, Duchess. I would have driven you here." He looked straight at the blond man and smiled before he turned Katie around and kissed her hard on the lips. "I missed you."

Bowie slung his arm over Katie's shoulder. A sign of possession. "What can I get you boys?" He emphasized the word "boys" because he knew it would irritate the men. "My brother says you're hiking today?"

"Your brother?" the brown-haired man said. "Is he the Neanderthal that runs the bed and breakfast and the bar?"

"That would be the one." Bowie snapped together a box like he'd done it all his life. Then again, he'd spent many an afternoon boxing up muffins just waiting for Brandy. "Muffins? Coffee?"

While he waited for their answer, he looked around the place. The layout was the same, but it didn't feel familiar. He expected it to be heavy with loss and sadness, but it was bright and happy, like the woman who stood next to him, looking at him like he'd lost his mind.

"Three muffins and three coffees."

Katie turned to start the coffee while Bowie boxed up the muffins. "My girl makes the best muffins in town."

The men were quiet. Bowie plopped the muffins inside the box and shoved it across the counter. "If you boys are looking for some action, you won't find it here. I'd suggest you look in Copper Creek. They don't have the caveman mentality you'll find here."

Katie's shoulders shook with her suppressed laugh. "Here you go." She rang up their order and took the money. After the three men left them alone, she turned to Bowie. "What was that all about?"

She rocked forward, then rocked away from him. He couldn't blame her. He'd sent conflicting messages since he'd met her. Telling her all she'd be was a good time wasn't fair. She was that. The best time he'd had in years, but she was more than that. His heart ached for the way he'd reduced her to nothing more than a pleasurable act. Bowie knew then he had a lot to make up for.

"That was me telling them you aren't available. Me telling you I had an amazing time last night. And me also telling you you're more than a good time."

She breezed past him into the kitchen. She dumped eggs and butter and vanilla into the large stand mixer. "This is me telling you I have to make more muffins." She walked up to him and stood on her tiptoes to press a kiss to his lips. "Me telling you that last night was amazing. Thanks for making me feel ..." She paused for a minute. "Whole."

She went about her business like he wasn't there, and for the first time in a long time, Bowie felt uncertain. He'd always been the one to make the rules. He gloved it, he loved it, and he disappeared. With Katie, he couldn't imagine a day without seeing her smile. He wanted to wake up next to her and feel the heat of her body clinging to his. He wanted more, and that scared the hell out of him. More was dangerous.

"Can I take the last muffin?" He looked over his back to the display case that held heart-shaped cookies, mini cakes, and one muffin.

"Knock yourself out." She hefted the large mixing bowl to the prep table and tilted it to its side while she scooped batter into cups. "Grab coffee, too."

He leaned against the doorjamb and watched her. She looked right in the shop. She felt right.

"I never thought you'd set foot in here." She picked up two

muffin pans and breezed past him to the oven. The door handle he'd fixed years ago had come loose. He made a mental note to fix it again.

"This wise woman taught me that neverisms are stupid, but I like them. My new mantra is 'Never say never.'"

"That's a good one."

He looked past her to the back door. "How did the apartment upstairs turn out?"

Her eyes opened wide. "You haven't seen it?" She wiped her hands on the apron tied around her waist.

"No. It was only a thought at the time. Brandy had wanted to convert the upstairs to an apartment where we could live. She thought it would be convenient while I ran the bait and tackle store and she ran the bakery, but it never came to pass."

"You're welcome to look around." She stocked the counter with boxes and opened a fresh packet of napkins. "It's a great place, with two bedrooms and a bathroom. There's a small kitchen and a living room. It's perfect. Go on up and see it for yourself."

Bowie shook his head. "I'll wait for the personal tour."

Katie stopped what she was doing and came to stand in front of him. "That would mean you'd have to spend more time with me."

"Duchess, after last night, you'll be lucky to get rid of me."

The way her smile lit up her face made his insides heat. If she didn't have muffins in the oven and he didn't have to open the shop next door, he'd carry her upstairs and start the tour with every surface he could have her on.

"Is that right?" She closed in on him and pressed her hands to his chest. "I once experienced something hard to get rid of, but I'm sure it was a virus."

Bowie laughed. "That's me. I'm a virus you're not likely to shake off too easily."

The timer beeped, and Katie pulled the oven door open. The

heat surrounded them both, but Bowie wasn't certain the air whooshing from the oven caused it. "You better leave before I close up shop and beg to be infected again."

"How about dinner tonight at the diner? Just you and me?"

Katie put her hands on her hips. "Bowie Bishop ... are you asking me on a date?"

He smiled at her. "I am. What's your answer, Duchess?"

She flung herself into his arms, hopping up and wrapping her legs around his waist. "One hundred times, yes."

"I'll be at your door at six." He relished the feel of her sliding down his body. She said he made her feel whole. She made him feel alive.

He gave her one last peck on the lips before he walked out. The rest of the day, all he would think about was their next moment together. Deep in his shredded but healing heart, he knew she was the one.

CHAPTER FOURTEEN

Three batches of muffins and ten dozen cookies later, Katie leaned against the counter, exhausted. The only thing that kept her going was the promise of a date with Bowie. A real date. For a man intent on a one-and-done experience, he sure changed his tune. Katie laughed. Maybe Grandma Pearl was right when she advised Katie to tempt men with the china before letting them drink the tea.

Bowie had gotten to know her before she spread out her good china and served her teacakes in the same night. Thinking about her grandma made her think of her mother. Hadn't she made her suffer long enough?

She dialed her mom's number and pressed send. It rang twice before her mother answered.

"Princess ... is everything okay?"

Katie had been called "Princess" long before Kate Middleton came on the scene and landed her prince. She couldn't remember a time where her parents hadn't used the moniker.

"Hello, Mama, how are you?" It was nearing three o'clock, the slowest time of the day for Katie, so there would be no interruptions. "How's Daddy? Isabella? Nick?" She listed off her siblings in order. Isabella was four years younger than Katie. Nick two years younger than Isabella.

"Everyone is fine, sweetheart. How's the weather?" Over the last two months, her mother had learned not to come out of the gate with *how's your health,* but Katie knew that was always her mother's biggest concern.

"It's wonderful. The skies are healthy. The clouds are rested. It's a beautiful, healthy day."

"I miss you, baby. We got your package. Your sister is just gaga over that lavender lotion you sent."

Katie watched as a family walked into the dry goods store. "It's made locally. A woman in town raises bees, and she uses the honey and wax for amazing things like lotions and candles and soap."

"You're liking Colorado?"

The minute she mailed the box, her location would be known. "I do. I like it so much."

Katie could hear the scrape of a chair on a wooden floor in the background. She could picture her mother sitting at the large stone island in the big country kitchen, looking across the massive back yard of their estate.

"Tell me about your life there." It was the first time her mother acknowledged that she had a life anywhere but Dallas.

"I'll tell you everything as long as you promise not to hop on Daddy's jet and fly here."

Another thing she had told no one was that she came from a wealthy family. Not new money rich, but old family Rockefeller rich. Her great-granddaddy made his money in oil. Her father made his in insurance.

None of that mattered to Katie because when she left Texas, she left it all behind. Being independent didn't mean dipping into the trust fund the minute things became bad. It meant living within her *own* means.

That first day she met Sage and told her she didn't have money for supplies, she wasn't kidding. She'd left with the cash she had in her pocket, which was barely enough to get her to Colorado.

"I promise. Tell me everything."

She moved from behind the counter and took up a chair in front of the window. It was the perfect perch to people watch. She told her everything, from the pink envelope to her muffin of the day.

"You own a bakery?"

"I do, and it's the most wonderful thing to mix up the ingredients and earn money for my masterpiece."

"Your father said you were keeping up with your insurance payments. You know we would have paid them, regardless."

"Don't you understand? I needed this. All my life, I've been Sophia and Tate's daughter—the poor thing with the heart condition. Here in Aspen Cove, I'm just Katie. No one knows about my heart. They don't know my net worth. All they know is, I'm a girl who came to town and learned to make treats. I love being normal."

The bakery was silent except for the hum of the exhaust fan above the oven. "I can see the allure, but you have to tell someone there about your health. What if—"

"I know, Mama. I'll tell someone soon, but for now, I feel great. I'm happy for the first time in years. I've even got a date with an amazing man. I want to pretend I'm normal for a little while longer."

"You've got a date? Who is this boy, and what does he do?"

"At thirty-four, he's a man, not a boy." Katie relived in her mind the things Bowie did to her body last night. No boy would ever have those skills. A shiver of excitement raced through her at the possibility of a repeat tonight. "He used to be a soldier but was injured and returned home."

"What does he do for a living?"

If Katie had been home, her parents would have had a dossier on Bowie. "He runs a bait and tackle shop." She could imagine her mom's eye roll. Sophia Middleton would never approve of Bowie Bishop. He wasn't white-collar and rich. While Katie was privileged, Bowie was a commoner.

"He's a good man. Works hard. Loves his family."

"A bait shop?" Leave it to her mom to hear what she wanted.

"Yes, he taught me how to fish. He went rowing with me. We ate bologna sandwiches. I'm doing things I only dreamed about."

"You could travel first class around the world. Why are you settling for bologna?" She could almost see the curl of her mother's lip. The look she made when she tasted something foul.

Katie let out a frustrated growl. She'd spent a good portion of her life in a hospital. Never once did her parents' money buy her health or happiness. When her heart failed, and machines kept her blood pumping through her veins, their money couldn't buy her a new heart. She waited on the list like everyone else.

"I choose bologna. Bologna may be common, but it tastes good. It feels right." They were no longer talking about food but lifestyles. "You're caviar and Cristal. I'm peanut butter and jelly. I always have been. I'm happy. Be happy for me."

"You know what?" her mom said with more joy and resignation than she'd heard in her lifetime. "You've been through hell and back. If heaven is a small town in Colorado, I'm happy you found it, but don't forget, caviar and Cristal will always be waiting for you."

"I love you." She pressed her lips to the receiver of the phone. "I miss you."

"I miss you, too, Princess. You let me know when I can visit you. Surely, there's an airport nearby."

Katie shook her head. One visit from Sophia Middleton would turn Aspen Cove on its ear. That might be worth the visit alone.

"There's an airport where Daddy's plane can land in Copper Creek. I'll let you know when I'm ready."

"Call me next week?"

"Of course." Katie hadn't missed a phone call with her mom yet. Despite her need to be independent, she also needed the reassurance that when push came to shove, her mom would be there for her. "Talk to you soon."

"Katie?" her mom said before hanging up. "I'm so damn proud of you."

Sophia Middleton never cursed, so when she said "damn," it emphasized the importance of her statement.

Katie looked around the old bakery. Although the building was a gift, she'd built her dozen-muffins-a-day business into a hundred-muffins-a-day empire. She was literally rolling in the dough that made her life here in Aspen Cove possible.

———

At six o'clock, she ran down the stairs to answer the back door. Taking up the entire doorframe was Bowie dressed in black jeans and a gray T-shirt. In his hands was a mixed bouquet of daffodils and tulips. An odd combination of flowers that somehow worked.

"Are you ready?" He turned to the side and offered his arm.

"I need my purse." She started up the steps, flowers in hand, but he caught her by the thin belt cinching the waist of her dress. She placed the buds on the steps by her feet.

"You don't need anything." He spun her around and pulled her into his chest.

"Not true," she mumbled against the soft cotton of his shirt. "I need a kiss."

He circled her waist with his hands and lifted her like a rag doll into the air until her lips were close to his. "You want a kiss, or need a kiss?"

"What does it matter?"

He kissed her forehead and let her slide down his body. "Oh ... it matters. Want comes from a place of selfishness. Need comes from a place of desperation."

With her chest glued to his stomach, she tilted her head back and looked into his eyes. "Which one gets me a better kiss?"

"Are you sure you were a data entry person and not a negotiator?"

"Kiss me." She tilted her mouth to his. "I'm desperate."

He pressed his lips to hers, and holy hell, if it didn't send a bolt of heat and desire straight to her core.

"Like this?" He left her lips and pressed open mouth kisses down the column of her neck until his lips rested on the pulse point.

Katie stepped back and lifted her hand to her heart. It pounded out a strong tattoo against her palm. "Help me, Jesus." Normally at one hundred heartbeats per minute, her heart raced beyond that now. "Your kisses are deadly."

"Maybe, but you'll die happy." He gave her a panty-dropping smile. She loved when his smile came from inside and lit up his outside. "Let's go. Dalton is making a special dinner for us, being as it's our first date and all."

Moments later, they were seated in the corner booth. Everything was special, from the cloth napkins to the tiny tea light set on top of an overturned wineglass in the center of the table. Bowie opened a bottle of her favorite sparkling water and poured them each a glass.

"You look beautiful," Bowie said. He lifted his glass in a toast. "To our first date?"

She tapped his glass and sipped. The cool bubbles tickled as they made their way down. The whole idea of a first date with

Bowie was both intriguing and ridiculous. The curls that lay on her shoulders shook with her blooming laughter.

"Do you think it's odd we kissed before we shared a meal?" She looked around the mostly empty diner, making sure no one could hear her. "We slept together before we had a date?"

Bowie reached across the table and covered her hands with his. "I owe you an apology, Duchess. I told you you'd never be more than a good time. I was wrong. You're more." He rubbed his thumbs over the tops of her hands. Each time he touched her, every cell in her body danced. "My words were disrespectful. I'm sorry."

Dalton appeared with two plates. They weren't the chicken-fried steak blue-plate special on the menu, but a perfectly cooked filet with grilled asparagus and a fully loaded baked potato.

"Save room for dessert," Dalton said before he turned and left them alone in their quiet little corner.

While they ate, Katie thought about his words. "You don't owe me an apology. I was on board. You can't claim to be a victim if you're involved in the crime."

"Maybe not, but you deserve more. I offered so little."

She picked up a spear of asparagus and licked the salty spices off. Bowie didn't take his eyes off her tongue.

"I knew you would be worth the risk." She bit the flowered end of the stem and hummed. "So good."

Bowie's cheeks blushed. "I loved those words last night. That and when you called my name are in a tie for the sexiest thing I've ever heard. Then there's the 'Yes, yes, yes.' That's up there, too."

Katie could feel heat rise to her cheeks. How many times had she closed her eyes today and relived the moments of plea-sure he gave her last night? Could she make it through a meal and not want more? Would her feelings be considered wants or needs?

"I need a kiss." The words came out throaty and sexy.

"Need or want?" He laid his silverware next to his half-eaten meal.

"Need."

The way her body vibrated inside was like the withdrawal of a drug. She was a Bowie junkie after one hit. She took a sip of water, hoping the cold carbonation would cool the heat bubbling inside.

He lifted himself from his side of the booth, moved next to her, and licked her lips. "You taste like a strawberry."

Dalton walked over mid-kiss. "Should I pack this shit up?"

Bowie's lips never left hers, but she saw him give Dalton a thumbs-up.

"Will do," Dalton said on the tail end of his laugh. "I see you got dessert covered."

The moment he left, Katie broke the kiss. "Bowie?"

"Yes, sweetheart?"

"Take me home and disrespect me some more."

CHAPTER FIFTEEN

"Mornin', son." Ben walked into the kitchen and pulled a mug from the cabinet. "Sleep well?" He lifted one eyebrow and smiled.

Bowie hardly slept at all, and it had been that way for weeks. He couldn't get enough of Katie. They spent every moment they could together. They worked next door to each other. They dined together each night and loved on each other every chance they got. When she slept, he watched over her and worried.

This was why he'd promised himself he'd never fall in love again. Love did crazy shit to the brain, not to mention the heart.

"Me? What about you?" He reached past his father for a cup and tried to beat him to the coffeepot, but Ben was too quick. He'd already popped in his K-cup and pressed the start button. "You just getting home?" His father hadn't been spending much there, which left the house for Bowie to use as he pleased.

"It's not like I can bring her here. First off, you and Katie seem to have the nocturnal lease on the place. Second, I don't think I could do that to your mom. This was her house."

Bowie understood that sentiment. Although he'd become comfortable with the bakery, he couldn't bring himself to go upstairs to the place that was intended to be his and Brandy's starter home. To make love to Katie in the apartment would seem disrespectful to Brandy's memory. He knew he was being ridiculous, considering it had only been a drawing on paper when she died.

Bowie picked up his dad's steaming hot mug of coffee and replaced it with his empty cup. "Do you think you'll ever get over the loss?" He leaned against the harvest-gold counter and waited while the machine spit and sputtered out a cup of perfection.

"Get over it?" His dad shook his head. "Nope. How could you?" He walked to the table and took a seat. Reaching into the fruit bowl, he grabbed a banana and peeled it open. "The best you can hope for is to live with it."

Bowie joined his father at the table. He turned his chair toward the window and watched the rising sun shine off the lake. The water was still and reflected the orange glow of the sun like a mirror, making the water look like fire. Only the ripples of feeding fish disrupted the glasslike surface.

"Is that fair to others?"

Ben took a bite of his banana and chewed. A thoughtful expression of calm crossed his face. "Life isn't fair, son." He pulled the peel down and took another bite. As he chewed the fruit, it appeared he chewed on his thoughts, too. "Was it fair you got shot? Was it fair life took away your mother and your fiancée on the same day? That your father turned into a drunk? You can't worry about fair as far as life goes."

Bowie pulled in a deep breath and exhaled. "I know life isn't fair, but I want to be. Am I being fair to Katie?"

Ben chuckled. "Katie seems pleased with the arrangement."

In the distance, Bowie watched a rowboat cut through the water, leaving a wake behind. That's what he felt like. Katie had cut through the calm he faked. Everything inside him felt unsettled and turbulent in a good way. She made him want more than mere existence. He wanted her.

"When I'm with her, I'm so happy, Dad. She's amazing. We have so much fun together. It's all so easy and so hard at the same time." He leaned back in the chair and kicked up his feet on the empty chair beside him.

"You deserve happiness, Bowie. You're too young to be alone. Hell, I'm too young to be alone."

"Being alone is safe."

His dad shook his head. "That's what I thought, too, but it's not safe. Being alone is simply lonely."

Bowie looked out on the lake and spoke in a whisper. "It's in the quiet moments when I struggle. I watch her sleep, and my gut twists because I'm afraid to lose her, too. Letting her in was dangerous."

Ben sat his cup down and reached out to Bowie. He laid a solid hand on his shoulder and kept it there. "How many purple hearts do you have?"

"Three."

"You didn't get those because you were afraid. You got them because, despite the danger you faced, you dove in headfirst." Ben squeezed Bowie's shoulder before he dropped his arm. "How many bullets did you take?"

He knew where his father was going with his line of questioning. He'd taken seven bullets, but not one hurt as much as the hole shot through his heart when Brandy died. "I don't know if I could handle another hit like that, Dad."

Ben sighed. "I get it. I've lived your pain. I tried to drown mine in alcohol. You tried to erase yours with adrenaline. How'd that work out for you? My solution got me a pickled liver and a bad reputation. What'd yours get you?"

"A few medals and a lot of scars."

"All I'm saying is, you're not the kind of man who hides. That was me. I hid behind a bottle. You ran into the thick of things and made a difference."

"I'm no hero." Bowie shook his head so hard, his brain ached. "Initially, I ran into the melee, hoping I'd be able to join Brandy. After a while, I ran in because I wanted no one to feel the profound loss I felt at losing someone."

"How many lives did you save?"

He shrugged his shoulders. "It's hard to say." Bowie lost count of the men he'd carried on his back. The flow of blood he'd staunched with as little as a shoelace. The hands he held while a medevac swooped in for rescue. The faces blurred together, and the names sounded the same. Saving his men wasn't an option—it was what he did.

"Son, you're a hero."

"No, I'm just a man." He finished his coffee and looked down at the grounds in the bottom of his cup. He was as significant and insignificant as one of the little brown specs. It took every single one working together to make a decent cup of coffee. One ground made nothing. He thought of that commercial that said, "An army of one." Everything good in his life came in multiples. There was no army if there was only one. That thought was the moment of clarity he'd needed.

"Do you love her?"

"I'm not sure I'm there yet. All I know is, she makes it easier to breathe. It's so confusing. How did you let go of Mom?"

Ben placed both hands flat on the table and leaned forward. "I'll never let her go. She's a piece of me. I've tucked her safely into a corner of my heart, where she'll live forever."

"My heart is crowded with two women battling for space."

A crease etched into Ben's forehead. "There's no battle, son. Brandy has a place in your memory and your heart, but she's no longer in your life. How lucky are you to find two women worthy of your love? When it comes to life and death, choose life, Bowie.

Katie is alive. Be alive with her. There is something magical about her. She's an angel who came here to remind us how to live." Ben stood and left his son to consider his words.

Bowie sat alone at the kitchen table. His dad was right. Bowie had lived in the past for so long, it had eaten into his future. He had denied himself everything, but he wouldn't deny himself Katie and what they could have. There was still time for them.

He'd spent years trying to hold on to a piece of Brandy, but he had to let her go. Tonight after work, he'd visit the cemetery and say goodbye to his first love so he could make room for his second.

It wouldn't be easy. He hadn't been to the gravesite since the day they buried her. He still had nightmares of the crash and how the icy water seeped into the car while he tried to open the doors. His dreams were always silent, except for the gurgle of water exchanging places with oxygen in the car. He broke the window and tore his cheek, trying to get them out. On the frozen shore, he covered them with his bloodied body, hoping to warm the death from their skin.

His mom had been gone since impact, but Brandy somehow hung on to life by the thread of a brain stem. She lingered in the hospital for three days, all but dead without the help of modern medicine. He never understood why Bea waited so long to let her go when the doctors said there was no hope. It was as if she expected resurrection on the third day, and when it didn't come, she pulled the plug.

He shook the macabre memory from his mind. That was the past. He looked at the sun dancing across the lake, at the birds swooping down to feast on a floating bug. The wildflowers were in full bloom. Today was the first day of the rest of his life.

Except for a few stolen kisses at the back door, Bowie didn't see much of Katie that day. She'd been busy baking cookies for a church group that was using the old campgrounds for a daytime youth retreat. Heart-shaped cookies covered every surface in the bakery. It was fitting because Katie had such a big heart. She never failed to offer a kind word, a warm smile, or a hug to whoever needed one.

He told her of his plans to stop by the cemetery to say his goodbyes. She looked both relieved and concerned. Before he left, she held him for a long time. In her embrace was where he found hope and courage.

When he arrived at the cemetery, he visited his mother first. On top of her headstone were trinkets his dad or Cannon had left behind. There was an arrowhead, a carved wooden angel, and a roll of cherry Life Savers. Mom used to say they were almost as good as a kiss.

He kneeled before the headstone and plucked at the weeds growing around his mom's favorite yellow flowers. He felt like an awful son for staying away so long. He told her about everything that had happened since she went away. Although there was no answer, he imagined her soft voice telling him it was okay.

Bowie moved several rows to where Bill, Bea, and Brandy were buried. Sprouts of green grass filled in the area around the new headstone. Three cement hearts sat intertwined. An inscription that read, "Gone but not forgotten," was etched in black in the stone. He dropped to his knees and leaned his forehead against the cold granite marker.

"Where do I begin?" He took in several deep breaths to clear his mind. "I think I loved you the day I met you. The day Bill and Bea adopted you. You were six, and you had me tied around your little finger. Who knew I'd be so easy to catch? Then again, I was only eight. We had a comfortable kind of love, the kind you get from knowing someone forever. It was everything until you were gone."

He leaned back and rubbed his thumb over her name. Although it was hard to see her name etched in death for all time and eternity, his insides didn't twist and turn with sorrow and anger or loss. He looked at the stone and remembered her with love and friendship.

"I've met someone. I think I love her, but she deserves all of me, not the shrapnel left of my broken heart. Katie brings light to my life. A smile to my face. Hope to my heart. She makes me feel whole. When you died, so did I. When I met her, I was reborn. I'm here to tell you I will always love you, but I have to let you go."

CHAPTER SIXTEEN

One of the many benefits of owning a shop was flexible scheduling. Seeing as how Ben was happy to close up to go to the diner and be near Maisey, Katie could sneak upstairs and change into something clean that didn't smell like snickerdoodles—not an unpleasant smell by any means, but Bowie loved it when she was bathed in the scent of strawberries and honey.

Showered and dressed, she crossed paths with Sage in the corner store. In her friend's hands were two frozen potpies.

"I swear that man's a saint," Katie said with a giggle. "Does he ever tire of Stouffer's?"

Sage held up the two boxes. "These are Marie Callender's. I'm bringing out the big guns tonight." She pointed to the ad copy. "It says right here, 'A Heritage of Homemade.'"

Katie supposed it was a nice change from the frozen lasagna Sage liked to serve. "That's as close as he'll get to real food, I suppose." She walked down the aisle to where the jars of spaghetti sauce sat on a shelf above the pasta. "I can't say I'm offering anything more spectacular." She grabbed the sauce that had meat in it, along with a package of spaghetti.

"Honey, the Bishop boys aren't complaining about what we're offering." She followed Katie down the aisle to where the green cans of Parmesan cheese were lined up like little Italian soldiers next to the other ingredients perfect for Italian food.

To look around the corner store, it would seem like the people of Aspen Cove had particular tastes. The rows were divided by ethnicity. There was the Italian aisle, the Mexican aisle shared space with the Asian aisle. American food actually had two aisles and had everything guaranteed to give a person high blood pressure or indigestion. Who needed ten varieties of Hamburger Helper? She glanced at Sage and swallowed her question. Obviously, Sage did.

"Do you love him?" Katie asked. The two women hadn't really talked about love. Katie had never been in love, so she couldn't be sure what she felt was the real deal.

"I do. It's funny because the first time I saw him, I wanted to throttle him."

"He was a piece of work."

Katie moved to the freezer section to find the ice cream. It wasn't often she indulged in sweets. Funny for a girl surrounded daily by sugary confections. She looked at the paltry offerings and decided Bowie would be dessert. There was no reason to settle for less. That thought shook her because all her life she'd settled for so little—even with Bowie. He was willing to give her his body, but she was uncertain if he'd give her his heart.

"He's at the cemetery today." Katie's voice sounded far away, like someone else was speaking.

"That will be hard for him."

"He said he needed to say goodbye."

Sage leaned on the Little Debbie snack display and sent the boxes tumbling to the floor like dominos. She scrambled to pick them up, but each time she put one back, another came crashing down.

"Oh, hell," she said. "I suppose I'm nervous and excited for you." She got them all lined up. "If he's saying goodbye, that has to be good. Right?"

Marge peeked around the corner and shook her head at the mess they made of her display. "You girls are trouble."

"Clumsy, maybe. Trouble ... not so much." Katie said as she moved with Sage toward the register. Marge's husband, Phillip, sat reading the newspaper.

Katie laid her items on the counter and turned to Sage. "As for saying goodbye? You'd think it's a good sign, but I'm afraid of what could happen."

Phillip rang up her order. She didn't worry about him hearing the conversation because he was basically deaf. He had hearing aids, but he didn't wear them. He said they were uncomfortable, but Katie knew it was because he couldn't stand the sound of Marge bitching at him all day.

"Have things been good? I didn't want to pry, but you seem to spend more time at his place than your own."

Katie closed her eyes and remembered the heat that washed over her body after last night's lovemaking session. "Things are *so* good. That's the worry. He seems to be moving forward, but going there could set him back."

"How long ago did he leave?"

Katie looked at the ridiculous cat clock hanging on the wall behind Phillip. Its tail moved back and forth with each second. "It's been at least an hour."

Bowie had closed the shop around two and left right away.

"Maybe you should check on him."

"Don't you think that might seem invasive?"

Sage reached in the bucket of water at her feet and pulled out the last bouquet. "Bring these to Bea." She pressed them against Katie's chest, leaving droplets of water darkening her pink T-shirt.

"You can say you wanted to thank her for bringing you to Aspen Cove."

"He'll see right through that."

Sage smiled. "Yes, he'll see you care." She waved her hand in front of Phillip's face, getting his attention, and pointed to the flowers and her potpies. "I'll get the flowers. You go get your man."

In truth, Katie wanted to visit Bea's grave. She owed the woman who had given her a second chance. She leaned in and gave her best friend a kiss on the cheek before she turned and walked to the door. "Wish me luck."

"Break a leg," Sage called from behind.

When Katie arrived at the cemetery, it differed greatly from the day they put Bea in the ground. The parking lot was empty except for Bowie's black truck, which sat alone in the corner slot. She scanned the area but saw no one. The only things standing were cement headstones.

Mixed emotions swirled inside her, making her stomach do flips. Was it wrong of her to check on him? All she wanted was the best for Bowie, and at that moment, she knew without a doubt, she was it. She'd fallen in love with the man and was infinitely more capable of taking care of him than a ghost from his past.

A part of her burned with jealousy. Who would have pined for her had she died eight years ago? Her mother. Her father. Her siblings. But there was no man to remember his love for her; no heart filled with treasured memories. She wanted that with Bowie. If she could persuade him to stay in Aspen Cove, she had a chance of reaching that goal. He acted like a man who would stay, but he'd never said the words, and words were important, too.

With the flowers in her hand, she climbed out of her SUV and wound around the path to where she remembered Bea's grave.

As she approached, she saw Bowie on his knees in front of a headstone of three hearts blended together. It was a beautiful tribute to a family filled with love. His fingers traced the black etched lettering of Brandy's name.

She knew her decision to look for Bowie was wrong. This was a private moment between him and his one true love. She had no right to be there. When she stepped backward to retreat, her shoe crunched down on a dried leaf. The sound echoed through the dead silence of the cemetery.

Bowie stood and spun around to face her. His expression went from annoyed to concerned to soft. "Hey, what are you doing here?"

Katie took another step back. "I'm sorry." She looked down at the flowers in her hand. "I thought I'd—" She shook her head. She hated to lie. "I was worried about you. I went by the store to pick up something for dinner and ..." She let out a huge breath that vibrated through her chest. "Are you okay?"

Bowie walked toward her, his hands reaching for her shoulders. He gripped them tightly. She was certain he'd try to shake sense into her, but instead, he pulled her to his chest. "Yes, I'm okay."

She buried her nose into the cotton of his T-shirt and took a deep breath. She associated his smell with everything good in her life. Her arms hung limply beside her, but her body pressed into his for comfort.

"I know this is hard for you. I want you to know that as your friend, I'm here for you."

Bowie seemed to laugh at all the right times, even when it was in the wrong place. They were in the middle of a cemetery, the least likely place to bring a smile to a face or laughter to warm a heart.

He thumbed her chin up and connected eye to eye. "I'd say we're more than friends, Duchess." He leaned down and brushed his lips across hers. He looked over his shoulder to the headstone. "This was about being able to move forward—to give you and me a chance at something more. I could never give you my heart if it belonged to another."

Katie could hardly breathe. He wanted more with her. "I hoped we could be more, but I was willing to settle for less."

He placed his hands on both sides of her head. "You really should set your standards higher. You deserve so much more than me."

She dropped the flowers to the gravelly path and wrapped her arms around him. "And you should see yourself as I do. You are so much more than you give yourself credit for."

They stood on the path and held each other. Katie closed her eyes and said a silent thank you to the universe for bringing this man to her. She said a prayer of thanks to Bea for bringing her to Aspen Cove. Her last silent prayer went to Brandy. She had to have been an amazing woman to have locked down Bowie's heart for so long.

He rubbed his hands down her back. "Shall we get out of here?"

Katie nodded but looked down at the flowers lying at her feet. "I brought these for Bea."

Bowie smiled, and the somber atmosphere of the cemetery lit up. "Then you should give them to her." He bent over and picked up the bouquet. He threaded his fingers through hers and led her to the grave. Her eyes followed the newly bloomed grass to the pristine headstone. Under each name were a birth and death date. Bill had died five years ago; Bea this year. It was when she looked at the date of Brandy's death that her heart stilled. It wasn't a decade past, like she'd been led to believe, but eight years ago on the same day her life began again.

Her lungs seized. Her heart raced, then all but stopped. The world spun around her and turned black.

"Katie." His voice sounded far away, like Bowie was calling to her through thick fog. "Katie, wake up, honey."

She moved along the gravel path in Bowie's arms. "What happened?" She looked up to see relief in his blue eyes.

"There you are." He set her down and propped her against his truck while he opened the door. "You fainted."

"I what?" She pressed her memory for an explanation. It all came rushing back. She had Brandy Bennett's heart.

"You fainted. Hit the ground like a cement block." He picked her up and placed her in his truck. "Banged your head good."

She reached up and touched the tender spot on the back of her head. "Oh, Lord." She had a lump the size of Houston forming. "I can't believe I did that."

"I'm taking you to Doc's. I want him to look you over."

She shook her head, but her brain hurt. "No. I'm fine." Her thoughts were scrambled. "I want to go home."

"Not happening until you get the seal of approval from Doc Parker."

"Seriously?" She leaned against the window. The cool glass tethered her to consciousness. "I'm fine." Her head spun, but her heart ached. Brandy's heart ached.

She was anything but fine. She'd fallen in love with Bowie. Once he found out she had his fiancée's heart, what would happen? She'd never been more frightened in her life.

Even on the day of her surgery, when they placed the mask over her nose and told her to count, she wasn't as scared as today. Back then, she had a life unlived. Now, she had a future to lose.

CHAPTER SEVENTEEN

Katie watched Bowie race around to help her from the truck. He walked her at a snail's pace to the pharmacy.

Attentive and loving now, but would that end the minute the truth was revealed? Did Katie want to reveal the truth? He'd never asked her about her scar. She'd told him she'd been sickly as a child, and they fixed her.

Did she owe him the facts, or was it good enough that she'd given him the gist of the situation?

Doc Parker came out of the back room with a mug of coffee in his hands. "You cleaned me out of condoms yesterday." He sipped at his coffee. "I don't get a delivery until next week. You ever hear of pacing yourself?"

"I'm not here about condoms." That's when Doc noticed Katie. "She fainted and hit her head hard."

Doc moved fast for an old fart. He rushed around the counter to open the door for Bowie. "Bring her on back."

"I'm fine," she said with little confidence in her voice.

"Stop being difficult," Doc said. He turned on the light to the examination room and patted the paper-covered table. "Climb up, young lady, and let me have a look at your melon."

Bowie helped her onto the table. He didn't leave her side, holding her hand while Doc Parker looked her over.

"You're pale, and your heartbeat is too high." He reached into the drawer and pulled out a stethoscope.

Doc must have seen the fear on her face. The pleading in her eyes. She wasn't sure if she was sending the message that said, "Don't do this here, not with Bowie around," but somehow Doc seemed to understand.

"Son," he said to Bowie. "I need to give her a thorough exam, and although I know you've seen the goods, I'm not into three-somes." He nodded toward the door. "See if the bakery has any muffins left. I'll call you when we're finished."

Bowie looked from Katie to Doc. There was a moment when she wasn't certain he'd leave.

"Do you want me to go?" Bowie squeezed her hand.

"I'll be okay." She swallowed the lump in her throat. "Steal a muffin for me, too. I probably didn't eat enough today, and my blood sugar got low." She hated the lie that flowed so easily from her lips.

Bowie narrowed his eyes for a second. Did he see the lie for what it was—a way to get him out of the office before Doc saw her scar and found out her truth? She thought he'd hold his ground, but instead, he pressed his lips to hers in a comforting kiss.

"You know where I'll be."

Doc waited until he heard the bell above the front door ring. "By the look you gave me, I was sure you didn't want Bowie in here. Was I wrong?"

She shook her head. "No. You will find out something in a minute that I've kept a secret." Katie pulled the hem of her pink T-shirt over her head.

"Holy heavens." Doc Parker took a step back and grabbed the side table for balance. "He hasn't seen that scar?"

Katie dropped her chin to look at the silver line that ran vertically down her chest. "He's seen it." She shrugged. "He never asked for specifics, and I didn't give him details he didn't require."

Doc Parker pointed to the scar. "That's why you have the bakery."

She nodded. "I didn't know until I went to the cemetery today to check on Bowie." Her eyes filled with tears. Her throat ached. "At Bea's funeral, there was no headstone, and you," she shuddered at the memory, "you said they died a decade ago."

"I rounded up. The exact details didn't matter."

"They did to me. I couldn't figure out why she gave me the bakery. I thought for a second I had her daughter's heart, but the timing didn't match because I was told Brandy had died ten years ago. I should have looked into it more thoroughly. Bea put it plain and simple on the page, 'you have a good heart,' she wrote. She would know. I have her daughter's heart," Katie cried.

Doc pulled a tissue from a nearby box and handed it to her. "She did it and told no one." Doc spread his fingers to massage the strain in his furrowed brows. "She donated her organs."

Katie sat on the examination table, exposed in more than one way. "You didn't know?"

He pushed off the table, put the earpieces in his ears, and pressed the cold cone to her chest. He listened for a while. When he stepped back, his expression was one of awe.

"She never said a word." He wrapped the stethoscope into a circle and put it on the table. "That's a fine heart you have, my dear."

Katie swallowed the lump in her throat. "It's served me well for the last eight years."

Doc Parker went into medical mode. "You have quite a lump on your head." He pulled a light from his pocket and shined it into her eyes. "Your pupils are even, but I won't rule out a concussion." He opened a drawer and lifted a white disk. With a twist, he activated the ice pack and pressed it to the back of her head. "You need to ice that to keep the swelling down."

Katie set the pack next to her while she pulled on her shirt. "Are you going to tell Bowie?" Just the mention of his name made her heart race and her stomach twist into knots.

"No, that's not my truth to tell, but don't you think you should?"

Katie sat for minutes in contemplative silence, or maybe it was shock. "I should."

"But ..." He walked to the sink and washed his hands. He looked over his shoulder at her. "You won't?"

Katie gnawed at her bottom lip. "What if it ruins what we have?"

Doc leaned against the table and crossed his arms over his chest. "What if he finds out somehow? I can't tell you what to do. Your secret is safe with me. It's part of the privacy act, but I think you should be the one to tell him."

Katie nodded and jumped off the table, the movement sending a wave of dizziness rushing at her. She gripped the edge with her free hand to steady herself. "I'll tell him, but I need some time to figure out how."

Doc's bushy white mustache dropped with his frown. "Give it a day or two to sink in." He reached into his pocket and pulled out his phone but set it on the table. "I want you to stay at your place tonight. That way, you'll be close by if you need me. Also, someone has to stay with you to keep an eye on things. Head injuries are tricky. If you showed more severe signs of a concussion, you wouldn't be standing here, you'd be in an ambulance on the way to the hospital." He looked down at the area between her breasts like he had X-ray vision. "Speaking of hospitals ... do you have a cardiologist you're seeing? Are you taking your anti-rejection drugs? Where's your family?" He rattled off so many questions, she couldn't keep up.

"I registered with Holland Cardiology in Copper Creek. I haven't seen them yet because I haven't needed to, and I take my meds as directed."

"Good. Good. Derek Holland is a skilled doctor. You couldn't have chosen more wisely."

"He came recommended by my last doctor."

"What about your family?"

"They live in Dallas. They know where I'm at, although they are less than happy with how I got here."

"Do they know?"

Katie wanted to laugh, but she knew it would hurt her already aching head. "How could they know before I did? Donors and recipients are anonymous. I wonder how Bea found me?"

Doc picked up his phone. "I've never known a woman more determined than Bea. She was like a dog with a bone." He smiled. "Wow." He shook his head. "Brandy had never left the state of Colorado until she went to meet you."

Katie lifted her palm to her chest. "I owe her everything."

"Bea used to tell everyone that Brandy might be gone, but she lived in others. We thought she was speaking metaphorically. Like her memories and spirit lived in others. I'll be damned." He punched in some numbers and waited until the person on the other line answered. "She's ready for you, son." He hung up, but his smile burned like a hundred-watt bulb. "What are the chances one man can find the same heart twice?"

The bell above the door rang, and the sound of heavy boots thudded on the linoleum floor in the hallway.

Bowie appeared in the doorway and smiled with relief. "It took you so long, I thought something serious happened."

Doc looked at Katie. "We were chitchattin'. She can tell you all about it."

Katie took a step forward and wobbled. Not that she was dizzy; she was scared. Everything she ever wanted stood in front of her. Bowie had finally said goodbye to Brandy. How would he feel knowing part of Brandy lived inside her?

It was confusing. Almost surreal. For the first time, she questioned her love for Bowie. Was it real? Or was it some supernatural oddity that Brandy's heart recognized Bowie's presence? She'd heard of stranger things.

"I'm ready to go home and go to bed."

"Nuh-uh," Doc said. "No sleeping for two hours." He looked at Bowie. "She needs to be woken up periodically to make sure she's okay. No sexy business either. She needs to rest. Those condoms will hold."

Katie groaned.

Bowie laughed. "I can do that." He stepped forward and wrapped an arm around her waist. "I'll take good care of her." He walked her a step forward.

"I want her at her house."

Bowie stopped. He hadn't been inside her house since they met. She wondered if having to be there would pose a problem.

"Not an issue." He looked down at her and whispered. "I let it all go today, Duchess. It's just you and me from now on. I'll never forget her, but Brandy no longer has my heart."

Inside, Katie died a little. They'd never be free of her because although Brandy no longer had Bowie's heart, Katie had hers.

CHAPTER EIGHTEEN

"Put me down." Katie squirmed in his arms.

"Stop it before I drop you and hurt your head again." He'd scooped her up and held her close to his chest. "You weigh nothing."

"Liar." She clutched her arms around his neck and hung on like she'd lose him if he let her go. "I weigh over a hundred pounds."

He cradled her while he raised and lowered her like he was weighing her. "I'd guess one hundred and thirty-two." It was only a guess, but when her jaw dropped, he assumed he was close.

"How did you know?"

Bowie laughed. "In the desert, my rucksack weighed just over eighty pounds without armor or ammo. I used that as a gauge. How close did I get?"

"Off by a pound." She rested her head against his arm and winced.

"Hurts bad, huh?" He adjusted her body so her face leaned into him, not the back of her head.

"It's not pleasant."

Bowie kicked open the door to the bakery. His father stood behind the counter, wearing a ruffled apron. "That's a look I never thought I'd see."

Katie lifted her head and smiled. "He looks good in ruffles."

"What did Doc say?" Ben opened the swinging door that led to the back room.

"He says she needs rest and that you have to run the shop the next few days."

Katie moved until Bowie was forced to put her down rather than drop her.

"He did not. He said he can't rule out a concussion, but that's all he said."

She lifted a broken heart cookie from the cooling rack. He watched her frown before she took a bite.

"Not true. She has to rest and eat well." He looked at his father. "I'll be staying here tonight."

Dad's eyes grew big with his statement. "Oh, okay then."

Bowie winked at his father. "Looks like you and Maisey have options." He'd never seen his father blush, but the red on his cheeks matched the trim on his apron.

"I'm going upstairs," Katie said while she snuck past him.

He reached out and wrapped his arm around her waist, pulling her to his side. "I'll carry you." There was no way Katie was making it up the stairs on her own.

"I can walk."

"Stop being so stubborn. You have a concussion. I'm carrying you." He looked at his dad, who laughed his way back to the front of the bakery.

"I *may* have a concussion. I don't need you to carry me. I don't want you to babysit me."

"Wrong." He bent down and tucked his arm under the crook of her knees and lifted. She crumbled against him. "Doctor's orders." The one thing he knew about Doc Parker was he didn't ask for anything that wasn't needed.

"Fine."

She held on to him while he took the back stairs two at a time. His heart beat rapidly, like a drummer in his chest. He couldn't decide if it was the exertion or the anxiety. As soon as she opened the door, he wasn't sure how he'd feel. This was supposed to be his and Brandy's place.

Though he'd said goodbye at the cemetery. Letting something go wasn't like flicking off a light switch. There were pieces of her that would remain with him forever.

When Katie leaned over to turn the knob, he held his breath. He felt like he was back in Afghanistan, walking through a minefield.

The door swung open, and Katie's sweet scent filled the air. He stopped at the threshold and put her down. The orange glow of the setting sun bled between the cream curtains across the room.

"It's small, but it works." She rocked forward and backward several times. He didn't know if she was feeling awkward for him or about him being in her place.

"It's great." He walked past her to the center of the living room. A blue sofa took up most of the space, but the essentials were there, like a coffee table and a television. He moved toward the window, where a small table sat covered with small pieces of paper.

He picked one up.

"Don't read it unless you plan on trying to help." She plucked it from his fingers.

"What are these?"

She pulled a folded piece of paper from a shoebox and opened it. "This one was granted, or it will be, so I suppose it's okay to share it." She opened the tiny folded square and handed it to him.

My only wish right now is to have an hour alone with my husband so I can show him how much I love him.

Louise Williams

"She wants a babysitter, and you found her one?" Bowie folded the paper and stuck it back into the shoebox.

"I will babysit."

"She's got eight kids."

Katie moved her head from left to right with slow deliberation. "She has seven. Maybe there will be eight if she gets that hour alone with Bobby."

"Don't tell, Doc."

Katie looked exhausted. She pulled out a chair and sat with a heavy thud. "I'm not telling anyone's secrets." She turned from him and looked out the window.

Since her fall, she'd lost her spark. "Beaten down" were words he'd use to describe her. "You look exhausted."

"I'm okay." She rose. "Let me show you the mansion."

Bowie had done all right with the little he'd seen. He didn't need a full tour, but if it was important to Katie, he'd suffer through it.

He looked around the living room. It wasn't anything like he'd imagined. When Bea had talked of the place, Bowie hadn't pictured it to look like a real apartment. In his mind, he saw a loft with open beams and exposed wiring. This place was an actual apartment. It was perfect.

Katie tentatively took his hand. He turned her palm over to see if she'd injured it during the fall. She'd never been shy about touching him, but her delicate touch felt foreign.

"Does your hand hurt?"

She looked down to where his hand covered hers. "No, it's fine."

She threaded her fingers through his and walked him through the tiny kitchen equipped with everything a person needed, from a microwave to a refrigerator covered in magnets. She had a space on the freezer door with cut up magnetic words and letters. Bowie caught his name amidst words like happy, content, and independent. There was one string of words put together, "I love Bowie." Before he could comment, she reached up and mixed the letters and words so nothing made sense, but even if she could erase the evidence, she couldn't erase his memory of it. She loved him. That was all he needed to know.

"There's stuff in the fridge if you get hungry."

"Sweetheart, I'm starved, but not for food." They had been dating for weeks now, but every time he used sexual innuendo, she blushed. With her skin so pale, the pink that rose to her cheeks made her look downright feverish. "Show me the bedroom where I won't be able to make love to you. I want to see the bed that won't squeak under my weight tonight."

Katie moved ahead of him down the hallway. She poked her head into the first room. "Spare." She moved down to the next door. "Bathroom." At the end of the hallway was her room. It smelled like her. "Convent."

A big bed sat against the wall. Bowie swallowed a stone of sorrow that seemed to lodge in his throat. His brother had custom made a headboard for Brandy and him. He wondered what had happened to it. This bed had a simple wooden frame and headboard.

Katie sat on the bed and fell to her side, curling up like a baby.

"Not yet. Doc says no sleeping for a few hours." He held her hands and pulled her into a sitting position. He understood how a head injury could change a person, but Katie acted like something had stolen her best friend. "You okay? You seem sad or depressed. Is there anything you want to talk about?"

She turned her head, and he could see tears collecting in the corners of her brilliant blue eyes. "No, I'm tired, that's all."

He had to take her word for it because one thing he knew

about Katie was, she didn't lie. She was like an open book, and if something was bothering her, he was certain she'd let him know.

"Tell you what. Let's go into the living room and see if we can't grant some wishes." He helped her to her feet and walked her to the table, where she'd been sorting through the tiny pieces of paper.

She opened one note, crumpled it up, and tossed it into a nearby trash can.

"Hey, that's someone's wish you're throwing away."

She pulled it out and handed him a note that said, "I want a twelve-incher." Bowie wadded it up and tossed it back into the can.

"Don't we all." He reached for a new note. "What are the rules?"

"You can't ask for something ridiculous, like a million dollars or a sports car. Most of the wishes are easy to grant, like this one." She picked up a pink sticky note.

I'd like a dozen heart cookies for my birthday.
Lily Dawson

"Or this one." She opened the yellow paper.

Please pray for my daddy. He really needs a job.

"This one is silly but doable."

Please paste a few stars above your door. I told Jackson that someday he'd kiss me under the stars, but the only place he goes with me is to your bakery in daylight.
Sadie
P.S. This Saturday would be wonderful.

Katie picked up a pair of scissors and cut out a handful of stars. "You started this?"

"When I was little. I wished for a lot of things. Things I didn't have a right to wish for, like becoming a royal or never getting sick again. I got my wish to skip the chicken pox and my parents bought me the Barbie Dream House, but most wishes went unfulfilled. That's why I started the Wishing Wall."

Bowie sorted the wishes into piles: One was a prayer pile. One was a silly-but-doable pile. The last one was the almost impossible pile. He would have put Louise Williams's request in that pile because no one in their right mind would babysit seven kids. Only Katie and she couldn't blame that decision on a concussion.

"When I told you I was a sickly child ..." She glanced at him and went back to cutting stars. "I didn't elaborate, but—"

"It doesn't matter. I learned long ago not to dwell on the things that can't be changed."

"It could matter. What if it changed everything?"

He leaned back in his chair and watched her fidget with the scissors. "Unless you have a terminal disease, nothing you can say will make a difference. What's the point in talking about the past? It's the past. What we should talk about is the future." He handed her a blank sticky note. "If you could wish for anything right now, what would it be?" He plunked a pen into her hand.

She thought for a few minutes and then wrote something quickly. He swiped it from the table before she could hide it from him. On the note, it said,

Pray for me that Bowie Bishop will love me anyway.

He knew the hit on the head had jumbled her brains. *Anyway?*

He took the pen and scribbled out the word "anyway" and replaced it with "always." He stretched his body across the table and kissed her. "I'll love you always."

CHAPTER NINETEEN

Two days of Bowie hovering over her were enough. Ben watched the bakery while Cannon stepped up to watch the bait and tackle store. Sage wandered over and mothered Katie while Bowie went home for a change of clothes.

"I promised Bowie I wouldn't leave you." Sage stood in front of her with her hands on her hips.

"You'll be across the street getting me a grilled cheese and fruit salad. I'll be fine for the time it'll take you to pick it up." Katie fluffed the pillow leaning on the blue sofa arm. Bowie insisted she lay down. She fought him on his overprotectiveness at each turn, but she always lost. "I'm more likely to die from starvation than a head injury." Katie looked around Sage and flipped through the channels. Daytime television sucked, and since she'd been on a budget, expensive cable wasn't an option, but each time her limited selection came up, she met it with a sense of pride. She'd paid for those stations with her money. Not once had she dipped into her trust fund to pay for anything, including her pricey insurance.

Sage gave her a "You win" look. "Okay, but don't move."

Katie pulled the plush blanket up to her chin. "Not going anywhere."

She glanced at her phone on the table. She'd been waiting for a private minute to call her mom. Although she craved independence, she needed her mom for the tough moments.

"You better not move. I don't want Bowie mad at me." Sage picked up her bag and walked to the door.

When Katie heard her footsteps disappear down the stairs, she called her mom.

"Mama?" She tried to keep her voice calm and swiped the tears running down her cheeks.

"Katie girl, what's wrong?" Panic rose to a high pitch. Mothers had that sixth sense about their children and never failed to pick up the small hints of something wrong.

Even after heroic attempts to temper her emotions, Katie couldn't stop the sobs from breaking free. "I don't know what to do."

"About what, honey?"

"I'm in love with Bowie."

Silence stretched between them.

"His name is Bowie?" Leave it to her mom to focus on the name and not the emotion.

"Focus. I said I was *in love*." Katie sat up and leaned her side into the armrest. "He's so amazing."

"The bait-and-tackle man?" In the background, the sound of a chair scraping against tile echoed through the line. "Let me get coffee."

Katie heard her mother walk around the kitchen of her Highland Park house.

"He's more than a bait-and-tackle man." Katie knew there was a large dose of sarcasm tingeing her voice, but she needed her mother to pay attention.

"Honey, that's wonderful. All Daddy and I ever wanted for you was to be happy and healthy. So why the tears?"

Katie started from the beginning, where a pink envelope changed her life. When she got to the part about having Brandy's fiancé and her heart, her mother cried with her.

"I want to kill that woman and hug her at the same time." She pulled in a shaky breath. "She gave you life and stress in the same gift."

Katie could picture her mother dabbing at her eyes with a Kleenex so she didn't mar the makeup that took an hour to put on.

"Mama, she gave me everything. A second chance at life. A way to live independently so I wouldn't have to remain childlike in your eyes. She gave me purpose and friends and the greatest man on Earth, but what happens when I tell him? What if he can't stand to look at me because it's just too weird?"

"He told you nothing could change his feelings for you. Give him a chance to prove it."

"I'm so scared."

Her mother let out a long sigh. "You've been scared before and survived. You've faced more in life than anyone I know. This is small stuff compared to dying."

That was the magic of mothers; they put things into perspective. Sophia Middleton taught Katie to look at life from a glass-half-full attitude. Unless that glass had fine champagne in it, then Sophia said it was better to look at it half empty and get in line to have it filled back up.

"What if he leaves me?"

"Then he never truly loved you."

"What if he only loves me because her heart is in me?"

Her mother rarely made unladylike noises. They weren't flattering, but she let out a growl that could scare a badger. "Honey, he said he loved you. He doesn't know that heart, only what's in it. It's your lifeblood that keeps it pumping. The minute that heart took residence in your chest, there was an agreement made. It would provide you with life, but not without your life-giving blood. Her part in your existence is no stronger than yours. You and she are partners for life."

Mom was right. Brandy's heart wouldn't beat without Katie's blood, and Katie's blood could not circulate without her heart. "I love you, Mama."

"You want me to come out there? I'm happy to hop on the plane today." Her voice was hopeful.

Katie teetered on the edge of saying yes, but she said, "No. I have to do this myself. I'll tell him the truth. You're right. If he's as good a man as I think he is, he'll understand. If not, he wasn't meant for me."

"That's my girl. If things don't go the way you expect, I'm here, Princess. I can have Daddy's plane there in a few hours to pick you up."

Katie told her mom she loved her and hung up. She reflected on their talk. Throughout that conversation, her mother never once commented that Katie had a head injury. She smiled to herself because that meant her mother was learning to trust her to take care of her own health.

The tap of Sage's shoes coming up the stairs meant food was here. She'd need to be fortified to face Bowie.

"I'm back." She rushed in the door with her red curls shooting out like flames around her head. "Dalton said to eat it all; he thinks you're too skinny. He added extras."

Katie swung her legs from the couch to the floor. "Dalton is a cook. He thinks everyone is too skinny. Skinny people don't pay his bills."

Sage plopped onto the center cushion of the couch. She spread out a feast on the coffee table in front of them. "Don't get mad at me. Dalton said the grilled cheese went great with tomato soup. That the fruit was better with real whipped cream and the whipped cream was lonely without his mother's famous cherry pie."

Katie looked at the buffet set before her and knew she'd eat every bite.

"Ran into Bowie and told him I was feeding you. He said he'd be up after he made his supply order." Sage opened her to-go box, which held a burger and fries. "He's worried about you. Said he thinks the hit on the head is more serious because you don't laugh or smile as much." Sage opened her container of ketchup and drowned an unsuspecting french fry in the cup. "I've seen it, too. Do you think we should take you to Copper Creek to get an MRI? Maybe you have a TBI."

Katie laughed at her use of acronyms. Sage used them all the time, and if Katie hadn't spent a lifetime in the hospital, she'd never know what her friend was talking about. "I don't have a traumatic brain injury. I've got a lot on my mind." Katie wondered if she should tell Sage first. It might be a good idea to practice her speech on her best friend.

"You want to talk about it? Is there something wrong between you and Bowie?" Her vivid green eyes showed concern.

"Yes ... I mean, no." Katie dropped her head. "What I mean is, I need to talk, but what I have to say should be said to Bowie first, except I fear that once I say it, he'll take off and never return."

Sage pulled her food box into her lap and turned to face Katie. "That boy loves you. You're the reason he's still here."

Katie slowly lifted her chin. "I may be the reason he leaves. I want to tell you because I need your 'Sage' advice, but you have to promise not to say a word until I talk to Bowie."

Sage chewed on a fry. "When are you going to tell him whatever this is?"

"Soon."

Sage set her food on the table and reached for Katie's hands. "I don't like to keep secrets, but I want to be here for you."

Katie took in three cleansing breaths. She stood up and pulled her sweatshirt to her neck. "I have this scar." Katie had hoped that with Sage's nursing background, she wouldn't have to say any more, that Sage would put the pieces together, but she sat in silence while Katie dropped her shirt into place and took her seat.

"Wow, that's a doozy. Heart? Lungs? Car accident?"

"Heart. A childhood illness that weakened my heart."

Sage smiled. "And look at you now."

"Remember how we sat in the bakery and tried to figure out Bea's connection to me? How she said I had a good heart?"

Katie knew the second Sage figured it out.

"Oh, shit." Her hand came to her mouth. "You couldn't figure it out then?"

Her mouth went Sahara desert dry. "No. I thought it was because I volunteered at the children's hospital. I knew I didn't have Bea's heart. I had no idea Bea had a daughter. Then when I found out about Brandy, everyone kept using a decade as the time-line for her death." She pounded against her chest. "I got this heart eight years ago." Katie pulled her hands to her face. "Eight years isn't a decade. It's eight damn years."

"Oh, shit," Sage repeated. "When did you find out?"

"When you gave me the flowers and told me to go get my man from the cemetery."

"Oh, shit. This is my fault."

Katie shook her head. "No. No, it's not. Whether or not I took the flowers doesn't change the fact that I have Brandy's heart in my chest. I found Bowie at the gravesite that day, and I walked up to him. He had changed. He'd let her go so he could be with me. I was so happy."

"Oh, shit."

"Stop 'oh, shitting' me. I had the flowers, and he walked me to the grave so I could pay tribute to Bea. I saw the date. Brandy died three days after Cannon and Bowie's mother because Bea kept her on life support until they found matches for her donated organs. She told no one she'd donated them. When I saw the date was the same day I got my heart, I fainted."

"Oh ... honey." Sage leaned in and pulled Katie in for a hug. When she leaned back, she smiled. "It's the most romantic thing I've ever heard in my life."

"Or the creepiest." Katie pulled free. "What the heck will he do when he finds out he's dating the girl who has his first love's heart? I even had a silly string of thoughts, wondering if her heart recognized him, and that's why I fell in love with him."

"You love him on your own. Brandy's heart has nothing to do with it." She said the words, but there was a moment when Sage looked unsure. "I don't know what he'll do. I don't know what I'd do."

"You're no help. Right now, I need your 'Sage' advice." She sat there and looked at her friend, hoping she'd be able to offer wise counsel in a difficult situation.

"You have to tell him. Bowie has a right to know."

The already open door swung wider to accommodate his body. "Tell me what?" Bowie stood in front of Katie, looking for answers.

CHAPTER TWENTY

Katie's face turned white when he walked through the door. He could tell she tried to hide her distress with a smile. A fake smile that didn't reach her eyes. Something was wrong. First instincts told him to run toward her.

"What's wrong?" He rushed to her, cupped her face, and looked into her eyes. The once bright blue had dulled to a stormy gray. "Is it your head?" He dropped to his knees, forcing the coffee table back to accommodate his size. He fluffed the pillow beside her. "Lie down and let me take care of you."

Bowie had all but forgotten about Sage's presence until she stood up from the couch. "That's my cue to leave." She gathered her meal and her bag and was gone before he or Katie said goodbye. He'd never seen Sage move so swiftly. It was like she was escaping.

Katie lifted her hand to his cheek. She always rubbed his scruff. Although she couldn't care less about his scar, the beard she loved had grown to cover it. "I'm fine." Her hand fell to the soft fabric of the couch. Katie turned her body so her back leaned against the armrest and pulled her legs close to her chest, securing everything in place with clasped hands.

"You're not fine. You're as pale as an egg white." He shuffled sideways and sat on the cushion Sage had vacated. "What's hurting you?"

She pulled her upper lip between her teeth. This was always her thinking pose. Not when she was debating between simple stuff like beef or chicken, but the look she got when her mind raced.

"Slow it down, sweetheart, before you chew a hole in that lip of yours." He reached over and thumbed her upper lip loose. "I have a fondness for your kisses. They would be less appealing if you only had one lip."

"So you're saying if I lost something you thought important, you'd love me less?"

He sat back. "Why do I feel like this is a trick question?"

"It's not. I'm gauging your perspective on what's important. You seem to like my lips."

He leaned forward and inhaled her scent, pressing his lips gently against hers. "I like all of you, but these lips …"

He closed his eyes and remembered the night she was on her knees before him. Her lips wrapped around him. The smell of her strawberry shampoo floated through the air and hugged him.

They hadn't been intimate since her accident. He missed the connection they shared. Despite spending nearly every minute with her since she fainted, he felt a divide between them. It was silly because they were so much more than sex, but somehow when their bodies weren't interconnected, it felt like their hearts were miles apart.

"You need to eat." He picked up her sandwich and offered it to her.

"I can't eat any more." Shaking hands pushed it away.

He looked down at the grilled cheese that was missing a single bite. "You have to eat more than this." Her lack of sustenance could cause her shaking hands, but his mind went back to the conversation he'd walked in on.

"You have to tell him," Sage had said.

She pulled her knees to her chest and rocked back and forth? "We need to talk."

The twist in his stomach caused physical pain from his gut to his heart. Those four words were never good. His mind raced for an explanation.

"Tell me what's wrong. What have I done?"

Her eyes grew wide. "You? Nothing. You're perfect. It's me."

"I'm far from perfect, so what the hell have I done?" The heat of anxiety made Bowie's neck feel like it was on fire. "Nothing good ever starts with 'We have to talk' or ends with 'It's me.'" He knew the flame of his fear rose from his neck to color his face.

Is she breaking up with me?

He'd just let go of his past, took a leap forward, and chose the woman he wanted to spend his future with. He was confused.

"Are we breaking up?"

"I don't want to break up with you. I love you, Bowie, but after what I have to tell you, you may not want my love."

There wasn't one thing he could think of that would change his feelings for Katie. "You can't say anything that will make me love you less."

She laughed. Not the kind of laugh that happened when a person heard something funny, but the crazy cackle of someone a breath away from losing their mind. He closed the gap between them and pulled her into his arms. She folded her body against his and sobbed into his shirt. The last time he'd heard someone cry that hard was when Bea came to the hospital and found out Brandy was brain dead.

Though Bowie needed to know what Katie had to tell him,

something gut-deep told him once she did, everything would change.

"I'm scared of losing you, Bowie."

"Not possible."

She pulled away but stayed seated in his lap. "What if you found out something that changes nothing, yet changes everything?"

He tightened his hold on her. His heart raced, and he wondered if she could hear how fast it beat against his ribs.

"I've never been good at puzzles. What are you trying to tell me?"

"Remember the chocolate chip muffins I made, and you said they would be better if I added orange essence?"

"I love the orange essence. It makes them special. Like that added ingredient is the secret to their magnificence."

Though he tried to hold her in his lap, she pushed away and sat beside him. "What I have to tell you may make you think differently about me."

"Jesus, what is it? You have a police record? A handful of kids hidden in the attic? Just tell me."

She pulled in a deep breath and let it out between O-shaped lips. "What if I told you I was a plain chocolate muffin years ago?"

"Not possible. You've got something special. There's nothing ordinary or plain about you. Not now, and probably not then."

"Remember when I said I got sick?" Her hand went to her chest. "It was a rough decade. I spent a ton of time in the hospital. In fact, I was nearing the end of my life, and something happened. I was offered something special, kind of like orange extract, but better."

The constant furrow between his brows made his eyeballs ache. "I've never asked about that scar because I don't care how you got it. Are you telling me you're not healthy? You're sick again?" He couldn't take losing another woman he loved.

"No," she whispered. "I'm not sick."

This had dragged out long enough. "Just tell me whatever it is you think will change my heart. I promise you can't tell me anything that would change my mind about you."

"That's a promise you can't make." She threaded her shaking fingers through her hair and tugged. Her palms covered her face before they fell to her lap. "On April twenty-third, eight years ago, you lost something. I gained something." Her breath quickened. "You lost the love of your life. Because she died, I lived." She placed her hand pledge of allegiance style over her chest. "I have her heart."

Bowie sat stone still. "What?"

"I'm telling you the orange essence in me is Brandy's heart. Sitting in my chest is a piece of the woman you loved and lost."

The world faded to gray before it came back in full color to tilt him sideways. He opened his mouth to speak several times, but nothing came out until his brain could process the enormity of her confession. "You knew and said nothing." He stood abruptly, hitting the coffee table, sending food in all directions. "You knew how broken I was." His throat hurt from the raw emotion. "How could you not say something before now?"

A flood of tears ran down her cheeks. "I didn't know. Not until I brought the flowers to Bea's grave." She fisted her already swollen eyes. "I saw the date, and everything made sense. The bakery, her list, it all came together."

Bowie backed away from her until he ran out of room and hit the wall. "That was days ago. Why didn't you tell me then?"

She fell into the pillow and curled into a ball. "I ... I tried, but you said to not dwell on the things that can't be changed. I can't change whose donor heart I received. Nothing's changed."

"Everything's changed." He looked around the apartment and back to the woman he'd fallen in love with. Why wouldn't he still love her? She had the best part of Brandy. "I have to go. I have to think."

Katie rushed from the couch to him and wrapped her arms around his waist. "You said you'd love me always."

Bowie saw the hurt in her eyes. His heart ached for her and for himself. "You prayed I'd love you anyway. You said that because you knew." He pulled free of her hold. "I love you, Katie. I still do, but I need time and space to figure it all out."

She nodded her head and inhaled a shaky breath. "I know ... too weird, huh?"

He stared at her, his eyes landing on her chest. "It's creepy." Would he see her as herself, or would he see her as the love he lost? He had to question his feelings for her. Did he fall so hard and fast because he'd already been intimately involved with her heart? Just when he thought he'd moved forward, he was catapulted back to hell. "Give me some time to process."

She stepped back and lowered her head in what could only be described as defeat. "Time would be wise for both of us."

He raced down the staircase and went straight to the bar, where he knew there would be plenty of alcohol and advice.

Sage was behind the bar when he took a seat on the center stool. "You knew?" He hated that his voice sounded so accusatory, but she was the one pleading with Katie to tell him.

She shook her head. "No, I found out two minutes before you came in."

"Found out what?" Cannon came out of the storage room with a full bottle of Jack Daniels in his hand.

Bowie reached for the bottle and twisted off the cap. "Katie has Brandy's heart."

Sage lined up a few shot glasses.

Cannon stumbled back and leaned on the back bar. "She what?"

The bell above the bar door rang, and in walked Doc. "Saw you running across the street. Thought you might like to chat."

Bowie turned to face Doc Parker. "You knew and didn't say anything to anyone."

He slid onto the stool next to Bowie. With his hands held in the air, he said, "I didn't know, son. She didn't know. No one in town knew. So if you're feeling you've been duped, you best tuck that feeling away because no one lied to you or kept anything from you long term."

Cannon pushed off the counter and came forward, taking the open bottle from Bowie to fill up the shot glasses. "You want one, sweetheart?" he asked Sage.

"No, I think I should go hang out with Katie." She pulled a bottle of wine from the cooler and turned to Doc. "Can she have a glass?"

"A glass won't kill her."

Sage swiped two stemmed glasses from the rack above the bar and walked out, leaving the three men alone.

"So let me get this straight," Cannon started as he pulled beer chasers for the group. "Katie, the girl you love now, has the heart of the girl you loved before. Am I close?"

Bowie tilted his head back and drank what would be the first of many shots. "Spot on." He turned to Doc. "Did you know Bea had donated her organs?"

Doc sipped at his whiskey. "Nope. She never said a word except to say Brandy lived among us. I always thought that was a figure of speech. Like she surrounded us in spirit."

Cannon poured Bowie another shot. "So for real, Katie has a donor heart, and that heart is Brandy's." Cannon laughed. "How damn lucky are you to fall in love with the same heart twice?"

"Lucky?" Bowie tossed back the second shot and shivered as the heat of it ribboned through his body. "It's a freak show."

"Now, now, young man. I won't put up with you calling Katie

a freak. I always knew that girl was special. Just didn't know she was extra special."

"Tell me this. Do I love her because I love her, or is it some cosmic thing? Does my heart know that heart?"

Doc rubbed at his bushy brows, making them point straight to the heavens. "Did you love her yesterday when you didn't know she had that heart? Did you ever ask her about the scar?"

"Yes, I loved her, and no, I didn't ask her about the scar; it didn't matter."

"But it matters now?" Doc asked.

"It's different now because I know she has the heart."

Doc finished his shot and turned the glass over on the table. "She's the same girl as she was yesterday. Let me ask you this. What if you needed a new engine for your truck, and the one that was available came from your dad's truck? Once it's fixed, is it your truck or your dad's truck?"

"It's my truck."

"That there heart is Katie's heart. It stopped being Brandy's when she died. It's just a part, son. We're a sum of all our parts. It's Katie's blood that runs through that heart, not Brandy's. It's Katie's brain that keeps it functioning. Somehow, Brandy's heart found its way into Katie's chest. You would have never known if Bea hadn't given her the bakery. What if Katie hadn't accepted? Is there a little fate happening here? I don't know. All I know is you've got one special woman who loves you enough to tell you. She didn't have to be honest."

"You wouldn't have said anything?"

Doc nodded. "I couldn't. It's doctor/patient privilege. But even if I could, I wouldn't. Katie had to tell you on her own. And she did."

"Two days later." A hint of agitation rose in his voice.

Doc picked up the now-closed bottle of whiskey and tapped

Bowie on the head hard enough so he would feel it, but not hard enough to cause damage.

"She had a head injury, you dolt. Let me hit you a little harder and see how clearly you think. That woman has faced death head-on and won. She's happy and healthy and in love. How hard do you think it was for her to risk it all by telling you the truth? That's integrity—another special gift."

Doc looked at Cannon, then nodded to Bowie. "He's paying tonight. I dished out enough wisdom to make it worth a shot and a beer." He picked up his mug and emptied it, the foam sticking to his mustache. "You're a smart man, Bowie; don't be stupid tonight." Doc walked out the door.

"Holy shit." Cannon let out a long whistle. "What the hell are you going to do?"

Bowie held up his shot glass. "I'm getting drunk."

"After that?"

"I'm going to tell Katie I'm sorry."

CHAPTER TWENTY-ONE

Wrapped in Sage's arms, Katie cried herself out of tears. "He looked so broken. I feel so bad." She moved her head to find a dry spot on Sage's floral button-down shirt.

"He'll be back. That boy loves you."

Uncomfortable with a button in her ear, Katie pulled back and looked at her friend. "He loved her, too. If he comes back, how will I know if he's back because of me or her?"

"Oh, honey. You'll know in *your* heart." She pressed a finger forward against the center of Katie's chest.

"That's irony for you. Her heart, my heart, where does one end and the other begin?"

"The heart in you is yours." Sage picked up the bottle and poured Katie more wine. "Doc said you could have a glass. I don't think another half will hurt."

On any other day, Katie would have declined, but she needed to reach the calm that a glass and a half of wine could bring. "I bet you're wondering why I didn't tell anyone."

Sage hopped off the couch and walked toward the kitchen. "If we're going to get deep, I'll need sugar. Where's your stash?"

Katie followed her and opened the cupboard. She reached to the top shelf for the tub of candy she stashed away for PMS and bad days. If any day qualified as bad, this one did. It was a bad week, and she hadn't opened the tub once. She peeked under the lid, then handed the bucket to Sage.

Sage dug right in. "Ooh, you have peanut butter cups and Skittles. My favorites." She hugged the container to her chest and went back to her seat on the couch. "I'll be good for hours now. Start at birth if you need to go back that far."

For the first time that night, Katie laughed. "You're easy."

"And cheap, but don't tell Cannon."

"He'd love you anyway." Those words came out of Katie's mouth without thought. They were a reminder of the wish for Bowie to love her anyway. She'd hoped and prayed so much, her brain hurt worse than her heart. There was nothing left to do but wait and see if he could come to terms with what she'd shared.

"Bowie loves you. He'll come around. Who knows? We could be sisters someday."

"Wouldn't that be awesome? Do you see Cannon proposing soon?" Talking about Sage's forever made the loss of hers less painful. To focus on joy made it hard to lament her loss. "Do you have a ring in mind? Marquis? Princess cut? Oval?" Katie spent years looking at rings, wedding dresses, wedding venues—things she never thought possible until a donor heart became available.

She'd walked down the aisle a thousand times in her mind. Always dressed in white, she had a long train and a massive diamond that weighed down her hand. She'd trade those dreams for one more ride on the back of Bowie's Harley. One more kiss of his lips. The sound of his voice saying he loved her. Katie shook the thoughts from her head.

"A ring? That man can't afford new jeans. He'd never be able to afford a ring, and I don't care about the ring, but if I could choose, it would be a simple gold band." Sage looked at her empty ring finger. "Big diamonds and nursing don't mesh well. The prong things that hold the diamond tear the gloves."

"You really are cheap and easy." Katie reached into the bucket for a chocolate kiss. It was the closest Katie would get to any kind of kiss, anytime soon. "I saw a beautiful headboard at the dry goods store. It has to be Cannon's work. If it sells, that would buy him plenty of pairs of new jeans and leave enough left over for something special. Maybe a ring?"

"We aren't there yet, but it's a nice thought for the future."

Katie didn't have the luxury of thinking about the future. It would be hard getting through the night. "You know, I considered purchasing it myself. It's so pretty."

"No. Don't buy it." There was nothing playful in Sage's voice. Not a hint of suggestion. It was a demand.

"Why not?" The headboard was beautiful and obviously Cannon's work. Why wouldn't she want it sold?

Sage reached into the candy bucket and pulled out two pieces. She ate them both before she said another word.

"That headboard was Cannon's wedding gift to Brandy and Bowie."

Katie gasped. She was grateful she hadn't bought it. She'd been seconds away from a purchase, but the store only took cash and she was short by several hundred dollars. "People have to talk in this town," she complained. "I really thought it would look nice in my room. Holy hell, could you imagine if I had bought it?"

"No, but speaking of talking, why didn't you tell anyone?"

"It's not a conversation opener." She took a drink of wine and liked the fruity tang that danced across her tongue. It tasted far sweeter than sorrow. "You don't shake someone's hand and say, 'Hi, I'm Katie, and I have a donor heart.'"

"You're right. Honestly, it's no one's business."

Katie took the candy bucket and rummaged through it until

she found a Snickers bar. "The problem is, once people know you're a transplant recipient, they treat you differently."

Sage got a sly smile on her face. "Should you be eating that with your condition?" She exaggerated the worry in her voice.

"Exactly. I was twenty-eight and had to run away from home to get freedom. Do you think I'd let strangers steal it from me? No way. I love being treated like a normal person."

"You are a normal person." Sage shrugged. She dug into the bucket for another fun-sized bag of Skittles. "Then again, 'normal' is a broad term."

"Thanks for making me feel better."

Sage tilted her head and gave a wide smile. "That's what I do; I'm a walking ray of light."

Katie touched a curl shooting from the top of Sage's head. "You're a ball of fire."

"Hair jokes? Just wait until I can Google bad transplant jokes." She popped a green Skittle into her mouth.

The laughter bubbled inside of Katie until she couldn't hold it back. "I've got one for you. Here goes." She sat ruler straight. "A doctor tells a man needing a heart transplant that the only heart available is that of a sheep. The man agrees, and the doctor performs the transplant of the sheep heart." Katie stopped for dramatic effect. She'd heard it was important when delivering the punch line, and she wanted to make Sage laugh. "A few days after the operation, the man comes in for a checkup, and the doctor asks him, 'How are you feeling?' The man answers, 'Not BAAAAD!'"

Sage tugged the candy back into her lap. "That was awful. Just for that, you get no sweets." She pressed the top onto the plastic container. "Who told you that *baaaad* joke?"

"My transplant doctor," Katie said between bouts of laughter.

"We need better material. You needed a different doctor."

"There's the one about the doctor telling the patient she had her choice of two hearts. A twenty-year-old athlete or an eighty-year-old lawyer."

Sage leaned in like Katie held a secret. "Which one did she take?"

Katie rolled her eyes. "The eighty-year-old lawyer, of course. She wanted the heart that hadn't been used."

Sage tried to suppress her laughter, but a giggle burst forth. "That's so much better. Same doctor tell you that?"

"No. That came from one of my nurses."

"Naturally. Nurses have it all, brains, beauty, and humor."

"I'd love to hear the jokes your sister tells."

"My sister has no sense of humor, especially lately."

"What's going on with her?"

Sage sank into the sofa. "She's entering the last lap of her residency. There's lots of stress. She expected the hospital to pick up her contract, but maybe it wasn't a good idea to sleep with the boss."

"Does she love him?"

"She thinks she does."

Katie caught sight of her phone's screen glowing. She picked it up and saw the message from Bowie.

Can I come over?

She read it twice. "He wants to come over."

"See, I told you he would figure it out."

The calm the wine provided disappeared. "You did, but I'm not sure how I feel about it."

Sage gave her a confused puppy look. "I don't understand. Don't you want to be with Bowie?"

Katie brought the screen to her nose and inhaled as if she could smell him. It was crazy. She knew she should type "yes, yes, yes," but she couldn't because a question loomed in her mind. When Bowie looked at her from this point forward, would he see her, or would he see Brandy in her?

"I do, but I need to make sure he wants to be with me. The real me." She pointed to her chest. "This little ticker has muddled it all up."

"What are you going to tell him?"

She skimmed her fingers over the screen. "I'll tell him the truth. I need time, too. He's not the only one processing new information." She typed a return message.

Bowie, I love you, but I need time to process all that's gone on. Give me a day or two.

His reply took several minutes.

I'm so sorry. I'll give you anything you need.

"You want me to stay?" Sage asked.

Every possible answer floated through Katie's head. Yes, no, maybe, but Katie knew no matter how wise her friend could be, given her name was Sage, she needed to search *her* heart for the answers.

"No. I need time to think." Katie rose without giving Sage a chance to change her mind. At the door, she hugged her tight. "Thank you for being here for me. I've never had a friend as wonderful as you."

Sage held on to her for a long minute. "You and I have a bond. Bea chose us. She had a hundred reasons to bring us here."

"Two hundred if you combine them." She gripped Sage's shoulders and turned her body to face the door. "Go find your man. Tell him I promise not to buy the bed if he promises to whittle more ornaments."

"I'll give him the message."

The minute Katie locked the door, her stomach took a turn. It coiled and twisted and tightened. Had she made the right choice? It would have been easier to say yes and fall into Bowie's arms, but easy wasn't always best.

The acid of the wine rose to her throat. She barely made it to the bathroom before she lost everything.

IT HAD BEEN TWO DAYS SINCE THE TRUTH CAME OUT—TWO lonely, awful days where Bowie was so close and yet so far. She heard him next door in the bait and tackle shop, moving things around. She caught him peeking in the window several times a day. Each time she got a glimpse of him, it made her heartsick. She'd never get over loving him and hoped she wouldn't have to because he was everything and everywhere. He was the air she breathed. Above the cinnamon and sugar of the snickerdoodles, he was there in the scent of amber, pine, and sunshine.

Sitting under the Wishing Wall, Katie filled out a pink sticky note for herself. She'd been up most of the last two nights, missing Bowie. Her decision for space was wise, but knowing didn't make it feel better. She printed her wish on the tiny paper and tacked it to the board.

The bell rang above the door. She lifted her head, expecting to see Ben, but it was Bowie in front of her, and he looked worse than she felt.

CHAPTER TWENTY-TWO

"I know you want space, but I had to see you and make sure you were okay."

"I'm okay." She walked past him and behind the counter. "Let me get you coffee and a muffin."

She hadn't kicked him out. That was a plus. The thin line of his lips softened into a smile. "Coffee and a muffin sound great." He leaned against the counter and watched her move gracefully like a leaf in the wind.

She popped a K-cup into the machine and plated up a muffin. "As life would have it, it's chocolate-chip-orange muffin day."

He inhaled the essence of orange. He'd never be able to smell that scent again and not think of Katie. "Unbelievable." He lifted his brow when she handed him the plate.

"Coincidence or fate?" she lifted her shoulders.

"Irony," he replied. Bowie cleared his throat. "You might not know this, but I like orange essence in my muffins."

"I heard that."

"You also might know I love special girls."

Katie leaned across the counter. "What makes these girls special?"

Bowie nodded to the coffee machine, and Katie handed him his cup. He looked to the table under the Wishing Wall. "Will you join me?"

He took a seat at the table, where a pile of wishes sat waiting to be granted. The only wish that hung from the corkboard was hers. He knew because he'd watched her pen it and post it.

"You didn't answer the question." She grabbed a bottle of water from the refrigerator and followed him—another good sign.

"Because the answer isn't short or easy." He pulled the top of the muffin from the base and took a bite. "So good."

He looked at her like she was the muffin. He'd missed her. That first night when he'd asked if he could come over and she said no, he was sure she was punishing him for acting impulsively, but now he knew better. Time to think was important for both of them.

"It's the orange."

"I used to think so, too, but I was wrong. It's more about the surprise. Even without the orange, it would be an excellent muffin. I'd still love it."

He looked at her with as much love as he could convey without touching her. "You would?"

"Yes." He played with the notes on the table and picked one up.

I wish we had a park.

He put it back face up, so the wish was seen. "We used to have a park."

"You want to talk about parks?"

He leaned in and cupped her cheeks. "No, I want to talk about wishes. You want to know mine?"

She handed him a sticky note and a pen. "There's a system here. Follow the rules."

"Never a fan of rules, but for you ..." He jotted down his wish and thumbtacked it to the wall. While there, he removed hers and opened it.

"Hey, that's mine."

"I know, and if I can't grant it, no one can." He opened it and smiled. "Really?"

"What?"

He flattened the note and read it. *I need Bowie to love me.*

"Duchess, I do. I love *you.*" He scooted his chair closer and pointed to her chest. "Can I listen?"

His request was odd, but she understood the need. She'd want to hear it, too. It once beat in another chest for him. "Sure." She tilted her head back, giving him room to place his ear to her breastbone.

He pressed his ear to her chest and listened. "Nope. It's not the same." He leaned back and smiled. "This heart is yours and yours alone."

"You believe those words?"

Bowie dropped to his knees, leaned forward, and lowered his head. "After the other night, I know it's hard to believe me. I spent the entire night thinking about a life without you. The you I knew before two days ago, which is the same woman you are today. I'm so sorry, Katie. It was a shock."

"For both of us, but I have to know each time you look at me, you won't see a piece of her."

He lifted his head, so they were face to face. "When I look at you, all I see is love. I see how much I love you and how much you love me."

"We need to talk."

He hated those words. "I don't want to talk. I want to kiss you and make love to you. Are you sure you want to talk?"

"We have to talk. You need to know things about me before you decide if you want to be with me." She wrung her hands together. "I owed you an explanation for my scar. My selfish act of withholding did not give you enough data to decide about a relationship with me."

"I don't need data to know I love you. All I need to know is that you love me in return." He sat up in the chair and leaned back, prepared to sit for hours if that was what she needed.

With outstretched arms, she took hold of his hands. "There are so many factors that can affect our relationship. I got so caught up in the excitement of it all, I forgot to see the reality."

"Are you sick?"

Her grip grew tighter, as if she feared he'd run away, but he wasn't running.

"No. I'm healthy. I've been healthy since the day I got her heart."

Bowie looked at the green cotton T-shirt covering Katie's scar. He forced himself to imagine it was Brandy's heart in there, but he couldn't. Doc was right. Having a part of something didn't make it that thing. "The only reality I see is that we are two people in love."

Bowie flipped his hands, so they cupped hers.

"Okay, but you need facts, and I will give them to you."

"All right, tell me these facts." She tried to pull her hands away, but he held on tight. She would never get away from him again.

"First, I've had this heart for eight years. It's been good. I take my meds every day so my body doesn't reject the gift. I've outlived the average person living with a donor heart."

His heart rate sped up. The blood pounded out a drum-like rhythm in his ears. "You said you weren't sick, now you're telling me you'll die soon?" He'd read as much as he could find on the internet over the last two days. Most of it was beyond his comprehension, but he found many cases where donors lived normal, healthy lives for decades. He'd already decided Katie would grow old. He wanted to see her wrinkle and turn gray with him.

"I don't plan on dying anytime soon. I feel great." She looked around the bakery. "Have you ever thought of your legacy?"

Bowie followed her field of vision. This was Bea's legacy. The bakery would have been Brandy's. "No, in all honesty, I never thought I'd make it out of the desert alive. The universe or fate or God had other plans for me."

"Thankfully. Ben tells me you have three Purple Hearts and a box of other medals and commendations. He says you're a hero. That is part of your legacy." She slipped her hands from his and picked up her water for a drink. "My point in asking is because legacies are stories and heirlooms and assets you pass down to the next generation. Do you want kids?"

Early on, Bowie had thought about a family. He'd wanted children, but when Brandy died, that dream died with her. "It's not something I've thought about in a long time."

"You need to think about it because I can't have kids." She shook her head. "That's not true. I can physically become pregnant, but I shouldn't."

"If you shouldn't, why not go on the pill? We've been using condoms, and although I've never had a failure, they aren't unheard of. In fact, a buddy of mine just had what he calls a 'desert baby.' Blames the condom failure on heat and sand."

"Makes sense." Once the water bottle was back on the table, she leaned forward with her elbows on her knees. "Guys think they are so smart to keep condoms in their wallet, but did you know the constant heat from their body breaks down the latex?"

"Really?"

Bowie considered the condoms they'd used the first night. They'd been in his wallet for a year, survived the squelching heat of a tour in Afghanistan. Thankfully, Katie's cycle had come and gone. She had a short one, but she had one.

"I just told you we could never have kids, and now we're talking about latex and Afghanistan. Don't you want children, Bowie?"

Did he? One thing he knew with absolute certainty was he wanted her; children or no children.

"We'll get a dog. I hear they're less trouble and won't cost us as much over the long term."

Katie rolled her beautiful blue eyes at him. "A dog isn't a son or daughter. It won't carry your name."

"Bullshit. We'll name it Bishop."

"I'm being serious. I come with limitations. I won't ever climb Everest. I won't give you a daughter or a son. I have a compromised immune system. Things can change fast for me."

Bowie pulled her into his lap so she straddled him. "I've never wanted to climb Everest or any other mountain." He dipped his head for a quick kiss. "We'll adopt if having kids is important to you." Another kiss. "I'll take care of you."

"What if things go terribly wrong one day?"

"I've lived through terribly wrong. I survived. We'll do everything we can to keep you healthy. I can live without high-risk activities, but I can't live without you. I love you. Let me show you how much." He pressed his lips to hers, but this time he didn't pull back. The bell above the door rang, but he didn't break the kiss. It was long and lingering. A kiss he wanted to last forever.

"You kids want to take that upstairs?" Ben said as he rounded the counter.

"Yes, we do." Bowie lifted her from the chair.

"Wait." Katie reached for his wish. She plucked it from the board and read it. "I wish for a second chance with Katie. She's my future." She wrapped her arms around his neck. "I can grant that one. I can attest that life is better the second time around."

Bowie adjusted her in his arms and took off for the back stairs. "Call Cannon and tell him he's got the bait shop today," he called over his shoulder to his father. "I'm spending the day with my girl."

When they got upstairs, Bowie took her straight to bed. "I want to make love to you."

She pulled him on top of her. "I want you, too." Her hands went to the button of his jeans. "Too many clothes." The husky, soft vibration of her voice ramped up his desire tenfold.

"Easy to take care of."

He toed off his boots and sent his clothes flying in all directions. Once he was naked, he went to work on her. First, the shoes came off, then her pants and underwear. Bowie worshipped her long legs inch by beautiful inch until he reached the velvet skin of her inner thighs. Oh, how he wanted to stop and spend the afternoon right there, but he had all day, so he moved north trailing his tongue to the edge of her shirt.

"This has to go." With care, he lifted the soft cotton over her head.

It was the first time he'd seen her scar after knowing the truth. As he took in the silver line that ran the length of her chest, she watched him. He knew she was looking for any sign that would tell her he saw something other than her. In the back of his head, he knew it was Brandy's heart that beat beneath her breastbone, but all he saw was Katie.

With a twist, the front snap of her bra unhooked, and the perfect globes of her breasts fell into his hands. Worry clouded her eyes. He needed to reassure her that she was the only one in bed with him.

"I see you, Duchess. Only you." He lowered his mouth to hers, kissed her, and loved the sigh she released against his lips. It shredded him that they'd been apart for days. Wasted precious minutes where loving her could have replaced her worry. "I never want to be apart again. Not even for a day."

Katie stroked his back, tasting his mouth as her hips lifted, searching for his body. He held himself up to keep from crushing her with his weight. He wanted this moment to last forever. A reaffirmation of their love to last a lifetime, but when he released her mouth and looked into her eyes, he saw the fiery heat that erupted between them.

She put her palm against his chest. "Bowie," she said, breathless. His name on her lips filled him with hope and such pleasure. His growing length pressed between her legs.

"We need to protect you, love." He slid down her body, over the flat expanse of her stomach and down her legs. He reluctantly pulled away. Inside her nightstand was a box of condoms he hoped to deplete tonight.

Once he was wrapped and ready, he made his way back up her beautiful body. At her center, he parted her legs and buried his face. Her intake of breath, the sweet sound she made, and the taste of her told him he was home. There was no place for him but with Katie, and all he wanted was to bring her pleasure. She moved beneath his mouth. When her breath went from slow to rapid, he left her little knot of pleasure pulsing and made his way up her body.

Positioned between her legs, he gazed down on perfection. She was scarred. He was scarred. They were made for each other. Although he didn't want Brandy to be a part of this moment, he couldn't help saying a silent thank you for her sacrifice and the gift of Katie.

His mouth captured hers in a soul-searing kiss. He entered her in one deep, slow stroke that caused her to gasp. Her hips rose to meet his with every thrust, and her sighs turned to moans as he moved within her.

It would be so easy to let the passion take over and find his release, but he was determined that her needs would come before his. He pushed and pulled, causing both to breathe harder and faster. The heat of her drove him out of his mind, but he held on steadily while her body sought satisfaction. He wanted more than anything to please her. To replace the pain of the last two days with pleasure. She stilled. Her breath caught as she waited for those shudders of fulfillment to begin. When her sweet voice called out his name, he pressed deep inside her and let the moment of immense pleasure wash over him.

Her breathing slowed, and her body relaxed. Short puffs of air became sighs. Her kisses pressed soft and sweet against his lips.

"I love you," she said.

He fell to her side, lying face to face with his future. He liked the way it looked.

"I love you, too."

They made love so perfectly, so closely, they felt like two bodies with one heart. He hoped his love for her would be etched into her soul because he knew, without a doubt, she had burned her love into every cell of his.

CHAPTER TWENTY-THREE

Doctors' appointments were not new to Katie, but this one was interesting. Bowie had asked her to accompany him to Doc Parker's so he could understand her condition and what his part would be in keeping her healthy.

It had been two days since he carried her into her apartment. She'd never felt so loved or been loved so completely.

"I can see why you didn't tell him." Doc turned to her and lifted his bushy brows.

"Right? Weeks ago I was safe to row a boat, but today he doesn't like me crossing the street by myself." Katie laid a hand on Bowie's back. She knew he was coming from a place of concern and love. "This kind of obsessive behavior made me run away from Dallas."

Bowie's head snapped in her direction. "You run away, I will hunt the ends of the Earth to find you."

"The only running I'm doing is *to* you, but you have to calm down. Tell him, Doc. I'm healthy. I can do almost anything a non-transplant person can do."

Doc let out a long exhale that warbled with the shake of his head. "To be young and in love." He dragged the chair from the corner toward the examination table and flopped into it. "Let her live, Bowie. She can do anything she wants."

"Okay, but she wants to babysit the Williamses' eight kids tonight."

"Seven," Doc and Katie said in unison.

"That's got to be unhealthy."

"Crazy, yes, but unhealthy, no. The Williams children aren't sick. The worse that can happen is they tire Katie out." Doc looked over at her. "Looks like you're doing a fine job of that yourself, son."

Katie felt the heat rise to her cheeks. Now that she and Bowie had made up, they didn't pass up a chance to make love. Doc ordered condoms in bulk and gave them a discount.

"See? I'm good, now stop worrying."

Bowie threaded his fingers through hers. "You can't fault me for wanting to hang on to a good thing. If I'm protective, it's because I love you."

"I love you, too."

"Have you made an appointment with Dr. Holland?" Doc put the stethoscope in his ears. The feet of the chair scraped against the linoleum floor as he stood. He pressed the cold instrument to her chest and listened. "That's a sweet sound." He looked at Bowie. "You want to hear how healthy she is?"

He'd laid on her chest dozens of times, listening to the drum of life beat out a steady rhythm.

"Yes. I do." He turned toward Katie. "If it's okay with you."

She no longer worried about what he would think. He'd proven in short order he loved everything about her, from the way she stole the blankets at night to how she called out his name in passion.

"It's fine. You can listen."

Doc cleaned the earpieces off with an alcohol wipe and placed them in Bowie's ears. She knew the second he heard her heart beating. His smile grew broad and bright. "It so fast," he whispered in awe.

"One hundred heartbeats a minute, just for you."

Doc took his stethoscope away. "I was never one for sickly sweet, but you two are a second away from relationship diabetes. You better grab another box of condoms and go back to bed. You'll eventually get that out of your system, too."

Katie jumped off the exam table. "No time. We've got seven little angels to watch over." She rubbed her hands together like a devious mastermind. "I can't wait to get my hands on baby Bea." Katie had long ago come to terms with the fact that she'd never be a mother, but that didn't stop her from wanting to be one or taking advantage of mothering other people's children.

Doc patted Bowie on the back. "Any more questions, son?"

"I think I'm set."

They walked to the door, and Katie stepped aside to give room to Bowie so he could open the door. She watched the two men exchange glances.

"You gonna open that door, Duchess? I'd hate to take away your independence."

Bowie's grin bloomed until Katie wound up and punched him in the arm.

"Bowie Bishop, I'm not trading my independence for your bad manners."

Doc howled with laughter. "You'll learn, son. Might take you fifty years, but you'll learn."

Bowie pulled the door open. "I need a manual just to learn how this independence thing works."

Katie fisted his shirt and pulled him behind her. "I'll write you one."

They hopped on Bowie's Harley and drove to the Williamses' house. Once parked, they stood outside the two-story Victorian on Daisy Lane. Flower beds bloomed with hydrangeas in pink, green, and blue. A white picket fence surrounded a yard littered with Little Tyke toys. A pang of regret sliced through Katie that she tried to push away. She'd never have this life, but one look at Bowie and her regret turned to gratefulness. She might never hold their child in her arms, but she'd hold him, and that was enough.

"You ready for this?" She buzzed with excitement. Louise said the kids would be bathed and fed, and all they needed to do was entertain them until bedtime.

"I've been to war multiple times. I can't imagine this is worse or different."

She wanted to tell him he was being silly, but his description was spot on. With seven kids to watch, there was no doubt there would be battles won and lost over the next three hours.

Bobbie and Louise met them at the door. Louise looked beautiful tonight dressed in yellow. Little Bea slept in the cradle of her arms.

By the way Bobbie looked at his wife, Katie knew if they didn't stay someplace public, Williams baby number eight would be on the way soon.

"We'll be at Bishop's Brewhouse if you need us." Louise kissed her daughter on the forehead before she passed her off to Katie, who snuggled Bea to her chest and breathed in the scent of baby powder and fabric softener.

It took all of two minutes for the calm of the moment to turn into chaos. Jill ran toward Bowie and threw herself into his arms. Big crocodile tears ran down her cheeks.

"David tore off my Barbie's head." She lifted a decapitated doll to his face.

Bowie's lost expression told her this was worse than war.

David claimed innocence, but the look of guilt shone from him like a beacon. Katie had seen that look of guilt on the faces of many children she'd visited in the children's hospital. When they were stuck in bed, mischief was all they had left.

She shifted baby Bea to one arm and held out her hand. "Give it to me." Her voice was stern despite the laughter that bubbled inside her. "Right now, young man, or G.I. Joe will meet a similar fate." She spied the man-doll gripped in his hand but didn't see the Barbie head.

"She made her doll kiss Joe. He's a soldier."

Lucky for Katie, soldiering was something Bowie could relate to. He gave Jill a hug and put her on her feet. "Go with Katie." He turned to David. "You and I'll talk about women and war."

As Katie herded the kids into the living room to watch a movie Louise had chosen for them, she heard Bowie tell David there were battles a man should wage and some that were better left lost. When David said something about kisses being gross, Bowie laughed and told him he'd change his mind soon enough.

Bowie returned some time later with the doll's head dangling between his fingers. He found the torso discarded on the coffee table. Once he reunited the two pieces, he tucked the doll into the arms of Jill, who had curled into a chair and fallen asleep. He squeezed into the spot next to Katie and wrapped his arm around her.

It took time to get them settled down. For a while, it seemed they all needed something different at the same time. Snacks and bathroom runs and Band-Aids applied to nonexistent wounds took up the first hour of the night. Getting six kids and a baby into the living room was like herding cats. She and Bowie had done it and were no worse for the wear. She looked at the seven children who either slept or zoned in on the cartoon and smiled. They'd survived, so far.

"You know," Katie said to Bowie. She glanced at David, who was lying on the floor, sandwiched between Melissa and Thomas. "You were wonderful with him."

"He's a good kid, and now he's ahead of the pack when it comes to women. I let him know the golden rule."

"There's a golden rule?" Her voice rose with each word. "What's that?"

Bowie seemed to consider whether he should tell her. "I told him the facts. When he's right, he's wrong. When he's wrong, he's wrong. He'll be much happier if he's always wrong. I also told him the right kiss from the right woman would make everything right. Then he and I and G.I. Joe blew up stuff in his room."

Every day, Katie fell in love with Bowie a little more. Her secondhand heart was full. She'd hit the lottery with him and worried he wasn't as lucky with her. It pained her that this man would give up the possibility of a family for her.

"Are you sure you're okay with not having one of these yourself?" She hugged Bea closer to her breast and bent over to rub her cheek along the baby's soft hair.

He looked around the room at the seven kids. "Watching this brood is the best birth control ever. It's a wonder their parents had time to make so many." Bowie turned and nuzzled his chin into her neck. "If we ever feel like we're missing out, I'm sure Louise will have a new one we can borrow."

"You're probably right, but I don't want you to make a sacrifice you'll regret."

"No regrets. All I want is you."

As the children dropped off to sleep one by one, Bowie carried them to bed. The only one left was Bea, who Katie wanted to cradle for a moment more until her bladder said enough was enough.

"Hold her for a second while I go to the bathroom?"

Bowie stared at the baby as if she'd asked him to hold a live grenade, but he held out his hands and took the tiny little girl. Bowie's arms dwarfed little Bea. She was barely bigger than his palms lined side by side. He looked perfect holding her. Katie stood in the hallway and watched him look down at the baby with wonder and awe. She knew right then her only concern would be never giving Bowie a child.

Bobby and Louise returned, holding hands. They were the kind of couple that emitted the light of love. Katie saw it in the way they looked at their children—the way they looked at each other. She saw the same look in Bowie's eyes when he looked at her.

"Bring that car over whenever you need an oil change," Bobby told Katie before he closed the door.

At the bike, Bowie placed the helmet on her head and said, "You got an oil change for babysitting? I helped. What do I get?"

"I'll show you when we get home." She hung on to Bowie as he raced back to her apartment, where she expressed her gratitude for over an hour.

They lay sated and wrapped in each other's arms. "We made it through that gauntlet. What's next?"

Katie turned to him. "You thought that was a gauntlet? Wait until you meet my parents. I've invited them here for my birthday."

CHAPTER TWENTY-FOUR

How did this happen?

Bowie sat in the corner booth at Maisey's, waiting for Cannon and his father. Never for one moment in the last eight years did he think he'd be this happy. Although he missed Brandy in many ways, there was more to what he'd found with Katie. She had life experiences that forced her to value the small stuff.

She woke up every morning ready to conquer the world. Her outlook was positive and infectious.

"You want some coffee?" Maisey walked over with the pot swinging in her hands.

"*Need* some coffee is more like it." Bowie overturned the clean cup on the table and slid it toward the edge.

"Late night?"

Bowie laughed. "Early morning." Knowing they wouldn't be sleeping together the next few nights, he and Katie had stayed up making love. It was silly to change their routine because of her parents. They were consenting adults, but he loved her enough to make the sacrifice.

Katie emphasized the point that her very Southern parents wouldn't be happy about the sleeping arrangements.

"Oh, to be young again." She poured coffee to the brim and slid into the booth across from him. "I wanted to ask you something."

"Anything." Bowie took his first sip and waited for Maisey to continue. He'd never known her to be shy about much, but he saw the vulnerability in her expression. The way she got smaller with each second she waited. "What's up, Maisey?"

"I'm in love with your father, and I want to make sure you're okay with that," she blurted.

"You're in love with my father? That's amazing. You know the Bishop men aren't easy to love."

"Maybe not, but you're worth the effort. Your dad's a good man. More so since he's not drinking. I know it's been a tough time for all of you, but I wanted his boys' blessings before I told him."

"You told me you loved him before you told him?"

She wiggled in her seat. "I wanted to make sure it was okay to love him."

Bowie reached his hand over and touched Maisey's arm. Although she was seated, she looked ready to bolt with her legs facing the middle of the restaurant and her hand still gripping the coffeepot.

"You love who you love. I want my dad to be happy, and he seems happy now that he's with you. I'm sure he would love to know how you feel."

She relaxed against the booth. "Things going well for you and Katie?"

"Well" didn't begin to explain what happened between him and Katie. "She's special."

"Are the rumors true?"

He knew the town would be abuzz about the whole heart thing. It was something people would ask about until the novelty of it wore off. He hoped something more exciting would come up and grab people's attention. For the last several weeks, he'd been busy at the shop, and Katie had been swamped at the bakery. They were a true love story, better suited for television.

"It's all true, but then you know that because you're in love with my father."

She lifted her chin. "I believe it's important to fact-check."

"I agree. Facts are important. Here are a few for you. Katie has a donor heart, but it doesn't matter to me who it belonged to; it's in Katie's chest, so it's hers. She changed my life with her love. I've been given a second chance at happiness. I'd be stupid to pass that up."

"Sounds like you're in love, too." She rocked forward and stood.

"That's a fact."

As Maisey walked away, the door opened, and Ben and Cannon walked inside. Since Bowie took up most of the seat, his father and brother sat across from him.

"Are you nervous, son?" Ben turned over a mug and nodded toward Maisey, who was on her way back with a full pot of coffee.

It didn't pass Bowie's attention when his dad reached out and wrapped his arm possessively around Maisey's waist. He watched his father's expression go soft the minute she looked down at him, and he wondered if he got that same goofy look on his face when Katie was nearby.

"Not really. I'm not sleeping with her parents."

Cannon laughed. "From what I hear, you're not sleeping with her either." He pushed his empty mug toward Maisey.

"From the way we look, no one is getting sleep." Ben waggled his eyebrows and gave Maisey a pat on the bottom.

She ignored the gesture. "Breakfast special for all of you?"

The three men nodded before she walked away.

Bowie picked up his knife and playfully pointed it at his

brother. "If the bed and breakfast had an empty room, they'd be staying there."

"You could have put them at the house, and Dad could have babysat."

Ben shook his head. "The only thing I'm babysitting is that three-legged dog of Sage's. He's about all I can handle."

"Wait until you get some grandkids."

It wasn't public knowledge he and Katie would never have children, so Bowie tried not to react. He would have loved to have a family with her, but it wasn't in the cards. He turned to his father. "Speaking of babysitting, are you good with holding my present for Katie until tomorrow?"

He hoped she liked the puppy he adopted for her. She'd mentioned more than once that she wanted a chocolate Labrador someday. She was never allowed a dog when she was little. He wanted to help her cross off that item from her bucket list. He'd found the furball at the humane society in Gold Gulch. Since he'd rescued the animal, it made little Bishop special. According to Katie, everything and everyone deserved a second chance.

"I'm good. He's locked in the bathroom right now. The little shit got out this morning and ran into the lake. It might be July second, but the water is still cold."

Bowie found it hard to believe he was sitting across from his brother and his father and all three were planning new futures.

"What about you?" He turned to Cannon. "You got kids on the radar?"

By the look on Cannon's face, a person would have thought he'd been asked to douse himself in gas and light himself on fire. "Oh no, I think I'll wait on that. I like the idea of practicing until we get our routine perfect." He fidgeted with his napkin, which was odd because Cannon was not the nervous type. "I did want to ask you something, though."

There were a lot of people asking Bowie questions this morning. "It's okay if you love her," he said.

"I'm not asking your permission to love her. That's a done deal." He tore at his napkin until it lay in shreds in front of him. "I put that headboard at the dry goods store on consignment, but I should have asked you if you minded if I sold it." Cannon lowered his head.

"Dude, that headboard was a masterpiece. It should be in a museum. I think it's great that you have it for sale."

"You do?"

Bowie nodded. He'd seen it the week before when Katie dragged him in to buy more soap and honey from Abby. She wanted his opinion on a scent, but he didn't care whether she smelled like strawberries or mango as long as she was with him and naked.

"What are you going to buy with the money if you sell it?"

"Money?" Dalton said as he approached the table. "I'll take your money." He put a plate of bacon, eggs, and pancakes in front of each of the three men. Behind him, he reached for a chair and pulled it up to the table. "Who's got money?"

"Not a damn one of us," Ben said. "One thing I've learned over the years is, you never need more than enough. We've got enough."

"Once my disability rating comes in, I should start getting a check from here on out," Bowie said.

"You're getting a disability check?" Dalton asked. "What part of you is disabled, outside of your brain?" He looked at Cannon and Ben. "You two, as well. You're a bunch of wusses for letting women get under your skin."

Cannon coughed on his bacon. "Says the man who went to jail for a woman he didn't know."

Dalton gave them a what-can-I-say shrug. "I'll protect a woman any day of the week, but fall in love ..."

"You will, and when it happens, it's like a Mack Truck colliding with your heart and brain at once."

Dalton looked around the diner. It was filled with locals, but not one single girl was in sight. "You took all the single women in town worth dating." He eyed Ben. "Not that I'd date my mom. That would be all kinds of wrong."

"Things in Aspen Cove are changing. You never know who might show up next," Cannon replied.

Ben swallowed his pancake and took a drink of coffee. "I don't think Bea owned any other property. Doc owns the empty shops on Main Street, so I wouldn't be expecting another pink envelope to steer a woman your way."

Dalton gripped the table. "That's my point. The pickings are slim, and those who are around stay clear of me. Who wants to date a felon?"

Bowie couldn't hide his amusement. It was true Dalton had killed a man, but there were extenuating circumstances. "Any woman who can't see the poetry in what you did doesn't deserve you. You did time for a woman you didn't know. You protected and most likely saved her life. If I were a woman, I'd be asking what you'd do to protect what was yours."

"I'd give everything to protect what was mine," Dalton said.

Bowie patted his friend on the back. "A good woman will know that."

"Speaking of women." Dalton looked between Cannon and Bowie. "Where are yours?"

"Copper Creek," Cannon answered.

"Another Target run?" Dalton reached over and swiped Bowie's last piece of bacon.

Bowie was too slow and couldn't nab it back before Dalton devoured it. "Nope, a parent pickup run. Katie's parents flew in this morning, and she and Sage went to pick them up."

"She hiding you?" Dalton asked.

"No. Since she's been hiding from them for months, she knew they would fuss over her and probably do a fair amount of complaining. She didn't want me to see that side of her parents. Worried that my first impression wouldn't be positive. In fact, she worried herself sick. Sage went along because I asked her to go. I wasn't invited to the homecoming, but I wanted Katie to have moral support."

"That girl domesticated you with efficiency." Dalton lifted his eyes in a challenge to say otherwise.

"Screw you. Your time is coming." Bowie pushed his empty plate to the center of the table.

"Not likely anytime soon." Dalton looked around the diner again. "I better get back to the kitchen." He rose and left the table.

"The plan is still to meet at the bar at five, right?" Cannon stole his father's napkin and wiped his mouth.

"That's the last I heard," Ben said.

Cannon laughed. "Dude, you're meeting the parents. That's huge."

He was right. It was huge. Meeting the parents was almost like buying a ring–something he'd considered over the last two weeks. Instead, he bought a puppy.

CHAPTER TWENTY-FIVE

"Let me get this straight, your parents have a private plane?"

Katie paced inside the tiny terminal of Copper Creek Municipal Airport. It wasn't a terminal as much as a small building close to the tarmac.

"It's a company jet." She pressed her nose to the glass and squinted her eyes. Off in the distance were the lights of an incoming plane.

"What company do they own?"

Katie walked back and forth in front of the glass. "Integrity Insurance."

Sage stepped in front of Katie and stopped her from wearing a path in the carpet. "'The insurance you can trust'?" She sang the jingle that played no less than twenty times a day on the television. "*That* Integrity Insurance?"

"Yes," she said sheepishly.

"Is there anything else you've been keeping to yourself?"

Katie hated she hadn't been completely transparent with anyone. She hadn't lied; she simply didn't divulge more than she had to. Even Bowie didn't know everything. Though he did know her father was an insurance executive, she hadn't painted the full picture.

"I wanted you all to like me for me. I didn't want you to feel sorry for me because of my health issues. I also didn't want my parents' money to be a factor in how people felt about me. To most people, selling insurance is almost as bad as selling used cars. A slimy profession."

"So when you said you were a data entry worker, was that true?" Sage leaned against the glass with her back to the tarmac.

"Yes, I refused any position I didn't earn. I grew up privileged, but I've always wanted to be independent." She looked over Sage's head at the plane touching down hundreds of yards away. "Imagine having to be dependent on someone for everything. That was me, and I promised myself if I got healthy, I'd stand on my own two feet."

"So that's why you drive a piece-of-junk car?"

Katie had bought the SUV used and loved it because she'd done it herself. "That piece of junk is my first large purchase."

"Surely, your parents bought you a car. They're as rich as God himself." Sage fidgeted with her top.

Katie noticed how self-conscious Sage was getting in the minutes since she told her who her parents were. It was the same with everyone. That's why she never said anything.

"Yes, I got a Range Rover for my sixteenth birthday. I was really sick then and couldn't drive it much because my mother was worried I'd pass out behind the wheel. It looked pretty in the garage, though."

"You had a Rover, and you traded it for a used Jeep?" Sage ran her hands through her curls, leaving one coiled toward the ceiling.

Katie smoothed out her friend's hair. "I didn't trade it. It's still in the garage. I think the housekeeper drives it."

"Housekeeper?" Sage shook her head. "You have a housekeeper?"

Katie laughed. "*I* don't. Have you seen my apartment?"

Sage let out an unladylike growl. "I meant ... you grew up with servants?"

The plane pulled up to the building, then a crew walked out to prep for her parents' arrival.

"We had help. You know, like a gardener, a cook, and a housekeeper."

Sage's smile bloomed brightly. "I had you pegged from the beginning as a beauty queen." She fist-pumped the air. "I was spot-on."

Katie smoothed out the wrinkle in the skirt of her dress. "I only won twice. Never got the trifecta."

"So you're rich?"

Katie's sigh sounded like resignation. "Technically, I'm rich. I have a trust fund I don't use." She pointed to herself. "Remember? Independent."

Sage shrugged. "We all need someone. I mean, you took the bakery from Bea. That's not an act of independence."

Katie knew Sage wasn't slamming her for the choice; just trying to figure it out. "I did take the bakery as a way to escape that." She pointed to the couple emerging from the plane like movie stars. Her mother was dressed in Prada, while her dad's suit screamed tailor-made. "Making it work—although not entirely on my own—was as independent as I've ever been."

Sage looked at her. Without warning, she pulled Katie in for a hug. "I'm so proud of you."

"Thank you."

She held her hand to her chest, her heart pounding out a million beats per second. She knew her parents would hate everything about her new life. She only hoped she could convince them it was right for her.

"I still think it's a shame you have a bunch of money sitting there doing nothing."

Katie smiled. "It's not doing nothing; it's gaining interest. Besides, I have a few ideas on where it could be used."

The door flew open, and Katie's parents walked in. Her mother rushed in for the first hug, while her father stood back and took everything in.

"Oh, honey, it's been too long." Sophia Middleton stepped back and looked Katie up and down. "Have you gained weight?" She walked around her daughter like Katie was on display. "You know being overweight is hard on your heart."

Sage gave her a what-the-hell look.

"Welcome to Colorado." Katie reached out and yanked Sage next to her. "This is my best friend, Sage."

"Nice to meet you, dear," her mom said.

Dad simply nodded in her direction. "Where's the car? We have luggage."

"Luggage? I thought you were only staying for a few days?"

"That's right, but I like to be prepared for anything."

"My place is really small, but it's a forty-minute drive to Aspen Cove, so you'll have time to prepare."

Tate Middleton wielded his wealth like Thor did his hammer. He raised a few bills and asked for help. It was amazing how loud money could speak to some people, but Katie had faced death. Once that happened, she knew money meant nothing.

It was funny to put her parents in the back seat of her Jeep. She couldn't remember a time where either of her parents were passengers in anything but a limousine.

"I don't understand why you couldn't take the Range Rover," her father said.

"It wouldn't matter; you'd still be sitting in the back." Katie looked to the side at Sage, who tried to hide her smirk. It was obvious she enjoyed this exchange.

Katie's mother leaned forward. "Tell me, Sage, what do you do?"

Sage turned in her seat to face Sophia. "I'm a nurse, and I work in the small clinic in town a few days a week. I also run the only bed and breakfast in town. It was also a gift from Bea Bennett."

Sophia sat up. "Are you a donor recipient as well?"

Sage shook her head. "No. I cared for Bea in her last days."

"Oh, that's lovely." Sophia waited for a minute. "I'm conflicted when it comes to Bea. I'm grateful her daughter was an organ donor. That gift saved Katie's life. However, her other gift took Katie away from us."

Katie knew this trip would be difficult. Her parents were used to getting what they wanted, and what they wanted right now was Katie living back in Dallas in the north wing of the house.

"Bea's gifts saved my life in all ways. I own a bakery, and I have a boyfriend I love. I have friends." She risked a backward glance at her parents, who sat emotionless in the back seat. "I still have you. I love you both, but when you gave birth to me, did you ever truly expect me to live with you forever?"

This time, it was her father who answered. His voice was board meeting serious. "When we had you, all we wanted was a happy, healthy baby. We got that for a while. Things changed, and so the plan changed. The secret to success is to adapt."

"Exactly. I live in Colorado now; you'll have to adapt." It was so easy to use his words against him. "Besides, you got your original wish. I am happy and healthy. I can't wait for you to meet Bowie."

"That is an odd name. I wonder how he got it."

Sage giggled. "In all honesty, the Bishop boys were named with the first initial of their parents' names, Carly and Ben, but I think Ben had a fascination with armament. He did name his first-born Bowie, like the knife, and his second Cannon."

"Names always fascinate me. Do you remember that boy you had a crush on in junior high school? His name was Teddy Bear."

Katie remembered him with fondness. "He was a chubby kid no one was nice to but me."

"You always had a soft heart," her father said. "Katie's motto is 'give me your poor, wounded, and downtrodden, and I'll give them my heart.'"

"She has a big heart. There's nothing wrong with showing love and compassion," Sage said in Katie's defense.

"When she was eight, she hid a homeless woman in our pool house."

Out of the corner of her eye, she saw Sage's mouth drop open. "You had a pool?"

Katie smiled. "And a pool boy."

They all but ignored her parents for a few minutes.

"Hot?"

"No. Old, but his son was cute. He gave me my first kiss at fifteen."

"He did not. You kissed Manny's son?" Her mother's voice reached the decibel level just below hearing loss.

A giggle welled up in Katie. "Have you seen him? He's gorgeous. Even then, he had the bones of a beautiful man in the making. He was a good kisser."

"Should I be aware of any other help I'll need to fire when I get home?" Tate held his voice in a monotone, but when Katie peeked at him in the rearview mirror, she caught the lift of his lip. He always found her mother's prudish edge funny.

"Don't you know? I kissed them all, even Delia, the house-keeper. Looks like you're going to have to do the dishes yourself from now on."

"Stop teasing," her mother said. "You know I don't do dishes."

Katie glanced at Sage. "Welcome to the Middletons'." All this banter made the drive go quickly. Katie pulled onto Main Street and parked in front of B's Bakery. "This is home."

Her mom pressed her nose to the glass. "You live in a bakery?"

"No, I live above the bakery. Come on." She looked at her father. "You'll have to carry the luggage yourself, Dad. I'm afraid we're servant-free here in Aspen Cove."

Sage hopped out of the car and opened the door for Sophia, who stepped out and looked around like she'd been dropped into the pits of hell.

"This is it? You left Dallas for this?"

Katie was out of the car and on the sidewalk. Her stomach turned, but after this morning, there was nothing left inside it.

"Behave yourself, Mother. This is home to a lot of nice people. It's home to me, too."

Her mother shook herself and pasted on a smile that could win an award. "Show me your castle, darling."

Tate grabbed only the essentials and followed them into the bakery. Ben was standing behind the counter.

"Katie, glad you made it back safely." He looked at her parents with a warm, genuine smile. "I'm Ben. Katie adopted me." He shook his head. "That's not quite the truth. Katie and Sage saved my life." He walked around the corner and hugged Sophia, who wasn't used to unexpected displays of affection. He then shook Katie's father's hand.

"Would you be a good man and fetch our bags from the trunk?" Tate palmed a hundred into Ben's hand.

"Dad, Ben is not your hired help."

Ben looked at the bill and handed it back. "I'd be happy to help with your bags, but I don't need your money." He pressed it back into Tate's hand. "I'm the richest man without it."

Katie felt a sense of pride toward Ben. He knew what had value—people. She wasn't responsible for his turnaround, but she was glad she got to see it. All she provided him was an opportunity.

That's exactly what Bea provided for her and Sage. What they did with her gift was up to them. Katie always hated when people accepted praise for the success of others. When her cousin Pat passed the bar exam, everyone told his parents they should be given praise for his accomplishment, but his parents didn't take the test. They didn't study for months on end. They didn't go to school to become a lawyer. Pat did, and he deserved the accolades. All his parents provided was an opportunity. Pat took that gift and turned it into something. It could have gone the other way.

"I'm going to leave you all for now. See you at the bar tonight?" Sage hugged Katie's mother and gave her father a nod.

"We'll be there." She guided her parents through the bakery to the back staircase. She looked down at her mom's four-inch heels. "No elevator, sorry."

At the top of the stairs, she held her breath before she opened the door. "Before you go in, you need to know I love it here and there's nothing you can do or say to change my mind. I suggest you love it, too."

She swung open the door and walked into the tiny space. Being there with her parents made it even smaller. Her whole apartment would fit in their master bedroom at home.

Her mother's heels tapped across the floor. "It's ..." she turned to her husband, "charming. Right, Tate?"

He walked around the living room and stood at the window, looking out at Main Street. "Charming," he repeated.

Katie looked at her place through her mother's eyes. There were no hand-knotted rugs. No antiques—unless you counted the can opener on the kitchen counter. The furniture was blue. The walls were beige. The carpet was brown. The kitchen floor was fabricated plastic, not Italian tile. The counters came from a hardware store; they were not honed from stone carved from inside a mountain. Katie scanned her home. It wasn't much, but it was everything, and she loved it.

Ben pushed open the door with one of her parents' heavy bags. "Here you go. Where do you want them?" Ben had never been up here as far as Katie knew. He looked around the place like he was checking out a model home. "This place is amazing. No wonder you kids spend so much time up here."

Before her parents could question him, she said, "Ben is Bowie's father."

Both of her parents smiled. "Charming," they said in unison.

"First door on the left, Ben." Katie looked at her mother. "Did you bring anything less ... pretentious?"

"I have everyday clothes." As Ben came out of the hallway, her mother entered.

"See you later." Ben closed the door behind him.

Her father opened his arms like he was showing her something she hadn't seen. "This makes you happy?" He moved from the living room to the small galley kitchen.

"It's not the apartment. I like it, and it does make me happy, but it's the town and the people. They're real. When they smile, it comes from deep inside." Honesty was one of the most endearing qualities of the town. A pang of guilt rushed through her when she thought about how much she'd kept from the people of Aspen Cove.

"You bake?" Her father lifted the plastic wrap from a paper plate left on her counter. Inside were leftover poppy seed muffins.

"I do. I made those." She leaned against the counter and waited for his approval. It was funny because even though her mother was the tougher of her two parents when it came to acceptance, it was her father's blessing that meant more.

He took a bite and chewed. His eyes closed, like somehow that action helped him taste better. "I'll be damned. You can bake."

Pride filled her with warmth. "I make cookies, too. And mini cakes." She reached into the refrigerator and poured her father a glass of milk. "I haven't mastered big cakes yet. They always seem to fall on one side."

"Princess, I have no doubt those will be mastered soon. You

may have a big heart, but you have a stubborn disposition. Your mother says you get it from me, but I'm not convinced."

"She gets what from you?" Sophia entered the kitchen wearing tailored slacks, a silk blouse, and patent leather pumps—her casual clothes.

"Her baking skills. Taste this." Tate handed his wife the second half of the muffin. "I'm going to change." He looked at Sophia, then at Katie. "Jeans okay?"

"Perfect, Daddy." She knew it was silly to use such a childish name for her father, but when she was with him, she always felt little.

Ten minutes later, her dad walked out looking like he belonged in Aspen Cove. Well ... almost, if it wasn't for the ten-thousand-dollar watch and two-hundred-dollar haircut.

Tate took a seat in the chair next to the couch. "When do we meet this boyfriend of yours? I thought he'd come with you to pick us up."

"He wanted to come, but I said no. I wanted you all to myself."

She knew it was a stupid answer because she'd brought Sage. Her parents didn't say anything to contradict her. By disappearing for months, she'd upset the balance in their totalitarian relationship. She was sure the minute she took charge of her life, her parents felt the repercussions of their total control parenting style.

"How are Isabella and Nick?" Both of her siblings were still in college. They were on the extended plan, and Katie hoped they'd found themselves in the time they'd spent away from home.

Her mom bubbled at the chance to talk about her kids. "Isabella is loving UCLA, and Nick is ready to come back to Dallas. They're both home for the summer but anxious to complete this journey in their lives."

Nick was attending NYU for a degree in business management. He'd take over the insurance business for her father when he was ready. Isabella, on the other hand, flitted between degrees.

First, she tried art history, then ecology, now she was studying film. Like Katie, Isabella didn't have to work. Unlike Katie, Isabella didn't like to work.

Katie looked at the clock that sat on the end table. "Speaking of lives, do you want to come meet the people in mine?"

CHAPTER TWENTY-SIX

"Have a beer; it'll calm you down." Cannon pulled a lager into a frosty mug and set it in front of Bowie. "You look like a trapped animal."

He'd been walking the length of the bar for minutes. "I'm not used to being away from Katie this long." He cupped the frosted glass with his hands, but he didn't take a drink.

"If you're not drinking that beer, son, pass it down," Doc said. "And stop warming my beer with your hands."

Bowie slid the mug down the slick bar. When it landed in Doc's hand, the suds splashed over the side and onto the bar.

"Sage is back safe, so they're fine. She went home to check on Otis."

Bowie's phone buzzed in his pocket. He ripped it free and looked at Katie's message. "They're on their way." He'd never been so nervous about meeting anyone, but when Katie told him this morning her father was an insurance executive, he looked him up. Seems a donor heart wasn't the only information Katie had been withholding. Her father was one of the richest men in the United States.

"Give me a beer," he called to his brother.

"I just gave you one, asshole, and you gave it away." Cannon pulled another lager and set it in front of Bowie.

He lifted the mug. "Here's to everything."

"I'll drink to that," Doc said.

The door opened, and Bowie's heart stilled. Katie looked beautiful in her dress. The receding sun caught her blonde hair just right, making her look like she glowed. Dressed in his best jeans and a button-down shirt, Bowie rushed over to meet the parents.

He offered his hand to her mother first because he had manners and ladies always went first. "It's a pleasure to meet you, ma'am. I'm Bowie Bishop, your daughter's boyfriend." As he said the words, they sounded wrong because Katie was so much more than his girlfriend. She was his everything. He turned to her father, who'd been sizing him up since Bowie walked over to them. "Sir, it's also my pleasure to meet you. I've heard a lot about you."

That wasn't the truth exactly. He'd read a lot about the man—enough to make Bowie feel unworthy of Katie's love. He'd never be able to provide her with what she was used to, but he reminded himself all day that she was here because she found something she couldn't find anywhere else. He hoped it was him.

"Can I get you a drink?" Bowie led them to a table near the bar.

"I'll take whatever kind of whiskey you've got," Tate said.

"I'll take a glass of Duckhorn, please," Sophia replied.

When he gave her a confused look, Katie piped in, "She'll take the house cabernet."

When he walked to the bar, Cannon laughed. "You are so screwed," he whispered.

"Shut up, asshole, and get me the drinks," he whispered back. He knew his brother had heard the order. Outside of Doc, they were the only ones in the place.

Bowie returned with fizzy water for Katie, wine for her

mother, and a glass of Jack for her father. He hated small talk, but he engaged in it anyway to break the ice.

"How was the flight?" He wanted to punch himself in the gut. He was sure the flight was great. How could it not be when it was a private jet?

"It was good. Do you know much about planes?"

Bowie sent up a silent *thank you* to the conversation gods. "I do. Planes have always fascinated me. I spent eight years jumping out of them."

"No kidding?"

"It's kind of a requirement to be a Ranger."

Tate looked at his daughter. "I didn't know he was a soldier, Katie."

She looked at her mom, who took a sip of the wine and made a face like she'd just eaten car wax. "I told Mama. I figured she'd pass that on."

Tate shook his head at his wife, then turned back to Bowie. "Seen any combat?"

The aches Bowie felt in his leg, his back, and his stomach were all reminders of how much combat he'd seen.

"More than I'd like to admit."

"He has a box of ribbons and medals." Katie threaded her fingers with his under the table. "He's a hero, Daddy."

"A hero?"

Bowie nudged Katie playfully with his shoulder. "She exaggerates."

"I do not. Seriously, he's got three of those Purple Heart ones."

Bowie was embarrassed because getting shot wasn't something he'd been proud of ever. Saving his people was where his sense of accomplishment rested.

Tate's hand slapped him on the back hard. "I'm so proud of you. I always wanted to serve, but my father had other plans for me."

"If you have a Purple Heart, then you've been injured." Sophia's voice held a drop of concern.

Bowie nodded his head. "Yes, ma'am. I've been shot and stabbed, but I made it back alive."

There was a moment of silence before Sophia spoke again. "This may seem insensitive, but it's my understanding that the heart in my daughter's chest once belonged to your fiancée."

Bowie had been expecting that. He was surprised it wasn't the first thing to come out of one of her parents' mouths.

"You're right. It was a shock, to say the least. Am I in love with your daughter's heart?" Bowie sat back and took a sip of beer. "I am, but not because it belonged to Brandy. I love your daughter because she has the biggest heart I know. It's *her* heart." He turned toward Doc. "This smart man I know asked me an important question, and I'll ask you the same. If your plane needed a new engine and your friend had one sitting unused in his garage and gave it to you, would it be his plane now, or still yours?"

Tate answered directly, "It's my plane."

Sophia nodded in agreement.

Bowie laid his hand over Katie's heart. "This is Katie's heart, and she owns mine, too."

They spent an hour at the bar, where they met most of the town. No one comes to Aspen Cove unnoticed. While Katie's mother was on the less friendly side, her father quickly became a local.

Once they finished their drinks, they walked down the street to Maisey's Diner. Maisey had hired seasonal help. A woman named Meg took their order, but it was Dalton who delivered it. He always came out when his friends were around.

Katie rose to her feet and threw her arms around his neck once he dropped off the plates. "This is Dalton. He was my second friend in town."

If it were any other man, Bowie would have burned with jealousy, but he understood the relationship between the two of them was more like brother and sister.

He pulled up a chair while the group ate and talked about cooking and the town. It was funny to watch such a big man get excited about chicken-fried steak and Aspen Cove, but Dalton had had a tough childhood. If it weren't for Aspen Cove's mantra, "We take care of our own," Dalton and his mom wouldn't have made it. It was Doc who thought the diner would be a good idea. He and his wife financed the place until Maisey could pay off the note. Growing up, Dalton had always seemed more like a brother to Bowie, too. Hell, if his father moved forward with his feelings for Maisey, Dalton would be his stepbrother.

When a group of tourists walked in, Dalton said his goodbyes.

Tate gobbled up his plate of comfort food while Sophia picked at hers. "Do you eat here often?" she asked Katie.

"Often enough."

"That's probably why you've gained weight."

The back of Bowie's neck heated with irritation. Katie was perfect.

"I'm not overweight, Mama. Doc Parker checked me out a few weeks ago and said I was as healthy as a horse."

"You're trusting the word of a country doctor? You left the world's finest cardiologist to see a man who probably tends to people, pigs, and cows."

"And birds," Katie quipped.

Rumor had it, he mended a bird's wing at Sage's. The way they tell it, that was the start of their relationship. Bowie only wished he'd seen Sage with that bird nesting in her hair.

"Seriously," her mother said. "Staying here will be the death of you."

Tate laid his hand over his wife's. "Now, honey, you can see she's healthy and happy."

Katie took a minute, then addressed her mother. "Daddy can

have the jet ready to leave in an hour if you don't stop. Aspen Cove isn't the death of me. It's the life of me."

When Tate pulled a large bill from his wallet to pay for dinner, Bowie stopped him.

"This is my treat, sir." He paid Meg and rose from the table. "I'll walk you and your parents across the street." It broke his heart to leave her alone with them. Her dad seemed fine, but her mother was something else.

Tate looked at his watch. "It's an hour later for us. Why don't you kids stay and enjoy each other?" He smiled at Katie. "I'll take your mother home and put her to bed. Maybe tomorrow she'll be rested and nicer."

Sophia gasped. "I'm nice. I'm just concerned about my daughter."

Tate laughed. "Look around you, Sophia. She can't get any safer here. Hell, her boyfriend is a damn Ranger. I think that earns him our trust." He helped his wife to her feet. "Is the door locked?"

Katie nodded but handed them her keys. "See you later, Daddy." She got up and kissed him on the cheek. "Thank you." She turned to her mother and did the same. "Love you, Mama."

As soon as they walked out the door, Katie pressed her face into his chest and breathed him in. "I'm so sorry. I told you she was impossible."

"Duchess, she's just being a mom." Bowie's mom had never been like that, but then again, he grew up in Aspen Cove.

They walked around town for the next hour until they got to an empty lot at the other end of Main Street.

"This used to be the park." He could still see the outline of where the baseball diamond had once been.

"What happened to it?"

He walked her to a grassy area and sat down, pulling her into his lap. His hands rested on her hips—his chin on her shoulder. He couldn't remember a time he'd felt more content. He would have loved to take her to his place and make love, but there was a little furry hellion waiting to make his debut at her birthday party tomorrow.

"When the paper mill went out of business, jobs dried up, and so did services. The town couldn't afford it all, so the Parks and Recreation Department folded." He'd been mostly grown by then, but he had fond memories of long days in this park.

She leaned against him and looked across the moonlit park. "What do the kids do now?"

"I imagine they stay inside and watch television or play video games."

"That's awful. They need a place to run and grow and play."

"I'd like to play." Bowie wrapped his arms around her middle and guided them both to the ground. "Maybe the kids make out in the tall grass like us."

He moved her to his side, so she faced him. She was so beautiful under the light of the moon. When he kissed her, she made that little moan that caused his blood to run like lava through his veins. No woman had ever made him so hot with a kiss.

CHAPTER TWENTY-SEVEN

"Happy birthday, sweetheart." Katie's father handed her a small white box.

Since Sage had taken her mom into the bed and breakfast for a tour, they had a minute to themselves. At the end of the dock of Bowie's childhood home, she opened her gift. On a bed of velvet sat a broken gold heart stitched together with the word "love."

"It's perfect."

She removed the necklace and turned around so her father could put it on her. It hung past the jagged scar that marred her chest—a scar she proudly wore now that she'd given her heart to Bowie.

"Where's the birthday girl?" Doc hollered from the end of the dock. He held a box in the air. "I brought gifts."

She looked at her dad.

"Go get your gift. It's your birthday." Katie raced to the end where Doc stood waiting.

"Don't open this in front of your father."

"Why?" She peeled back the corner and knew immediately. "Really, Doc? Condoms?"

"What do you get a girl who has everything?"

She threaded her arm through his and walked him to Sage's deck, where Cannon was barbecuing burgers and brats.

"Hey, birthday girl. Where's my brother?"

Katie looked around her. "He disappeared with your father a few minutes ago." She looked at the jumbo box of condoms. "Can you hide these for me?"

Cannon looked to where she had opened the end. "Ahhh. I'll put these away for later." He handed the barbecue tongs to Doc. "You're the new grill master."

Katie walked down the steps and looked at the water. Its surface rippled with the slight breeze. The aspens and pines shot up around the shore, enclosing the lake in a green hug. She'd been all over the world, but no place was as peaceful and homey as Aspen Cove.

"There you are." Bowie walked toward her with a gift in his hand. "You have to open this now. I'm not sure who's more excited, me or the gift."

She laughed because Bowie had once told her he wasn't good at riddles, and yet he managed to tell a few himself. Behind him walked Sage and Cannon, Ben, and her parents. Doc raised a beer and the tongs from his position on the deck. Maisey and Dalton pulled up the rear. In Dalton's hands was a cake on fire. It was amazing how much heat twenty-nine candles could create, but she felt it from a distance.

When the group came closer, they sang to her. She took a big breath and blew out the candles. It took her two tries, but she did it. Some would say she didn't earn her wish, but looking at the people surrounding her, she'd already been granted it.

"Who made the cake?" It was perfect. She knew there wouldn't be an inch of frosting on one end to cover a mistake.

"Dalton made the cake," Bowie said. He stumbled sideways and almost dropped the box. "You need to open this now." The box bobbled in his hands again. "I'll hold it. You take off the lid slowly."

Katie gripped the lid. "Bowie Bishop, if something jumps out at me, you're in so much trouble."

"We'll see." He gave her a smile that could stop a weaker heart.

Afraid he was pranking her in some way, she leaned to the side before she pulled off the lid. "Oh my God." She lifted the brown bundle of wiggly fur into her arms. "You got me a puppy!"

Bowie threw the box to the ground and wrapped his arms around her and the puppy. "I gave you a child." He reached between them and lifted the dog tag that had "Bishop" etched into a metal bone.

"I love you." She tilted her chin up for a kiss.

Bowie met her in the middle and gave her a kiss she'd remember for a long time. She ignored the crowd around them and got lost in his love.

When Doc yelled, "The weiners are ready," everyone laughed.

A leash appeared from Bowie's back pocket, and he snapped it on Bishop's collar. "Dad's been teaching him to walk on the leash. He's a smart dog."

Katie smiled at him. "Of course he's smart. He's our son." She lowered Bishop to the ground and walked him to the deck where Sage had tables set up with salads and chips and buns. Everyone piled food onto their plates and claimed chairs.

Katie sat close to Bowie. Bishop lay at her feet. She was giddy with happiness, but she was tired. All the excitement of the day had worn her out. She signaled to Sage, who walked right over.

"You need something, birthday girl?"

Katie felt the world tilt to the right. "I need to lie down for a minute. Can I use your room?" Sage had a full house this week due to the Fourth of July holiday.

A look of concern creased her brow. "Let's get you there."

Katie handed the leash to Bowie. "Can you take care of our child? I'm going to go inside for a few minutes."

"You okay?"

She nodded and pushed herself off the chair, but the world tilted again. "Bowie?" A flush covered her skin, and her knees buckled as she reached for him for stability.

In seconds, she was in his arms, and Sage was leading them into her and Cannon's bedroom. "I don't feel well."

Bowie put her on the bed and placed his hand on her forehead. He turned to Sage. "Get Doc, she's got a fever."

In seconds, the room was filled with people. It reminded Katie of the night before her surgery, when everyone came in to see her.

"Move away, everyone." Doc shuffled in and set his black bag on the nightstand.

"You do house calls?" Katie asked with a weak voice.

"Not if I can help it." He pulled the stethoscope from his bag. "You want an audience?"

Katie looked around the room. Her mother's hand covered her mouth. Her father seemed to hold Sophia up.

"I'm fine, just tired. Go enjoy the barbecue. I'll be out in a few minutes."

Katie's dad all but dragged his wife out of the room. The rest followed, except for Bowie.

"I'm staying." It was a statement of fact. He wrapped his big hand around her small hand and sat on the edge of the bed.

Doc lifted Katie's shirt and pressed the cold stethoscope to her chest. His head bobbed quickly while his eyes watched the second hand on his watch.

"Ticker is fine." He slung the instrument around his neck. "How have you been feeling?"

Katie scooted back and sat against the headboard—one similar to the one Cannon had made for Bowie and Brandy.

"I've been tired, but other than that, I've been great."

Bowie shook his head. "She threw up this morning."

Doc frowned. "Was it just this morning, or have you been sick before today?"

Bowie glared in her direction.

"I've been sick a few times."

"Mornings?"

"What? No?" She looked at Bowie, whose tawny skin turned ghostly white. "Seriously?"

Doc opened his bag and tossed the stethoscope inside. "Condoms have a failure rate of two to fifteen percent. Two if used properly."

Katie sat up. Her hands went to her stomach. Was it possible she was pregnant? "You think I'm pregnant?"

"Whoa, whoa," Bowie said. He rose from the bed and ran his hands through his hair. "She had her cycle."

"Normal?" Doc asked.

Katie shrugged. "I'm not sure what's normal. With my immunosuppressant drugs, nothing is ever normal."

"You're pregnant. I got you pregnant." The words were like a painful howl. "Shit. I've killed you."

"What? No, you did no such thing. You didn't have sex by yourself."

"Maybe he should have, and you wouldn't be in this predicament."

"Wait a minute," she yelled. "You don't know I'm pregnant."

The door opened wide, and Katie's mom stood there with a look of horror on her face. "What do you mean she's pregnant?" The last word came out in a cry.

"I'm not pregnant." Katie kicked her feet off the bed and tried to stand, but the change in position caused her to falter.

Bowie rushed to her side and scooped Katie into his arms. "She is pregnant. I know it."

"Only one way to find out." Doc closed his bag and walked to

214

the door. "I'll meet you at the clinic."

When Doc disappeared down the hallway, Sophia surged toward Bowie. "If you really loved my daughter, you would have looked after her. Pregnancy is as good as a gun to her head."

Katie struggled from Bowie's arms and stood beside him. "Mother. I won't put up with you ruining everything for me. You need to leave now." Katie pointed a finger at the door.

"Me, ruin everything?" Sophia stood defiantly in front of Bowie. "He's ruining everything." Sophia pulled her hand back. When she swung it forward, she connected with Bowie's cheek with enough force to snap his head back. "If she's pregnant, I'll kill you myself."

"Sophia!" Tate stood in the doorway. "Come with me now."

Katie's mom walked toward her husband.

"Mama. You listen and listen well. I'd trade every minute of my life for one more with him."

The door closed behind them, and Bowie fell to his knees in front of Katie. "I'm so sorry."

Katie had only seen a man cry once. It was the day they wheeled her into the operating room. Her father had held her hand until the last minute. When she looked at him, his eyes couldn't hold the tears anymore. She looked down at Bowie, and his eyes looked the same.

"I can't live without you."

Katie dropped to her knees in front of him. "You don't have to live without me. Now go get our son and let's find out if you're going to be a daddy."

"Katie, you can't have this baby. Even you told me it wasn't recommended. It isn't safe. It isn't right."

"Bowie Bishop, have we done anything the right way?"

She leaned into his chest and breathed in his comforting scent. She'd never been so afraid, but it wasn't for her life she feared. It was for the life of the unborn child that might live in her womb.

CHAPTER TWENTY-EIGHT

Walking into Doc's was like walking in front of a firing squad. Bowie held Katie's hand in his. Although she was the picture of calm on the outside, the way her body shook gave her away.

"We'll take care of this so we can take care of you."

She shot him a look as deadly as an on-target bullet. "Haven't you learned anything?" She pulled her hand from his. "I can take care of myself."

She marched through the doorway that led to the examination room. He was hot on her heels, followed closely behind by Tate and Sophia. The latter had been tossing verbal grenades his way since she'd barged into Sage's room. No doubt Sophia had been standing there the whole time with an ear to the door.

"I know you can, but is it a bad thing that I want to care for you?"

"Care for me? No. Control me? Yes." She hopped onto the table. "If you want to help, tell Doc we're here."

Bowie nodded and walked out, but he heard Katie lay into her mom. With Doc's shop empty, he didn't miss a word she said.

"You know why I left, Mama?"

"Yes. You wanted independence."

"That means making decisions for myself. If you want to be a part of my life, you need to step back and let me live it."

Their voices faded as Bowie ran upstairs to Doc's apartment. He had a setup similar to Katie's, although hers was by far nicer.

"You okay, son?"

Bowie plastered his body against the wall so Doc could slide past him in the narrow stairwell. "No, not really. I finally opened my heart and found love, and I've planted a death sentence inside her."

"Don't put the cart in front of the horse. Let's go see what's up. If she's pregnant, we'll concoct the best plan."

"She needs to get rid of that baby."

Doc expelled a heavy breath. "Have you learned nothing about women—that woman in particular? She doesn't want to be controlled; she wants to be supported. The decision is not yours. It's hers. If she's pregnant and wants to have that baby, she will. I've never met a more determined woman in my life. She rivals Phyllis for stubbornness." Doc sucked in a long breath and sighed out a loud exhale. "You love her?"

Bowie followed Doc down the stairs. "More than anything."

"Then you support her, no matter what."

Bowie swallowed the lump caught in his throat. "I will."

Doc swiped a few pregnancy tests from the shelf and walked into the room where Katie was still talking to her mom.

"You had your life, Mama. Let me have mine, no matter how long it is." She looked past her parents to Bowie. "I'm happy. I'm in love."

Bowie walked up to her and wrapped an arm around her shoulder. "You okay?"

A weak smile lifted the corners of her lips. "Yes, but can you help me clarify something?"

"Anything for you, Duchess."

She put her hand to her heart. "Was Brandy healthy?"

"Yes. She had no medical issues I knew about."

Katie reached her free hand to her mother's. "She was healthy, Mom. She woke up that day healthy and happy and in love."

Her eyes turned toward Bowie. He could see the love in her brilliant blue eyes, but he also saw sadness. He wasn't sure if it was because they were potentially facing a crisis or because she hated to bring up his wound. Knowing Katie, it was because she didn't want to hurt him.

"What's your point?" Sophia asked.

"My point is, no one is guaranteed anything. Brandy woke up to a normal day. She went about her business and climbed in a car to run an errand, and in the blink of an eye, her life was gone."

Bowie lifted his hand to the scar on his face. It was a visual reminder of how fast things could change.

"I have a donor heart. My life is risky, but no more at risk than any other life. So stop it." She looked around the room at her parents and him. "Shall I take this test and see where the next chapter leads?"

"I'm going to take blood and send it off to the lab, but let's see if we can't get a preliminary result with these." Doc handed her two different pregnancy tests and pointed to the bathroom.

Bowie dragged in several chairs from the hallway and lined them up against the wall for them to sit on. He took a seat and turned to Sophia.

"I really do love your daughter, and no matter what the outcome is, I will support her and take care of her."

Bowie could see the moment defeat and resignation claimed Katie's mom. Her features softened, and the visual daggers she'd been slicing through him dulled.

"I know you do. And she loves you. Not having a child of your own, you can't understand how I feel. I've spent twenty-nine years protecting her."

Tate cleared his throat. "Maybe it's time you spent the next phase of her life enjoying her. She's right, you know. Life isn't a guarantee. Live in the moment."

Katie emerged from the bathroom carrying two sticks. One in each hand. "What if we get mixed results?" She handed them to Doc, who set them on the counter and prepped to take her blood.

"I've got a third one out there we can use as a tiebreaker." He tied a rubber strap to her arm and had her hold on to a rubber ball. After a few taps at the crook, the needle went in the vial and filled up. Doc put on a Snoopy Band-Aid and popped a Life Saver into her mouth before she could say a word.

They waited. Katie and Bowie stared at the tests on the counter while Doc, Tate, and Sophia had their eyes on the clock. When the recommended time had passed, Doc read the results.

"It's unanimous." He raised the two tests, facing the group. One had two bright pink stripes, and the other clearly said pregnant 3+. "You can return your birthday gift for diapers since you won't be needing what I gave you for a while."

Bowie didn't know how to feel. A part of him wanted to crawl into a ball and die right there. Another part of him wanted to leap into the air with joy. His child was growing inside Katie, but could he risk ending one life in the hope of bringing another into the world? Then he remembered what she'd told them minutes before. Nothing in life was guaranteed.

"Oh my God ... I'm pregnant?" Gone was the weak smile, and in its place was the sun that burst forth from within her. "I never thought to put that on my bucket list." She reached for her bag and pulled out the journal where she recorded her dreams.

Bowie watched as she penned "have a baby" on a blank line.

Sophia stood and came over to her daughter. "Katie, are you—"

"Mama, I know what you're going to say. Don't."

Sophia gave her a grunt of frustration. "You're wrong. I was going to ask if you could clear a week next month so we can baby shop."

"Really?" Tears ran down Katie's cheeks.

"I'll send the jet," Tate said. He looked at Bowie. "Son, what are your intentions toward my daughter?"

"I intend to love her and care for her for the rest of my life."

"That sounds great, but will you marry her? We're old-fashioned that way."

"Daddy," Katie squeaked. "Bowie and I don't do anything the traditional way."

She was right. They'd kissed before they'd held hands. They'd slept together before they'd dated. They'd created a baby before they'd considered marriage. It was unconventional, but it worked for them.

"I'll marry her today if she'll have me."

"No way," Katie said with a hint of humor. Everyone looked at her in surprise. "If you think I'm going to make it easy on you by having my birthday and anniversary the same day, you're nuts. I'm not cheating myself out of an extra present or an extra day to celebrate."

Bowie cupped her face with his hands. "I love you. Every day is a day to celebrate, but I will marry you." He lowered one hand to her stomach. "I will be the best father and husband I can be."

Her father turned to Doc Parker. "What do I owe you, Doc?" Tate pulled out his wallet and tried to hand him a big bill.

Doc waved him away. "Nothing. Money isn't the most valuable currency here in Aspen Cove. We take care of our own."

"Surely, I can pay you somehow?"

Doc smiled. "Did I hear you have a jet?"

Tate laughed. "At your disposal."

Katie's parents stayed long enough to visit her new cardiologist, Dr. Holland, in Copper Creek. After he gave her a full physical, he told everyone that although heart transplant recipients were at a high-risk for pregnancy, there was no reason to believe Katie wouldn't deliver a healthy child.

While he set up the ultrasound, he outlined the risks from infection to early delivery. He explained Katie's fever and the need to adjust her anti-rejection medications. When he gelled her stomach and placed the wand over her belly, the room fell silent except for the fast thumping beat that floated through the air.

All eyes went to the monitor where a clearly defined baby snuggled inside Katie's womb, its heartbeat a fast flicker on the screen.

"Your baby looks perfect," Doctor Holland said. "He or she is about eleven weeks along, weighs about an ounce, and is the length of your little finger."

Sophia burst into tears, followed by a laugh. "I told you you'd gained weight."

Everyone smiled at her joke.

"Can you tell what the sex is, Doctor Holland?" Tate asked.

"With this machine, it's too soon to say, but we should be able to see at your next appointment. That is, if you want to know."

Katie looked at Bowie. "You want to know?"

"Of course he wants to know," Sophia piped in. "It makes shopping easier."

"Let's decide then," Bowie said.

The doctor printed several copies of the baby photo and passed them out to everyone. Bowie folded his up and placed it in his wallet. Whereas he'd once kept a picture of Brandy to remember his past, this was a glimpse into his future.

"Let's go home," Katie said. "I miss our fur baby."

Turned out Otis was a fine father figure to Bishop. He'd taken to the puppy like they were raised together. Mike, on the other hand, wasn't a fan of the little furball, but that could be because Bishop was teething and decided Cannon's one-eyed cat was a good chew toy.

They dropped off Katie's parents at the airport, with a promise to visit Dallas after the results of the next ultrasound.

On the way home, Bowie reached for Katie's hand. "This is all my fault."

"Are we back to that?"

Bowie thought back to his friend Trig's conversation about Sledge and his sand baby. "Yes, but not how you think. You got pregnant the first time I made love to you. I think I knew in my heart I loved you then, but I wasn't ready to admit."

"My heart has always loved you." There was a lot of truth to that statement. "What makes you think it happened on that night?"

"I used a condom that had been in my wallet for a year. It had been through the heat of the desert and a dozen sandstorms. When you warned me about heat breaking down latex, you were already pregnant."

She laid her hand over her belly. "A desert baby, huh?"

"Our desert baby," he replied.

CHAPTER TWENTY-NINE
TWENTY-SIX WEEKS LATER...

The frozen ground was unforgiving as the backhoe dug into the dirt.

"Are you sure this is the best time of year to be doing this?" Bowie asked as he wrapped his arms around her stomach. Katie felt the ripple of her child's swift kick move all the way to her back.

They stood with Bishop in the middle of the old park and watched the construction crew break ground. Katie wanted to pass her good fortune forward. Rather than use her trust fund to build a house or buy things she didn't need, she put a chunk of the money to community improvements like Hope Park.

She turned to her husband and looked into his eyes—eyes the color of a spring sky. "It has to be now. I want the children of Aspen Cove to have a place to play this summer." She walked to his right and pointed. "That's where the new baseball diamond is going." She turned and pointed behind them. "They're putting a jungle gym and swing sets over there." She pivoted to the left. "Right there will be a pavilion where the town can hold events like picnics or concerts."

"How much money is in this trust of yours?"

Because the money never mattered to her, she never brought it up until now. She had remembered the scripture recited at Bea's funeral that said something about money being used to do good. That people should give generously to those in need, always being ready to share what they have. Money in a trust didn't help anyone, but this park would.

"We're rich."

"How rich?" he asked her.

"We won't make the world's top ten, but we're okay."

"You want to spend your money on a park?"

She leaned in to him and breathed in his scent. "I want to invest in people. I want to pay the gifts given to me forward."

"You don't want a better house? A nicer car?" He looked to her wedding ring. "A bigger diamond?"

Though the diamond was small, the gesture was huge. She knew Bowie had spent every dime he had on this ring, and she'd wear it to her grave.

"I'm the richest woman in the world, and it has nothing to do with money."

She rubbed at the ache in her lower back. She was certain it was the cold January day that caused the persistent discomfort.

"Let's go home, and I'll make you your favorite tea."

"Home sounds good."

It was no longer the apartment above the bakery. Ben had taken that over and given them the lake house as a wedding gift. Most of Katie's favorite moments happened there. It was the place they created the new life inside her.

She had so many favorites with Bowie, but the day they stood on the end of the dock and said, "I do," topped her list. It was the same place where she threw an empty hook into the water and somehow caught the man of her dreams. Doc put on another hat that day and officiated over their vows.

Since then, she'd marked off hundreds of items from her

bucket list, from roller skating to making love under the stars. In her twenty-ninth year, she'd lived a lifetime.

They walked together to the truck, and Bowie lifted her into the seat. Bishop curled up on the floorboard by her feet. He barely fit. The poor dog was convinced he was still a puppy.

When Bowie climbed in, he turned up the heat. "Let's get you defrosted." He leaned over to help with her seat belt and stopped. "Duchess?" His eyes went to the space between her legs. "You're melting."

Katie looked down just as a gush of warm water released. Bishop leaped from the floor onto the seat.

"Uh-oh."

Bowie grinned. "It's time."

Doctor Holland expected the baby to come around week thirty-seven, but they were turning the corner on week thirty-eight. All was right in the world except the incredible pain that gripped her middle.

Bowie immediately went into military mode. He was trained for high-stress situations, which was a good thing because Katie wasn't prepared at all. In that second, she felt completely unprepared to be a mother.

"Oh my God, what if I suck as a parent?"

She gripped the door handle and panted through the next contraction.

"You'll be an amazing mother. You already have the cookie-making down pat." Bowie dialed Sage and Cannon and told them to meet him outside for the handoff. Cannon would get Katie's suitcase, and Sage would take the dog.

Next he called Sophia and Tate and told them to get the jet ready. Their grandchild was coming. Much to Sophia's disappointment, they didn't know the sex. The baby was a gift, and it didn't matter if it was a boy or a girl. It's not like they could send it back.

The final call, which should have been the first call, was to Dr.

Holland, who promised everything would be ready when they arrived.

When they got to Copper Creek General Hospital, Dr. Holland was waiting with a wheelchair.

"How are you doing there, Mom?" he asked Katie. Then he turned to Bowie. "What about you, Dad? Ready to meet your baby?"

Bowie relayed pertinent information while Katie puffed through another contraction. Four hours that seemed like a lifetime later, her parents rushed into the delivery room. They stood by her head while Bowie coached her through the last phases of labor. Because she was a high-risk pregnancy, at least a half dozen specialists were standing nearby. Katie was grateful for their presence but confident she wouldn't need them. She had Bowie, she had her parents, and she had the strongest, most loving heart in the world.

When Dr. Holland told her to push, she felt an extra surge of strength. Ten minutes later, Sahara Brandelyn Bishop was born. When she grew old enough to understand, Bowie and Katie would tell her about all the people who made it possible for her to exist. How dreams can come true and how the only currency worth collecting is love.

She looked down at her daughter, who had eyes like her father and a scream loud enough to wake the dead, and she smiled. In her mind, she checked off another item from her bucket list.

As she took a deep breath, she felt warmth flood her chest. Call her crazy, but she knew Brandy was with them. Looking down on them with love. She was certain her gift would beat for years to come.

Katie reflected on the last few months. She was certain of so many things when she arrived in Aspen Cove, but she'd been taught many lessons along her journey.

Hope didn't come in a pink envelope. It was visible in the eyes of the man who loved her and in the heartbeat of the child in her arms.

Prince Charming may ride a Harley, but he also drove a truck and drove her crazy.

Secrets were never best left unspoken. The truth set her free.

There was a final thing she'd learned, maybe the most important since her arrival. Being independent didn't mean being alone. It meant surrounding herself with people who cared, people who valued her opinion, and who celebrated her successes along with her failures.

Bowie looked down at his wife and child. She saw the tears in his eyes—tears of joy.

"Your bucket list is empty," he said. "What's next?"

While Tate and Sophia counted Sahara's fingers and toes, Katie giggled. "How about a boy?"

ACKNOWLEDGMENTS

Where do I start? There are so many people that must be recognized. I always say it starts with an idea but that's not actually true. It starts with the love and support of a village. Family and friends and fans are what fuel the words. Without them it's like owning a car and having no gas.

Special thanks to my writing bestie Mel, who never fails to be a cheerleader no matter what.

Hugs and that mushy stuff to everyone in Kelly Collins's Corner and the Kel's Smut Junkies. They all play well in the sandbox and help me make the tough choices like what couple to put on the cover.

Speaking of covers. These covers were not what I envisioned when I wrote the books. When *One Hundred Reasons* won in Kindle Scout, it was suggested strongly that I put a couple in scene in Aspen Cove and so a new vision had to be created in record time. Thank you Victoria Cooper Art for coming to my rescue.

Thanks to the ladies who proofread this book. Judy and Sabrina, I'm grateful for the hours you devote to making sure my work is the best it can be.

Last but never least, I thank you the reader for being loyal fans. Because you continue to ask for more, I continue to write. I hope you enjoy your time in Aspen Cove. There's so much more to come.

KELLY COLLINS

ONE HUNDRED
Wishes

AN ASPEN COVE ROMANCE

Copyright © 2018 by Kelley Maestas

All rights reserved.

No part of this book may be reproduced in any form or by any electronic or mechanical means, including information storage and retrieval systems, without written permission from the author, except for the use of brief quotations in a book review.

Cover photograph by Darren Birks Photography

Cover design by Victoria Cooper Art

To my family. I hope your wishes come true.

CHAPTER ONE

Samantha White looked into the mirror but no longer recognized herself. She'd come a long way from the girl who lived in the back seat of her mother's car. With blue hair and a five-thousand-dollar leather jacket, she hardly knew the woman staring back at her.

"Indigo, you're on in five," Brenda, the assistant to her assistant called from the door.

She looked into the mirror. "You can do this," she said to the scared girl who lived inside her. The young woman she'd buried under hair dye and designer clothes. "You *have* to do this." She pulled her ID card and a wad of cash from her purse and shoved it inside her back pocket. "I *will* do this," she said to herself as she walked toward the stage.

At the edge of the curtain stood her agent, Oliver Shepherd, and her manager, Dave Belton. One handled her career, the other handled her life. She was tired of being handled—*man*handled.

"You ready?" Dave gripped her arms too tightly. She hated it when he was pumped up on something. She wouldn't call him abusive in her opinion. She'd seen what abuse looked like firsthand when her drunken father beat her mother nearly to death. No,

Dave was a control freak and a cocaine freak—not a good mix when the star of your show wasn't keen on continuing to be an indentured servant. That's why Oliver Shepherd was here tonight in Denver. He was present to secure their futures.

"Don't forget the playlist. None of that slow, lover's-lament shit you want to sing lately. No one wants to hear sad stuff. These are hard times, and people look to you to lift them up." He turned her around and gave her a push toward the stage.

"Knock 'em dead, Indigo," Oliver said. "We'll meet up at the hotel to sign the new deal."

She smiled on the outside and put on her headset. Her hand reached to her back pocket to confirm the presence of phase one of her escape plan, a plan that took her years to put into place. There was no walking away from the power of the Shepherd Agency or the grip of Dave Belton.

It wasn't an easy decision to run away from her life when so many people depended on her, but Samantha knew she'd never survive another year like the past one. Thirty-six countries and two hundred and ten concerts in fifty-two weeks. Add two new albums and three music awards, and she was done. While her alter ego Indigo was a powerhouse, Samantha White was burned out.

The sold-out venue hummed with the deafening chant of "In-di-go, In-di-go, In-di-go."

Her heart raced. The rush of blood to her head dizzied her. The minute she walked on stage, she earned five hundred and sixty thousand dollars, but it wasn't enough. There wasn't an amount large enough to keep her in the spotlight. There were at least three things Samantha wanted more than money.

She wanted a life.

She wanted to love.

She wanted the freedom that came from being invisible.

She'd get none of those things living under the microscope of fame or the strong arm of her manager.

She was America's sweetheart. At twenty-nine, she still looked sixteen, which was a curse because the public's perception was everything when you were famous. She wanted to act her age, but having a glass of wine or a date went against her squeaky-clean brand.

Her real life wasn't too far off from the lie they told the public. She drank, but she did it alone in her hotel room or on her bus. She dated, but only in secret, and she was limited to band members and stage hands. When she complained, Dave offered her his magic elixir—a concoction of drugs and alcohol he guaranteed would cheer her up. She knew then it was time to go. She didn't want to be another Amy Winehouse or Janis Joplin.

When the drummer started the distinctive beat of her last platinum single, "Your Way" she walked out onto the stage for what she hoped would be her last contractual live performance.

For an hour and forty-six minutes, she gave the audience everything she had. For her final song, she walked to the band and told them what she wanted to sing. They gave her that look, the one that said Dave would be furious, but if she was going to walk away, it would be on her terms.

Gary, her lead guitarist, counted off the beats to start the song "Empty Box". She glanced over her shoulder to stage right, to the red-faced Dave flailing his hands in the air. Behind him, Oliver Shepherd frowned. It wasn't what they wanted, but it was what she wanted. After ten years of contract slavery, wasn't it time she got her way?

She belted out the song about a life not lived, and on the chorus she walked down the steps and disappeared into the crowd.

The fans swarmed around her as she pushed her way toward the back of the arena.

"Ohmigod, Ohmigod, Ohmigod!" a blue-haired teenage girl, dressed in jeans and a gray hoodie screamed. "It's you! It's really you!"

Samantha smiled. "It's *almost* me." She pointed to the girl's hoodie and then back to her studded leather jacket. "Want to trade?" Samantha heard the security team closing in, telling people to, "Move aside." She had minutes to make her escape.

"You want to trade with me? Ohmigod, Ohmigod, Ohmigod! Yes!" The teen stripped her jacket off like it was on fire and traded it for Indigo's custom-designed look. While the girl stood putting her new fashion-forward coat on, Indigo pulled the hoodie over her blue hair and blended in with the crowd.

She felt bad for the girl who would soon be accosted by her security team in seconds and whisked away to the back room. Eventually, they'd figure out she wasn't Indigo, but a super fan who had the perfect shade of blue hair and the same physique. She couldn't feel too badly because whoever the girl was, she'd get her fifteen minutes of fame and a rockin' hot custom leather jacket.

At the front of the arena with Indigo left behind, Samantha White flagged down a cab and gave him the address to the second phase of her plan. He drove her to the airport, where a used front-wheel drive was parked in space number nine-three-seven.

She tipped the cabbie and watched him drive away. Inside the front right wheel well, she felt for the keys her assistant Deanna promised would be there. They fell off the tire and into her palm. She opened the door, sank into the driver's seat and sent a silent thanks to her assistant and only real friend. Deanna had watched Samantha wither under the constant stress and abuse. She'll never forget the day they sat down and planned Samantha's escape. She'd be forever grateful for her loyalty and help.

It took over two years because she needed to fulfill her public engagements or face multiple lawsuits. She couldn't believe she'd made it out alive and mostly well.

Samantha was young and naïve when Oliver Shepherd discovered her singing in a honky-tonk bar in Nashville. He saw what she didn't. She had star power, and he took advantage of her by offering her a ten-year deal. She thought he was being generous, but in reality, he was hedging a sure bet and locking down his talent.

While Samantha thought how freeing a steady paycheck could be for her and her mom, the management team added up the millions she would make them.

She bought her mom a house and gave her the life she'd always wanted. Samantha continued to dream about her life ahead. While her mother enjoyed the fruits of her daughter's labor, Samantha was a workhorse who didn't get a second to breathe.

She couldn't complain about her life too much because she'd been the one to sign her name on the dotted line. She was slow to investigate and quick to act.

One bright note was her management team was fair with compensation, but they were relentless when it came to work ethic. They would get their pound of flesh from her one way or another. At five-foot-five and down to a hundred and four pounds, she had no more flesh to offer.

She glanced around the car. The back seat was filled with suitcases of clothes. The front seat held a bag with more cash than the car was worth. It was risky to leave it all out here in a parking lot, but what price could she put on survival? She opened the cooler on the floor and found her favorite drink, a sugar-free, calorie-free lemonade that tasted almost as good as the real thing. For the next five minutes, Samantha White sat in silence and enjoyed freedom and anonymity. In the glove compartment was a knit cap, along with a pair of sunglasses she wouldn't need until tomorrow.

She pulled off the hoodie and stuffed her sapphire locks into the hat. She laughed at how they'd come up with her name and brand. No wonder she was blue.

"You can't be Samantha White. It's a boring name," Oliver said. "Let me see your eyes."

She lifted her face into the light. Her mom always said her

eyes were blue, while drunken Daddy said they were black as tar, like her soul. Then again, he didn't see straight after having a fifth of hard liquor for breakfast.

"Indigo," Dave said. "Her eyes are a black-blue." By that time, Dave was hired to be her manager—really a babysitter because she had recently turned nineteen. Not old enough to know better, but old enough to make legal decisions. It made her dangerous in their eyes.

Once they'd named her "Indigo," her future was set. She'd adopted a persona with blue hair, edgy clothes, and a squeaky-clean image. It was the dichotomy of her appearance versus her persona that drew attention. She was every parent's nightmare and dream in the same girl. Throw in a voice with a range to rival Whitney Houston, and she was a hit. All she had to do was show up. That was where Dave Belton came in.

Dave's superpower was his ability to instill fear. He scared the hell out of her. After the first time she mouthed off at him and found herself locked inside her hotel room, she rarely gave him trouble. He reminded her of her father. If he could hold her hostage, he was capable of anything.

Mixing attitude with alcohol made the impossible possible. She'd learned that lesson the hard way. She thought of the time her father put her mother into the hospital. Yvette White was unconscious for three days. After she was released, she packed her and Samantha's belongings and moved from place to place, never staying anyplace long enough for Harlan White to find them. Funny how life had come full circle; now she had packed up her stuff and was hiding again.

"Welcome to your life, Samantha." It was odd to hear her real name, even from her own voice. Everyone called her Indigo, even her mother. She turned on the dome light and pulled down the visor to inspect herself in the mirror. "You're almost you." She plucked the false lashes from her eyes and flicked them out the window. That was her past. This was her beginning.

"Aspen Cove, here I come."

She took an hour to get used to driving. Although she maintained a driver's license, she rarely got behind the wheel. The last time she went out for a drive, she was swarmed by paparazzi and had to call her security team to come and get her. She loved the fans, but there was something to be said for freedom.

Before she entered the mountain pass, she pulled into a fast-food drive-thru. It was her first test at being invisible. She checked herself in the mirror and tucked the remaining strands of blue away.

"Welcome, what can I get you?" said the young female voice through the speaker.

"One second, please." Samantha couldn't remember a time when she'd sat in a drive-thru looking over the menu. Her food was portioned, calorie-counted, and delivered. She'd spent the first year starving and the next nine pretending food was poison. It made it easier to not eat. Now a menu of burgers and fries were staring at her. She was the proverbial kid in a candy shop. "I'm ready."

"Me too," the girl called back.

"I'll have a cheeseburger and fries and a chocolate shake. Oh, and can I have a box of those animal cookies, and maybe some apple slices?" She didn't know if she'd get to the apple slices, but she ordered them because it at least made the meal seem balanced.

The girl gave her a total and told her to drive around.

Samantha held her breath when the window opened and the teenager looked at her. For a second she thought she'd been recognized, then the girl said, "I have the same cap."

"Cool." Samantha handed over a twenty and took her food. She was on a roll. She pulled into the parking spot reserved for to-go orders and texted Deanna.

Operation Indi-go-go is a success. She shot a picture of her food and laughed.

Dave would have an aneurysm if he saw what you are eating, she wrote back. **I'm glad you're safe. Everything is taken care of. The key is under the mat. The furniture is in place. The place is basic, but the view is nice. You'll need lots of stuff once you get settled. I found a cool headboard at a consignment shop in town. It was closed for the season, but when I said I had cash, some lady named Abby was happy to open for me. You'll love it.**

She pulled the phone to her chest and hugged it.

I appreciate everything you've done.

Deanna took a vacation and traveled to Aspen Cove to accept a delivery of basic furniture and a bed before she started her real vacation hundreds of miles away in Alaska.

You might not thank me when you don't have coffee in the morning, but there's a diner in town and the food is decent. Now turn off your phone or they'll track it. Enjoy what time you get. Hugs.

Samantha powered down her phone and headed for Aspen Cove. She turned on the eighties station and sang to the old-school music she loved while she had her first burger and fries in years. She knew this wasn't a permanent vacation. She still had commitments left to fulfill. Her last real planned public event was important. Although her management team was pissed off she was doing it for free, the event was for victims of domestic abuse, and she was excited to help. She had a final album due for the record label, but at least she'd get downtime until they found her. They *would* find her. That was a certainty. Between now and then, she'd need to come up with a plan B.

Nearly three hours later, she pulled into the tiny town of

Aspen Cove. Everything was dark except the diner where a group of people seemed to be celebrating. If it weren't so late and she weren't so tired, she'd consider crashing their party. She had a lot to celebrate, too.

She pulled into the driveway of 7 Lake Circle and took in a deep breath. This was it. She danced her way to the front door. Under the mat, like Deanna said, was the key. She slid it into the lock and opened the door to a whole different world.

CHAPTER TWO

"Can I have everyone's attention?" Dalton Black stood in the center of Maisey's Diner and let out a whistle that could be heard across the lake. "We're here to celebrate a lot of things." He picked up the glass of wine in front of him. "First, I want to thank Cannon and Bowie for supplying the alcohol."

The raucous group yipped and hollered. Everyone loved free booze.

"Second, I wanted to say I love you to my mom, who made this diner possible along with the help and support of Doc Parker and the community." He shuddered to think where their lives would be if the people of Aspen Cove hadn't protected and cared for them. That was the best thing about living here. Everyone was family.

When Dalton was a teen and his mom was beaten and bruised, Doc Parker offered up the building for their future. Although her outer shell had recovered, Dalton knew even as a teen the internal scars from years of abuse would take the longest to heal.

Despite it all, Maisey Black moved forward. She'd made the

diner a success and paid back the note owed to Doc in record time. Maisey's Diner belonged to his mom, though she insisted he was a full partner.

"I want to welcome my new brothers, Cannon and Bowie, to my family. I want to give my new dad a hug." He pulled Ben Bishop to his side and gave him a squeeze. If Ben, who spent years drunk and pining for his dead wife could turn himself around and make Maisey Black fall in love with him, anything was possible.

"In a matter of moments, I went from being an only child to one of three sons." He looked at Bowie and Cannon, his new step-brothers and longtime friends. Next to Bowie stood his wife Katie cradling their newborn daughter Sahara. "I also became an uncle." He found Cannon in the crowd and gave him a knowing look. "I have one more thing to say, and then I'm done." He glanced between the two sets of newlyweds in the room, Ben and Maisey and Bowie and Katie. "Stop with this love shit. It's like a virus in this town, and I don't want to catch it." He lifted his glass and said, "Cheers!"

Dalton shook his head at his friends who were all laughing and enjoying a night of friendship and camaraderie.

Ben had carted his mom Maisey to Denver last week and married her at the county courthouse. He could have tied the knot here where Doc would have been happy to officiate, but Ben wanted it to be special, so he sprung for a weekend at the Brown Palace Hotel.

Dalton had never seen his mother so happy, but tonight was about something else altogether, and his part in the charade was to make it seem like it was Maisey and Ben's night to celebrate— again. Since they'd been celebrating every night since they returned, no one would be the wiser.

Cannon brought Sage to the center of the crowd. "I have a few things to say myself." He nodded to Dalton, which was his cue to get Sage's sister, Lydia, who'd been hiding in the kitchen for almost an hour. It was a good thing she was hungry when she arrived because he didn't know what to do with the woman besides feed her. Dalton had a soft spot for Sage, but her sister was a whole other beast. Never had he seen two people come from the same set of parents and be so different. Sage had flaming red hair, while her sister was blonde. Sage had green eyes, while her sister's were blue. Sage was no bigger than four stacked milk crates, while Lydia came to his chin, which meant she had to be five-foot-six or seven. Sage was always happy, but her sister spent most of her time crying over pie. Dalton didn't do well with teary-eyed women.

He snuck into the kitchen and said, "It's time." Lydia scooped another bite of Maisey's famous cherry pie into her mouth and followed him out.

As soon as Cannon saw Lydia, he dropped to a knee in front of Sage. She looked at him like he'd had a stroke and fell to her knees in front of him.

"You okay? Are you sick? Too much wine?" She lifted her hand to his head and felt him for fever. The nurse in her never took a break.

He laughed. "I am sick, and I'll never recover," he said with dramatic flair. "I caught the bug Dalton talked about."

She tilted her head the way her three-legged dog Otis did when he was confused. Then she looked behind Cannon to see her sister. Sage jumped to her feet and ran past him to Lydia. Poor Cannon might never get those four words he wanted to ask out.

Sage threw her arms around Lydia's neck. "You're here." She stepped back with a look of concern. "What are you doing here? Are you okay?"

Dalton thought it was funny how everything around him had changed so fast. How his two friends who were sworn bachelors had fallen hard and fast.

When Sage and Katie arrived in town, nothing stayed the same.

He looked across the darkened street to Bea's bakery and thought about the old woman responsible for this love fest. How her gifts of the bed and breakfast to Sage and the bakery to Katie brought the town together. Her act of selflessness had healed so many hurts.

Lydia wiped the tears from her eyes. "I'm fine. I'm here because..." She nodded her head toward Cannon, who was still on one knee but facing no one. "Go to your man, he has something to ask you." Lydia widened her eyes and made a face.

"Oh my God." Sage looked at all the nodding heads and raced back to stand in front of Cannon. "I'm sorry. You have my full attention."

Cannon chuckled. "I'll take whatever piece of you I can get, even if it's your short attention span." He wiped his hands on his jeans and reached into his pocket to pull out a small white box, then he cleared his throat.

Dalton wasn't sure if Cannon was trying to gain his composure or get the attention of everyone in the room. Either way, all eyes were on him.

"Sage, I wanted to do this on Valentine's Day, but I heard it was a cliché. Then I wanted to do it last week on lucky St. Patrick's Day, but Dad beat me to it by marrying Maisey. So, today is it, sweetheart." He reached for her hand and held it to his heart. "I loved you the day I met you. Well, I hated you in my head, but I loved you in my heart."

The room erupted in laughter. Dalton hadn't been present that day, but rumor said they had a doozy of a first meeting.

Sage pulled back and looked down at him. "Cannon Bishop, if this is the way you're going to propose, I'll walk out of here with what's in the box, but you'll walk out with a black eye." She fisted her hands on her hips. "You can do better. Give me the best you've got."

Doc Parker walked up and placed his hand on Cannon's

shoulder. "You're screwing this up, son." He looked at Sage. His white brows arched toward the ceiling. "The boy loves you. He wants to marry you. What do you say, young lady?"

"Thanks, Doc, I got this." Cannon turned back to Sage. "I do love you. I can't imagine a life without you. I want to marry you so I can love you forever." He opened the box to reveal a gold band imbedded with tiny diamonds. Cannon's attention drifted to Katie and then back to Sage. "A certain blonde baker told me a gold band was all you wanted, but it wasn't enough. You need a little sparkle in your life. Sage Nichols, will you marry me?"

Her sister Lydia burst into tears. Dalton wasn't sure if they were happy tears or sad tears. He was betting they were a little of both.

Sage dropped to her knees in front of Cannon and threw her arms around his neck, sending the box and ring flying into the air. Dalton caught it mid-flight and hoped it wasn't like catching the bouquet at a wedding. He needed a woman like he needed another six years in prison.

"You're the only sparkle I need, Cannon Bishop," Sage said. "Yes, I'll marry you."

Dalton tossed the box back to Cannon. "Get the ring on her finger before she comes to her senses and changes her mind."

Cannon slipped the band on Sage's finger. The crowd lifted their wine glasses to toast.

This time, it was Sheriff Cooper who had something to say. He pointed at all the Bishops in the house. There were six now that Katie, Maisey, and baby Sahara took the last name. "We're being taken over by Bishops." He looked to Bobby Williams, who stood in the corner with his wife Louise. "Dude, they're giving you a run for your money."

Bobby gave everyone a sly smile and placed his hand on his wife's stomach. "Number eight is cooking."

Doc Parker groaned. "We know what causes that."

After everyone closed their open mouths, the group went wild. If there was one thing the Williamses did well, it was breed. They had the cutest kids, but Dalton couldn't imagine having one child, nonetheless eight.

One more look at Bowie and Katie, and he erased the thought. Sahara was a miracle baby born to a mother with the biggest heart he knew. It was a donor heart of a woman he'd grown up with. Looking at Bowie, he knew the man was one lucky bastard to have fallen in love with the same heart twice. Dalton would be lucky to find love once. Who'd fall in love with a man like him?

Katie handed Sahara off to Bowie and picked up the cake she'd baked for the occasion. She brought it to Sage and Cannon. "I did it. I mastered high-altitude cake baking." She handed Sage the pan, then jumped up and down like she'd discovered the cure for cancer. "It's even—I didn't have to balance it out with extra frosting!"

Bowie came up behind his wife and pressed his lips to her cheek. "I loved my lopsided cake." Bowie's homecoming cake had an extra quart of frosting on one side to cover up Katie's baking inexperience.

"You loved me," Katie reminded.

Dalton groaned. "It's getting far too thick and sweet in here." He gave his new dad a test. "Hey, Pops," he called to Ben. "I'm outta here. Can you lock up when everyone is finished?"

"Sure thing, son," Ben replied.

Dalton walked toward the door with a smile on his face. It wasn't the life he'd envisioned for himself all those years ago, but it was *his* life, and somehow it seemed to work.

Sheriff Cooper caught up to him. "Keep your eyes open on the way home. I think the kids suspected of burning down the house across the lake are from Copper Creek. Arsonists rarely stop with one. If you see anything, don't act on it, call me."

Dalton gave him an I'm-not-an-idiot look. "It's all good. I'll call you if I see anything." He walked outside into the chill of the March night. The sky was clear, and a million stars guided him toward home.

The sheriff needn't worry. Dalton took no chances with his freedom these days. If he had a drink, he walked home or got a ride. If he saw a fight, he stepped aside. Six years in prison for killing someone was enough for him.

Although life seemed to throw him a lot of curve balls, family and friends remained a consistent source of comfort. He looked over his shoulder at the crowd he left at the diner. Those were the people who mattered most in his life.

As he walked the mile up Main Street to Lake Circle, he thought about his future. There would be no falling in love. No engagement. No wedding. No babies. Dalton's life was fine the way it was, he liked the status quo. He liked the peacefulness of living in a town where he wasn't judged. In Aspen Cove, he was safe and invisible.

He rounded the corner and walked to his back porch. There were lights on in the cabin next door. Odd because it had been vacant for over two years. There had been no mention of anyone moving in. Cannon told him he thought an investment banker bought it for future development. Dalton would have ignored the light in the window and walked inside his cabin if it weren't for the smoke billowing from under the back door.

CHAPTER THREE

She expected rustic, but Samantha never expected *Little House on the Prairie.* The place was cold, damp and dull. She pulled her knit cap tighter over her head and zipped up the hoodie all the way to her neck. She found the thermostat on the wall and cranked it to high, but nothing happened.

Several years of vacancy and neglect showed. There wasn't an ounce of homeyness to the cabin except for the flowers Deanna left on the new coffee table she had delivered.

It wasn't as if Samantha was used to homey since she spent most of her life in hotel rooms and tour buses, but she liked heat. Right now if she could get warm, she'd be happy to skip homey altogether.

Feeling the chill of the cold mountain air in her bones, she zeroed in on the fireplace already set up to burn with logs stacked in the opening and a few cones of newspaper peeking out between the chopped wood. On the mantel sat a box of wooden matches. *Thank you, Deanna.*

She hurried over and grabbed them hoping she could get a blaze started before she unpacked her car or froze to death. There was nothing worse than being exhausted except being cold and exhausted. Her stomach rumbled, and she experienced a new worst. Being tired, cold and hungry was a trifecta.

It took a dozen strikes of the match to get it lit. Her icy cold fingers shook as she held the flame to the newspaper. Pure joy raced through her as the tiny flicker turned into a flame and built into an inferno. Her joy was short-lived when rolling clouds of gray and black smoke filled the room.

Not knowing what to do, Samantha took the metal poker leaning against the stone fireplace and shifted the wood. Her thought was it needed to be pushed deeper into the opening, but the action caused a wall of black smoke to rush at her.

"Great, just great." She looked around the cabin, hoping for an answer to her problem. The only solution was to put the fire out and open the door. Her moment of success turned into a crushing defeat when she realized the only heat she'd feel was from the flames threatening to burn down her secret retreat.

Without further deliberation, she grabbed the vase on the table and poured the water and flowers onto the flames. The hiss and sizzle brought with it another burst of smoke that burned her throat and threatened to choke her.

Sorely in need of fresh air, she ran for the door. As she reached for the knob, the door swung open with force. The power behind it sent her flying across the room to land flat on her ass.

A hulk of a man raced inside. Samantha was certain he was a kidnapper, or worse, a murderer. If the angry look on his face was any sign of his intent, she'd go with a murderer.

"Who the hell are you?" Over six feet of solid muscle stalked toward her like a bobcat closing in on its prey.

She spider-crawled backward until the wall stopped her progress. She was good and trapped.

He loomed over her big and scary while he pulled out his phone and dialed a number.

She tried to stand up, but he gave her a look that flattened her back to the floor. "I live here," she whispered.

"Right." He narrowed his eyes and shook his head. "Coop. I'm at the vacant next to mine. I've got your arsonist."

There was a moment of silence.

"I'm no—"

Her words halted when he raised his hand.

"Some scrawny little boy. Can't be over sixteen." He pointed to her and mouthed the words "Stay," then stepped back and rubbed his beard. "I haven't touched him—yet." Steely blue eyes held her in place.

He ended the call and shoved his phone inside his pocket. "Sheriff's on his way."

"Good," she said. She sat up taller and pulled the cap from her head, letting her blue hair tumble across her shoulders. "I'm not a scrawny little boy, you idiot. I'm a full-grown woman. Who the hell are you?"

Though his eyes gave way to surprise, his voice didn't waver. "Neighborhood watch."

He gave her a black look while his eyes traveled up and down her body.

She could see why he thought she was a little boy. Dressed in jeans and an oversized hoodie, her shape was straight and boxy. When her long hair was tucked inside a gray cap, there was nothing about her that screamed woman.

"Girl? Maybe. Woman? Doubtful. Arsonist? Most likely."

Samantha pulled her knees to her chest and ran her fingers through her hair. "I'm not an arsonist. I own this cabin. I was trying to get warm."

He nodded. "Right. Tell your story to the sheriff." He backed his big body toward the door and leaned against the frame like a sentry on duty.

A breeze whipped through the room and wrapped around her

like an icy cloak. Teeth chattering, she asked, "C-c-can you at least shut the d-d-door?"

He shoved his hands into his pockets. "Nope."

She saw the flashing lights reflect off the window. "Great. All I wanted was a warm place to camp out for a few weeks, and now my mug shot will be posted everywhere." She buried her head against her knees. "Perfect."

"You picked the wrong neighborhood—and the wrong neighbor."

Seconds later, a big man dressed in beige and brown entered the cabin. Mr. Neighborhood Watch nodded toward him. "Hey, Coop. This little waif said she was looking for a place to squat for a few weeks."

Samantha scrambled to her feet and pressed her body to the wooden wall. "I said no such thing."

"You can add liar to her list of infractions."

She wasn't sure if it was him or the cold that got her moving, but she knew one thing for certain. She was no longer freezing. In fact, she was hotter than a cinder. She'd been called many things, but liar wasn't one.

"My name is Samantha White, and I own this damn cabin." She stomped forward until the sheriff placed his hand on his pistol. Then she stopped dead still like road kill.

"I'm Sheriff Cooper, and you need to stay right there." The sheriff eased his hand from his weapon. "Do you have identification? Proof you are who you claim to be?"

Thankfully, Deanna was an efficient assistant. She'd had the utilities, homeowners insurance and cable put in Samantha's name. The papers were supposed to be in the top drawer in the kitchen. Besides those, she had a driver's license.

"Yes."

The sheriff looked at the other man. "Dalton, you got coffee at your place? I could use a cup."

No way. Samantha couldn't believe the big oaf standing by the door was Dalton. Could it be the same Dalton Black she remembered as a child? She'd spent the entire three months living in Aspen Cove staring at him. He was five years ahead of her in school, but so handsome. Something raw and vulnerable drew her in back then. There was nothing vulnerable about Dalton Black these days. He was a cross between cover model and serial killer.

She peeked around the sheriff to get a better look at Dalton the man. She could see it was the same person. Dark hair. Cold, steely eyes. Dark, brooding personality. He was at least a foot taller and a foot wider, but the scar that floated over his brow was still there. Covered by his beard, she could imagine the cleft in his chin also remained.

Before she could say anything, Dalton was out the door and down the steps. Gone.

"You say your name is Samantha White?"

"I am Samantha White."

The sheriff gave her a full head-to-toe inspection. She knew he was calculating the risks. Would she run? Would she do something worse? She'd watched enough *CSI* in hotel rooms to know he'd started his investigative profiling of her the minute he arrived. Looking like an out-of-control teen wouldn't help her case.

"All right, Samantha White with the blue hair, show me your identification?"

She pointed to the bag on the table. The only thing she'd brought into the cabin. In it was a stash of cash and her ID. The cash would make her look guilty of something, but her ID could at least prove she was telling the truth. "You want me to get it, or do you want to get it?" She didn't want her first taste of freedom to end in death.

He looked at the small duffel bag. "You can get it. Just move slowly."

Relief flooded through her. She didn't want to have to explain the thousands of dollars she had in cash, but when she opened the bag, she realized she'd have to wade through the bricks of twenties to get to her driver's license at the bottom.

The sheriff stood over her. When she dared to glance at him, his left brow nearly hit his hair.

She shoved the money to the side while she fished around. "I don't believe in credit cards, and having cash isn't illegal." She rummaged through the bag until she came up with the wallet where Deanna had stored her documents. "Here." She pulled out her driver's license and passed it to the sheriff's opened palm. "I'd offer you something to eat or drink, but I just arrived. I'm not set up for company."

He nodded toward the sofa still covered in protective plastic. "Have a seat."

She sat at the edge, the plastic crinkling under her as she took up the corner and once again pulled her knees to her chest. At least when Dalton left, he shut the door. The room wasn't warm, but there was no longer an icy breeze blanketing her. She glanced at the fireplace where sooty water leaked from inside. Her once pretty flowers lay wilted on top of charred wood. Not exactly how she envisioned her first night in town.

Sheriff Cooper pulled out his phone and dialed. In the silence, she heard a male voice on the other end. "Run this number for me," the sheriff said. He recited the numbers written on her California driver's license.

She made a mental note to give Deanna a bonus. She'd insisted Samantha keep her license up to date although she drove nowhere. She could hardly leave her house on her own. There were too many fans wanting an autograph, a picture, or any piece of her. That's why she came to Aspen Cove—to preserve the pieces she had left.

She remembered the townspeople as being friendly. A small town where everyone knew each other, but no one paid much attention. That was the impression from a glassy-eyed twelve-year-old girl, but she'd been wrong. It would appear Dalton Black paid attention to everything.

"So Samantha, what brings you to Aspen Cove?" He walked around the living room taking note of the new furniture. In front of the couch sat a coffee table that still had protective cardboard on the corners. He brushed his fingers across the mantel, but there was no dust.

"I needed a break—a vacation. I bought this house several years ago, but things have been crazy in my life."

He stared at her blue hair like she was going through a phase. "You say you bought the place a few years ago?"

She let her legs down and inched toward the edge of the sofa. Beneath the plastic, she could see it was a pretty cognac-colored leather. She wondered if she'd get to see the true warmth of the material or if she'd be spending her first night of freedom inside a jail cell. "If you let me, I can get you some proof I belong here."

The sheriff stood taller. "I'd love to see it."

She looked at the gun in his holster. "Promise not to shoot me?"

He chuckled. "I make no promises. Don't give me a reason to pull the trigger."

Her eyes went to the kitchen behind him. "I'm going to the kitchen where I have documents that will help."

He followed her to the small galley kitchen.

She held her breath when she opened the first drawer and let it out when she found a blue folder with everything she needed inside. In the left-hand pocket was a copy of her purchase agreement.

As soon as this was cleared up, Deanna was getting a hefty raise. Samantha handed over the documents and leaned against the old yellowed Formica counter. While the sheriff looked through the papers, she glanced around the kitchen. It didn't even have a microwave.

The stove was gas, which she liked. It was an old four burner like the one they had when she and Mom lived in the house on Gladiola Lane. That house was a dump, but she loved it because it meant she was no longer living in the old Toyota.

The sheriff's phone rang. He had a brief conversation with the man on the other end. "She is. Okay. That's great, Mark." He turned to Samantha and smiled. "Why Aspen Cove?" he asked as he folded the papers and slid them into the folder.

"I lived here as a kid."

"Welcome back." He pushed off the counter and walked toward the door. He opened it to reveal Dalton coming up the stairs with two cups of steaming coffee. "She owns the place." Sheriff Cooper breezed past Dalton. "Give her my cup of coffee and teach her how to start a fire." The sheriff trotted down the steps and disappeared into the night.

CHAPTER FOUR

Nothing shocked him more than the sheriff's comment. The woman owned the house. Dalton didn't know if he should be relieved or worried. He'd accused his new neighbor of being an arsonist. Not too neighborly.

He stood at the threshold of the door with two cups of steaming coffee. "It looks like I owe you an apology." He eyed the mess in the fireplace. "I'm told a lesson in lighting a fire is in order."

She wrapped her arms around her body and tried to stop her teeth from chattering. If their positions were reversed, he would have slammed the door and walked away, leaving her on the porch, but she didn't. She looked longingly at the steaming coffee mugs and glanced at the mess in her fireplace.

In a small voice, she said, "I could use the coffee and a fire."

He gave her a half smile. "I'm sorry." He stepped inside and kicked the door shut with his foot. "A house on the other side of the lake burned to the ground last week. It's under investigation for arson. When I saw the smoke ..." He shrugged. "I'm sorry."

"Nice to know you pay attention." She reached for a cup and

held it cradled in her hands. Raising it to her mouth, she didn't take a drink. She breathed in the steam to warm her.

His chest tightened when he saw her fingertips were blue. "Lord, let's get you warm." He led her to the couch and tore open the plastic covering. He yanked and tugged until it came loose. "I'm assuming you wanted that gone."

She climbed into the far corner and leaned against the soft leather of the armrest. "You assume a lot of things, but yes, it needed to go."

He hated that her first impression of him would be that of an unreasonable man. He'd never been so quick to judge, but he'd learned from example. He hated how going to prison had changed him. He wanted to see the best in people, but he was a realist. Most people weren't that good.

Her body shook from the chill, but it was no wonder. She was as thin as a piece of dental floss. If not for that blue hair, she'd be easy to miss. Turn her sideways, and she'd all but disappear.

Funny how only minutes before he wanted to throttle her, and now his instinct to care and protect kicked in. He wanted to feed her, and fast, but first things were first. She needed to get warm. He unzipped his jacket and wrapped it around her. "This should keep you warm until I get the fire going."

She set the coffee down and snugged his jacket beneath her chin. "The fireplace won't work. Something's wrong with it. I had a nice blaze going until the whole room filled with smoke." She looked toward the muddy mess on her floor. "It's a miracle I didn't burn the place down."

Dalton laughed. "Good thing you didn't burn it down because then you would have proven me right. You would have been an arsonist."

"A homeless arsonist."

"I'll be right back." He dashed out the door and returned minutes later with a broom, a metal dustpan and an old metal trash bin. He made quick work of cleaning up the sodden mess that had been her fire. The wilted flowers lay on top of the debris.

"You have something against flowers?"

Her lips quirked into a smile. "No. I love them. I have something against burning my place down. The vase was filled with water, the flowers were a sacrifice."

Minutes later, he'd stacked new wood, shoved in bits of kindling and paper, and pointed to a metal handle inside the opening.

"The flue was closed. You need to make sure it's open, and the air is circulating, otherwise, you get a back draft and a lot of smoke."

He loved the way her cheeks blushed. "I've heard of a flue." She leaned forward and picked up the coffee. One sip had her face twisting.

"Too strong?"

"Elixir of the gods. Super hot, but I appreciate it."

"You could cool it down with cream, sweeten it with sugar." He looked past her to the kitchen. "Do you have any?"

She shook her head and took another sip. This time, she smiled and her expression turned soft.

"I have little in the way of provisions." She tucked her legs close to her body. She nearly disappeared under his jacket.

"You got furniture." He found the matches sitting on the coffee table and pulled a single stick out. "How did you sneak that past me?"

She shrugged. "My ass—, I mean, my friend took care of it."

"I've got a few friends I'd call asses too. Nice that he or she could get things moved in here for you."

There was that smile again. "It's a she, and her name is Deanna."

Something about that pleased him. He wouldn't have been

surprised if it had been a he. On closer inspection, Samantha was a pretty woman. Pretty women didn't stay single for long.

He struck the match and started the kindling on fire. He watched as the heated air moved upward and out through the now open flue. One look at her wood supply, and he knew she'd be out soon. "This isn't going to last long. I'll bring over enough wood to get through a day or so. You'll want to call Zachariah Thomas. He can hook you up with wood and moonshine. Both of which will get you warm."

She laughed. "I'll stick with the wood. I can pay you for what you give me."

"Unnecessary, but call Zachariah soon. The days may be warming up, but the nights are always cold."

"Is that the same old man that lives up in the mountains?" She leaned forward to put her cup on the table. "He's still making shine?"

"You've heard of him?" Dalton took another good look at her. He didn't recognize her. He'd never known a person with blue hair, but even if he mentally ignored her colored head, she didn't seem familiar. "How is it you came to Aspen Cove?"

She pulled her upper lip between her teeth. She looked at him as if testing to see how trustworthy he was. As if she would divulge a big secret. When her lip popped free, she said, "I lived here seventeen years ago."

"No way. I would know you."

"You know everyone who's lived here?" She giggled. It was a sound that vibrated through his rigid walls and settled inside his chest.

Except for the time he spent in prison, he could say yes without a second thought. He knew everyone. If she were here seventeen years ago, he would have been seventeen. He should know her.

Now that the fire was burning well, he placed the metal screen in front and came to join her on the couch. He sat at the opposite end and stared in her direction.

He expected something to come to him, some glimmer of recognition, but nothing did. "You don't look familiar, but then again, I'm pretty sure you didn't have blue hair back then. How old were you seventeen years ago?" An hour ago he wouldn't have given her over sixteen, but now he could see she held herself like an adult. She was well-spoken and reserved. When she smiled, faint creases showed in the corners of her eyes. A sign of maturity, his mom told him when he asked her what crow's feet were.

"I was invisible. I was twelve, and I rode the school bus to Copper Creek with you."

He envisioned the forty-five minute bus ride and pressed his memory for familiar faces. He'd hated that bus, but it was the most economical way to get to school. Economics were important when being raised by a single parent. Money was tight.

His dad had recently passed away. Although the town was supportive, not one person would miss the bastard. The logging company said it was a freak accident, but Dalton was certain someone got tired of his father's bullying and felled him and a tree at the same time. Thankfully, the small life insurance policy buried the asshole and left a little extra to get Maisey's Diner open.

He searched his memory again and came up with a little girl with brown hair and eyes the color of a starless sky. "I remember you. You sat in the second row on the right and stared toward the back of the bus every day."

"That was me," she said, sounding pleased that he'd remembered. "I stared at you and wondered how long it would take for me to become one of the cool kids."

That was a lifetime ago. "I was never one of the cool kids."

She peeled his jacket from her body and rose to stand in front of the fire. "You were to me."

"So that makes you what?" He calculated the years. "Wow, you're like twenty-nine now." Time had been kind to her.

She nodded slowly. "Yep. That's a far cry from the sixteen you gave me earlier." She turned toward the fire and rubbed her hands close to the flames.

Her sweatshirt lifted to her hips when she bent over. Dalton laughed inside. Had he seen her ass the first time, he would have never confused her with a boy. She was definitely thin, but every muscle of her lean body was solid. He was certain he could bounce a quarter off that ass. It was round and firm and would fill his palms nicely.

He shook that thought from his mind. Generally, women were nothing but trouble for him. He had too much going on in his life. He didn't need other distractions. He'd be neighborly, but he wasn't getting involved with Samantha White.

"What are your plans?" The longer she was here, the harder it would be for him to keep his distance. He couldn't take his eyes off her backside and how those jeans hugged every tiny curve she had.

"I'm not sure yet. I don't have a solid plan. Eventually, I'll have to go back to work, but I'm here now."

"Cannon said a broker made the purchase of this property. He thought it was an investor waiting to scoop up a piece of land here and there until they had enough to put a resort on the lake."

Her eyes opened wide. "Lord no, that would be a shame. It was purchased under my company's name, but it's for personal use."

Her company? That meant the little quiet girl from Aspen Cove did all right for herself. Dalton loved it when he heard stories of rags to riches. Not that buying a house in Aspen Cove made her rich by any means, but if she could afford a vacation home, she was doing better than most. "What do you do?"

She turned toward him. Her lower lip sank between her teeth.

When it popped free, she said, "I'm in public relations. A small company called Ignite."

One look at the fire had him laughing. "I sure hope you do a better job igniting your clients' businesses than you do a fire."

She moved directly in front of the fire and backed herself against the screen. "We do okay. What about you?"

Dalton expected her to erupt into flames at any minute. He wasn't sure how much to tell her. It wasn't like she'd be a long-term resident. He believed in honesty. He had integrity. He wouldn't lie to her, but he wouldn't provide more truth than she asked for or needed.

"I studied culinary arts." That was true. He'd attended Escoffier in Denver before he went to prison.

"So, you're a chef. Lucky me—you cook food, and I eat it!" She came back to the couch and sat in the corner.

Now that he knew she wasn't an arsonist, he liked her. She was easy to be around. He'd accosted her in her own home, and here he sat on her couch, drinking coffee and talking about careers.

"I'll make you something before you leave to go back to where it is you live full-time."

"That sounds great. Who knows, I could live here full-time if the food is good."

He let his eyes travel over her body. "I have a feeling you don't eat much." He rose from the couch. "Is there anything else you need? Any other crimes I can accuse you of? Any more insults I can toss your way before I leave?"

She rolled to her feet and walked to the front door to open it. Shivering when the cold wind whipped inside, she said, "I think I've been sufficiently humbled for the day. Thank you."

"Perfect. Glad I could help." He stepped outside and rubbed his arms. The T-shirt was poor protection from the biting cold.

"Oh my God, I almost stole your coat. I can't imagine the sheriff wanting to make another trip for a petty crime." She rushed to the couch where his coat lay and picked it up. She brought it to her nose and inhaled. "You smell nice."

He didn't think he'd ever been told that before. Some said he was handsome. He was strong. He was an ass. Good in bed. A great hugger. Compassionate. He never had a woman tell him he smelled nice. He liked it.

"Thanks." He pulled on his jacket. "I'll set some wood by the door."

"I appreciate that." She slowly closed it behind him.

He walked away smiling and turned his head to smell his collar. It didn't smell like anything to him. Scratch that. It smelled like her. Sweet and fruity and all woman. Something told him his status quo had changed.

CHAPTER FIVE

Samantha stretched her arms over her head. One by one, her vertebrae popped into place. At twenty-nine, she felt more like sixty. Years of pushing her body to the limit were taking their toll.

Last night she was strung too tight to sleep, so she unloaded her car and organized what little she had. Thankfully, Deanna thought about essentials like bedding and towels and toilet paper and hangers. She'd bought soap and shampoo and even put a six-pack of diet soda in the refrigerator. But a can of carbonated liquid wasn't going to stop the growling in her stomach. She needed food, and right away.

After a quick cold shower, she pulled on a pair of yoga pants, a plain pink T-shirt and the hoodie she acquired at last night's concert.

A jog into town would get her blood pumping and warm her up. She knew she had a small window of time to remain unnoticed. Someone was sure to recognize her, and then her peaceful retreat would turn into a paparazzi paradise. She had to take advantage of her anonymity while she had it.

After a quick peek out the door to make sure she hadn't

already been discovered, she tucked the strands of her hair into the hoodie and took off at a slow pace.

The altitude and lack of oxygen made her breathe deeply. The cold air burned her lungs. Her tennis shoes crunched the pine needles underfoot. She couldn't remember the last time she'd felt this good. There was no one here to control her choices. Today, she was the ruler of her world.

One foot in front of the other, she listened to the thump of her shoes hitting the hard ground. The air smelled like Christmas, with a hint of pine mixed with campfire.

First stop would be the beauty shop. She had folded a handful of twenties and tucked them inside her pocket in case they had an opening. Would it be the same owner, Kathy, who had fixed her hair years ago? She thought back to that day.

In hopes of saving her mom a few bucks, Samantha decided to cut her own bangs. How hard could it be, she thought? She lifted them up and took the scissors to them. Too bad she had a crooked eye. When she let them loose, one side hovered above her eyebrow and the other skimmed her cheek. She knew she shouldn't have another go of it or she'd be bald when she finished. She walked to the shop and told the owner she'd work for a trim. After cleaning up the hair from the floor, Kathy not only fixed her bangs, but she washed, conditioned and styled it. For Samantha, it was her first spa-like experience.

A strand of blue hair slipped from the hoodie. She tucked it back inside as she neared the town. Yep, getting back to her natural color was a priority. She'd have a better chance of remaining hidden if her hair wasn't so bold.

As she approached the shop, her heart sank. It no longer had the images of scissors and a comb on the window. No lights were on. The glass was whitewashed to hide the vacant interior. Kathy's was no longer in business. *Now what?*

Her stomach gurgled, then growled to remind her that a

hamburger and fries from yesterday couldn't hold her forever. She lifted her nose in the air and breathed in the sweet aroma of baked goods. Figuring the smell came from the diner, she moved down the street and found it was also closed.

Hands fisted on her hips, she looked around the town. It wasn't the bustling place she remembered. There were no kids running on the sidewalk. The stores weren't open selling their goods. It was like the town had dried up and disappeared. Her day moved from bad to worse.

Against her better judgment, she looked at her phone this morning. The first ten messages were from her manager, demanding to know where she was. She sent a quick text, informing him she was taking a break. After the next five messages arrived filled with expletives and threats, she powered down her phone and went about her day. What she didn't see couldn't hurt her, or so she told herself. She banished thoughts of work from her brain and went in search of sustenance.

Wanting something sweeter and more satisfying than bad news, she followed the yummy aroma filling the air. Bea, the nice woman who owned the bakery at the end of the block came to mind. On the way down the sidewalk, Samantha reminisced about her short stay in Aspen Cove.

Two days a week, she had walked into town. Mondays she picked up milk from the Corner Store, and Thursdays she bought a loaf of bread. She supposed she could have done it all on the same day, but that would mean one less cookie and one less hug from Bea. She could use a hug about now.

Her heart leaped with joy when she looked across the street at the end of the block to see the bakery open. Would Bea remember her?

Feeling buoyed by fond memories, she skipped across the road and picked up her pace. The closer she got, the sweeter the air smelled. She closed her eyes and breathed deeply. If she was right, it was banana nut muffin day.

One thing Samantha could count on was consistency when it came to Bea. Every day of the week had a specific muffin. You could schedule your life by the muffin of the day. Today was Sunday.

The bell above the door rang when she entered. A voice from the back called out, "I'll be right with you." It was too young to be Bea, but maybe her daughter. She remembered the girl who worked side-by-side with her mom. A friendly girl with a heart of gold, brown hair, and eyes the color of maple syrup.

One look around told her things had changed everywhere. The pinstriped wallpaper was gone, as were the needlepoint pictures Bea stitched while waiting for her next customer.

The coat of yellow paint made it fresh and bright, but it still felt warm and welcoming. The iron tables with their torn plastic cushions were the same, along with the glass display case and turn of the century cash register. Those little pieces of history made it feel right.

Next to the window sat a woman with her head hung low. She hovered over a sticky note and scribbled while she nibbled on a muffin.

"Hey, sorry about that." A blonde came out of the back wiping her hands on her apron. "I can't figure out how to have the dishes wash themselves."

"That would be awesome." In Samantha's case, it was magical. One minute they were there, the next they were gone. It was like a dish fairy waved a magical wand, but that kind of magic came with a high price.

The blonde stared and gave her a knowing smile. "You're—"

"Starving," she said. Samantha gave her a pleading look and nodded toward the woman at the table. "Banana nut muffin day, right?" Samantha looked at the case that was chock full of treats.

There were cookies and brownies and mini loaf cakes. She'd entered the forbidden temple and wasn't leaving until she'd tasted something she wasn't normally allowed.

"Yes. How do you know? You're not—"

"From here?" She picked up a sample from the tray and popped it into her mouth. The banana flavor rushed over her taste buds. She swore she'd tasted heaven. "I lived here for a brief time when I was a kid."

The blonde's eyes lit up. "No way. I can't believe it. Aspen Cove has its own ..." she leaned in and whispered, "superstar."

Samantha gave her an aw-shucks look. "It's not as glamorous as one would think. Besides, there are quite of few memorable people here in Aspen Cove." She thought about Dalton Black and how he looked with muscles rippling and bulging in front of her while he tended the fire. Ink she wanted to explore peeked from under his cotton T-shirt. Dalton started more than the blaze in the fireplace. He'd stirred a spark inside her she thought had died long ago. "Is Bea around?"

The blonde's face fell. "You want a muffin and a coffee?"

Samantha nodded. "Yes, that sounds good." It wasn't often she got to be around strangers and enjoy being anonymous.

"I'm Katie. Katie Bishop. You might remember the Bishop boys, Cannon and Bowie. Bowie is my husband." She put a few muffins on a plate and a pod in the coffeemaker before pressing start.

"I remember them. Big handsome boys."

"Now big, handsome men." Katie smiled. "We have so much to talk about." She pointed to the table opposite the other woman.

A minute later, she came from behind the counter with two cups of coffee and a plate full of goodies.

"You asked about Bea?" There was a minute of silence as she seemed to weigh her words. "I'm afraid she's no longer with us. She passed early last year."

Samantha's heart sank into her empty stomach. As hungry as she was, she wasn't sure she could eat after hearing such sad news.

"That's heartbreaking. She was kind to me."

"Everyone has nice things to say about her."

"Along with her cookies, she always had a smile, a hug, and something positive to say. What about her daughter? I can't remember her name."

Again, Katie frowned. Her hand went to her chest. "Brandy. She's also gone, but she remains in my heart."

"Oh lord. How?"

"Car accident."

"So sad."

"It is, but their memories live on." Katie leaned forward and in a hushed voice said, "Since you're trying to remain incognito, what do you want to be called? I can't very well call you Indigo."

Samantha reached under the hoodie to make sure none of her hair had fallen loose. "I would appreciate it if you didn't. That's not who I am, only who I pretend to be. My real name is Samantha."

"Well, Samantha, since we're going to be friends, eat up and tell me why you're here."

"I needed down time. I'm tired. Burned out, really."

"Where are you staying?"

"I bought a small cabin on Lake Circle next door to Dalton Black. Do you know him?" Samantha imagined everyone knew everybody, but since she didn't know Katie, there was a slim chance Katie didn't know Dalton.

Katie plucked the top off one muffin. "Not only are we friends, we're neighbors. I live on the other side of Dalton." She took a bite and swallowed. "I'm sure glad I covered for Ben today, otherwise, I would have missed you. He normally works Sunday, but he's taken the week off."

"Ben? Cannon and Bowie's dad? I remember him. Nice man. His wife taught at the school."

Another frown. "She's gone, too. Same car accident."

Samantha sipped her coffee and leaned back. "So much has changed."

"Change is the one thing you can always count on."

"Speaking of change." She reached inside the hood and drew a strand of hair free. "I can't lie low with this." She twisted the hair around her finger. "What happened to the beauty shop?"

Katie shrugged. "More change, I guess." In a normal toned voice, she said, "There's a place called Gracie's in Copper Creek. I haven't been there, but I pass it on my way to Target."

The woman across the room rose. Her chair scraped against the linoleum floor. "Don't go to Gracie's." She walked over to Samantha and Katie's table. "You'll pay too much, and she doesn't do good work." With one tug, she yanked down Sam's hoodie and touched her hair. "I can do it for you. You need a touch up, or are you going for something different?"

Katie tilted her head and looked at the woman. "You do hair?"

She nodded. Samantha noticed the dark circles under her eyes and the fading green bruise on her cheekbone. Although Samantha had never been hit, she saw firsthand what it did to a person. Covering her mother's marks was a superpower no eight-year-old girl should have to master.

"Have a seat," Katie offered.

The woman shook her head. "I was leaving my wish. It costs nothing to wish, right? It's like dreaming out loud." She reached over Katie's head and thumbtacked a folded note to the corkboard.

"Your wish?" Samantha asked. She looked above her to the sign on the corkboard that read 'Wishing Wall'. "What's the Wishing Wall?"

Katie laughed. "I started it as a way to get to know the people of Aspen Cove. It was a simple way for people to make reasonable

273

wishes come true. If it's a request for prayer, I pray. If it's something easy, I figure out a way to grant it. All I can do is try. I can't solve all the world's problems, but I can fix a few."

The woman looked at her wish and hung her head. "I fear mine is unobtainable, unreasonable really, but I believe thoughts are important, and I'm trying to find inner peace and a positive outlook." She looked at Samantha and Katie. "I'll leave you two alone."

"Nonsense." Katie rose from her seat and rushed behind the counter for another cup of coffee. "Join us." When she returned, she patted the chair next to her. "Please. Come sit down. What's your name?"

'Skittish' was the only way to describe the dark-haired woman. She looked at them and then at the door as if calculating how many steps it would take her to get there. She took a seat and brought the fresh coffee to her lips.

"I'm Marina."

They introduced themselves and went back to talking hair.

"I want to go back to my natural dark brown."

Marina touched Sam's hair again, moving it between her fingers. "It's healthy despite the heavy processing. I can stop by your place Tuesday if you don't mind me working from your kitchen."

"You don't work in a shop?"

Marina chewed on her inner cheek before she spoke. "Like you, I'm in transition."

Samantha groaned. The more people who recognized her, the less time she'd have. "You women from Aspen Cove are too observant. I'm begging you to please not give me away."

Katie covered both Samantha's and Marina's hands with hers. "Aspen Cove takes care of its own."

Marina shook her head. "I'm not from here."

"You're an honorary resident. Besides, maybe someday you'll

move here. There's an empty beauty shop across the street." Katie touched her blonde hair. "We're all in need of your services."

For the first time since Samantha entered the bakery, she saw Marina smile. She had a strong urge to hug her but didn't want to send her running.

"Tuesday sounds great." She took a wad of twenties from her pocket and laid them on the table. "Here's money to get what you need. I live at 7 Lake Circle. What time are we doing this?"

Marina glanced at the pile of cash on the table. "I can be there at eleven. You want a dark rich brown, right?"

Samantha flicked the hoodie back over her head. "I'll settle for anything other than blue."

After she finished her muffin and coffee, she paid her bill and made her way home. When she arrived at the cabin, she was greeted with a pleasant surprise. Maybe her day was turning around.

Pantry staples like bread, eggs, milk, and sugar sat tucked inside a cooler on her porch. Next to it was a vase of flowers and a note.

Welcome to the neighborhood, Samantha. Thought you could use a few items for your empty cupboards. The flowers looked like a nice add, too. Wanted to say I'm sorry one more time for bulldozing you.

Dalton

She brought the mixed bouquet to her nose and inhaled. For a second, they didn't smell like flowers at all. She imagined they smelled like him. Raw energy mixed with hot male and evergreen.

A lot had changed in Aspen Cove, but one thing remained the same. Just like when she was a kid, Samantha would be happy to spend hours looking at Dalton Black.

CHAPTER SIX

"You realize I'm not really a killer, right?" Dalton leaned forward and placed his arms on the parole officer's desk. She was a nice woman who insisted he call her Lucy. In his head, she'd always be Ms. Warwick. He'd never had a parole officer before her and didn't know if they were all as kind and flexible, but he appreciated her meeting him on a Sunday afternoon.

"I'm not here to judge you. I'm here to make sure you toe the line. You behaving yourself, Dalton?"

"Yes, ma'am. Can't get into too much trouble in Aspen Cove."

She leaned back and kicked her boots up onto the table. "It's been my experience that if you're looking for trouble, you can find it anywhere."

He shook his head. "I'm not looking for anything but an end to this nightmare."

She pushed off the desk, sending her chair rolling back. Leaning forward, she opened his file. "It's been a year without problems. I don't imagine I'll be seeing you as much next year."

She pulled a black pen from the edge of her desk and marked up the page. "Have you done anything about that anger problem?"

"I had six years of incarceration. Do you think that helps anger issues?"

"You telling me you're still angry?"

He shook his head. He was pissed, but it wasn't something he'd share with her. "What I'm telling you is, I didn't have anger problems going in, and I didn't have them coming out."

She laughed. "Good line. I'll write that one down." She shuffled through his papers. "I know what went down that night. I've read all the transcripts. Some would call you a hero—others a vigilante. Me, I'd call you a nice guy who thought he was doing the right thing."

He couldn't argue, she was right. People either loved him or hated him. There was no gray area to killing a person. "Imagine that. Chivalry is dead."

"It isn't dead. Just misunderstood. Don't stop caring for people. That's when the trouble *really* begins."

Trouble for him started when he cared. He'd played out all the roles he could have taken that night in his head again and again. He could have been the pretender who ignored the woman's cries when that asshole punched her. He could have been the ignorant ass who stood to the side and watched it all go down while laughing and saying she probably deserved it. He could have been a lot of things, but he was the only man who stepped forward to stop another man from beating a woman because she ignored his advances.

Dalton caught Andy Kranz's fist midair as he tried to deliver the second blow to Bethany Waters. When Andy turned around, it wasn't to apologize. He swung with his other fist and landed a solid blow to Dalton's gut. Dalton fisted up and took one swing at the drunk bastard. He hit him right between the eyes. The jerk dropped like a boulder. The problem was, he never got back up.

"Bethany Waters wrote at least a hundred letters to the courts and parole board." Lucy pulled out a stack of photocopied letters.

Dalton and Lucy had never talked about the crime, only the sentence. It was interesting to hear her take on things.

"I know. She sent me about two hundred in prison." He had them rubber banded together. It helped him to know he'd done the right thing even though the outcome wasn't what he expected. "She still writes occasionally to say thanks. She's married and has two kids."

"What about you? You seeing anyone?"

Lucy was pushing sixty. Life hadn't been kind to her. Her leathered skin was marked by the lines of a life lived outdoors. Her calloused hands were rough enough to sand wood. During one of their talks, she'd told him she raised champion horses. Serving as a parole officer was her way of giving back.

"You flirting with me, Lucy?"

"Darlin', I'd rip you to pieces. You couldn't handle me. Go find yourself a nice young thing and make babies."

This time, he laughed. "My dating resume is tarnished. Few women are looking for ex-felons who cook blue plate specials part-time at a diner."

"You don't come out of the gate with 'Hi, I'm Dalton Black, and I did six years for killing someone.'" She pursed her lips, which made her entire face prune up. "That's like telling a guy you have herpes before you even kiss him."

His mouth fell open. The one thing Dalton liked most about Lucy was her candor. She didn't pussyfoot around or tell him life would be wonderful. She usually told him to get his shit together, and she'd see him next month.

"You got herpes?"

"No, I'm giving you an example of what *not* to do. Here's a good one. Don't annoy your PO, or she'll revoke your parole."

"Got it. Are we done?"

She turned to the first page of the folder. "Sober—check. Employed—check. Housed—check. Cute as a button—check." She closed the file. "You can let your past define you, or you can define your future. Who will you become, Dalton Black?"

"Good question, Lucy. I'll give it some thought."

"Don't waste too much time. You're thirty-four. That clock only moves forward."

"Got it." He rose from his chair. "Same day next month?"

"Nope, I'll see you in six." She walked him to the door. "Enjoy your life. Not enough that I'll be barking up your ass, but enough so the years don't pass by with regret."

Dalton climbed into his truck with a lot to think about. Actually, it was a little—a little blue-haired woman who'd been on his mind since he busted through her front door and accused her of a crime.

That bothered him. He'd been quick to judge and condemn. He knew better. He'd been found guilty before he had cuffs on. Visits with Lucy always brought that day into focus. Did he feel bad that Andy Kranz died? Sure. He hadn't intended to kill him, but it came down to Bethany or Andy. In Dalton's mind, the woman would almost always win. Especially when the man was being an asshole.

Having lived in a violent house, the odds were in favor of Dalton being an abuser, but he wasn't. He'd taken a punch or two or twenty from his old man by stepping into the fist before it hit his mother. He had the scars to prove it. The one above his eyebrow was a constant reminder. A reminder of who he never wanted to be.

The three-hour drive from Denver back to Aspen Cove gave him plenty of time to think about the trajectory of his life, but he couldn't clear his head. His mind kept going back to Samantha. He wasn't sure if it was the memory of her staring at him from the front of the bus in their youth or the exhaustion he saw when she collapsed onto her couch. All he wanted to do was feed her and make her happy because for one second last night when she smiled, his entire world seemed brighter.

When he pulled into his driveway and hopped out of his truck, he glanced to the right. The house looked empty and lifeless in the twilight of the night. That was until he heard a soft lilting voice and the strum of a guitar coming from the beach.

Instead of going inside like he planned, he walked quietly around the back to find Samantha sitting on the ground, facing the lake. The sun had set, and the bruised sky hung above her head with wisps of pink and purple and blue.

Too far away to hear the lyrics, he leaned against his deck and listened to the blend of chords mixed with her angelic voice. There was a beautiful woman, good music, a picturesque setting. The only thing missing was a glass of wine. That was one thing he could provide.

He returned to the beach in minutes with an opened bottle of cabernet and two glasses. The damp dirt ate up any noise his shoes made. Behind her, he cleared his throat. She jumped six inches into the air.

She swung around, brandishing her guitar like a weapon. When she saw it was him, she lowered it and tugged it to her chest. "Holy hell, you scared me near to death. I could have hurt you."

Dalton had never seen a person move so fast. "Are you going to bludgeon me to death with your guitar?"

She lowered herself back to the folded blanket. "Murder doesn't look good on a resume."

Never a truer statement had been said. He lifted the wine and the glasses. "I saw you and thought a good wine would go great with the sunset."

"Dalton Black, be careful, or I might think you're wooing me."

"Well, that's something I've never been accused of." He walked over and took a seat on the damp ground beside her. "Care for a glass?"

She set her guitar down and slid over to make room for him. "Get off the wet ground. If you're sharing your wine, I can share my blanket."

He was twice her size and took up most of the space. The urge to pick her up and sit her on his lap was strong, but he controlled his desire. Under the half-hung moon, he filled the glasses and offered a toast. "Here's to celebrating."

"What are we celebrating?" She turned to him. Her eyes were almost black, with a hint of blue around the edges.

"Milestones," he said, and touched his glass to hers, letting the clink ring in the air.

"Do tell ..." She smiled, and that warmth and light he experienced the night before radiated through him and settled like a fire in his chest.

"Mine are complicated to explain." He heard Lucy's warning about coming out the gate with an *I'm-a-felon* introduction. "What about you? What do you want to celebrate?"

"I have some difficult-to-explain milestones as well. Let's simply agree to celebrate."

"Sounds like a plan."

They sipped their wine and looked at the still water.

"I don't remember the weather being so temperamental. Last night I nearly froze to death, and tonight I barely need a jacket."

"It's early spring. It might have been close to sixty degrees today, but next week we'll get a foot of snow."

"Really?" She leaned forward and rested her chin on her knees. "I lived here from August to early November. At the first big snow storm, we headed out." She shivered and pulled down her sleeves.

He wasn't sure if she was cold or living a dark memory. He moved closer until their bodies touched on one side from shoulder to ankle.

"It's been a light year for snow. People talk about climate change. And when we go from this to a foot of snow, I get it."

"Other than the possibility of freezing to death, I'd love to see that much snow." She looked to the cloudless night. "To sit in front of a blazing fire with hot cocoa and a good book. That sounds like heaven."

He picked up the bottle and topped off her glass. "You have simple wishes."

She sighed. "I live an incredibly busy life. I'm afraid it will be over before I really get to enjoy it."

"I get the impression you're a workaholic."

She laughed. It was a sweet sound that sent a ripple from his chest to the space between his legs. He was grateful the moon wasn't full. Otherwise, his attraction to her couldn't be hidden.

"Not by choice."

"It's all a choice." Dalton knew that life was a series of decisions. Some set you up for success. Others could ruin you. "You can choose differently."

"Hence the milestones. Coming here was a risky decision." She leaned into him and traced the tattoos on his arm. "Bet these took thought."

He let out a low, rumbling laugh. "Not at all. Most of them took a night of too much alcohol."

"Seriously?"

"Not all the decisions I've made were wise." He took a chance and wrapped his arm around her shoulder. "Not sure if this decision is wise either, but I really want to kiss you."

"You want to kiss me?" She turned her body and faced him. Her crisscrossed legs caged him from hip to knee.

"More than anything." It had been a long time since he'd kissed anyone out of desire rather than need. That first week of man-whoring after prison didn't count. He'd had six years of celibacy to make up for. All the faces blended together. No one was looking for anything but a good time. Tonight was different. Wanting to kiss her meant something to him.

She lifted her chin in what looked like defiance, but her eyes softened into submission. "I'd like that." She closed them and leaned in.

He pressed his mouth to hers. His tongue slipped out to taste the sweetness of her lips. The angle was awkward. He was too tall. She was too small. This wasn't working. After he lowered his glass to the ground, he took hers and set it aside before he lifted her onto his lap. The exact place he wanted her earlier.

She straddled him and wrapped her legs around his waist. Stone hard thighs pressed into his hips. His hands moved down her too-thin body and gripped an ass made of steel.

"I've never kissed a girl with blue hair."

She whispered against his lips. "Me either."

He chuckled. "That's a relief."

"Are you going to kiss me or talk about my hair?"

"Oh, I'm going to kiss you like you've never been kissed before." He lifted his hands to cup her face and lowered his lips to hers. He knew this was a bad idea, but he'd be damned if he could stop himself from indulging. He nipped at her bottom lip and pulled it into his mouth. He tasted wine and desire ... and maybe a little fear.

Her tiny hands moved up his chest, over his shoulders, and ran through his hair. He reminded himself that women were trouble and the only reason he kissed her was because she said she was leaving. She wouldn't be around long enough to cause him harm.

Samantha opened her mouth and moaned. It was deep and throaty and sexy as hell. That was all the invitation he needed to intensify the kiss. One hand slid up to the back of her head where he threaded his fingers through her hair. He pulled her closer. His tongue stroked hers softly at first and became more demanding as the kiss lingered. He continued his assault on her mouth until he could no longer breathe. The desire he felt for her had sucked all the oxygen from his lungs.

Despite the temperature dropping outside, he was hot. *She* was hot. He pulled away with regret. All he wanted was to get lost in her touch and her taste, but he knew better. He expected a simple kiss, but this was way more than he bargained for. "I should get you inside."

She leaned back and looked at him. What did he see in her eyes? Under the night sky they were like a wishing well, full of dark desire and endless possibilities. Dalton hadn't felt this turned on since he was a teen.

Her legs lowered to the ground, and she rose to her feet. "You're probably right. Thanks for the wine." She looked to her deck. "Oh, and the flowers and eggs and bread and stuff. That was sweet."

"I was being neighborly."

She picked up her guitar. "I think I might like this neighborhood."

He walked her to her door. "I'd like to kiss you again."

"Now?" She turned the knob and let the door swing open behind her.

"Hell yes, but I won't because I wouldn't stop at the kiss. Racing to the finish line would be a shame when there's so much to explore in-between." He looked past her to the fireplace. "You want a fire?"

She shook her head. "No, thanks. I'm already warm."

He reached past her and waved his hand through the air. Her cabin was colder inside than it was outdoors. "You're warm now, but it won't last. You have gas heating. You know that, right?"

"I turned it on. It doesn't work."

He pressed into her until she backed into the living room. "My cabin is the same model as yours, only we have flipped floor plans." He walked past her to a hallway closet. "Bring me the matches.

The pilot light to your heater probably isn't lit. Didn't you use the stove?"

"No, I went to the bakery." She handed him the box of matches and stood back as he turned on the gas and lit the pilot light. On the hallway wall, he adjusted the thermostat to sixty-eight.

"That should do it. You'll *stay* warm now." He closed the door and looked down at her grateful expression.

"Or you could kiss me again. That seems to heat me up."

"You're trouble." He shook his head and walked out the door.

As he walked toward his place, he mentally kicked himself for walking away from a sure thing. Carelessness sat on one shoulder, screaming, "Turn around!" Common sense sat on the other, demanding he walk away.

He wanted to turn around and run back to her cabin. The problem was, he knew that the minute he did, a kiss would lead to more. And something told him that when he pressed himself inside her body, Samantha White would own his heart.

CHAPTER SEVEN

Even an hour-long run couldn't clear her mind of last night's kiss. The way Dalton's body melded to hers. How his hands sent sparks of awareness racing across her skin. His touch was the final thing she thought of last night and the first thing she had on her mind this morning.

He wanted to explore what happened between the beginning and the end. *Had she ever had that?* The last beginning she had was with the lead singer of Granite Soldiers.

The short fling started last summer when the band opened for her in Europe. Thankfully, it never went further than a few kisses. She'd shown up at his bus unannounced, only to find him the meat between two blonde honey buns.

She ran down Main Street toward the bakery, but the smell of coffee and bacon stopped her in front of the diner. It was Tuesday, which meant breakfast was served. She calculated the distance she had run and imagined she'd burned off enough calories for an egg or a bowl of oatmeal. Old habits were hard to break. *Screw healthy eating.* Today she'd have bacon and whatever else she wanted.

Swiping the sweat from her forehead, she ran her hand around the knit cap that imprisoned her hair. There were no escapees.

Through the swinging doors, she entered a different world. The diner was probably around when she lived here, but she and her mom didn't eat out much. Restaurants were not in their budget. It was funny to think how far she'd come.

A woman approached. She'd recognize Dalton's mom anywhere with her bouffant hairstyle and fire engine red lips. She realized Maisey Black in fact owned Maisey's Diner. Why she hadn't already put that together, she had no idea.

"Have a seat anywhere."

"Thanks, Ms. Black." Samantha looked around the near-empty eatery. The only occupied table was one in the corner. Tucked against the wall, an older man read his paper. The only thing visible was his white hair peeking out in tufts above the pages.

Samantha took the corner booth on the other side of the restaurant.

Maisey followed her, carrying an empty mug and a full pot of coffee. "It's Bishop now... Do I know you?"

"Congratulations." Besides Cannon and Bowie, there was only one Bishop remaining. She must have married Ben. "I doubt you know me, but I remember you. I lived here briefly with my mom, Yvette."

She put the pot and cup on the table and slid into the bench across from Samantha. "I remember your mom. She worked at the paper mill."

Samantha nodded. "Yes, but then it closed, and the first snow fell and we left."

"And now you're back." She pushed the mug forward. "Coffee?"

"I'd love some." Samantha lived on black coffee and adrenaline.

"How's your mom?"

It had been a while since she'd seen her. Between the travel and recording, she didn't get much time to relax or visit.

"She's great. She lives in San Diego now." The first thing Samantha purchased once she'd made it was a house for her mom. She never wanted her to have to live in a car or a rent by the week motel room again.

"She married?"

She laughed. "Oh no, she said once was enough for her. My father wasn't a particularly nice man." Samantha recognized the knowing look that spread over Maisey's face.

"I understand." She lifted her hand to her cheek like she had remembered a painful moment. "I hope she's happy."

With a nice little nest egg and a fully paid for house, Samantha hoped she was happy too. "Seems to be."

"You might know my son, Dalton."

Oh boy, do I know him. "Yes, he's my neighbor."

"Is that right? He didn't tell me." She rose from the booth and picked up the pot of coffee. "I'll tell him you're here."

"Wait. He's here?"

"Of course. He's the chef."

Of course he was. It made sense. He told her he was a chef. Only he didn't say where.

Samantha was thrilled with the coffee. Add in a side order of Dalton, and it was a perfect day. The only thing that could make it better would be some of that in-between stuff he spoke about.

She fidgeted in the booth while she waited. Without a stitch of makeup on, she wasn't pretty to look at, but Dalton didn't seem to notice last night. Then again, it was dark. She pinched her cheeks to pink and chanced a side sniff to make sure her deodorant was working. All seemed to be in order when Mr. Tall, Dark, and Delicious walked over.

"Good morning," he said. Those two words that could have been a lover's sonnet to a woman who had so much, and yet so little.

"Hey, you." She knew she looked at him like he was breakfast. "I didn't know you worked here."

"The exchange of resumes didn't seem necessary."

She blushed under his gaze. "I suppose we shared enough."

He laughed loud enough for the old man in the corner to lower his newspaper and frown.

Dalton hovered over her. "You think that was enough? Baby, that wasn't even an appetizer." His breath floated over her. Goosebumps rose on her skin, but the heat of desire pulsed through her veins.

She took him in from head to toe. His hair was covered with a dark bandana. The black cotton of his T-shirt stretched across his broad chest, reminding her of every muscle her fingertips skimmed over last night. Worn jeans hung low on his hips and led to black boots more suited for a motorcycle ride than a kitchen.

Her hands tingled to touch him. Afraid she'd act on her desires, she tucked them beneath her legs.

"Why are you hiding in the corner?"

"I'm not hiding." In fact, she was. With her back to the window and her body pressed against the red vinyl, she hoped to disappear into the décor. One reason she chose Aspen Cove was because it was the last place anyone would look for her. Few people knew of her connection to the small town. "I smelled bacon and came in to investigate."

"You hungry?" He licked his lips like he could taste her on the air.

"Are you going to stand over me and tease me or satisfy my hunger?"

His big body pushed into the booth, trapping her between him and the wall. His arm fell over her shoulder while his lips traced her jaw to the shell of her ear. "What are you hungry for?"

Laughter bubbled until it burst forth. "Does that work for you?" It worked for her, but she wasn't ready to strip down and be devoured in a diner. Someone had to put an end to the madness before she asked him to kick everyone out and hang out the 'closed' sign.

He sat back and watched her with his soulful blue eyes. "I'm a little rusty in the seduction department."

She twisted so her knee pressed into his thigh. "Are you now?" She lifted her hand and brushed it across his perfectly trimmed beard. "You're selling yourself short. I loved the flowers. The eggs and milk were a unique treat but much appreciated. The wine and the kiss on the beach? That was foreplay."

He twisted his lips in a thoughtful expression. "Flowers, food, and wine, huh?" He scooted out of the booth and stood. "I've got you covered." He whipped around and walked into the kitchen.

Something told Samantha she'd unleashed a monster. As she drank her coffee, she powered up her phone and read through the next twenty-two emails that started with "Where the hell are you?" and ended with her agent pleading for her to contact Dave.

She knew she started a panic when she left. They wanted a new contract. A five-year deal that would give them control over her life again. It wasn't happening. She'd given them enough.

She dialed Deanna and waited for her to pick up.

"Are you okay?" were the first words out of her mouth.

"I'm perfect. Still incognito. Getting hair color today."

"Ooh, what color?"

"Boring brown."

"Nothing about you is boring."

"Oh please. Boring is my middle name, but I'm working on that." She touched her lips and sighed. "I met a guy my first night here." She refused to say he accosted her because what came next was far more exciting. "We shared a bottle of wine and an amazing kiss."

"Does he know who you are?"

"No, and that was what made the kiss that much more amazing."

"Don't get your heart broken. You're not staying there. Aspen Cove was supposed to be like rehab for your soul. You can't keep him."

Deanna was right. Aspen Cove wasn't part of her long-term plan. The plan was to rest so she could get back into the recording studio to sing what she wanted to sing. She needed to find a studio willing to piss off Oliver Shepherd. Ending her relationship with the music mogul could blacklist her for life. It might come down to her starting her own label.

"I know, and it's been good so far."

"Tell me about that kiss."

"The kiss," she closed her eyes to remember it better, "was amazing."

A plate of food appeared in front of her. "'Amazing,' huh?" His warm molasses voice seeped into her cells, heating her all the way to her core.

"Got to go, Deanna. The kisser is here." She hung up before her assistant could say another word.

Dalton sat across from her and plucked a piece of bacon from her plate. She looked down at what he brought to the table. It was more like a platter than a plate.

"You better have more than a piece of bacon. Who do you think will eat all of this?"

"You are. You're way too thin. While your ass is perfection, the rest of you is like a piece of knotty pine."

Samantha's chin nearly hit her chest. "That can't work for you."

He rose from his seat and moved next to her. "It's not my

intention to offend you, but you have to know you're painfully thin."

Barely over a hundred pounds, she was thin. "I have a killer metabolism."

"Then eat up. You'll need it."

"For?"

"There's a bonfire and barbecue tonight on the beach. We're celebrating Sage and Cannon's engagement. I thought maybe you could go with me?"

She looked up into his eyes. Eyes that threatened to melt her. "Dalton Black, are you asking my knotty-pine ass on a date?"

He thumbed her chin so she couldn't look away. "No. I'm inviting the woman who has an ass created in heaven and hip bones as sharp as anvils on a date."

"So, I'm *not* knotty?"

He pulled his lower lip into his mouth and rolled it between his teeth. When it popped free, he leaned forward and brushed his mouth over hers. "God, I hope you're naughty."

The bell above the door rang, and a large family entered.

"That's my cue to leave. See you tonight?" His expression was full of hope.

"I'll be there."

She'd say whatever he wanted to hear in order to see that smile again.

Samantha glanced at the family and thought the mom and dad looked familiar, but she couldn't come up with a name. The double doors to the kitchen swung closed when Dalton walked through them and opened again when Maisey walked out and greeted the couple and their seven children. That was a couple who spent a lot of time enjoying the "in-between."

Maisey hugged the woman and patted the telltale bump on her stomach. Baby number eight was on its way.

As a performer, she never had the time to consider marriage or children, but looking at the family in front of her caused a pang of jealousy to thread through her. She never asked for fame and fortune. She asked for a life. Maybe she should have been more specific.

CHAPTER EIGHT

An hour later, Samantha sat at her kitchen table while Marina inspected her hair. She talked about a two-step process that included bleaching and dying or something of that nature. All Samantha cared about was blending in.

"I appreciate you making a house call."

Marina gave her a weak smile. "I could use the distraction." She lifted her arms, making her shirt rise up. The bruises on her stomach had faded to a pale yellow.

"There are places you can go for help."

At first, Samantha thought Marina would ignore her comment, but in fact, she considered her answer. "This is not what you think."

"My imagination is pretty active and often accurate. My father abused my mother. We escaped but looked over our shoulders for years. How sad is it that the day he died was the day our lives began?"

Marina unpacked a bag of supplies and covered Samantha's shoulders with a navy blue cape. Why did women insist on protecting their abusers? It was obvious Marina had suffered some kind of trauma. "Are you running from something? Someone?"

"Are you?" she countered. "There are many kinds of abuse. They all hurt the same."

Samantha considered her words. Bruises healed, but the words stayed inside and beat you up repeatedly. Abuse was abuse no matter what form it came in.

Cool liquid gushed from a bottle onto her hair. "Why do you stay?"

"Why did you?"

She hated it when people answered questions with questions. "It took time to get a plan together."

"Ditto." That was the end of the conversation. Marina worked in silence as Samantha thought about her own life. Coming to Aspen Cove was the beginning, but not the end.

Two hours later, she looked at herself in the mirror. Samantha White was back.

Marina had breathed new life into her tired persona. She couldn't wait to show off her true self. Would Dalton like her hair now that it was brown, or was it the edginess of the blue that attracted him?

"You have no idea what you did for me today." Samantha handed her several hundred dollars.

"That's too much." She tried to pass back everything but a hundred.

Samantha closed her hand over the hand of the woman who had given her a fresh start. "Put it to work in your plan."

Marina looked down at the pile of twenties. When her head lifted, tears filled her eyes. "You have no idea what this means."

Samantha pulled her in for a hug. "You'd be surprised."

As soon as the hairdresser left, Samantha found herself back in front of the mirror, staring at her reflection. How had things gotten so out of hand that she'd let another person define who she was?

Her thoughts went to Marina. Desperation made people do crazy things. Samantha didn't know why smart women stayed in bad situations. Society would say they were dumb, but when the options came down to living or dying, the choice got easier. When your choice is between dying by starvation or dying at the hand of an asshole, the choice was less clear because the outcome remained the same.

In many ways, Samantha had already experienced death. The beatings her mom took were the death of her childhood. Signing a long-term contract was the death of her choices. Now Samantha White was back and ready to live again.

She applied blush, mascara, and lip gloss before getting dressed for the bonfire. An internal debate warred inside her on whether she should wear nice jeans or worn jeans. It was funny how worn jeans cost twice as much for less fabric. A good shredding cost big bucks these days. She paired the torn jeans with a white T-shirt and hoodie. The weather had stayed in the mid-sixties all day and only now dipped down to the fifties. With a fire pit and a hot man, Samantha was certain she'd stay plenty warm.

Dalton said it was a date, but did he mean a *date-date* or a *come-hang-out-with-me date?*

Deanna's words echoed in her head. *"You can't keep him."* Maybe not, but she could enjoy him for a while, couldn't she? At least she could enjoy his kisses. That was probably the smartest plan. Don't let it get past a hug or a kiss or two … or ten. He was an excellent kisser, and Samantha found no reason to waste those talents.

She heard voices and music coming from the lake side of her property. Her stomach grumbled, and she hoped they would serve food. All she'd eaten was the breakfast Dalton had cooked. It was enough to feed an army, but not enough to last her all day.

She grabbed a piece of bread and walked outside. Several people milled about the property two doors down. She leaned against the deck rail and watched as Katie talked and laughed with a tiny redhead.

A tall man came up behind Katie and kissed her on the cheek. She'd recognize him anywhere. Bowie Bishop always commanded attention. When he stepped around his wife, he handed her a baby.

Katie never mentioned a child, but then again they had shared little beyond baked goods and hair stories. The way she cooed over the infant twisted Samantha's stomach into knots. It was obvious the child was adored, and the parents were in love. Had her mother ever had a single moment of such bliss? Would she?

Out of the corner of her eye, she saw movement. A big lumbering bear of a man hopped off his deck and headed her way. She could smell his cologne before he arrived. It was a mix of clean linen and citrus.

"You ready?" He took the steps up to her deck two at a time. In front of her, he stood still and stared. "Wow." He ran his fingers through the hair that floated over her shoulder. "Done with that phase of your life?"

Phase was right. "Yep, this is the real me. Still want that date?"

He pulled his lower lip between his teeth. It was the sexiest thing she'd seen in a long time. There would definitely be more kisses.

"You're beautiful."

She'd been told that a lot, but not by anyone that mattered, and somehow, Dalton mattered. Was it because she'd had a twelve-week crush on him as a kid? Or was it because he still didn't know who she was and he liked her anyway?

"I am?" she asked sweetly. "I wasn't sure you'd like it."

He pulled her back from the rail and pressed her against the wall in the dark corner of her deck. "This is how much I like it." Hidden in the shadows, he kissed her senseless. How his kisses could suck the air from her lungs and weaken her knees was a mystery. No kiss she could remember had ever been so powerful. It was like she found her next breath in his lungs. She never wanted to break the kiss.

He stood back and licked his lips. "Grape?"

She nodded. Cheap lip gloss was her guilty pleasure. Deanna bought it in bulk from Walmart. "I have watermelon, too."

She felt like a teenager, not a twenty-nine-year-old woman.

"I'd love to taste that as well."

"It can be arranged." He looked over his shoulder at the group growing around the bonfire. "Are you ready to meet the gang?"

Am I? Indigo screamed, "No," but Samantha stood tall and said, "Yes. I can't wait to meet everyone." A knot of fear tugged at her insides. Had Katie told anyone who she was? That was the problem with fame. It was hard to tell who were true friends. Hard to know who was trustworthy. Hard to get close to people.

Dalton ran his tongue across her lower lip. "I think I got it all. I'm ready to test the watermelon."

She pushed at his chest. "You ate all my gloss." She pulled the tube from her back pocket and applied a new coat.

"I knew you'd have me covered." He dipped down for another quick kiss before he folded his hand around hers and led her to his friends.

Katie was the first to rush over. She adjusted her hold on her baby and gave Samantha a side hug. "You came. Dalton said he invited you."

Dalton let his fingers run languidly across her lower back. The touch sent a kinetic energy zipping through her. She felt truly alive. "I'll be right back," he said and disappeared into the house behind them, leaving her missing him already.

"I hope it's okay that I'm crashing your party."

"You're making it better." Katie's eyes went to Samantha's hair. "Marina has some skills." She walked around Samantha, checking out the color from all angles. "It looks so natural."

"She did a good job. It's exactly how I remember my hair used to be." Samantha couldn't stop twirling a lock around her finger. It felt so soft and thick and ... like *her.*

"Did she say much to you while she was at your house?" Katie looked down at her bundled up baby and smiled.

"No, she was friendly but reserved."

Katie's smile turned upside down. "I looked at her wish."

"It's none of my business, but is it grantable?"

She shook her head. "Not really. It was cryptic. All it said was she needed a plan B. Did you get the impression that she was in trouble?"

"The bruises on her face were my first clue, but she has to help herself before anyone else can help her." Samantha knew that from experience.

She looked down at the baby sleeping in Katie's arms.

"You want to hold her?"

As strange as it might be, Samantha had never held a baby in her life. They appeared so tiny and frail and complicated. "No, that's okay."

Katie had already shifted the baby forward, leaving her no choice but to offer up the cradle of her arms. "She won't break. Her name is Sahara. She's my little miracle."

Samantha held the baby with stiff arms. Although differently shaped, she wasn't much heavier than Deanna's poodle—but Sahara was so much cuter. "How old is she?"

"About three months."

"She's beautiful." Samantha lifted the bundled baby and smelled the scent everyone talked about. Babies had a smell all their own that was pure heaven. "You say she's a miracle?"

"Long story, but I'll give you the short version." Katie told her tale about two women, one heart, the perfect man, passionate love, and faith.

"Holy shit. I can't even write stuff that good."

"You did." She looked around as if to make sure no one was in earshot. "Your song 'Empty Box' is one of my favorites."

Dalton approached carrying a glass of wine and a beer. "Which one would you like?"

Samantha gave Katie the baby back and took the wine from Dalton. "I'll stick with what I know. Besides, wine has fewer calories."

Dalton quirked a brow and switched drinks with her, handing her the beer. "You need the calories. Did you eat anything else today?"

Katie looked at them with curiosity and smiled. "Got a protector already. Dalton's a keeper."

With little thought, Samantha blurted, "Oh, I can't keep him. I won't be here that long."

If frowns could darken the moment, Samantha stood in pitch black. Katie shrugged and nodded toward the redhead walking toward them. "That's what Sage said, and it's been a year."

"I hear we have a new resident." Sage walked over to Samantha and offered her a handshake.

"Yes, I'm Samantha White."

Sage laughed a full belly laugh. "We've got a White," she looked at Dalton, "and a Black." She stood next to Katie and wrapped her arm around her shoulder. It was obvious they were friends. Samantha hoped that someday she could stay somewhere long enough to make lasting connections. "Looks like we have to be the gray in-between."

Katie shook her head. "No way, gray isn't my color."

Samantha watched Sage for any hint of recognition. There wasn't any. If she knew who Samantha was, she was good at hiding the knowledge.

"Doc is on the deck, grilling burgers," Sage said.

Katie looked over her shoulder. "Last time he was the grill

master, I found out I was pregnant. Who's next?" She looked at Sage and Samantha who had stepped back several feet.

"I know what causes that," Sage said. "I'm protected from that particular problem." They all turned toward Samantha.

"Don't look at me. There are certain activities that one has to take part in to ... you know. I haven't taken part in quite some time." The heat of a blush raced across her cheeks. She'd just told several strangers she'd been celibate.

Katie and Sage looked surprised. Dalton looked pleased. "Let's feed you." He rested his hand on the small of her back and walked her up the steps to where an old guy manned the grill. The man from the diner.

"Doc, this is our newest resident, Samantha White."

Doc looked her up and down and shook his head. He plated her up a hot dog and a burger, then reached inside a bag of chips and dumped a super-sized serving on her plate. "Eat up, young lady. You're too thin."

Samantha gasped and looked at Dalton. "Have you been talking to him?"

Doc laughed. "You think she's thin too?" Doc gave her another look. "I'd guess a hundred pounds fully clothed."

Feeling the need to defend her physique, she said, "One hundred and four, bare-assed naked."

Doc forked another dog and slapped it on her plate. "Eat up, young lady. From the look on Dalton's face, you're going to need it."

"Oh my God." She marched away with two hot dogs, a hamburger, and a mountain of chips. She took a seat on the ground a few feet away from the frozen lake.

Before she knew it, two dogs bounded forward. She held her plate of food in the air while the canines tried to lick her to death.

"Otis. Bishop. Down, boys." Dalton shooed the dogs away. The chocolate lab chased after the three-legged retriever.

"I wanted to be the one to kiss you before dinner." Dalton sank to the ground beside her.

She tried to mimic the stern tone of his voice. "Dalton. Down, boy."

He looked at her plate, piled a mile high. "How about we share that?"

"What? Are you afraid my knotty-pine ass will get too big if I eat it all?"

"Your ass is perfect. Let's forget I said you were skinny. I'd like to take it back." He took the plate of food and set it next to her. He pushed the beer bottle into the soft ground beside her where he also put the glass of wine. "Let's start over."

"Okay." She smiled. "Hi, I'm Samantha White, and I heard you are a perfect kisser."

He held her hands. "Hello, Samantha White, I'm Dalton Black, and I think you're perfect all around." He leaned in and brushed his lips over hers. "I know you're not staying, but maybe while you're here we can be friends." He gave her a heart-stopping smile.

"Does that friendship include kisses?"

"We can negotiate as we go."

They sat together in front of the lake, which quickly became her favorite place. They ate and laughed and talked. All the Bishop couples joined them. There was Sage and Cannon, Ben and Maisey, and Katie and Bowie. Then Doc joined, followed by Otis, who was happy to gobble up leftovers until Bishop took over.

She'd escaped to Aspen Cove to rest, or so she thought, but maybe she'd come here to think. Being surrounded by people who cared about each other was plenty to provoke her musings.

At the end of the evening, Dalton walked her back to her place. He hadn't kissed her once since that brief touch earlier. He'd been the perfect gentleman. She wondered if her intent to leave was the reason he kept his distance.

"How are those supplies holding up?"

"You want to talk about food?"

"No, I wanted to tell you I'm heading to Copper Creek to pick up a few things tomorrow. Do you want to come with me?"

Everything about Dalton screamed "sexy"—from the way he licked a drop of wine from his lips to the way he watched her eat her hot dog. He said, "Come with me" like it was an offer of more than a ride into town.

"Mr. Black, are you asking me out on a second date?" His boyish smile belied the hulking man in front of her.

"I think I might be. That leaves us one away from our third. You know what they say about third dates ..."

She knew exactly what they said. Third dates were the put-out-or-get-out date. "Are you really a third-date-rule man?"

"There are rules?" He kissed her cheek. "I was going to say on the third date, I'd show you my skills." He waited a moment, knowing full well what that implied. "My culinary skills, that is. I'll cook for you." He turned and walked away.

He was long gone, but she stared at where he had stood. Dalton Black knew she was leaving and planned to woo her anyway.

CHAPTER NINE

Normally, he didn't pay much attention to what he wore. Today, he stood in his closet and looked at the rainbow of T-shirts in front of him. He was spending the day with Samantha. He didn't know why that made him so happy, but it did.

She said she was leaving, which he understood. Aspen Cove didn't have much to offer, but he hoped she'd change her mind.

He tugged the bluish gray T-shirt off the hanger. Something about Samantha pulled at his natural instincts to nurture. He remembered the sullen little girl who looked at the world from the outskirts. She was skittish and unsure—almost afraid. Behind her brassy persona he saw glimpses of that same fear, and he wondered what she was running from.

He whipped up a few breakfast sandwiches and grabbed a yogurt from the refrigerator before he walked over to her cabin.

She answered the door wearing yoga pants, a long shirt and a smile. "Come in, I have to grab my watermelon lip gloss." She looked over her shoulder as she walked away. All he could think about was making sure she had to apply that all day long.

"I brought you breakfast." He walked in and stood next to the doorway.

She returned holding the tube of gloss in the air. "Still trying to fatten me up?"

He shook his head. "No. Eating in front of you would be rude, so I brought you food." Truth was he wanted to fatten her up. She was beyond underweight, but he could see she was fit and seemed healthy. He pulled one sandwich from his coat pocket. He unwrapped it and took a bite. Nothing went together better than bread, cheese, eggs and bacon.

"You got one of those for me?" She moved toward him like a bug to a light.

He teased her. He took another bite and slowly chewed before he swallowed. All the while, she watched the bacon peeking past the sourdough bread. "I brought you a yogurt. Seemed more your thing." He reached into his right pocket for the strawberry yogurt.

She deflated in front of him like a punctured raft. "Oh, yes, that's probably a better choice." She reached forward to take what he offered.

He held it out of her reach. "Or ... you could have what's behind door number two."

Her chin lifted, and her eyes sparkled with interest. "Ooh ... I'm intrigued."

"Are you now?" With food in both hands, he lifted them into the air. "Tell me, what intrigues you?"

She looked him up and down like he was a tasty meal and for a minute he wished he were.

"Everything. I want everything." She sounded so excited and happy. He would have a hard time denying her.

"Let's start with breakfast." He walked into her kitchen and set the yogurt on the table before he pulled the other sandwich from his pocket and offered it to her.

"I think I may love you already." She unwrapped it and took a bite. The humming sounds of satisfaction she made sent his heart racing and body parts pulsing. So as not to embarrass himself by the swell in his jeans, he turned around and opened the door.

"We should go." The cold air hit, and any evidence of his desire disappeared. "It's chilly, so grab a jacket." He zipped his up to his chin. Yesterday was hot. Today was cold. Weather was as confusing as women.

Dalton led her to his truck where he opened her door and helped her inside. When she raised the sandwich to take a bite, he took one instead.

"Hey, that's mine." She pulled it aside like it was something to be treasured. Something more than a simple egg sandwich.

"We can share." He'd finished his in four bites. Hers looked better, but maybe that was because she looked at it like she looked at him—with hungry eyes. He shut the door and made his way to the driver's side.

By the time he buckled in, she turned in her seat to face him. "You want more of what I got?"

One thing Samantha was good at was the art of double entendre.

"What are you offering?" After last night's kiss and the declaration that she was leaving, Dalton wasn't sure how to proceed. He didn't know how to do short-term unless it was *really* short-term, like one night. Before incarceration, he had a long-term girlfriend. Casey had been at the bar that fateful night. She'd stuck with him through the trial, but as soon as he went away, so did she. On their final visit, she said his reputation would ruin her. He knew that to be true. No one would give him the chance to prove he was something other than a killer.

He'd decided then to be a hit-it-and-quit-it guy, but Samantha seemed different. Outside she gave the impression of a good-time girl, but her kisses weren't those of a woman who practiced hit and run.

There was an innocence and awe about the way she responded to him. Like she'd never been truly kissed in her life. That made him think ... just maybe he could risk more with her. Until she said she couldn't keep him.

They sat in front of the fire last night. Everyone paired up except Doc, who'd remained single since his wife's death. Dalton didn't want to be like him, old and alone. His friends were blissfully happy and moving forward with their lives. He wanted that for himself, but he didn't know how to get it. He was on pause.

"Where do you need to stop today?" he asked as he backed out of the driveway.

"We can stop where I need to go too?" She said it like it was a shock. "I thought we were running your errands."

"Doesn't mean we can't run yours too. What do you need?"

She rolled those pretty dark eyes. "The real question is, what *don't* I need?"

"All right. Let's phrase it this way. What do you want?" He knew what he wanted. He wanted her. In his head, it made sense. They could have fun while she was here. His heart knew better. He finished one kiss and wanted the next. She was like that extra piece of pie you wanted but knew you shouldn't have because there was no stopping once you tasted it.

"I want a television. I want groceries. I want a new cell phone."

"All right. That helps with logistics. We'll hit the phone store first, then the electronics store. I'd love to take you to lunch at my favorite burger place, and then we'll grocery shop before we head back to Aspen Cove. Sound good?"

"Perfect. Grocery shopping was all you had on your list?"

"And lunch."

"It's always food with you."

"Not always." He turned the radio on. "But I like to taste

307

things." He risked a quick glance at her. "How much lip gloss did you bring?"

Her wide smile told him she had plenty. She wet her lips with a single lick. It was sexy and seductive and super hot because Dalton knew she wasn't trying. She was responding to her base instincts. Samantha didn't have to try. She was stunning. He liked women who didn't require much maintenance. Samantha was that girl. She could wear a trash bag cinched at the waist and make it look good.

A song played on the radio he recognized. It had the same rhythm as the music Samantha played that night on the beach.

"You were playing this song."

Out of the corner of his eye, he could see her nod. "I like it."

"Do you know the lyrics?"

She laughed. "By heart." She fidgeted in her seat and pulled at the belt across her chest. "It's a song about looking like you have it all but knowing inside you're hollow."

"Sounds grim." He didn't know what it looked like to have it all, but he sure knew what hollow felt like. It felt like six years in prison. Coming home to find that life went on without you was brutal.

"No, not so much grim as honest. I think we all hide behind the truth that people make for us. It may not be the truth as we see it for ourselves."

He thought about that for a few minutes. He knew how people viewed him. He also knew he wasn't that man. "Yes, but once you're labeled, it's often who you become."

She nodded. "A shame, really, because I think we are so much more as a whole than as the various parts people focus on."

He knew he liked her, but that statement confirmed it. "What do you think is worse, lying to yourself about who you are, or lying to others?" He'd spent the last year telling himself he was fine being an island. He didn't need anything but his job or anyone other than his friends and family. Those were lies. He'd had dreams that were dashed by a dose of gallantry.

She turned her body to face him and leaned against the door. "I think we all lie to ourselves, and in lying to ourselves, we lie to others. Don't let your lie become your truth." She hummed along with the song until the music faded into the next.

"You have a beautiful voice. Have you considered a career in music?"

She laughed until she choked. "Sure, it's crossed my mind."

"You laugh, but you are good." She had a voice like a lover's caress. He could listen to her serenade him all day. "Seriously, sing me something."

"You want me to sing you a song?" She reached into her pocket and slicked on more gloss, which only made his mouth water for another kiss. "What song?"

"Whatever, but I love the oldies." He could picture her singing anything from Stevie Nicks to Aretha.

She leaned forward and changed the radio station until it landed on his favorite music channel. When the Lynyrd Skynyrd song "Freebird" played, and she belted out the lyrics like she'd written them. He was a goner.

"Wow."

"I can't do the original justice, but what a great song. Kind of sad when you think about the lyrics. It's about a man explaining to a woman why he can't settle down and make a commitment. He has to let her go."

He hated to ask, but he needed to know. "Speaking of leaving, how long do you plan to stay?"

"As long as I can. Work can be demanding and unpredictable."

"Do you love what you do?" He turned onto the highway that led to Copper Creek.

She pulled her upper lip between her teeth. Over the last few days, he'd seen her do that when the question was tough.

"I love many aspects about my job. I dislike others, but isn't that the nature of work? Some days are good. Some days are bad. Do you like your job every day?"

He did. He loved to cook, but cooking at Maisey's wasn't the dream. "I love what I do."

"Lucky you. You're living the dream."

"I didn't say that. I said I love what I do, but cooking in my mom's diner wasn't the dream." He gripped the steering wheel until he felt the texture of the leather on his palms.

"So, what was the dream, and why aren't you going after it?"

"It's complicated." He gave her a quick glance and saw the softness and acceptance in her expression. Would she be that accepting if she learned the truth? He didn't want to find out. She was leaving, so the truth didn't matter. "I wanted to open a culinary school."

"So why don't you?"

It all sounded so easy when she said it, but it wasn't easy. "I never finished school. I was about to when I got into some legal trouble." He waited for her to ask for more details, but she didn't.

"You can still finish." Her voice lifted in excitement. "What's stopping you?"

Her excitement bled into him. "You're right. I could. I'll give it some thought. I've got stuff to take care of first." Prison gobbled up the best years of his life. The years he could have used to make a name for himself. Who wanted to learn to cook from a guy who spent more time in a penitentiary than a kitchen?

Conversation ate up the rest of the trip, and before he knew it, they were pulling into a place where she could get a phone and a television.

When the salesperson offered to back up the old phone to the new phone, she said she wanted a new number. She said it with such desperation that Dalton was sure Samantha had secrets too.

CHAPTER TEN

The whole point of getting a new phone was so she wouldn't have to see the sheer number of missed calls and emails from her agent and manager, not to mention auxiliary staff and the few reporters she knew well.

Turns out that walking into a crowd after a concert and disappearing wasn't the way to lie low. Indigo was the new *Where's Waldo.*

With a phone in hand, she followed Dalton to where televisions lined the walls.

"If you were trying to hide, you could have gotten a burner phone. It would have cost less than setting up a new account."

Her heart hammered in her chest. Hiding was the objective, but she hadn't realized she'd been so transparent with her actions.

"I'm separating work from my personal life. I've been here for a few days, and my phone has been on fire with a work-related crisis." The crisis being her disappearance. No less than fifty calls and emails had been flooding her phone daily.

Desperate measures were propelled by desperation. At the risk of losing herself completely, she needed time to let herself settle back into a normal life. Getting a phone where the only people to call were vetted was part of the process.

With her brown hair and toned-down clothes, she hoped to blend in. After one glance around the electronics superstore, she realized no one paid her any mind. Maybe she considered herself more important than she was.

"They say size matters." Dalton looked at her with a devilish grin. "How big do you like yours?"

She held in the laughter and played along. At the end were the small screens. She stopped and stared at the monitors no bigger than a laptop.

"This one lacks length and girth. While it would do the job, it doesn't impress me. I fear the experience would be unsatisfying."

Dalton barely controlled his laughter. His shoulders shook as she followed him down the row.

"What about this?" He pointed to a wide screen television. One that was long and narrow.

She stood in front of it and analyzed the proportions. "Do you really think length is more important than width?"

He rubbed his finely trimmed beard with his calloused hands. The scruffy sound filled in the surrounding silence. "This size makes sure in the long run you don't miss an inch of what's there. Having said that, I imagine having a balance between the two is more important." He moved all the way to the end, where eighty inches hung on the wall in front of them. "Now this is a beast. It's got it all."

Samantha looked at Dalton. As much as she tried to keep her eyes on his face, they rolled down his body.

Tension skirted through her the second they talked length and girth. It appeared he wasn't unaffected either. Hanging toward the right between his legs was the growing evidence. If Dalton Black had been a television, he would have been a high-definition big screen.

She cleared her head and looked at the beast hanging on the wall in front of her. "That would never fit."

He moved behind her and rested his chin on the top of her head. She wanted to lean back into his body but was afraid she'd be poked by his specifications.

"You can always make room for what you desire." He left her in front of the massive television with her mouth hanging open. Were they still talking about TVs? Had they ever been talking about TVs?

She couldn't deny they shared a mutual attraction. She knew it before the first kiss. Hell, she knew it when she was twelve. He was like a live wire that skirted over her skin.

Hot.

Tingling.

Powerful.

When she got to where he stood in front of another large unit, she said, "I have little experience with this kind of thing." Again, not talking about televisions. "I'm used to the standard size you find in hotels and such."

He turned to face her. "You don't want to settle for small. You'll walk away feeling disappointed."

"I get that, but if it's too big, I may not walk at all." She grabbed the salesman and asked him to ring up the size in the middle.

At the register, the cashier told her she owed $1842.36. She pulled out a brick of twenties wrapped with a purple band.

"Cash?" Dalton asked. The scar above his eye lifted.

She stared at him and smiled. "It's easier to use." She paid, and they took her purchases to the truck.

He helped her inside. While he rounded the front of the truck, she texted Deanna and her mother the new phone number.

"You hungry?"

"Starved." Who knew electronics could give her such an appetite?

Ten minutes later, they pulled in front of a little hole-in-the-wall diner called Chachi's. It was modeled after the sitcom *Happy Days*. He raced around to help her out. She loved how he could be so chivalrous and yet not. His talk was anything but gentlemanly, but he treated her like she mattered. Not as a means to influence his portfolio, but as a human. Her value wasn't dependent on her net worth. He seemed to appreciate her for who she was in that moment.

"My treat," Samantha said. She took the seat in the far booth where she could see everything around her. She was feeling brazen and brave having made it through a store without the slightest nod of recognition.

"You're not paying. I don't care how many bricks of cash are in your purse. I pay for my date."

She felt giddy inside. "So exciting." She'd never been on an actual date. She'd ordered room service and watched movies on pay-per-view, but all of those 'dates' ended up on her hotel tab.

"You're easy."

She giggled. "Yes, but not cheap." She took the menu from the stand and looked over the offerings. She would be easy and cheap since the most expensive item on the menu was under ten bucks. "What do you recommend?"

"You want me to order for you?" He slid the menu from her hands and turned it to face him. "You trust me?"

She trusted him, which was odd because she didn't trust most men. "It's food. You're a chef. I trust you."

When he smiled, she knew her trust in him was important.

A young male waiter named Todd came over and stood in front of them. He looked at Dalton, then at her, but his eyes focused on her. He stared for what seemed like an eternity before a grin took over his face.

"You're—"

"Starving." She hoped that line hadn't lost its magic. It worked at the bakery, and she prayed it would work here.

Todd nodded his head and pulled a pen from behind his ear. "What would you like?"

Samantha looked to Dalton who cleared his throat to get the waiter's attention. "The lady will have the Joanie, and I'll have The Fonz. We'll share a plate of Happy Fries. Bring us two chocolate malts."

Todd scribbled the order down and took one last long look at Samantha before he left.

She knew she'd been recognized but hoped he'd respect her privacy. She was on a date and didn't want it ruined.

"You shouldn't be carrying so much cash around. Purple bands means two grand. People get mugged for less."

"How would you know what a purple band holds? Are you a numismatist?"

His long arms had no problem reaching across the table to hold her hands. His thumbs brushed over her knuckles. "No, I like money but not enough to collect it or study it. I had a roommate who knew a lot about how the banks bundled money. Talked about it all the time." He ran his thumbs across her unadorned fingers. She'd never worn a ring. Had never been one for much jewelry.

The day her mom pawned her wedding ring to get food, Samantha promised herself she wouldn't let a ring grace her fingers until she was one hundred percent certain about the giver. It was an unrealistic expectation because it was impossible to be one hundred percent sure about anything or anyone.

"Yeah, money is good to have when you need things, but it's not the panacea for the world's problems."

"If you had the solution to the world's problems, you wouldn't need money. You'd be filthy rich."

"Is that what you want? To be filthy rich?" She liked that she could sit with a man who had no idea of her worth. At the last tally, it was over a one hundred and twenty million. It wasn't like she had that much money in the bank, but her talent was bankable. She had enough that she wouldn't have to work again. It wasn't her future she worried about these days. Lots of people depended on her. Her mother and dozens of employees would suffer without her. It was their future that kept her on stage.

"I'm not motivated by money," Dalton said as the waiter delivered everything they ordered at once. He picked up a fry drenched in a cheesy meat sauce. "I'm motivated by food." He looked at Todd, who stood staring at Samantha. "We're good," he said and waited for the waiter to walk away before he looked directly at her with those beautiful steel blue eyes. "Oh, and kisses. Not any kisses though. I particularly like yours."

She lifted the top bun to see what was hiding beneath. Turns out, the Joanie burger was a fully loaded cardiac arrest waiting to happen. Massive patty, covered in cheese, bacon, grilled mushrooms, and green chili. She wasn't sure she'd be able to get it into her mouth. Then she remembered what Dalton said in the electronics store. *You can always make room for what you desire.* She wanted it all.

When Todd came back to collect their plates, he stared once more. "I like your hair."

Dalton lifted his palms in the air. "Dude, are you trying to be annoying, or does it come naturally for you?"

He gave Dalton a look that could kill, and then he addressed Samantha. "I see why you'd need protection, but surely you can afford someone with better manners."

Dalton's fingers folded into fists. She wasn't sure what he'd do if Todd continued. Didn't want to find out.

"You have a phone?" she asked. "I'm not who you think I am, but what the hell. I get mistaken for her a lot." She moved out of the booth and stood next to Todd who pulled his phone from his apron pocket and lifted it for a selfie.

"Who does he think you are?" Dalton asked.

Samantha waved his question away with a flick of her wrist and stood next to Todd. She put her standard peace sign in front of her chest and smiled. On tiptoes, she kissed his cheek while he snapped the picture.

"I'm a huge fan. Like, obsessive."

"I'm sure she appreciates it." Samantha turned so Dalton couldn't see the wink she gave Todd. "Have a great day. Be cool."

"Ready?" Dalton startled her with his voice whispering in her ear.

"I am."

When they were both in the truck, he asked, "Does that happen a lot?"

She sighed. "More than you could imagine."

Their next stop was Walmart. Samantha hadn't been in one since she was a kid, but they were perfect because it was a one-stop shopping experience. Hell, she could have bought her phone and television here as well. Then again, it might not have been as much fun.

"What do you need?" she asked him.

"Food for an overnighter times two."

"You're leaving?"

"I'll be close. Bowie, Cannon, and I will do some ice fishing tonight and tomorrow before it gets too warm. We like to fish the cove."

"I'm kind of sad that you won't be around. You're like my guilty pleasure."

"You haven't seen pleasure yet." He picked up a bag of oranges and a bunch of bananas.

"Like you, I like our kisses a lot." She lowered her head to hide the blush of truth.

He pushed forward, and then waited for her to catch up. "That's only the beginning, but here's the problem. You're leaving, and that means we probably have to skip the in-between. And I kind of like the in-between."

She pushed her cart down the aisle and tossed in various varieties of fruit, from grapes to apples. *This shopping stuff is awesome.*

"Can't we go with it and see where it leads?"

He left his cart alone and sidled up next to her so his body touched hers on one side. "You already know where this will lead. The question is, how long will it take for us to get there?"

"Since you're leaving, at least two days."

He nuzzled his beard into the crook of her neck. It felt deliciously good.

She ducked away from his touch. It was too ticklish and tantalizing. She wanted him in a place where she could savor every whisker that brushed against her skin.

"We haven't hit the third date yet. You know there's a third-date rule. Besides, outside of breakfast, I'm not sure you can cook. I haven't seen it yet."

"I'll show you my skills, but you'll have to wait until I get back."

"It will be so hard." She emphasized the last word.

He groaned. "You have no idea."

She raced ahead, tossing whatever looked good in her basket. If she couldn't have him, she'd have chocolate and cake and chocolate and pie and chocolate.

CHAPTER ELEVEN

What the hell was he doing? Dalton popped the cap off another beer and stared across the lake to the cabin next door to his. Shadows in her window caught his attention.

"What's she like?" Cannon asked.

"She's nice." He took a deep drink and savored the bubbling burn as it moved down his throat. *She was nice. Nice to look at. Nice to be with. Nice to talk to. Nice to kiss.*

"Is this already a thing between you two?" Bowie pulled up a chair and sat next to Dalton.

It seemed funny they were sitting on a sheet of ice in the middle of a lake, but that's where they were. How crazy was it that he left a woman happy to share her warm cabin—and most likely her bed—for the company of two dudes, a six-pack of beer, and a case of frostbite?

"Are we a thing? I don't even know what that is. Do I like her? Yes. Is it going to get serious? No. She's leaving." His voice sank on the last word.

"You say that like it bothers you." Cannon tossed a piece of cardboard onto the ice and sat on top of it. "She *says* she's leaving, but so did Sage. That woman had nothing but an exit plan when she arrived. Maybe you can change Samantha's mind."

"You're forgetting the details. Sage was unemployed. Samantha owns a PR company or runs it or works there. I don't know exactly. All I know, is her life isn't here in Aspen Cove."

"You kiss her?" Now it was Bowie's turn to ask the stupid questions.

"What am I, fifteen? I don't need a year to get to first base." He'd rushed straight for first, but held off stealing second and beyond.

The brothers looked at each other. "I guess that's a yes," Cannon said. "Since you're our brother and all, we're looking out for you."

He cut them a sharp look that dared them to argue. "Like you did for each other? No, thanks. One of you went from monk to married. And you," he pointed to Cannon, "are running to catch up."

"Don't knock it until you try it," Bowie answered.

"Not happening." He'd given it a lot of thought over the last year. He'd seen the faces of the women who heard about his past. One moment they were sharing a beer, the next he watched their taillights fade into the distance, never to be heard from again. "Marriage. It's not for everyone." Newlyweds surrounded Dalton. Like a bad case of the flu, no one in Aspen Cove seemed to be immune. "Can't believe my mom ran to the altar again. I never thought that would happen—and not with Ben. Your dad is great, but he has an ugly temper."

Cannon laughed and then slapped his hand over his mouth. "He only has an ugly temper when he drinks, which he no longer does. He's never hit a woman until Sage, and that was an accident."

Dalton cringed at the memory of that day when both Cannon and Sage showed up to Bea's funeral sporting black eyes. "Still, most people don't forgive and forget, but my mom did." He hoped he could get there someday. He craved the day when he could look at any person and see the good in them without trying to figure out their angle first. He wanted a day to come when people could see him for who he was, not the crime he committed.

Bowie nodded his head while an "Ahh ..." left his mouth. "Samantha doesn't know about your incarceration."

"No, and I'm not telling her. If she were staying, it would be a different matter, but she's not. It's not like I'm Charles Manson and get off on killing people. It was a one-time event." He considered Lucy's advice and spoke it out loud. "I'm not going to strip down and blurt out I have herpes."

Bowie leaned back too far, and his chair tumbled, sending him to the ice. He scrambled up. "You what? Who the hell gave you herpes?"

Dalton let out a growl that could frighten a bear. "I don't have herpes. It's a figure of speech." He explained the conversation he had with his parole officer.

Cannon shook his head from side to side the whole time. "I definitely would *not* use that one again. If I were a girl, I'd much rather you be a felon than have an STD."

Bowie grabbed another beer. "I don't know. Take the proper precautions, and it's no big deal."

"So is this where I get the brotherly talk on safe sex?" Dalton finished his beer and tossed it into the plastic bag they'd set out for trash. "You know I'm older than you, right?"

Bowie handed him another. "You've got me by a month."

"Still makes me older." He lit the stove they'd set up to cook hot dogs. It wasn't more than a Sterno can on a stand, but it worked. He glanced back to the shore and wondered what Samantha was up to. *What was she doing? What was she eating? Most likely sitting in front of her big screen TV, eating fruit and chocolate, since that was what filled the bulk of her cart.*

"As for safe sex ... no glove, no love, brother," Cannon said with a chuckle.

"Am I going to regret coming fishing?" He popped the top on his beer and listened to the hissing carbonation escape.

They both shrugged and said, "Probably," in unison.

This was the first year in many that any of them had been ice fishing. Dalton's time in prison and the accident that killed Bowie and Cannon's mom and Bowie's fiancée had stalled their lives for years.

At yesterday's bonfire, they decided they had to do it now since the days were getting warmer and the ice would melt soon. They'd already wasted so much time.

Before they settled on a place, they drilled through the ice to make sure they wouldn't end up wet by morning. The cove was always the last place to melt since it sat on the shady side of the lake, surrounded by walls of granite and aspen trees.

"Is it weird?" Dalton turned to Bowie.

"Is what weird?"

In the fading light, he could see Bowie's scowl. He knew that Bowie couldn't hear his thoughts, but Dalton wondered about lots of things. He'd been curious about Katie, her wealth, her heart, and their life together. Most of all, he wondered what it felt like to be a dad.

"Being a dad."

The scowl turned into a smile. "Oh man, you have no idea what it's like to look at a tiny human being and know she's half you."

Cannon slapped Bowie's knee. "The bad half. Sad for you because babies have a no return policy. Good thing she's half Katie, or Sahara would be in trouble."

They took a package of hot dogs from the cooler and speared them onto sticks they'd found.

"You're right. Everything good about Sahara comes from Katie.

She'll grow into the bad shit later when I teach her how to fight and protect herself."

Dalton took a swig of his beer. "I'll protect her. It's what I do."

They all sat in silence. "Maybe next time you can pull a different tool out of your box other than the fist of death," Cannon said.

Dalton raised his right hand into the air. "But it's so effective." No one could argue with that.

How many women had cried over the death of Andy Kranz? How many let out a sigh of relief? How many wouldn't have to find out something sinister lay under his smile because Dalton had killed him?

Bowie rotated his hot dog over the fire and glanced toward the shore.

Dalton could tell a part of him wanted to race across the lake to get back home to Katie and his daughter.

Bowie sat up tall. "You know what I can't wait for?" He reached for a bun to cradle his charred dog. "I can't wait to hear her first laugh." He took a bite.

"Will that be soon?" Dalton knew nothing about babies. He knew they ate and pooped and slept. That was the extent of his knowledge.

"The book says it happens around three months. We'll see."

Dalton sat forward and took his dog from the flame. It was perfect, not charred like Bowie's, or undercooked like Cannon's. His was hot, sweating, and juicy.

"They come with a manual? When did that happen?" He squeezed a line of mustard on each side of the meat and took a bite. A good hot dog was almost as satisfying as a good kiss. Almost. He stared back to Samantha's cabin. *I'm such an idiot.*

"They have this book called *What To Expect The First Year.*"

"Sounds like a riveting read." Dalton continued to stare across the lake.

Cannon kicked at Bowie. "This asshole read the first tome too. It's called *What To Expect When You're Expecting*. I opened it up and took a peek. Made me want to tuck my Johnson away forever."

Bowie eyed Cannon with a marksman stare. "You're next, unless big brother over here knocks up number seven."

Dalton choked on his food. "Number seven? I've never hit the target. No babies under my belt."

Cannon impaled another hot dog onto a stick and let it sit on the flame. It took time for the small fire to cook, but building a blaze on ice wasn't recommended. "I wouldn't put *can't hit the target* on your resume either. He was talking about her address. Samantha lives at 7 Lake Circle."

"No, don't reduce her to a number. She's Samantha White." If she were getting a nickname, he'd be the one to give it to her.

"Hard to believe she used to live here." Cannon kicked back and lay on the ice facing the darkening sky. Thousands of stars flickered above them. The moon cast a glow across the white surface. A beacon leading to her door.

"I remember her mom," Bowie said. "She was a classic battered woman. I came up behind her in the Corner Store, and she knocked over three displays trying to distance herself from me. I didn't recognize it then, but in hindsight I see it now. I was big, and she was scared."

Anger coiled inside Dalton. He knew that kind of fear. He'd lived it. His mom had lived it. Now he knew Samantha had lived it. She was more than the little girl from Aspen Cove who did well. She was a survivor. She was strong. He was weak because he wouldn't survive another minute without her kiss.

CHAPTER TWELVE

Nothing cured a lonely heart better than Ben & Jerry's Chunky Monkey ice cream and binge watching *Supernatural*. It probably wasn't the best idea to watch a show about angels, demons, and any other nightmare an active imagination could conjure while being alone in a cabin on a lake, but after the first two episodes, she was hooked.

In between ice cream, candy, and an apple as her healthy addition, she peeked out the window across the lake and wondered which of the small fires glowing in the darkness was Dalton's. Shadows played with her mind and imagination. Every once in a while, she swore she heard footsteps on her deck or a knock at her door. Each time she looked, there was no one and nothing but the sway of pine branches and the whisper of the wind racing between the cabins.

Though she'd slept alone in the house since she arrived, knowing Dalton was next door comforted her. That sense of comfort now sat somewhere on the frozen lake. Thoughts of him had invaded her dreams since that first night. How could they not? He kissed like a rock star still trying to impress groupies.

Tonight, the memory of his kisses wouldn't go away. Maybe it was because he planted the seed of more to come. His words about knowing where this would end made every cell in her body spark with hope that he'd be right.

As she pressed play for season one, episode nine, the thump of heavy footsteps sounded on her porch. Her heart leaped inside her chest. Maybe those shadows in the dark weren't her imagination after all.

Had her manager found her? The press? What if it was some evil entity she conjured by watching episode after episode of a show where demonic intentions ruled the day? She looked around the cabin for a weapon, but all she had was a bag of miniature candy bars and a half-finished pint of ice cream.

A soft tap on the door had her moving forward in her stockinged feet. She crept silently forward hoping she wouldn't be heard. Maybe she could ignore whoever was there, and they would go away. When she dared to look through the peephole, her heart nearly exploded. Dalton stood on her doorstep. His hair mussed. His cheeks rosy. Sexy as ever. No way she could, or would, ignore him. He was here for more.

She swung the door wide and threw herself at him.

"Hey, good to see you too." He wrapped his arms around her until they were glued chest-to-chest. He shuffled both their bodies through the doorway and closed it behind them. "I missed you too."

"You did?" She pressed tighter into his hold, not wanting to pull her face from his chest. He smelled so earthy and manly. One deep inhale and the scent of him filled her. He was citrus and pine and campfire with a hint of hot dog.

"Yes, I did." He brushed his lips to the top of her head. "I can't get you out of my mind."

"Do you want to?"

He placed his hands gently at her waist and lifted. Instinctively, she wrapped her legs around him, feeling his desire press between her thighs. If that fire didn't ignite her flame, she didn't know what would. They were body-to-body and now mouth-to-mouth as he kissed her with such intensity, she thought she'd implode. His tongue slipped between her lips, causing her to melt in his arms. He made love to her mouth, giving her a taste of what it would be like when he made love to her body. Energy passed between them, raw, hungry, and carnal.

With her glued to him, he walked her to the couch and fell onto the soft leather, pulling her down but not once breaking the kiss. His hands explored her body, first over her shirt until he found his way beneath it. His rough, calloused fingertips left a blazing trail of desire wherever he touched.

Seconds turned into minutes as they enjoyed the feel and flavor of each other. A shift of her body pressed her into his hardness. The firmness she felt told her they were pressing hard and fast toward more.

There were so many things she should tell him before they crossed that threshold. She pulled back, heaving for breath.

"Dalton, there are things you should know about me." While her mind told her to wait, her fingers pulled down the zipper of his jacket. His help was appreciated when he yanked the coat off and tossed it into the corner. She ran her fingers over the cotton covered, rippling muscles of his chest.

Quick as a flash, his hands moved under her shirt to her bare belly and grazed her heated skin from waistband to breasts. He stopped at the edge of her bra.

"Are you married?" his deep voice murmured.

"What?" It was so hard to think when his fingers skimmed under the lace. "No."

"Engaged?" He brushed his thumbs across the soft material. "No."

"Then I don't care," he growled. "All I care about is this thing burning between us."

"There are things you should know."

He sat up until she straddled his lap and their chests touched. Her pebbled nipples sent code to her core, which sent the message of *shut up* to her brain.

He quirked a sexy brow at her. "You want to exchange resumes?" He ran his lips over her collarbone, biting down with enough force to make her gasp. "There are things you should know about me too. You want me to stop kissing you to tell you?"

Hell no, her inner voice screamed.

"Are you married?" she teased. Her hand slipped beneath the cotton of his shirt to feel the heat of his skin.

He nipped at the sensitive area that sat between her neck and shoulder. "Not married, not engaged. Tonight, I'm yours ... if you want me." His breathy reply sent shivers racing across her body. His hands dipped past her waistband and caressed her bottom.

She was done. There was nothing he could say to change her mind. He was Dalton Black, her first crush. She would have him, and she would enjoy him.

"I've got a bed."

He chuckled. "Do you now? I'd love to see it." He was beastly strong. He twisted his body so his feet hit the floor, but hers stayed glued to his.

With his hands still inside her pants, he said, "You have the nicest ass." He grabbed handfuls of it and rose while Samantha held on for the ride. He stepped between the coffee table and couch and made his way to her room.

She expected him to toss her onto the bed. Her experience was, once a bed came into play, everything went quickly from that point forward. Dalton surprised her when he lowered her gently to the edge.

Steel blue eyes once hard were now like molten glass that held a sizzling, electric heat. Although she wore an oversized shirt and leggings, he looked at her as if she wore sexy lingerie or—better yet—nothing at all.

Hungry eyes took her in, from her high ponytail to her fuzzy socks. "You're so beautiful."

She tried to stand, but he shook his head. "Let me look at you for a minute."

While he stared at her, she drank him in. He wore a colored T-shirt that would become her favorite because the silver blue of it brought out the passion in his eyes. The material stretched across his broad chest. Mountains of muscle rippled to a narrow waist. Jeans that fit him perfectly hung low on his hips and hugged thighs she knew were honed from stone.

He could take all the minutes he wanted because the view was damn fine from where she sat.

"I thought you were staying the night on the ice." Her voice barely registered above a whisper.

"That was my plan, but every time I looked across the lake and saw the light on, I knew this was where I wanted to be."

"What about your brothers?" She inched back on the bed until her entire body rested on the soft mattress.

"They're men. They get it." He bent forward to unlace his boots. Once he toed them off, he climbed onto the bed beside her. The mattress dipped under his weight, making her roll toward him. She didn't fight it. She loved the feel of being next to him. He was so large. She was so small. Together, they were perfect.

"We're breaking the third-date rule," she said.

He splayed his hand across her stomach and pressed her to the mattress. "I don't like rules."

As his palm inched up to cup her breasts, she let out a sigh. It had been so long since anyone had touched her. She nearly wept with joy.

"Our rules, our way." She pulled the hem of her shirt over her head and threw it aside. Dalton groaned at the sight of her. One good thing about having money was being able to afford nice underthings. The black lace bra was made from the finest, softest material. Though her breasts were small, his palm seemed to like the weight.

"So pretty." He leaned down and breathed heat over one tight, aching nipple. Her back arched, forcing the lacy cup against his lips. "There's no hurry. We've got all night." He left one breast and moved to the other to repeat his hot, tortuous tease.

Being all about equality, Samantha tugged at the hem of his shirt until it bunched around his chest. "I want to see you. I want to taste you."

A slow, sexy rumble vibrated through the air. Dalton reached behind him, grabbing a handful of cotton and pulling it forward and over his head.

She tugged it from his arms and lifted it to her nose. "I love the way you smell."

He shrugged. "It's a body wash Abby makes."

"Abby?" She had no idea who that was, but a thread of jealousy twisted inside her. "Who's Abby?"

"Is that jealousy in those pretty eyes?" He lifted his body and straddled her hips.

The heavy hardness of him rubbed against her, the friction was better than anything she'd felt in ages.

"No, I don't have a right to be jealous." She bit her lip, thinking about Abby and conjuring all sorts of images. Pretty blondes. Dynamic redheads. Tatted up biker chicks. She released a telling sigh. "All right. I'm a little jealous. This is my first time with you, and I don't want to share you with anyone else."

With his palms flat against her body, he caressed her skin with long, soft strokes. "There's no one here but us. Abby Garrett is a local woman who raises bees and makes soaps and stuff. It's only you and me." His hands floated over her skin. A shiver of pleasure raced through her cells, slamming straight to her core.

She sucked in a cleansing breath, trying to settle her nerves. It was sex. She'd done it before, but somehow this was different. Dalton wasn't stripping down or impatient for her to do the same. He was enjoying every second.

Rather than rush through the mechanics of joining their two bodies, Samantha got in touch with the emotions she was feeling.

Fear.

Passion.

Excitement.

Anticipation.

Love.

The last one floored her. *I don't love Dalton.* She loved the way he made her feel.

No matter where he touched—her stomach, her hair, her arms, her face—the needy ache inside her grew. Her body was already humming, and they'd barely begun.

"God, I still have my pants on, and I'm close to being finished," she panted.

He chuckled. "We're only beginning."

She traced the lines of his tattoos. "Boston? When were you there?"

A smirk of a smile graced his face. "Not the city. The band."

She needed the distraction of conversation, or she'd erupt in seconds. "You had the name of a band tattooed on your arm?" She wondered if some poor fool was sporting the name Indigo on their body.

"Bad decision. Too much alcohol." He fell forward, catching himself on his arms. While one held his weight, the other snaked around her back to unhook her bra. Dalton was dexterous—one try, and it was loose. But he didn't strip it from her in one quick movement. He peeled it from her body inch by inch. She was a gift he unwrapped, revealing the treasure slowly.

Her nipples were hard and painfully tight. His lips covered one, and the heat of his mouth sucked it in. She no longer felt the tingling discomfort. It was replaced with the most amazing sensation created by his superior oral skills. A frenzied fire that raced through her body.

Her hips pumped against him, trying to find the release she craved.

"In such a hurry," he said. His lips touched her breast. The vibration of his words coursed through her. "Don't rush to the end when the middle is so much fun."

Dalton showed her how much enjoyment floating in the middle could bring. He spent minutes raking his whiskers over her breasts. Little nips and sucks added in between for her pleasure. He moved down to make love to her belly button with his tongue. Who knew that she would quiver and shake so hard? He leaned back and put his thumbs into the waistband of her pants and tugged, stripping her naked. She was grateful for the distance from his tongue, and yet she couldn't wait until it returned to torture her again.

Her labored breath slowed as the cool air rushed over her skin. She was on fire, and all she wore were fuzzy socks. Scratch that, Dalton pulled those off with his teeth and climbed up her naked body.

"Feel good?" His hands were back on her. They seemed to be everywhere. His lips and tongue teased her from her collarbone to what he'd referred to as her anvil-sharp hips.

"Be careful. I'd hate for you to poke an eye out." She ran her fingers through his hair and followed his movements down.

He looked up at her with hunger. "Heading for softer ground." His large hands rested on her legs to open them wide—wide enough for his shoulders to fit between the cradle of her thighs.

Good thing she was limber. All thoughts of being a contortionist ended when the heat of his mouth and the scruff of his beard made contact. The rough hair on his jawline scratched her delicate skin and left a delicious burn in its wake.

She'd been a taut string—a coiled mass of energy ready to spike at any moment. She never expected to come undone so fast and so furiously. He stroked her with the velvet of his tongue. Suckled her with his lips and hummed his satisfaction at her taste. She climbed higher and higher until the sensation tore through her. Dalton stayed with her for every glorious, pulsating moment.

Not to be rushed, he kept her quivering and moaning and praying for it to end and continue at the same time. When she lay next to him, wiped out and limp, he pulled her into his arms and held her tightly to his chest. He hugged her like she was important. Like she mattered.

"How is it that I've had the best sex of my life and you aren't even naked?" She stroked his dark, hair-dusted chest and followed the trail to his pants, where his quick reflexes stopped her progress.

"Sweetheart. That wasn't sex. That was foreplay."

"Oh holy hell."

He climbed off the bed. She was too weak to move. By the light of the hallway, she watched him walk away and return with a glass of water and a bowl of grapes.

He dropped his pants but not his boxers and climbed into bed beside her. She drank the water and shared a few grapes before she turned to him.

"Your turn." She covered her yawn and then dropped her hands to his magnificent chest. Her fingers touched every ridge of muscle until he threaded his fingers through hers and pulled them to his mouth for a kiss.

"I'm not keeping tabs. We've got more than tonight. We have all the nights until you leave."

After the best experience in her existence, she wasn't sure

leaving would be possible. How could a woman walk away from his talents—his tongue?

He reached over her and turned out the light, then scooted down next to her and pulled her close to his body. She'd never felt more cherished in her life. This was special. He gave more than he took. She felt happy. She felt satisfied. She felt loved.

CHAPTER THIRTEEN

Best night of his damn life, and he didn't even get laid.

The sun hadn't risen when Dalton trudged across the lake toward Bowie and Cannon with a pound of bacon and a dozen eggs tucked under his arm. He figured since he chose babe over brothers, he owed them something. Maybe a hot breakfast would reduce the variety of ways they would call him "whipped".

A layer of frost crackled beneath his boots while his breath turned to fog. What were they thinking when they planned to stay on the lake for two nights? *Idiots.*

Another decision made after too many beers. Definitely a chest-pounding Neanderthal moment of increased testosterone.

Holding Samantha in his arms all night would be worth the razzing he'd get all day. Hell, it was hard to leave her. Double hell because he was hard all night, but something told him that Samantha gave more than she received, and he wanted to let her know how it felt to be cherished.

He'd walked longer than expected and stopped to look around. He backtracked across the ice, certain he hadn't passed camp among the tents dotting the lake. They had been the only group camped at the edge of the cove.

Something melted into the ice caught his attention. It was the piece of hot dog Cannon had tossed at Bowie last night. "I'll be damned."

He spun in a circle. "I'm not the only one whipped," he said out loud.

He turned back and crunched across the ice, hoping he could make it back to Samantha's before she got up. He'd kissed her goodbye and told her he'd be back. His plan was to warm her bed again tonight. *Still the plan.*

He considered their conversation. The one they had in the throes of arousal where they both agreed to keep their secrets. Although Dalton believed relationships should be built on honesty, he was a realist. Samantha made it clear she was leaving. At best, he could see her when she vacationed in Aspen Cove. Given she owned the house for over two years and this was her first visit, he imagined those times would be few.

He made his way back to her cabin, only to realize he was too late. Dressed in sweatpants, sneakers, and a Hollywood T-shirt, she jogged in place, warming up her muscles.

"Going somewhere?" he called from the edge of the lake. He hopped from the thinning ice to the shore. His walk turned into a jog straight toward her. Once there, he set the breakfast fixings on the stairs.

"Yes, Katie wanted to go for a jog around town. Sage and Lydia are joining us."

"I thought you'd still be in bed." He looked at her with disappointment. "Thought I could make you breakfast. You must be hungry after last night." The way her body shook had to have burned off a thousand calories.

She blushed. "All my motivation to stay in the bed got up early and left." She put a hand on his chest, using him for balance, and pulled her right leg up behind her. Grabbing her toes, she gave it a good stretch before switching to the other side. "Besides, my muscles are sore and could use loosening up."

"I could have helped with that."

She pushed against him, making him stumble back a step. "You caused that." She peeked around his body, looking for her group, but they hadn't arrived. "I've never felt anything so intense. It was like the worst muscle spasm in the best way." She lowered her head to hide the new bloom of pink flooding her cheeks.

"And you'll feel it again."

"Not sure I can handle it." She used his body as exercise equipment, gripping his hips and leaning into him for a deep lunge.

Up and down she moved, and it nearly killed him. Her head bobbing near his zipper made the motion appear almost pornographic.

He stroked her cheek, stopping her movements. "You want to try that while we're naked?"

She hopped up. "Oh. My. God. I get near you, and I lose my mind."

"You're not alone." He heard a commotion behind him and knew he had mere minutes before she disappeared into a group of X chromosomes.

"Dinner tonight?"

She hopped on the step so they were face-to-face. "Can't, I hear it's karaoke night at the bar."

Dalton was confused. "Bowie closed the bar while we were fishing."

"And you're not fishing anymore, so it's back open." She pressed a quick kiss to his lips. "Come to the bar tonight. It should be fun. I'd love to hear you sing."

He gripped her hips to keep her there a moment longer.

"Why would I punish you like that when all I want to do is

pleasure you?" Not caring that the three women approached like a storm, he pulled Samantha against him and claimed her mouth. If she was leaving him for the day, the least she could do was leave him with a kiss.

When he released her, there was a sigh from behind. He turned to see Sage, Kate, and Lydia standing there. Katie and Sage had big smiles. Lydia looked like she'd eaten something bad. Then again, with the way she reacted to affectionate couples, Dalton didn't imagine things were good in the love department.

"Tonight. Okay?" Samantha said as she rushed past him.

"Yep, I'll pick you up at six."

She hopped into the air like she'd won something special.

He watched her perfect ass jog out of sight. When he glanced at the front of his jeans, he groaned. She left him with more than a kiss. He adjusted his discomfort and picked up the bacon and eggs.

Someone was going to eat his damn breakfast, so he marched next door to Bowie's house and walked inside. Though he knew a compromising situation wouldn't present itself with Katie gone and Bowie left home alone with the baby, he didn't expect to find his friend reduced to goo. On the floor, bench-pressing his daughter was the big man himself.

"Who's Daddy's little girl?" he crooned. "My baby. Little miracle. My treasure. Yes," he grinned at the baby, "that's you."

Dalton leaned against the wall and took it all in. Over the last year, he watched a bitter and angry man turn into marshmallow.

Katie brought peace and purpose to Bowie's life. She kept him on his toes. Who wouldn't want to be a better man when you had a woman worth fighting for?

Bowie had fought for both of them. It was funny because people say love heals everything. He didn't believe that until a little girl was born and her daddy's life changed. There wasn't a day Bowie didn't smile. Not a day he didn't have a positive thing to say to someone.

Dalton even noticed that Bowie's once pronounced limp had disappeared. He figured it was because he walked with purpose, determination and pride. Bowie was surrounded by love.

"You forgot to add 'perfect' and 'princess.'" Dalton walked into the room. "You better get started on that one now. I hear girls like that."

"Katie hated it, so I called her 'Duchess.'"

"And now you call her 'Queen'. Tell me again who's whipped?" He lifted the food he brought. "You hungry?"

Bowie sat up and cradled Sahara in his arms. "I could eat."

Dalton walked to the kitchen where he spent a lot of his youth. He knew it almost as well as his own.

"Call your brother. He might be hungry too."

Ten minutes later, Cannon walked in. "Is that bacon I smell?"

They sat at the small table by the window looking over the lake. "You two gave up last night too?"

Cannon picked up a piece of bacon and laughed. "You were gone less than thirty minutes before we packed up. We left two beautiful women sleeping alone. How stupid was that?" He pressed the entire piece of bacon into his mouth.

Bowie added to Cannon's response. "Yeah, you were walking toward a hot body, and we were looking to freeze our sacks off. Not the smartest move. You get the smart brother prize for the night." He forked a bite of the egg, the yolk dripping to the plate as he held it in front of his mouth. "You get lucky?" He lifted his brows with ridiculous exaggeration.

"Any time I spend with Samantha feels lucky."

Cannon picked up his coffee and took a swig. "No, man, he wants to know if you got laid?"

Something fierce and protective roiled inside him. "Don't talk about her like she's some common girl. She's not. She's more than a lay."

Bowie and Cannon looked at each other and then back to Dalton.

"You got it bad, bro," Bowie said.

"Start saving now," Cannon added, "the ring will set you back big time. If someone hadn't bought that headboard, I'd be in debt for a long time to come."

"You can thank Samantha for that. Your headboard is firmly affixed to her bed."

"No shit? Firmly affixed you say? You give it a rocking?" He held his hand up for a high five. "Congrats man."

That didn't sit well with Dalton. He didn't want Bowie and Cannon thinking Samantha was easy.

"We slept."

"Yeah, after you rocked the bed, right?" Bowie wiped up the remaining yolk with the last piece of bacon.

Dalton shook his head. "Nope, we slept. Best damn night of my life. I've never done so little and been so satisfied."

He looked at his new brothers who sat there silent with heads shaking. "He's got it really bad," they said in unison.

CHAPTER FOURTEEN

Samantha's run with the girls was amazing. They rounded the town and headed toward the old paper mill at Samantha's request.

"Heartbreaking to see it empty." She looked into the vacant building. "So many people left when it closed." It nearly broke her heart when her mom came home and told her she'd lost her job.

"Wouldn't it be great if someone could breathe new life into the place?" Katie asked. "What a great project this would be."

Sage wiped at a dusty window and glanced inside. "This would be a huge undertaking. You stick to the park and your family. Leave this to someone else."

Lydia stepped back and looked at the brick structure. "Get someone to build a hospital, and I'll come and run it."

"We've got the clinic. You can join me there. Doc is getting older. I'm sure he'd love more days to fish." Sage wrapped her arm around her sister. "Don't worry. Something will go your way soon."

"Small town life is not my thing. I have big dreams that can't be found in a place like Aspen Cove." Lydia looked at them. "No offense, but there's nothing here for me."

She was so wrong. Everything worth having was here. Friends, families, and Dalton. Especially Dalton. "That can change. Someone could buy this and turn it into something amazing." She closed her eyes and pictured the building divided into shops, an art gallery, and maybe a culinary school.

While they ran, Samantha listened to Sage and Lydia talk about the shortage of job offers in Denver, and Lydia's frustration with her boyfriend's lack of attention and assistance given he was in charge of the emergency room staffing.

They ran past the park Katie funded. It would be finished before the warm weather hit and provide a safe place for the local children to play. It would offer an opportunity for mothers and fathers to leave their houses and engage with others.

There wasn't much to do in Aspen Cove, so people hibernated inside their homes. Most likely, they weren't eleven seasons behind on *Supernatural. What could they be watching?*

As they neared their homes, they said their goodbyes. They were all excited about karaoke night at the bar. Even Samantha thought it would be fun to sing without expectation. The only one in the group who knew her true identity was Katie, and she hadn't talked.

Samantha's phone buzzed with an incoming message from Deanna because her mother would never text.

Trouble

She wasted no time texting her when a call would be quicker.

"What's up?" Samantha asked as soon as her assistant answered.

Deanna let out a long, breathy exhale. "A few things. Dave is furious that you're not returning his calls, emails, or smoke signals."

Samantha ran up the stairs and entered her cabin. "I'm on vacation, he can wait."

"That's the problem. He's not good at waiting."

She walked back to her room and sat on the edge of the bed.

"That's where you come in as my loyal, hard-working assistant with integrity made from steel and resolve made from titanium."

While they talked, Samantha looked through her closet. She didn't miss her stage clothes, but there was a pair of thigh high boots she was certain would knock Dalton flat if he could see them on her. She wished Deanna had packed those.

"That's another problem."

"What? Tell him I'm on vacation, and I'll be at the charity event as planned."

"I can't tell him."

"Why the hell not?" Samantha rarely swore, but anything to do with Dave Belton gave her selective Tourette's.

"He fired me today."

"He can't fire you!" Her voice rose two octaves. "You work for me."

"Yes, but I'm paid by them. So technically, I work for them."

There was no way Samantha could live without her assistant. The woman was a wonder of the world. Without her, Samantha's life would crumble.

"All right, you're hired. Whatever you were making before, give yourself a twenty-five percent raise." Money was the least of Samantha's worries—Dave Belton was her primary problem. If he thought he could bully her into the studio before she had time to relax and regroup, he had another thing coming.

"Thanks, Boss," Deanna said. "There's another problem."

Samantha leaned against the wall and tapped her head gently against the surface. Too hard, and she'd leave a mark and that wouldn't go well with whatever she planned to wear to seduce Dalton tonight.

"I'm ready. Tell me."

"So, apparently you were at a restaurant called Chachi's, which sounded awful until I looked up the menu. I mean, Happy Fries? Those sound amazing."

"They were." She loved Chachi's. It was her second date with Dalton. She pulled a pink, low-cut cashmere sweater from the shelf. She had a friend in high school who reserved a certain sweater for third dates. This little pink number would be hers. With that solved, she returned to the problem at hand.

"Dining at Chachi's was a problem?"

"Only because you walked off stage and disappeared. The tabloids offered up cash for your location. It would be a problem if a waiter named Todd, who has an unhealthy obsession with a once blue-haired singer who happened to snap a selfie with him, threatened to blackmail you if you don't agree to a date with him."

She threw the pink sweater on the bed and rummaged through her jeans to find the perfect pair. Muffins and ice cream and candy along with bacon and pancakes and Happy Fries weren't weight-maintenance foods.

"Are you there?" Deanna asked.

Samantha shook the thoughts of Dalton and Happy Fries from her head. "Yes, and he's ridiculous if he thinks I'm going on a date with him."

"He wrote, and I quote, 'I'm prepared to keep her location secret if she'll meet me for dinner.' Which means he'll sell the picture and your location if you don't."

Samantha knew her time to remain anonymous was coming to an end, but she refused to toss in the towel right now. She also refused to let a pimply-faced teenager blackmail her.

"Tell him no. Chachi's is in a town almost an hour away. He only knows I was there for lunch. I could have been passing through."

"Okay, Boss. What do you want me to tell Dave?"

"Nothing. I'll take care of Dave. You no longer answer to him. Pass on your promotion to the team and let them know to contact you directly if they have questions."

"Will do." There was a breath of silence between them. "Any more of those hot kisses?"

Samantha smiled knowing Deanna couldn't see her bigger-than-life grin, but she knew she'd hear it in her voice. "Those lips have skills, girlfriend. He's so freaking hot."

"I need pictures and details," Deanna squealed.

"I'll see what I can do. Are we good?"

"For now." They hung up.

Samantha sat on the bed and thought about the high-handed tactics Dave used to get her to behave. There was so much abuse in the world.

Abuse of power.

Verbal abuse.

Physical abuse.

Emotional abuse.

She'd seen it all. Experienced much of it. It was time to stop it. Here she thought Marina needed to deal with her problem, and yet Samantha hadn't dealt with her own. Things would be different from now on. Dave Belton could no longer hurt her.

She pulled her old phone from the drawer and powered it up. It sang with the ring of incoming messages for minutes. She ignored them all.

She thought about what she would say, but there was no way to say everything that needed to be said in a text, so she wrote what was in her heart.

Dave,

You have worked me to death for ten years. Add to that the verbal abuse and the total disregard for my general health and welfare, and you can't fault me for wanting to take a break.

If you think firing my assistant will earn my submission, you're wrong. You've fired the first shot

in a battle you won't win. Try to sell a concert without a singer.

My commitment to you ends after the charity event and the final album.

Let me rest and find clarity, and maybe we can negotiate a path forward.

Samantha

She powered down her phone with shaking hands. Not once had she had the courage to stand up to him. Even now, she took the coward's way out by texting. If they were face-to-face, she would have seen the vein bulge in his forehead and she would have caved. That's why she needed time and space. Dave Belton kept her close to keep her under control. *Baby steps.*

Walking off that stage and into the crowd was the bravest decision she ever made. But it was also a cowardly move because instead of facing the enemy, she hid from him in a crush of twenty thousand fans. *Baby steps.*

It took five minutes for her racing heart to settle. She calmed her nerves with a glass of wine and went to work getting ready for her date. They hadn't categorized it as an actual date, but he texted her and reminded her that he'd be there at six. That sounded like a date.

She squeezed into a pair of skinny jeans, pulled on the softest sweater she'd ever bought, and slipped on the same ankle boots she'd worn at her last concert. Though the boots looked fine, she still wished she had the calfskin, leather thigh-highs.

Hair down, watermelon gloss applied, she waited by the door for Dalton. Something told her tonight would be one to remember.

Who would have believed that Indigo was nervous? Then again, Indigo wasn't here. Samantha was, and she had a taste of perfection when she slept in Dalton's strong arms. Arms that did nothing but hold her tight and cradle her while she slept. He asked nothing of her. He didn't take advantage of her. He laid beside her and made her feel like she mattered.

At exactly six o'clock, he knocked. She counted to ten, not wanting to seem too eager. When she opened the door, he stood in front of her wearing jeans that made her body tingle. The denim hugged all the places she wanted to touch.

In his hand was a bouquet filled with yellow roses, irises, and baby's breath—a beautiful combination of flowers. He pressed them forward.

"They're beautiful. Thank you." He followed her to the kitchen, where she filled the biggest glass she had with water and arranged the flowers before she set them on the table.

"They reminded me of you."

"These reminded you of me?"

"Yes, the irises are so dark blue, they're almost black, like your eyes. The yellow roses are like the sun, warm and happy—like your personality. The baby's breath flowers are tiny, with a touch of innocence, but so beautiful. And ..." He rubbed his hands over them, and they sprung back into place. "They're resilient too." He thumbed her chin so she looked up at him. He brushed a tender kiss over her lips. "Shall we go?"

She picked up her purse from the table. "Yes. I'm ready to hear you sing."

"Not happening, sweetheart."

She exaggerated a pout. "And I thought you would serenade me."

"Later I'll make your body sing, but me sing? Not on your life. Let's go before I change my mind and lock us inside." He stepped back and took her in. "You look so damn hot, I don't think I want to share you with anyone."

"We could stay here ..."

"It's karaoke night. No one misses it unless the owner is ice fishing, which he's not, so it's a go. If we don't show up, someone will send out a search party, or the sheriff will come since he's such a fan. This town takes its showmanship seriously."

"We should go before Sheriff Cooper comes again with lights flashing."

Dalton helped her into her jacket and walked her to his truck. Once inside, he leaned in and kissed her dizzy. "Just a taste of what's coming."

"Are you sure we have to go?"

"We do, but we'll leave as soon as we can. You can claim to have a stomachache. Sage is bringing dinner."

She reached across the space and gave him a soft punch to the arm. "That's an awful thing to say."

He pulled out of the driveway and headed downtown. "Tell me that after you've eaten her lasagna."

"It can't be that bad."

He chuckled. "You'll see."

In minutes, they were there. Samantha was shocked to see how many people lived in town. The bar was full. Cannon, Bowie, and Sage stood behind the bar, pulling pitchers of beer and filling shot glasses.

The man she knew as "Doc" was on the stage singing "Hound Dog" rather poorly. They made their way to the bar, where a glass of wine and a beer sat waiting.

Sage took Samantha's purse and served her a plate of lasagna. "I brought dinner."

Samantha looked at the tinfoil baking tray on the back counter, then glanced at Dalton. He gave her an I-told-you-so look. She forked a bite from her plate and put it into her mouth. Not only was it horrid, but it was still frozen in the center. "So good." She faked a smile and washed it down with a sip of wine, then passed the plate to Dalton. "I ate already, but Dalton said he was famished."

He pulled her barstool next to him. "You're going to pay for that." He took a bite and smiled. When Sage turned around, he fed the food to Otis, who sat begging at his feet. The dog wasn't picky.

When Doc finished his song, he called the next victim. It was a quirky Aspen Cove tradition to choose the song and the next singer. After much help from the girls, Doc chose Bowie as the next one up in the round robin. Then Katie took the stage to sing an old Freda Payne song called "Band of Gold."

Samantha knew she was in trouble when Katie pointed to her and smiled. She knew she wouldn't get away without singing. The question was, would she get away unrecognized?

Dalton reached for her. "Don't go. It's a trap. She'll give you some impossible song to sing just to break you in."

"I've got this." She gave him a passing kiss and went to the small stage to take the mic. When the Whitney Houston song "Queen of the Night" played, she groaned. Katie would pay for this somehow.

There were two ways to attack this song. Belt it out like the pro she was, or croak it out like everyone expected. She'd given nothing less than her best performance, so why stop now?

The words flowed from her so raw—so true. As she sang, everyone in the bar faded until only Dalton remained. His eyes connected with hers. The lyrics poured out of her like they were written for him. He had the stuff that she wanted—the stuff that she needed. She knew it was too early to feel such strong emotions, but he was the first man to see her as a person.

She couldn't keep him—that was a certainty. Her life was so far removed from his. All she had was now. She would leave nothing behind and carry no regrets forward.

When she hit the chorus, the crowd cheered. Dollar bills floated through the air. She'd never been paid so little for a performance she enjoyed so much. The music had become a burden, but tonight it freed her.

When the song finished, she tossed the mic to Sheriff Cooper and walked over to Dalton. "I'm ready to leave."

Dalton nearly fell off his chair. He pulled a twenty from his pocket and set it on the counter. Sage passed him Samantha's purse, and all eyes watched them as they worked their way through the crowd. This time, she wasn't running *away* but running *to*—the best night of her life.

CHAPTER FIFTEEN

Her beautiful voice continued to replay in his head all the way home. Her eyes pierced his soul as if she sang the words to him. A song about what she wanted and needed.

"Wow." He reached over and held her hand. "That was ... that was amazing. You have quite a voice."

"Thank you."

He couldn't believe that voice inside her tiny body could be so big. "You should be a singer."

She giggled. "I sing. I am a singer. I sang to you."

Knowing that song was for him filled him with warmth. Though she didn't choose it, she sang it like she meant every word. He got all choked up when she looked at him like he was special. It felt so real that a lump the size of Wyoming lodged in his throat.

It was too soon to think about love, but he knew if there was ever a chance of falling in love with anyone, it would be easy to fall in love with Samantha. Hell, he was halfway there already. Bowie and Cannon were right. Dalton was whipped, and he hadn't even been inside her yet.

He pulled up in front of his cabin and killed the engine. "I thought we could stay at my place tonight." He held his breath. It was a forgone conclusion that they'd be together tonight. He wanted it. He thought she wanted it.

"Are you inviting me for a sleepover, Dalton?" She looked at him beneath long onyx lashes.

He wasn't the blushing type, but he swore there was heat on his cheeks. "I'll make you breakfast in the morning."

Everything about Samantha was near perfect. She was by far too skinny, but he could solve that with home-cooked meals. Most perfect was her ability to take him out at the knees with a smile.

"Pancakes?"

"Are you negotiating?"

"I'd be silly not to."

"Anything. You can have anything." He jumped out of his truck and rushed around to her side to open her door.

"I need a few things from my place."

He stood in front of her while she slid from the truck into his body. They walked hand-in-hand to her door. On the porch was a single daisy. She bent over to pick it up. "Must have fallen from my bouquet." She twirled it around and brought it to her nose.

Dalton knew for a fact the flower didn't come from her bouquet. He looked around and wondered whose ass he'd have to kick.

Once inside, she pressed the flower into the glass with the others and walked back to her room. The only thing she came out with was a toothbrush.

"Low-maintenance. My kind of girl." In the silence of the cabin he heard her stomach growl. She'd only had a bite of poison lasagna. "And you're hungry. I can fix that too."

"Are you going to solve all my problems tonight?"

"I'm going to try." He squatted down and wrapped his arms around her bottom before he stood. She lifted her hand so she wouldn't hit the ceiling, but she knew he'd let nothing happen to her. When he loosened his hold, she slid down his body until they were face to face. One quick kiss in the middle of her entryway would not satisfy the hunger he had for her. A kiss wouldn't fill her belly, but it was a kiss that spoke of their need for each other. When she ran her hands through his hair and pulled him deeper into the kiss, he knew he had to get her out of here or they'd never leave her cabin.

He loosened his hold until her boots hit the scarred wooden floor.

"Ready?"

She licked her lips like she was savoring the taste of him. "So ready. You have no idea."

Every time she was near him, he got hard. That alone gave him plenty of ideas. Before he changed his mind and stayed, he led her to the doorway. He glanced back at the flowers on the table. *Could there have been a daisy in the mix?*

He held his breath when he opened the door to his world. He'd never had a woman in his house or his bed. This was his safe haven. A place where the outside world wasn't invited in. And yet … here he was opening it up to her.

She walked past him into the entryway. He closed the door behind them. He'd never felt so right about something or someone.

"Wow. This place is amazing."

He looked at his home through her eyes. It was pretty amazing. More so because while he sat in prison, the work on his house continued. His mom oversaw the laborers as they turned his run-down shack into a home. *"That's what moms do,"* she told him when he tried to argue with her about the time and expense.

They were partners at Maisey's, and during the tourist season they made a killing. The building was paid off. Other than utilities and taxes, the place was pure profit. He wasn't rich by any means, but he didn't need much to keep him happy.

"You like it?"

She held up her toothbrush. "I should have packed all my stuff and moved over here. Your house is a five-star hotel. Mine is more like a bunk house at summer camp."

"You went to camp?"

Her head shook. "No, we couldn't afford it, but I looked at brochures. Dreaming costs nothing." That statement reminded her of Marina.

"Our lives weren't much different. Abusive fathers and determined mothers. No camp for me either."

She nodded. "And we survived." She thumbed the scar above his eye.

"Yes, we did." He lowered her hand and wrapped it in his. "Want the tour?"

"Absolutely."

They walked across his shiny oak floors into the living room, where his leather couch took up most of the space. A wall of glass looked over the lake. He lowered the blinds to give them privacy. He had a big screen television on his wall hanging above the fireplace.

"Yours is so big." She teased him, and he loved it.

"Size matters."

"I've heard that."

He squeezed her hand and led her into the galley kitchen. Only his was filled with top-of-the-line appliances.

"You have a microwave." She never thought she'd ever get excited over something as simple as an appliance, but the stainless steel box sitting over his stove made her giddy.

"I've got it all." He stood tall as he bantered with her.

"We'll see." She brushed past him, running her fingers over the granite counter.

"I'll show you after I feed you." He placed his hands on her hips and lifted her onto the countertop next to the stove. "Sit here. Watch and be amazed."

"Is the tour finished already? I thought maybe ..." She bit her lip. "Maybe I'd see your bedroom."

"Sweetheart, if we got to the bedroom, we'd never leave it. Let me be chivalrous and feed you so I can keep you in bed until I have to go to work on Tuesday."

"You're making promises you better be able to keep."

He drew an imaginary X across his chest. "Cross my heart. I'm a man of my word."

She squirmed on the counter while he pulled the ingredients for chicken piccata from the refrigerator. After he put a pot of water to boil on the stovetop, he went about mixing the ingredients for the sauce.

He slid past her and pounded the chicken breasts thin.

"You're killing that chicken."

He hit it a few more times. "That's what I do. I kill things." He was referring to food, but the irony wasn't lost on him.

Each time he had to pass her, he stopped for a kiss. Each kiss became more than the one before it. She tasted like fine wine. It could be because he had poured her a glass while he cooked or maybe because she was a fine vintage all on her own.

"How is it that you're not with someone?" He drained the pasta he'd cooked and plated up their dinner.

"I'm far too busy. My job takes me around the world, but I'm making some changes. It would be so nice to make a living *and* have a life."

After the final sprinkle of fresh herbs, he lowered her to her feet and walked her over to his small dining table by the window that overlooked the lake like hers. Everything beautiful about the cabins could be found in their back halves, on the lakeside. The front door led to nothing more exciting than a hallway.

He pulled out her chair and served her dinner. Watching her eat was an orgasmic experience. She hummed and moaned, and each bite made him harder.

"I take it you like it?"

"Oh my God, can I keep you? You want to go on tour with me?" She swallowed a sip of wine. "I mean go on my business trips. You can be my personal chef."

"Does the job pay in kisses?"

"Are you negotiating?"

Dalton chuckled. "I'd be silly not to."

"Then I'd ask for more than kisses."

He poured her another glass of wine and cleared her empty plate.

"I'll interview you tonight before I decide what goes on my list of demands. A comprehensive benefit package can make a difference."

She offered him her hand. "Shall we begin?"

CHAPTER SIXTEEN

Thump.

Thump.

Thump.

Samantha's heart beat like a tribal drum. She wasn't normally so forward and brazen, but her time was running out, and she wanted what she wanted. That was Dalton for as long as she could keep him.

Something about sending that text to Dave Benton freed her. Like ten years worth of chains simply broke loose. She deserved to be happy. Dalton made her happy.

He was selfless and kind and sexy. He kissed like a master. When his hands roamed her body, it was as if he'd wanted to memorize every part of her.

"Stay here for a second." He left her standing by the window, looking out over the lake. Small fires dotted the ice where diehard fishermen grabbed on to the last chance to pull a trophy from beneath the frozen surface.

Dalton returned in minutes and walked her down the hallway. Shadows of light danced across the walls of the room. He'd lit candles. Her heart burst with happiness. When had anything been so perfect?

"Do you do this for all your women?"

He cupped her cheek and looked into her eyes. His hard blue eyes softened. "No, you are the first woman in my house. The first I've invited to my bed. The first to break through my icy heart."

She couldn't breathe. His words had twisted inside her, tightening a hold on her heart. "I've never been treated like this. You're going to spoil me."

"I plan to."

He walked her to his bed until the mocha brown comforter hit the back of her knees. She leaned back and let his soft mattress hug her body. Her hands flattened onto the fabric. This is where she wanted to be, and she hoped he kept his promise of keeping her here all weekend.

Propped on her elbows, she watched him remove his shirt. The soft light created shadows that only increased her awareness of how toned and fit he was. The candlelight danced over the ridges and valleys of his carved-from-rock body.

"You work out?" She felt stupid for asking. With a body like his, he had to spend hours in the gym.

"I used to. I don't so much now. There was a time where all I did was work out."

"You're beautiful." She wanted to take the words back. What man wanted to be called beautiful?

"No, you're beautiful." He lifted her feet one at a time and tossed her boots aside. "Even when you had blue hair, I thought you were beautiful."

"You like it better blue?" She watched him unbuckle his belt and pull it through the loops. He rolled it up and walked it over to his dresser. Dalton wasn't what she expected. His house wasn't what she expected. He was put-together. His house was clean—

almost military or institutional in its organization—but there was a warmth to everything he did. He invested himself.

"No, I like this better, but I still thought you were beautiful."

She rolled to her side to stare at him. "Was that before or after you called me a skinny, blue-haired boy?"

He stalked toward her. She rolled onto her back in time for him to straddle her hips. With one motion he pulled her pink, cashmere, third-date sweater over her head and cupped the pink lacy bra she wore.

"These," he said with a heat and gravel voice, "would never belong to a boy."

"No? Just the hair, huh?"

He rubbed his thumbs over her aroused peaks. "Was that a phase?"

A ten-year phase. "I was definitely going through something. I'm working through it." She was making headway through her life. It wouldn't be easy, but she knew it would be worth it. Maybe she could figure out a way to keep Dalton.

"I'll work you through it." He reached behind her to unhook her bra. "As pretty as that little piece of lace is, I find you even more beautiful naked." He made fast work of removing her clothes.

"We are not doing this again." She rose up and tugged at the button of his jeans, then pulled the zipper down. "You may have the patience of a saint, but I don't. It's been a very long time for me, and you've been stroking my libido since the start."

He rolled off the bed and pulled down his pants until all he wore was a pair of clingy boxers. Her eyes went straight for the goods.

Oh shit. She knew he was well-endowed, but she never imagined that what she saw outlined down his thigh would be so big.

He opened the drawer to his nightstand and pulled out a strip of condoms. Magnum size, of course. "I stocked up."

"Oh shit."

He tugged his boxers off, evening the playing field. They were both naked. And she was scared to death.

"Changing your mind?" His lips twitched in amusement.

She pulled a deep breath into her lungs and thought of the words he'd told her days ago. "No. A really sexy man told me I could always make room for what I desired. And I want you. All of you."

"That's my girl." He climbed onto the bed beside her.

She knew Dalton wasn't a dive-straight-in kind of guy. He'd told her more than once that he loved the in-between. As he left kisses across her body, she grew fond of it as well. She'd never had the time to lie in bed and be worshipped by a man. Never had she wanted a man to kiss her as much as she wanted Dalton.

"This thing between us is dangerous," he said against her neck. "You're fire, and I'm accelerant."

Not wanting to be a taker and not a giver, she switched places with him. As she straddled his waist, his length sat heavy and ready between her legs. It would have been so easy to lift up and let it all happen, but she wanted Dalton to feel as cherished as she did.

Her fingers ghosted over his skin until goose bumps rose beneath her touch. She traced his tattoos. He was a work of art. "Did these hurt?"

He opened his heavy lids to look at her. "Not like you'd think. It's a good kind of pain."

Leaning forward, she pressed her breasts to his chest. The fine dusting of dark hair grazed her sensitive peaks. "If you gave me a tattoo, what would it be?" She drew her tongue over his nipple, and he hissed.

"Can't think." His hands reached for her bottom and squeezed. He pulled her harder against his length and groaned.

His expression was a mixture of pain and pleasure. "Don't

think." She shimmied down his body and kissed him where he needed attention the most. "Just feel."

"You're killing me."

She ran her tongue down the length of him. "Maybe, but you'll die happy," she purred against his silky soft skin.

Before she could take him inside her mouth, she was flat on her back and Dalton was over her. He reached for a foil wrapper and tore the end off with his teeth.

His breath sucked in when she helped him roll it on. Settled between her thighs, she opened to invite him in, more than ready for this moment.

At first, she was certain he'd split her in half, but he took his time coaxing her body to relax around him. He eased into her slowly. He was right, there was always room for what she desired.

Never in her life had she felt so complete. They moved together the way a melody and lyrics complemented each other.

"So good," she whispered against his chest. She rose to meet his thrusts.

She gripped his hips and pulled him in as close and deep as she could get him. She wanted him to live inside her. He was right, this was dangerous because now that she knew how it could be with two people who shared a connection, she wanted more. Did she dare to dream for more?

His steady rhythm pushed her passion forward. He never took his eyes off her. That alone pushed her to the edge. Possessive and feral was how he looked as he claimed her. For that moment in time she belonged to him. She was his. She wanted to be his forever.

Writhing and panting beneath him caused a sheen of sweat on her brow. His glorious body pumped into her with a purpose. Shocks of pleasure stole what breaths remained in her lungs. He pushed her to the limits, pulled her to the edge, and eased her back countless times. He didn't hurry. It was as if her pleasure was more important to him than anything in the world.

So close to falling off the edge. So close to falling in love. She held her breath for a moment, hoping to capture every feeling racing through her. As her body took control and her muscles ceased and then shook, she exploded around him. Her vision blurred, then blackened until prisms of light danced behind her eyelids. She knew she'd seen heaven.

She held tight until Dalton's hard body heaved forward and stilled. Most men have an expression when they climax. Often, it's not attractive. She swore she'd never seen a smile so beautiful as the one Dalton gave her when he found his release.

He didn't collapse on top of her but gently pulled out and lay down beside her. She curled into his arms, where she was content to stay forever.

His fingers brushed over her skin until he came to the place above her heart. He lingered there. She leaned back and looked into his eyes—eyes that told more than he did. Their experience went far deeper than good sex. It spoke of their deep connection. She saw it in his face. Felt it in her heart.

"Your tattoo would say, 'Dalton's.'" He pressed his hand over her heart. "Right here."

Never had she been so moved. People wanted her talent. They wanted her money. No one had ever asked for her heart. "After what you did, my heart belongs to you." She didn't mean to say it out loud. She spoke without thought, without fear—something she rarely did because she'd learned from watching her mother that speaking the truth was often painful. "You've ruined me, Dalton Black."

He brushed the damp hair back from her forehead. "Likewise, Samantha White."

"You're black, I'm white, but it's the gray in-between where the magic happens."

He nuzzled her neck. "I'm a fan of the gray."

Over the next several days, he showed her how lovely the color gray could be. When Sage and Katie and Lydia stopped by, he told them she was his until Tuesday. Little did he know, he'd claimed her for life.

CHAPTER SEVENTEEN

Dalton knew he had to share Samantha when Sage and Lydia banged on the door early Tuesday morning requiring proof of life. Lydia was heading back to Denver to continue her job search and wanted to say goodbye. She'd been tight-lipped about her prospects, which made him think they weren't good.

It was Tuesday, which meant Dalton was cooking at the diner. As he flipped pancakes, he thought about the tiny little firecracker he'd loved on all weekend. Pulled in two different directions, he was in a quandary about telling Samantha about his past. They agreed to keep their secrets, but it weighed heavily on his mind. What she thought of him was important. Would the truth bother her? He didn't want to spoil what they had. They connected on a deep level. After a week, they were finishing each other's sentences. He'd never had that with anyone. Not even Casey, the woman he'd dated for two years.

Maisey walked through the swinging doors. "Your girlfriend is here with the gang."

He liked the sound of Samantha being called his girlfriend. It was the furthest thing from the truth, but it warmed him through and through to consider the possibility.

"I wish." He put Doc's pancakes on the counter and brushed his hands on his apron. Making sure nothing would start on fire while he was gone, he left the kitchen behind him to get a kiss from his 'girlfriend'.

She never ceased to take his breath away. Today, she was dressed in jeans and a black T-shirt that hung off one shoulder. On closer inspection, he realized it was his T-shirt, and that did something to him. Seeing her in his clothes made him want to stick out his chest and pound it.

He lengthened his stride to get to her faster. At the table, he ignored Sage and Katie and gave Samantha a kiss.

"I'd say get a room, but then we might not see you two for months." Katie poked Dalton in the arm. Since she and Sage were on the same side of the booth, he slid in next to Samantha.

"You hungry, sweetheart?" She nodded. Lord knows she must be because they had burned enough calories.

Sage waved her hand in front of his face. "We're here too."

"I see ya." He didn't really, but he knew they were there. "What do you want?"

Katie let out a growl of frustration. "No sweetheart for us?"

He looked at Katie. "Bowie's across the street for you." His eyes went to Sage. "No idea where you've hidden Cannon."

"How have you missed him? He's like you, big as a tank. Not likely I can hide him anywhere. Today, he's in our garage whittling."

Katie jumped up and down in her seat. "I get all the ornaments. I'll pay double." She'd bought every ornament he'd put on consignment. By the time Christmas rolled around, she had the tree covered in whittled wood wildlife and angels.

Dalton turned to Samantha. "How about a waffle and bacon?"

He cupped her face and ran his thumb across her cheek. "Or I can make that omelet you love."

"Waffle, please."

"Anything you want, baby." He slid out of the booth but not before claiming another kiss. He turned to Sage and Katie. "Have you decided?"

"Waffles and bacon all the way around." He was several steps away when he heard Katie declare, "That boy has it bad for you."

He couldn't argue an obvious truth. He was falling in love with Samantha White. He loved the feeling yet hated the situation because what they had could never be long-term. He had commitments and responsibilities in Aspen Cove, not to mention four more years of parole check-ins. She had a life outside the little cocoon she'd created here. A life without him.

With the waffles done and the bacon crisp, he placed a strawberry on the top of each except for Samantha's. On hers, he made a smiley face out of several berries because that's how he felt with her around. He had finally found happiness.

With a few more orders to fill, he flicked at the bell to alert his mom to an order up. When he was free again, he peeked out the swinging doors to find the table vacant and a feeling of emptiness echoed in his heart.

In his favorite booth in the corner sat Doc, reading his paper.

"You gonna stare at me or come and chat?" No one ever got anything past Doc. He was old, not blind, and he had a spooky sixth sense about these things. He knew more than Abby Garrett—and she knew everything.

"What's up?" Adding "Doc" to the end of the sentence seemed cliché, so he let it end there.

"The population of Aspen Cove is up." He chuckled. "Soon, we'll be back to where we were twenty years ago." He sat back and placed his hands on his belly. "Those were the days."

"For some of you. Not so good for Mom and me." Twenty years ago, his dad was still alive.

"It's a good thing your old man died immediately because I'm not sure I would have tried to save the bastard."

Dalton's eyes grew large. He'd never heard Doc talk negatively about anyone. "Yes, you would have. That's what you do."

Doc pruned his lips and nodded. "You're probably right, but I would have made sure his recovery was long and painful."

"I never understood how some people could be so evil."

"Like the man you hit?"

Dalton's shoulders sagged. "You mean the man I killed."

Doc's eyebrows lifted. They always seemed ready to take flight. "Now, son, I don't see it that way."

Dalton knew from experience that if Doc started with "Now, son", he was in teaching mode. It was a good thing the diner had slowed down because Doc's lessons rarely finished fast.

"It is what it is."

Doc shook his head. "Things are seldom what they seem. That man killed himself. There are lowlifes, and—no offense to your mom—I'd have categorized Ben in that group when he was drinking. Not so much now. Andy Kranz was worse. He was a *no* life. That man was rancid hamburger meat. You did the world a favor by tossing out the trash. It's a shame you had to do time, but I'm not sure it was a bad thing, either."

"You think the time I did served me well?"

"I think it could have gone several ways. I think you spent a lot of time deciding the type of man you wanted to be. You got a degree in business management, which can't hurt running Maisey's. You grew up."

"I also have a felony conviction and no real earning potential."

"Should I get you a Kleenex? I've never known you to whine. Why now?"

The statement made him bristle because never once did Dalton take the time to have a pity party.

"You're right. The problem is, I've never had to worry about it. Now that Samantha is in my life … it changes things."

"She's a keeper. She's tough like you and knows life's not fair. Does she have a problem with your record?" Doc looked at the empty booth where she'd once sat. "She didn't look like she had a problem when you two were canoodling."

"I haven't told her. Do you think I should?"

"Can't say. Only you know the answer to that question, but I'm sure it would be easier hearing the truth from the person who lived it."

Doc pushed his legs to the edge of the bench and started a rocking motion that propelled him up and forward. His age was showing.

"Damn body won't work like it used to."

Dalton picked up the dirty dishes and walked behind Doc. "Good thing your mind's sharp as a tack."

"If my mind ever falters, kill me." His eyes popped when he realized what he'd said.

"You'll have to find someone else. I'm out of that business."

Doc walked out. Dalton went back to the kitchen.

His mom leaned against the prep table eating a piece of apple pie.

"Samantha says she'll be at the bakery when you get off."

He looked at the clock and frowned. He still had two hours left on his shift. His disappointment must have been obvious. "Thanks, Mom." He walked behind the burners to start his breakfast cleanup, but it was already done. "You cleaned my station?"

Maisey ignored his question. "You like her, don't you?"

"More than I should."

"I like her too. Go get her and have fun. Life's way too short. I got this."

Dalton was already untying his apron. "Are you sure?"

"The only one coming in is Abby, and she'll want coffee and pie. Ben will be here, but he can help himself. He's getting handy in the kitchen."

"You replacing me?"

She walked up to him and kissed him on the cheek. "Not possible. Now go get your girl."

He didn't have to be told twice. He tossed his apron on the prep table and bolted for the front door.

He found Samantha sitting under the Wishing Wall, filling out notes. So immersed in her task, he went unnoticed until he kissed her cheek.

She looked up, startled. "You're early."

He sat in the chair across from her. "I couldn't wait."

"I'm glad."

She had dozens of folded notes in front of her. Dalton wondered if they were her wishes.

"Can I grant any of those?"

Her lush lips broadened into a bright smile. She rummaged through the pile and pulled out one and handed it to him.

Across the center of the pink paper it read:

I wish for endless kisses from Dalton Black.

"Granted. You want to start those here and go back home?" It was funny how his place had become their home in days. It felt right.

She passed another note to him.

I wish Dalton would take me for a ride on his motorcycle.

"You're easy."

"Yes, but I'm not cheap."

He looked over his shoulder. The day was perfect for a ride. "Let's go. I'll give you the ride of a lifetime."

She gathered her notes and stuffed them inside her bag.

"I think you've given me one already. I'm interested in a

simple trip around the lake with my body pressed to yours. Katie tells me there's nothing like the wind in my hair and a Harley between my legs."

"I used to think that was nirvana. That was before I met you and settled between your legs."

"You're such a flirt." She walked to the door and opened and closed it several times. The bell rang a few times before Katie walked in from the storage room.

She came forward, patting Sahara on the back. "You leaving?"

Dalton's heart stopped when she wrapped her arms around him and said, "My man's taking me for a ride."

Her man. If there were ever a chest-pounding moment, it was that second she claimed him.

"I like being your man."

When they got to his cabin, he didn't go inside because he knew once they were behind closed doors, the first kiss would lead to more, and they'd never leave. Samantha's wish was to ride on the back of his Harley. That was easy to grant. When they got back, he'd work on the endless kisses.

CHAPTER EIGHTEEN

Never in her existence had she been so free. On the back of
Dalton's Harley, she held on for dear life, let the wind blow in her
hair, and lived honestly—well, mostly honestly.

They stopped at points along the way where Dalton pointed
out landmarks like the cove surrounded by aspens for which the
town was named.

On the far side of the lake, he pulled into a parking lot where a
single wooden shack sat surrounded by picnic tables and trash
cans. An old tin sign that read, 'Sam's Scoops' hung over the open
window. Leaning across the counter was a middle-aged man who
hadn't seen a razor or scissors in years.

"Dalton, my man." He nearly fell out of the shack trying to fist
bump Dalton.

"Sam, what's the flavor of the day?"

"I'd say it's her." He nodded toward Samantha. "She looks
good."

"She's mine." Dalton wrapped his arms possessively around
Samantha.

"Well, then." He turned around and pointed to the sign, "if

you're talking ice cream, I've got Breakfast in Bed, which is maple ice cream with donut pieces and glazed bacon; Lickin' Lizard, which is vanilla ice cream and gummy worms; and Unicorn Poop, which is basically rocky road with the addition of Pop Rocks." He smiled at them like he'd recited a Pulitzer Prize–winning novel. "What's your poison?"

The horror on her face must have been obvious. Who in their right mind wanted to eat anything called Unicorn Poop, or worms —gummy or not? The breakfast flavor didn't sound half bad if the ingredients were served individually.

"Trust me?" Dalton winked at her.

Her trust wasn't given lightly, but she did trust him with everything. "I do."

"We'll take a scoop of each." He looked at Samantha. "You haven't lived until you've tasted Sam's ice cream."

"My fear is I won't live *after* I've tasted it."

"I heard that, young lady." Sam's gravelly voice gave her the impression he hadn't missed a smoke in years. He pushed a plastic bowl forward and sprinkled something chocolate coated on top. "A little something extra." He smiled wide enough for his overgrown beard to split and show his lips and teeth. "Chocolate covered ants. You'll love the texture."

Dalton paid, picked up the bowl and led her to a table where they sat side by side.

Her lip curled in disgust. "I'm not eating bugs."

"No ants, only chocolate covered crispy rice." Dalton scooped a spoon of Unicorn Poop and pressed it to her mouth. "Open up."

Her tongue darted out to grab the tiniest taste. When the chocolate hit and the Pop Rocks burst, she was sold. "That's amazing."

They shared bite after bite until the bowl was empty.

"Did I lie?"

"I'm not sure you have it in you to lie."

His expression turned serious. "Not about ice cream."

There was something behind his statement—something that he was keeping to himself. She couldn't fault him. She hadn't divulged everything about herself either. Rather than dwell on the past, she dug right into her critique. "I love Unicorn Poop." She made a face. "Can't believe I said that." She dipped her finger into the bowl to swipe up an 'ant'. Before she could put it into her mouth, Dalton wrapped his lips around her finger and sucked it clean. Every cell in her body lit on fire. His tongue had the kind of talent that should be boxed and sold. "Breakfast in Bed was good, but I prefer yours. Not a huge fan of the worms, only because they're hard to chew when they're cold."

He looked at her with lazy bedroom eyes. It was the same look that melted her into the bed each night.

"And I thought you were a fan of hard worms."

"Really?" She knuckled him in the chest. Not hard enough to hurt but enough for him to feel it. "You're not giving yourself enough credit."

"Are you defending my manhood?" The aw-shucks look didn't fit the big man at her side.

"Just telling it like it is. Now take me home and show off your worm."

Dalton moved quickly when motivated, and anything to do with her and him naked had him focused.

The forty-five minutes it took to get there seemed like only twenty to get home. He pulled into her driveway so she could run inside and get some clean clothes. When she got to the door, Samantha stopped cold. It was cracked open, and her latest album played in the background.

She scurried backward.

Dalton watched her return. "Looking for one of those endless kisses?"

Her heart pounded in her chest. Blood pumped so hard, she

heard nothing but the *whoosh* in her ears. Words caught in her throat.

"What's wrong?" He looked past her to the opened door, and he was gone.

She pulled her phone from her bag and dialed the sheriff. She croaked out that someone was in her cabin and Dalton was confronting the intruder.

Sheriff Cooper let out a string of expletives that could make a hooker blush before he said he was on his way.

Samantha was torn between staying put and offering Dalton help. Her mind raced as she played out every scenario. What if it was her manager? What if it was a robber? What if Dalton was in danger? That was the thought that moved her forward and up the steps.

"Get out!" She heard an unrecognizable voice scream. The voice was too high to be Dalton and too low to be female.

She snuck inside the doorway with her phone in her hand. It was ridiculous that her only weapon was a palm-sized plastic box. She shouldn't have worried. Dalton was there, and if he could, he would protect her.

In the corner by the lit fireplace, he towered over a cowering young man. When the intruder saw her, he hopped to his feet and yelled, "Indigo! You're here."

"Todd?" She recognized the kid from Chachi's. "What are you doing here?" Samantha knew what he was doing. He was demanding his date. As she looked around the room, she would have been touched if she weren't so freaked out. A bottle of cheap wine and two glasses sat on the coffee table. A bouquet of daisies replaced the flowers Dalton had given her. That brought a level of anger she didn't know she was capable of, but the worst thing was the framed pictures he'd set around the room. He'd photoshopped a life for them. He'd taken publicity shots and put himself in each one.

Before Todd could answer, Sheriff Cooper burst inside the cabin with his hand on his weapon. He noticed the young man cowering in the corner. "Thank God." He walked to Dalton, who seemed to grow larger by the second and shoved him back. "Go home, Dalton. You don't need this trouble."

"No." The word came out in an angry growl. "I'm not leaving Samantha."

Todd shook his head. "She's not Samantha. That's Indigo." He looked at the sheriff. "I can show you." He pointed to his back pocket.

The sheriff nodded, and Samantha knew everything good about her life would end in seconds. The kid pulled out his wallet and let a strip of photos fall like dominoes. It was an act more suitable for a proud parent than a fan. But Todd wasn't any admirer; he'd proved himself to be a true fanatic.

Dalton lunged forward to grab the photos.

Samantha saw the recognition in his eyes. "It's you."

What could she say but the truth? "Yes, it's me, and I can explain."

He stepped back and looked at her, then did something unexpected. He smiled. "I like the brown hair better."

"Dude, that's Indigo." Todd moved forward, but the sheriff stopped his progress. "Have you heard her sing?"

Dalton's smile widened. "Yes, I have, and it's almost a religious experience." He wrapped his arms around her and whispered, "You could have trusted me with the truth."

"I wanted you to like me for me, not for who everyone thinks I am."

"I more than like you Samantha. I lo—"

"What do you want to do about this one?" Sheriff Cooper interrupted. His hand circled Todd's arm. He dragged him forward. "There is a list of charges you could file, including breaking and entering."

"She can't press charges. I'm a fan."

Samantha stepped forward. Dalton stepped in front of her protectively. Before her eyes, he morphed into a mass of agitation. The tension rolled off him in heated waves.

"I could have killed you." Dalton exchanged looks with the sheriff. "You don't walk into someone's house uninvited. What the hell were you thinking?"

"It's okay." Samantha slid in front of Dalton and placed her hand on his chest. Immediately, his tension eased. "I remember another man rushing into my house uninvited." She turned to Todd. "How old are you?"

"Twenty," he said proudly.

Sheriff Cooper pointed to the alcohol. "Who sold you that?"

"I stole it," Todd said, and then blanched. "I mean, I found it."

"Right." The sheriff turned to Samantha. "You pressing charges?"

Part of her wanted to press charges so Todd would learn a lesson. Part of her figured everyone needed a second chance. "No, but I better not see him again unless he's in the front row of a concert." She tried to give him a wicked mean scowl but couldn't pull it off.

"Let's go." Sheriff Cooper led Todd to the door. The young man reached for a picture he set on the entry table. "Can you sign this?"

"Out," Dalton bellowed.

Todd didn't stall. He rushed out of the house with the sheriff giving him a list of laws he'd broken.

When Samantha turned around, Dalton was scrolling furiously through his phone.

"What are you doing?"

He flopped his big body onto the couch. "I just found out my girlfriend is famous. I'm downloading all your music."

She laughed. "You're crazy."

He pulled her into his lap. "For you."

"Perfect answer." She crawled out of his lap and collected the photos of her fake wedding, her fake Valentine's Day, her fake Christmas, and tossed them into the trash can. The same trash can where Todd had thrown Dalton's flowers. After she exchanged the daisies for the discarded bouquet, she climbed back into Dalton's lap.

"You're not mad?"

"Mad for you." He flipped her around to straddle him like she weighed nothing because in truth, she didn't weigh much. Although, she was certain she had put on a few pounds. How could she not with Dalton constantly feeding her?

"I should have told you the truth."

"You hinted at it in so many ways. If I were a smarter man, I would have listened and understood."

"You pay attention to the important things." She snuggled close to his chest, grateful that her lack of transparency hadn't ruined what they had together.

"How about I take you to bed and you sing me a love song?"

"How about you take me to bed and make my body sing?"

"That'll work." He rose with her in his arms and carried her to her bedroom, where Dalton wasted no time making her body sing.

Exhausted after a night of passion, she fell asleep in the arms of the only man she felt safe around. The only man she trusted. The only man able to unlock her heart.

When a knock on the door woke them both the next morning, Dalton pulled on his T-shirt and his pants and grumbled all the way to the door. "This better be important, or you're dead."

She thought nothing of it until she recognized the click of cameras and the shouts of pushy reporters. This was all Todd's doing. Now she wished she had pressed charges. At least she would have had an additional day or so before the shit hit the fan.

She rushed out the door to rescue Dalton.

"Indigo! How do you think your fans will respond to your relationship with Dalton Black, a convicted killer?"

She staggered back. She was hit with a question that completely floored her, and she had no answer.

"Assholes!" Dalton yelled at the dozen or so reporters camped in front of her house snapping photos. He pulled Samantha into his arms and took her inside where it was dead silent.

CHAPTER NINETEEN

The pain in his chest was so profound, he thought he was having a heart attack. The horror on her face sliced through him like a rusty blade ripping out his soul. In reality, his heart had broken.

Samantha squirmed from his grip. "Tell me what they said is a lie."

Dalton ran his hand through his hair, gripping and pulling until his they dropped to his side. "It's not what it seems." He moved toward her. She shuffled back until she hit the wall. Trapped, her eyes grew large, her face pale. She reminded him of an animal caught in a cage.

It gutted him to know she feared him when he'd never do anything to harm her. He loved her. Almost told her last night. Now he wished he would have because she'd never know the truth.

The one thing he'd always tried to be was the hero, and not the villain. He'd promised himself that his actions would never cause a woman to shake from terror, but Samantha was quaking like a leaf caught in a violent storm.

She slid down the wall like her bones had softened and could no longer hold her up. "Did you kill someone or not?" She didn't ask for details, just the facts.

"Yes."

"You need to leave." She scrambled back into the corner and curled into a ball.

"Please, Samantha, you have to listen to the facts."

"I need space," she yelled. "I need a minute to think."

"Dammit, would you listen to me?" He didn't mean to yell, but she had to give him a chance to explain.

"You know what my past is. You know I came from an abusive background. A man with a violent past is a deal breaker."

"I'm not that man." He dropped to his knees, feet from her, palms up so she wouldn't feel threatened. "I've never hit a woman. I lived in that environment too. I'm not my father. I'm not your father."

"How can you say that? You killed someone. They said a convicted killer."

He couldn't argue with her words or logic.

"Let me explain," he pleaded again.

She looked up at him with her soulful eyes, and all he saw was hurt and distrust.

"Now that it's out in the open, you want to explain? Why didn't you tell me?"

"We both kept truths from each other. Why are your omissions okay and mine aren't?"

The look of hurt fell away and was replaced by anger. He'd rather have her furious than afraid any day.

"You're right. We did. Let's say them out loud. I'm a pop star. You're a killer. How are those equal?" She laid her head on her knees. "Oh my God, the press will have a field day."

"Screw the press. This has nothing to do with them."

"Have you not heard a word I said? I'm a public figure."

He wanted to laugh at the hypocrisy of it all. "Until last night, you were in hiding. Why is that?"

"Because of stuff like this. I can't have a life."

He inched his way forward. "We had a good life until this morning. I'm not any different from the man who made love to you last night. It was love Samantha. Don't think for a second that you don't own my heart. That you haven't impacted me."

"This changes everything."

His shoulders sagged, and his arms dropped lifelessly next to his body. "It changes nothing."

When she chewed her lip for a minute, he knew there was still a chance. He only hoped she'd let him back in.

"Would you have pursued me if you'd known I was famous?"

Would he have? He wanted to be honest with her. "I would have fought my attraction to you because what happened out there is everything I don't want. I like my privacy. I like being invisible."

She laughed. Not the laugh that comes from a joke, but the laugh spurred on by disbelief. "Dalton, you're lying to yourself if you think you've ever been invisible."

"Well, it looks like we've both been lying to ourselves and to each other." He risked inching forward. If he saw any apprehension or fear in her body language, he'd move back, but he saw none.

"I lie to myself all the time." Her voice became whisper soft. "I tell myself that I love what I do. I tell myself that I can make it another year. I tell myself that I'll be fine." She burst into tears. "I'm not fine."

He couldn't stand the distance any longer. He moved closer and pulled her into his lap.

She curled into him. Maybe her grief was greater than her fear, but he loved how she clung to his body.

"Tell me more." He figured if he could get her talking, then maybe when she was finished, she'd be willing to listen.

"I love it here. For the first time in my life, I felt like I fit."

"Sweetheart, you fit." He pressed a kiss to the top of her head.

"It seems like I've been on the road for a decade. I'm tired, Dalton. I'm tired of being Indigo."

"Indigo isn't here; Samantha is, and she has a heart of gold. She's kind and forgiving. Last night, she let a stalker go free because she said everyone deserves a second chance." He lifted her chin so she had to look at him. "I'm part of everyone." He pulled her tight against his chest. "Give me a second chance."

She cried until his shirt was wet. "I'm sorry. You're right. Tell me your story."

He lifted her up and carried her to the couch. "I'll make some tea. Stay put." She nodded and tucked her tiny body into the corner. He pulled the soft throw she had folded over the arm and covered her.

While he was in the kitchen, he pulled his phone from his pocket and dialed the sheriff. "We've got a situation at Samantha's. We need to circle the wagons."

With two cups of tea ready, he returned. It crushed him to see her eyes red and swollen. He promised himself he'd stop at nothing to put a smile back on her face.

They sat in silence for minutes while he built up the courage to talk about a time he wished he could forget.

"Six years ago, I was in Denver at a bar called The Empty Keg. It's a dive bar, but it was close to school. On Fridays and Saturdays, the alcohol was cheap. I was playing pool with my buddies when I saw some guy grab a woman by the arm and drag her outside. They had been arguing off and on all night. He had been harassing her for attention. She ignored him. He didn't like the word no."

Dalton closed his eyes and relived the moment that changed his life.

"No one did anything. Everyone saw what was going on. It was obvious they weren't a couple. He'd been trying to pick her up all night, without luck." He opened his eyes and looked at Samantha, whose face was unreadable. "She fought him all the way out the door. She begged and pleaded for him to let her go. It was like listening to my mother when my father pulled her by her hair across the yard. I couldn't stand by and watch. I rushed out to help. By the time I got to her, he'd already punched her once. Told her she asked for it." He shook his head. "No woman asks for it." He set his tea down and tucked his fists under his legs. The replay always upset him. No matter how hard he tried, he could never come up with a different ending. "As the asshole wound up for another hit, I stepped in. He turned around and swung at me, connecting with my stomach. I hit him once. He never got back up."

When he looked at Samantha, fresh tears were running down her cheeks. Through a shaky voice, she asked, "You only hit him once?"

"That's all it took. Those six seconds got me six years in prison."

She set her cup down and pulled him close. It was time for her to comfort him. He was grateful for the gesture. She tugged and pulled at him until his head was in her lap.

"It sounds like self-defense." She ran her hand through his hair.

"That's what my lawyer pled, but a man was dead. There were lots of witnesses saying I hit him. No one saw him hit me."

"What about the girl?"

"She testified. It's probably why I got the minimum sentence." He remembered the judge's words verbatim. "A 'heat-of-passion' crime provoked by something that caused an ordinary person to become angry and act irrationally by killing someone." He let out a shaky breath and rubbed his head into her lap like a puppy craving attention.

"You gave me hints." She stroked his cheek with affection. "I'm so sorry I didn't listen."

"I'm sorry I didn't tell you right away. I thought about it, but everyone told me I shouldn't come out of the gate with 'I'm an ex-felon.'"

Despite the sorrow, she giggled. "That was probably wise counsel."

"We're both guilty of wanting someone to see us for who we are, and not who society has made us out to be."

"Where do we go from here?" she asked.

To bed, Dalton's inner voice screamed. If only they could go back an hour, he'd make love to her again and ignore the knock at the door. Despite the turn of events, he was relieved that the truth was finally out. Brutal as it was, he was still here with her. She wasn't shaking with fear but touching him with compassion.

This next part was going to kill him, but he knew it needed to be done. She came to Aspen Cove for clarity. She'd never get it if he was around. Their relationship was anything but clear. All he knew was that he wanted her, but he wouldn't keep her if it wasn't in her best interests.

She had a reputation to uphold. Last night when he'd looked up her music, he read more than once that she was America's sweetheart. The reporter's voice echoed in his head. *"Indigo! How do you think your fans will respond to your relationship with Dalton Black, a convicted killer?"* Samantha might be willing to forgive, but the press would never forget. He didn't want that for her. He didn't want it for himself.

He rolled to a sitting position. His body glued to her side. "You came here to get your thoughts straight. You wanted to find yourself. You won't be able to do that with all this noise around you." Her look of defeat told him he was right.

"I called the sheriff. He should get rid of the crowd."

"Thank you." She leaned her head on his chest and sighed. "I'm going to leave you."

Her hands gripped his shirt like he was a lifeline. "I don't want to be alone."

"I don't want to leave you alone, but I know if I'm here, my presence won't give you the space you need to think and make sound decisions."

Her voice cracked with emotion. "I know you're right, but I hate it."

"I know I'm right, and for what it's worth, I hate it too. But I'll do it because I ... care."

He saw the words he wanted to say on her lips, She had fallen in love with him too, but he couldn't say them, or let her say them. If he heard the words or said them and couldn't have her, it would crush him. Instead, he pressed his lips softly to hers before he rose from the couch and went into the bedroom for his shoes.

When he came back, she was still sitting in the corner of the couch, staring into space.

"You're really leaving me?" Her wavering voice tugged at his heart.

"Not for good. Just for now." He pulled a smile from deep inside himself. "I'm free-birding you, baby."

She cocked her head. "You're what?"

"I'm letting you go. If you come back, I know it was meant to be." He pulled on his boots and put on his coat. "I texted the girls and told them you needed support."

She nodded. When he opened the front door, he saw that the press had been pushed back to the street. Sheriff Cooper walked toward him.

"You okay?"

"Not really." Dalton looked beyond him to where the reporters pulled long lenses from their bags.

"I can keep them off her property, not off the street. I'll send Mark over to keep an eye on things until it all settles down." He adjusted his hat and looked at the ground. "I looked her up. She's a big deal."

"She's everything."

CHAPTER TWENTY

The buzzing of her phone was relentless. Since only her mother and Deanna had the number, she had to look. She padded barefoot back to her room and sank onto her bed. Dalton's pillow cradled her head. It smelled like pine trees and pure man, like him.

She looked at the lit screen to see a dozen messages from Deanna all with the subject: **Trouble.**

Understatement. She pulled up her assistant's number and pressed call to connect. Deanna answered immediately.

"Oh. My. God. It's all over the news. Are you okay? Did they arrest him? Sweetie, it's not your fault."

"What?"

"The news said you were harboring a criminal." She heard the *tap tap* of a keyboard in the background. "Holy smokes. He's hot."

"They put his picture up?" She wanted to die right then. Not only had her career ruined her chance at a normal life, it had taken Dalton's peaceful existence away.

"Are you safe?"

"I was never in danger." Her stomach twisted from the guilt of cowering from him. The look on his face when she crawled into the corner of the room would slice her to pieces each time she remembered it. "It's not what it seems."

Those were his exact words, and she didn't listen to him. Why would anyone listen to her?

"We've got a lot of PR work to do. This is a huge mess. Dave Belton has called at least ten times in the last hour. I'm supposed to tell you you're in breach of contract. Something about protecting your image."

"Dave Belton can screw himself. He's all talk and no action."

Deanna let out a groan. "He's acting. He told me for each day you don't return, he's firing a member of your team."

Samantha shook her head to clear it. "How is that supposed to help? Let's say I come back next week. What do I come back to if my team is gone? Has he fired anyone else but you?"

Her silence was the answer. "Cohen got the ax thirty minutes ago."

"What?" Cohen was the best sound technician out there. "Hire him and give him a raise."

Deanna laughed. "Okay, but he doesn't get as much as me. He only gets ten percent."

"Fine." Her life was falling apart. She didn't need the extra bullshit Dave Belton was dishing out. She knew what his next game would be. He'd tell her how her career image was ruined, but if she stayed with him, he'd turn it all around.

"Are you coming back?"

The smart answer would have been yes, but the honest answer was no. "I can't. I'm not done here yet."

"You're in love with him, aren't you?"

Saying it out loud made it real. "Yes. He's not the man they say he is."

"I'm sorry I jumped to conclusions. The press rarely gets it right. You want me to put out a statement?"

"Not yet."

"Poor guy probably only has a parking ticket."

It wasn't funny, but Samantha couldn't stop the laughter bubbling inside her. "No, he killed someone."

"Okay, so you're in shock. A statement isn't probably wise. Have you distanced yourself?"

Samantha stood up and peeked between the cracks of the blinds of her bedroom window. Across the street, the paparazzi lay in wait. Unless she stayed a prisoner in her cabin, she would never get the peace and quiet she craved.

"He free-birded me."

"What? What does that mean?"

She walked through the house, pulling all the curtains and blinds closed. "Oh you know, that crap about loving someone and setting them free."

"I'm confused. He's a killer, but you love him anyway. He loves you, but because you're a rich, sexy pop star, he let you go?"

"Something like that." Samantha gave Deanna a shortened version of Dalton's story.

"Oh ..." Deanna's said with a dreamy voice. "I may be in love with him too."

"Find your own felon. He's mine." She'd come to Aspen Cove to find something. She thought it was clarity, but the only thing she was clear about was how much she loved Dalton Black.

A soft knock sounded at the door.

"I have to go."

"Wait, is there anything else I can do?"

"Make sure my band and crew know they have jobs. Other than that, keep an eye out about what people are posting. I refuse to let my fame ruin a good man."

"Got it, Boss."

On the next round of knocks, Samantha peeked out the peephole to see Sage, Katie, and baby Sahara on her doorstep.

She opened it a crack and disappeared behind the door so the press wouldn't snap her photo while her friends entered.

"Thanks for coming. I hope I didn't take you away from anything."

"You saved me. Doc can deal with that case of hemorrhoids by himself. No one should see that before lunch." Sage opened her purse and took out candy bar after candy bar. She picked up the peanut butter cups and handed them to Samantha. "These are particularly helpful in a time of crisis."

Samantha took the candy gratefully. She'd been shaking for the last half an hour. It could have been nerves or low blood sugar. "What about you?" She looked at Katie. "Shouldn't you be at the bakery?"

Katie walked over to the chair by the couch and sat down. Her diaper bag fell on the floor. She reached inside and took out a box of muffins. "That's the beauty of owning something. No one can tell you what, when, or how to do anything. Besides, Ben was happy to take over."

Sage and Samantha took positions on opposite ends of the couch.

Sage leaned in and looked at Samantha closely. "Yep, you're her. I didn't recognize you without the blue hair."

Katie pulled a bottle from her bag to feed Sahara. "I knew right away. Why do you think I saddled her with that song on karaoke night?"

"Which, by the way, you killed," Sage added. "Every man in that room envied Dalton."

"Is anyone looking after Dalton?" Samantha knew he was trying to protect her, but who was protecting him?

"He took off on his bike," Katie said. "He's a private person. He needed to get away."

"From me." That blade of guilt cut deeper, making her hemorrhage inside.

"He'd never leave you unless he thought it was what was best for you." Katie lifted the baby to her shoulder and patted her back until she released a belch twice as big as she was. "She burps like her daddy."

"Why does everyone think they know what's best for me? When do I get to choose for myself?" That fire of fury burned inside her. All her life her choices were taken away. First by an abusive father that kept her mother and her on the run for years. Next it was her manager, who thought he could strong-arm her into submission. Now it was Dalton, who walked out of her life because he thought it best.

"Choose now and choose us." Sage took the peanut butter cups from Samantha. "If you're not going to eat these, I will." She tore open the wrapper and hummed at the first bite.

Samantha threw her hands into the air. "Will life ever be easy?"

Katie passed Sahara to Sage and stood in front of Samantha, where she pulled her T-shirt up to reveal a scar that ran the length of her chest. "Not easy, but worth it." She flopped back into her seat and told Samantha her story. She covered everything from her illness to her donor heart to Bowie, and then Sahara. "If you want it, you have to fight for it. Sometimes you have to take scary steps to get what you want."

Samantha wanted to crawl under the couch with the dust bunnies—she felt as useless as one. "I asked him to leave before he explained. He wouldn't leave. He fought for me."

"Will you fight for him?" Katie asked.

Would she? "Without a doubt—but then what happens to us? We have such different lives."

Sage bounced the chubby baby on her knee. "You think Cannon and I were anything alike? Opposites attract, and if you don't kill each other falling in love, it's a beautiful thing."

"I'm such an idiot."

"Only if you let someone amazing slip away," Sage said.

"You guys have to go."

They both looked at her in surprise.

"You want us to leave?" Katie asked.

"I'm texting Dalton. If you want to be here when I ask him to forgive me and take me to bed, then you can stay. If not you should go, but before you do, I want to tell you both how much I value your friendship and advice." Samantha rolled to her feet and hugged both of them before she herded them toward the door.

The paparazzi snapped pictures right away. This time, Samantha didn't hide behind the door or her friends. It was time to fight. She stepped out with Sage and Katie, who looked at each other and laughed before they gave the press the bird.

She leaned over the rail and pointed to the only reporter she recognized and told him to come forward. He looked at her with skepticism. Sitting to the side of her house was the deputy sheriff.

She walked to the cruiser and told him she needed to see one particular reporter. He exited his SUV and escorted the man to her.

"What's up, Indigo?"

"Ray, you've always been fair to me. If I give you an exclusive interview, will you continue to be fair to me? Most importantly, you need to be fair to Dalton."

"You're going to give me an exclusive?"

"Yes."

"Do you know how famous that will make me?"

"Be careful, fame isn't all it's cracked up to be."

"Can I quote you?"

"Yes." Wasn't it time to be honest with herself and everyone around her? Her statement would anger many people. Most would trade their lives for hers. She'd trade everything she had for another night with Dalton. "I'll call you when I'm ready to talk."

He fished for a card from his pocket. "I can't wait."

"Neither can I." She wasn't talking about the interview. She was talking about seeing Dalton again.

She went back inside and picked up her phone to text a message.

Dalton,

I've made a lot of mistakes in my life, but the biggest was letting you walk out that door. Please come home. I miss you. I miss the gray.

With love,

Samantha

She set down the phone and raced to the bathroom so she was showered and ready when he came back. If he came back.

CHAPTER TWENTY-ONE

Dalton zipped toward Silver Springs on his Harley. He would have gone to Copper Creek, but it was too close and held fresh memories of his time with Samantha. Besides, he couldn't be certain he wouldn't end up at Chachi's, ready to wring Todd's neck. That little asshole was responsible for this whole shit show. Without a doubt, he posted her picture and disclosed her location.

The crisp mountain air whipped around him as he drove too fast through the pass. Carelessness outweighed caution. His phone vibrated inside his pocket. He ignored it while he weaved between cars, taking risks that could kill him. He realized how stupidly he'd behaved. His death wouldn't solve anything except possibly the ache in his chest since he walked out of Samantha's cabin. He wasn't sure he could go back to his status quo when he'd been given a taste of heaven.

Besides, it would break his mom's heart if he died. He knew his friends well enough to know they'd bring him back to life so they could kill him again for his stupidity.

The driver in front of him slammed on her brakes to avoid hitting a deer. He averted disaster by a hair when he swerved right and missed eating the back end of the midsize sedan by inches. Sadly, he caught his tire on the soft shoulder and down he went. The fall wouldn't kill him, but it would hurt like a bastard.

The denim of his jeans tore as he slid across the asphalt. The loose gravel bit into his skin. His Harley, with the momentum of a freight train, sped ahead of him, hit the guardrail, and flipped over the edge. The sound of metal crashed and crumbled as his prized possession flew over the cliff and tumbled down the embankment.

Dalton came to rest on his back near the metal rail. He took a mental and physical inventory. He could move both legs, both arms, and all his fingers. His head was still attached and safely inside his helmet until he unbuckled the strap and tossed it aside. Once he knew he'd survived, the pain kicked in. His entire left side was on fire from his ankle to his hip. Thankfully, he'd worn his leather jacket, or else the road rash would have claimed more real estate on his body.

"Are you okay?" An older woman rushed to his aid. "You were tailing too close. I almost hit the deer. You almost hit me."

She rattled off facts he couldn't deny. He'd been tailing her.

"I'm fine. It's a scratch." He glanced down at his blood-soaked, shredded jeans and groaned.

"That's more than a scratch."

"I'll be all right." He pulled himself up to a sitting position and leaned against the cold metal barrier.

She peeked over the edge where his bike had taken flight. Her eyes grew big, and her face blanched almost as white as her hair. "You're in better shape than that death mobile. I'll never understand the attraction to motorcycles. You don't see people riding on the outside of planes, do you? It's not safe."

He didn't want to argue with her, but in early aviation lots of people flew without being encased in tons of metal. After a closer look, he was pretty certain she'd been alive when the Wright brothers took their first flight.

"Yes, ma'am. I'm sorry I scared you. I'm all right." A few snowflakes dropped from the sky. "Great. Just great." He leaned back and thunked his head on the metal. Until that point, it was the only thing that didn't ache.

"You need a doctor."

"I've got one." He knew if he showed up to Doc's like this, the old man would skin what hadn't been skinned already.

"My name is Agatha Guild." She pulled on his arm to help him stand. "I'll give you a ride. What's your name?"

"I'm Dalton, and I'm okay. I'll call for help."

"Oh fiddlesticks, you young ones can be so stubborn. I'm taking you home." She yanked and pulled until he had no choice but to comply or have his arm ripped from the socket. For being an antique, she was quite strong, and Dalton feared he'd lose a limb if she kept tugging.

He managed to stand. The pain of the fall sliced through him. Each step he took was worse than the last. Bits of dirt and gravel rubbed against the denim and dug deeper into his skin.

"Really, I can call a friend."

"Dalton whoever you are … I don't want any lip from you." She led him to her car and opened the trunk. "I don't want you bleeding everywhere."

Dalton's head shook slowly back and forth. "Agatha, I'm not riding in your trunk."

"Of course not." She leaned in and grabbed a blanket. "Are you sure you didn't hit your head?" She covered the upholstery of the front passenger seat. He climbed inside. "Where are we going?" She buckled in and adjusted her seat. She was a tiny thing, much like Samantha, only Ms. Guild could barely see over the steering wheel.

"I live in Aspen Cove."

"You don't say." She pulled a U-turn and headed in the opposite direction she had been traveling. "Your doctor wouldn't happen to be Doctor Parker, would it?"

"You know him?"

"Oh, yes," she said, all dreamy. "I know him. He was my square dancing partner last year."

"Doc square dances?"

She smiled. "A man of many talents."

Maybe he imagined it, but Ms. Guild seemed to imply she'd been the recipient of his talents. Then again, Dalton's body hurt so bad, he wasn't thinking clearly. He imagined a lot of things, like the smell of chocolate chip cookies and the sound of Samantha's voice telling him to come home.

He remembered the vibration in his pocket prior to the crash and pulled out his phone. There was one text message. It was from Samantha.

Dalton,

I've made a lot of mistakes in my life, but the biggest was letting you walk out that door. Please come home. I miss you. I miss the gray.

With love,

Samantha

Her message gutted him. He wanted to race back to her, but he wasn't racing anywhere. Agatha Guild drove thirty in a fifty, which was why he was riding her ass in the first place. At least that's the lie he told himself. He knew if she were going eighty, he would have still been on her tail. All he wanted to do was gain distance from the situation and the pain, not from Samantha.

He thought about what he could say to her when he saw her again. He wanted to make this better, but the facts were the facts: He was an ex-felon. She was a pop star. There would never be a place for him in her life as long as the public continued to try him.

The hardest thing to do was to let her go. The kindest thing to do was to let her go. He had to let her go.

Samantha,

We had the beginning. We had the end. I wish we'd had more of the in-between. Take care of yourself. Be true to yourself.

With love,

Dalton

He hovered over the send button. When he pressed it, his heart hollowed out. He leaned his forehead on the window and watched the pine trees pass until the glass fogged and everything seemed hazy. They crawled toward Aspen Cove. The closer they got, the heavier the snow fell and the slower Agatha drove. Outside of the need to ease the pain in his leg, it didn't matter when they arrived. There was nothing to rush toward.

"Almost there." Agatha pulled in front of Doc's clinic. "Stay here."

For an old woman, she moved faster on her feet than she did on the road. Not wanting Doc or Sage to rush a gurney out to him, he exited the car and hobbled into the building.

The first person he saw was Sage, who helped him to the examination room. He limped past Doc and Agatha, who were exchanging niceties. Agatha blushed when Doc Parker told her he'd call her.

"What happened?" Sage rushed around the room, pulling out scissors and tweezers and a metal pan.

"I'm not pissing in that."

She laughed. "Wouldn't think of asking you to. It's for saline. We have to clean out the wounds."

"Agatha said you were flirting with death." Doc walked in and washed his hands. He made quick work of cutting off Dalton's jeans. "Flirting with pretty little brunettes would be a better choice."

"Like you were flirting with Agatha?" Dalton tried to tease through his pain.

He let out a curse when Doc peeled the denim from his wound. He looked down and saw what looked like ground beef.

"You could be with Samantha if you weren't sitting here." Doc yanked another piece of denim loose.

Anyone who said quick was painless was full of shit. Dalton sucked in a fortifying breath before he replied, "Obviously, you haven't heard the news."

"Heard it. Can't say I liked it. They got it all wrong."

Dalton hissed as Doc flushed the abraded skin with saline, then went to work with the tweezers. "Dammit Doc, do you have to dig to my spleen?"

Doc turned to Sage. "Make the necessary calls."

Dalton tried to rise from the table. "Don't call anyone." He didn't want anyone to make a big deal out of this. The faster he could become invisible, the better. He couldn't be invisible if Sage sent out the 4-1-1 on his 9-1-1.

Doc's cuff to the side of his head was swift and uncomfortable. He still had great reflexes for an old fart. "You don't get to make the rules inside my clinic." He jabbed a little deeper and came out with a pebble that pinged when it hit the metal pan.

He glanced at Sage and shook his head, hoping she'd heed his request. "Really, Sage, I'll be fine."

His plea fell on deaf ears as she left the room.

"Agatha says your bike is at the bottom of a ravine. Trying to kill yourself?"

"No, trying to put some space between me and the press."

"Now, listen here, son."

Dalton groaned. "I'm all ears."

"It's about the only thing you have left. Too bad you're not using what's between them." Doc found a rhythm, and the ping of pebbles in the pan became the backdrop to his lesson. "Do you like her?"

"Samantha? What's not to like?"

"Did you tell her about your past?" Doc dropped the tweezers into the basin and flushed Dalton's injury with more saline.

"She heard it from the press first."

"And?"

"After I explained, it was okay."

"I knew I liked that girl."

"Don't you get it? We can't be together. We knew going in there was an expiration date."

"You're wrong. The only true expiration date is sour milk and death. The rest is logistics."

"We come from different worlds."

Doc slathered soothing salve on the raw skin and wrapped gauze around Dalton's leg from ankle to hip. He tugged tight for emphasis. Not because he needed to but because he wanted Dalton's attention.

"Puppy brains." He shook his head. "She comes from your world. You think she came here to be Indigo?" Doc reached into the cabinet and pulled out a pair of scrub pants. "She came here to find herself again. Go show her who she is and show the world who you are." When Dalton opened his mouth to argue, Doc pulled a cherry Life Saver from his pocket and popped it into Dalton's mouth. "Get dressed. I think I hear your mother coming."

As he struggled into the pair of scrubs, his mother burst through the door. Ben, Sage, Bowie, Cannon, and Katie, carrying Sahara, followed her. Dalton craned his neck to see if Samantha came after. She didn't. Why would she? They were no longer a thing.

Disappointment filled his empty heart. After everyone reprimanded him for his carelessness, Cannon led him outside to his truck.

"Sheriff Cooper called in some favors. The Silver Springs Police Department is going to get what's left of your bike." They drove down Main Street to Lake Circle, but instead of turning right toward Dalton's cabin, Cannon pulled up close to the steps in front of the bed and breakfast.

"What are you doing? Just take me home."

"No can do. I've been given directions from Sage. Do you have any idea what kind of trouble I'd be in if I didn't follow instructions?"

"You're so whipped." Dalton looked around before he climbed slowly out of the truck. He didn't want to attract unwanted publicity to the bed and breakfast.

Cannon looked past him. "They're still camped out in front of Samantha's cabin. They can't see you here."

It seemed an accurate statement. If he couldn't see them because of the bend in the road, then most likely they wouldn't see him. "Is she okay? Is she safe?"

"*Okay* is a relative term, but she's safe."

Dalton limped up the steps.

"Why am I here?" He stepped into the unusually darkened room.

In the shadows, a silhouette moved in his direction.

"Because I needed to see you." Samantha rushed to him and wrapped her arms around his waist. She filled the cold, cavernous hole in his heart with her warmth and presence.

CHAPTER TWENTY-TWO

"What were you thinking?" She stepped back to take inventory of him. When Sage called and said Dalton had laid his bike down on the highway, she'd nearly had heart failure. She'd only just found him. There was no way she was losing him.

"I'm fine." He limped forward and cupped her cheek. "Better now that you're here. I'm so sorry."

Cannon cleared his throat behind them. "That would be my cue to leave." He backed up toward the door. "Sage says the last guest room is yours to use. She also said she'd bring home dinner."

Samantha and Dalton tried to stifle their groans, but it was hard to silence the sound of terror. "Man, I need to teach that woman how to cook."

Cannon laughed. "Been there, tried that. What we need is one of those places that sells prepared meals for the busy family."

Samantha's eyes brightened in the dim light. "That's a brilliant idea. I wonder if there are enough people in Aspen Cove to keep it open?" She imagined the town could figure it out. They managed to keep a bakery, a bar, and a diner in business.

Cannon left them alone. They stood in the middle of the living room, staring at each other.

"Let's get you to bed." Samantha led Dalton down the hallway. He moved slowly, favoring his left side. He inched onto the bed and sighed when he was settled.

"How did you get here without being seen?" He shifted to his right to get comfortable. His left side was on fire. She could feel the heat rising from his skin.

"Katie choreographed it all. She contacted the sheriff, who had his deputy distract the reporters while I snuck out the back door. Real cloak-and-dagger kind of stuff." She laughed at how she'd hunkered down and ran from cabin to cabin until she cleared the deck and dove inside the opened back door to the bed and breakfast. Cannon closed the blinds, and she waited and worried. "If you weren't already shredded to pieces, I'd skin you alive myself. You left me."

"I'm sorry. I was trying to protect you. I still want to protect you."

Samantha climbed onto the bed and curled up next to his body. She was careful to stay away from the left side he favored. "I know, and I love that you wanted to save me. I can't remember a time when anyone gave up something for me, but I don't want you to give me up to save me. I don't want to give you up."

"You know you can't keep me. You've said so yourself."

"What if I could? Would you want me to?"

He wrapped his arm around her and tugged her tight against his chest. "Yes. I'll always want you."

She tilted her face toward his, and he kissed her softly and slowly. A lingering kiss that said he was happy to see her.

"We'll figure it out." She had no idea how it could work, but she had to find a way. She knew the press would hound her. They would also hound him. That's what worried her the most. She'd signed up for it. He hadn't.

His past and his presence could ruin her career. Maybe it

already had. The headlines were full of stories and pictures. The latest one was of her and Sage and Katie giving the press the finger. Right next to it was Dalton's mug shot, but she cared less about her career than she did about his privacy.

"You need to rest." She reached for the quilt folded at the foot of the bed. He hissed as she pulled it over him. "I'm sorry. How bad is it?"

"I'll survive."

"What can I do to ease your pain?" Her hand ran up and down his chest until it settled on the waistband of the scrubs Doc had sent him home in.

His beautiful blue eyes turned from blue to a stormy, gunmetal gray. "Don't tease an injured man."

Her hand slipped below the elastic band and stroked the length of him. "Maybe if I made you feel good somewhere else, you'd forget how much you actually hurt." When he opened his mouth, she gripped him tighter. Instead of a rebuttal, she got the sweet moan of pleasure.

"Let me make you feel better, Dalton. Let me take your pain away, if only for a minute." She didn't wait for permission. She carefully inched his pants down and gasped at the extent of his injuries. Gauze covered him from hip to ankle. "Oh honey, I had no idea it was this bad." Her fingers skimmed the bandage. "Maybe I shouldn't touch you."

"Please," he begged. "Touch me." He lifted his hips. "Samantha. Touch me."

She started at his lips and kissed her way down his body. She wasn't sure if it was the wisest thing to do, but his throaty hum of pleasure told her it was the best thing to do. Hovering over his silky hard length, her tongue darted out for a taste.

"Christ, Samantha." He let out a long, shaky breath and stilled.

"Shh. Let me love you." His body was hot, hard, and ready.

Dalton didn't speak. He didn't move. He gripped the bedspread in his hands and held on for the ride.

She stroked him with the heat of her mouth. Taking as much of him in before she hummed a song.

Dalton released a low and throaty groan that was so sexy, it made her body quiver to give him such pleasure. As he tensed beneath her touch, she increased the pressure, quickened the pace. His hands threaded through her hair, guiding her where he wanted her.

She looked up to see his eyes closed and a look of pure pleasure on his face. His breath quickened, and his muscles tensed.

"Samantha, I'm—" He tried to pull her away. He sank his hips deeper into the mattress.

She ignored him and continued until her efforts wrenched a groan. His muscles tensed, then shook, and he came with a curse. She didn't let up until his body finished shuddering and his muscles relaxed.

He reached for her and pulled her up and next to him. "God, Samantha. That was … everything."

Samantha knew the sentiment well. Each time Dalton loved her body, it was everything. She feared without him, she'd have nothing.

"I'm sorry I left you. I really thought I was doing the right thing."

"Dalton, we are stronger together." Samantha curled into his side until she heard his breath deepen and slow. When she knew he was asleep, she rolled out of bed and sat in the chair in the corner with her phone.

Deanna had been texting her regularly throughout the day. Each hour, she'd sent a message with the name of the newest sacrificial lamb. Dave was firing a person an hour. Samantha was hiring a person per hour. By the end of the day, she'd have her own crew. All she needed was a label and a recording studio.

The next hour, she traded messages with her accountant. He wasn't pleased with the turn of events, but he wasn't a fan of Dave's, so he understood her need to protect those loyal to her.

She dozed for a minute, dreaming about a future that didn't seem possible. In the dream, she and Dalton walked hand in hand down Main Street. It was spring, and her friends peeked their faces out of the shops to say hello. Children played in Hope Park. Businesses moved into the Guild. It was perfect until she woke up and realized it was a dream. The beauty of dreams was, they cost nothing and anything was possible.

Dalton stirred, and she rushed to his side, climbing onto the bed to snuggle next to him. "You okay? You need anything?"

He wrapped his free arm around her. "I've got everything I need."

FOR THREE DAYS, THEY HID OUT AT THE BED AND BREAKFAST. No one was the wiser that Dalton had returned to Aspen Cove or that Samantha had left her cabin. Sage and Katie pretended to visit each day. They'd stay a few minutes and bring clean clothes. Bowie made a middle-of-the-night visit to Dalton's and picked up a few things he needed.

Three beautiful, blissful days were spent in each other's arms. It was like putting her life on pause while they caught up. It was easy to get to know a person when you spent every minute of every day with them. She liked what he did for her body, but she loved what he did for her soul. She'd come to Aspen Cove to find clarity. For those hours Dalton was gone, nothing was clear. The minute he returned, it came together. She may have had it all, but she had nothing without him.

Come Sunday, they had to vacate their room at the bed and breakfast. Sage had a group arriving that afternoon. Samantha and

Dalton braved the world together. What was done was done. She was getting a lot of backlash from her relationship with Dalton, but if she let society decide who she could date, she was no better off than when she allowed Dave to be a dictator.

She had heard nothing from him in two days, which was simultaneously nice and terrifying. Dave was not the type of man to go down easy.

Dalton was stiff and sore, but each day he moved more fluidly. At night when he made love to her, she couldn't even tell he was injured.

They looked outside. They had two choices: They could walk proudly out the front door and up the street into the throng of persistent reporters, or they could sneak back along the edge of the water to their cabins. Samantha decided their path when she said she would not hide the best thing in her life.

Hand in hand, they left the bed and breakfast and walked down Lake Circle. About a half dozen photographers turned in shock to see the couple appear. Shutters clicked, and the questions came nonstop.

When they reached the front of Dalton's cabin, Samantha's heart dropped to the hard ground. Spray painted in red over the exterior of his cabin was the word 'Killer'.

She turned toward the reporters. "Where were your cameras when this was going on?" She stomped forward until she was in front of Jake. "I expected more from you. You have a responsibility to report the truth. Report the damn truth, and do it with fairness and integrity." Her voice rose until it hit near hysteria. She pointed to Dalton, and then looked back at the reporters. "He killed a man, and by definition that makes him a killer, but do your damn homework. He's not a killer. He's the best man I know."

She marched toward Dalton and threaded her fingers through his in a sign of unity. "My house or yours?"

"Mine. I'll make you an edible meal." She followed him inside.

The cameras clicked, and she knew the next picture posted would be of her and Dalton walking into his home, beside them the red paint, running down the wood like blood.

In minutes, Dalton was in the kitchen whipping together a meal worthy of Michelin's highest three-star rating. Samantha set the table. They sat in front of the window overlooking the lake. Days ago the water was solid, but today cracks and fissures marred the once smooth surface, proving that everything changed.

"In a few weeks, you won't even know the lake was ever covered in ice." Dalton poured them a glass of white wine and sat down next to her to enjoy the salmon and grilled veggies.

"Hopefully in a few weeks, all of this other stuff will be a memory too." Samantha laid her hand on top of Dalton's. "I'll get someone to fix your house."

"It's not a big deal." Though his words were positive, the lines on his face were etched with concern.

She sipped her wine. Actually gulped it. She needed the alcohol to numb her anger. Name-calling was one thing. Destroying someone's property was another. Why did his crime count and the vandal's didn't?

"It's a big deal to me. If I wouldn't have come here, your life wouldn't have changed."

He dropped his fork, and his tight expression softened with such love and passion. "If you hadn't come here, Samantha, my life *wouldn't have changed*."

"Yes, that's what I said." She picked up her glass and emptied it.

"Change isn't always a bad thing."

"I don't want to be bad for you." She forked a bite of perfectly cooked fish.

"Baby, you're so bad, you're good."

"Get me drunk, and I'll show you how bad I can be."

He topped off her glass.

CHAPTER TWENTY-THREE

Dalton left his house early in the morning. Thankfully, the paparazzi weren't early risers. The only cameras present belonged to the reporters sleeping in their cars. In his rearview mirror, he watched as the red paint on his house faded from sight.

Not wanting to cause his mom or his business problems, he snuck into the kitchen from the back entrance and went to work. He liked to visit their patrons, but he knew he'd be stuck in the kitchen all day.

When his mother walked in, she did what all good mothers do. She wrapped her arms around him and gave him a hug. It was the same hug she'd given him seven years ago after sentencing, and the same hug she gave him last year when he came home. The hug that said, "I love you unconditionally, and I wish I could improve your life."

No words were exchanged. They didn't need words. It was always them against the world, and both knew they had each other's back.

Maisey stood back. "How's the road rash?"

"Feels better than it looks." He'd inspected the scabbing after his shower. There were a few deep places where he'd scar, but all in all, considering he'd slid about fifty feet across the pavement, he was in good shape.

"How is Samantha?" Maisey had visited them in the bed and breakfast several times. Dalton wasn't sure if it was to spend time with him and Samantha or save them from frozen lasagna, because she always came with food. One night it was chicken fried chicken with mashed potatoes and gravy. The second time, it was spaghetti and meatballs, the kind that simmered on a stovetop for hours.

"She's good. Her life is a mess. Her manager is a jerk. The press continues to hound her. They're trying her for my crime."

"She seems tough enough to handle it all."

"For a tiny thing, she's filled with tough stuff. I worry that my presence in her life will ruin her career. Fans are fickle."

Mom prepped several coffee filters, filling them with grounds and stacking them up so they were ready when she opened the door. One positive thing about the influx of press was that it would bring more customers to the diner. So far, no one had put two and two together and figured out that Dalton was Maisey's son. She was a Bishop now, and that would help. Plus, they were too focused on Samantha and Dalton to give other family connections much thought.

He hated that one act years ago would define his life forever and possibly ruin the lives of those he loved.

"I like her, Dalton. It takes courage to be the one percent."

Samantha was part of the 'one percent' that saw him for the man he was, and not the man the press made him out to be.

"I like her too." He liked everything about her, from the way he fit inside her body to the way she sang when no one was looking. Those were the songs from her heart. She spent hours each day curled up next to him, scribbling on a notepad. She said she was writing her next album and that it would be a secret.

Maisey took the stack of prepped coffee filters and walked through the swinging doors. It was seven o'clock and time to open.

Business was booming. Dalton didn't have time to slow down until the doors closed at two. He was scraping the grill when the back door opened and Samantha walked inside.

"How did you get away?"

"The sheriff came and got me. He said he had some errands to run and thought I might like lunch. He told the reporters that if they followed him, he'd cite them for interfering with an investigation. When they asked him what kind of investigation, he spouted off a dozen things that started with invasion of privacy to slander. They packed up their bags and left. If I wasn't there, there was no story. I'm sure they'll be back."

"Are you hungry?" Dalton lifted her and set her down on the stainless-steel prep table. He stepped between her legs and pressed a soft kiss to her lips. "I can make you that omelet you like. Or how about a waffle?"

"I hoped you could start your culinary school and make me your first student."

"You want to learn how to cook?"

"I want to learn how to cook something you like to eat."

Dalton's mind went straight to the gutter. His hands traveled up the thighs of her worn jeans and settled at the juncture between. "My favorite thing to eat requires absolutely no prep. The only ingredient is you."

"Men." She shook her head. "One-track mind. Besides, that's dessert." She winked at him and slid from the metal table to the tile floor. She wrapped her arms around his waist. He expected her to squeeze him tight like she always did. Instead, she removed his apron and tied it around her waist.

"Your student is ready."

He laughed. The hem of his apron reached the tops of her

tennis shoes. "You're going to trip." He rolled it up and retied it to her waist. "Can you boil water?"

She fisted up and slugged him in the arm. "I'm not Sage. I've got water boiling down to an art. I can also make a mean grilled cheese and an awesome mystery loaf."

"Mystery loaf?"

She smiled. "Like you, when I was a kid, I did some cooking. Mom worked all day, so I made dinner, but I was limited to three things. It was cheesy potato and ham casserole, meatloaf or what I called mystery loaf because I tossed in whatever we had, or grilled cheese. I can't say I mastered any of them, but grilled cheese was the best. The rest, I mostly ruined." Her shoulders slumped forward. "I'm good at ruining things."

He lifted her chin and kissed her sweetly. "Not everything."

The sound that left her was a cross between a snort and a groan. "Look at your life now. Two weeks ago you were living a happy, quiet life, and now everything is a mess."

"Sweetheart, two weeks ago I wasn't even living. I didn't know it until you arrived."

She pulled a hair tie from her pocket and fastened her hair into a high ponytail. "You can't say it's been boring. I mean, I've brought *a lot* to Aspen Cove." She said it in a tongue-in-cheek fashion. "There's the pestilence that camps outside our cabins." She walked around the kitchen, checking out the spices, the equipment, and him.

He nodded. "There's that."

"I sang you a song or two." She hummed something he didn't recognize.

Dalton thought about how much he liked her humming when her mouth was full—of him. "I like it when you sing." He reached above the grill for a loaf of bread.

"And we can't forget about the art."

He placed the bread on the counter and pulled a block of cheese from the refrigerator below. "The art?"

She opened her eyes and tilted her head. "I like the band The Killers, but I wouldn't have chosen to spray paint it on my cabin."

He laughed even though it wasn't funny. No one wanted to live in a place that was vandalized in such a way. "No accounting for taste."

"Speaking of taste, what are you going to teach me to cook?"

"I thought we'd learn from each other. You teach me how to make a mean grilled cheese sandwich, and I'll teach you how to make roasted creamy tomato soup from scratch."

They went to work side by side. Her secret recipe was to throw in several varieties of cheese, and instead of butter, she slathered the bread with mayonnaise and cooked it to a golden brown. Dalton fire roasted several tomatoes, added them to the blender with stock and cream and a few spices.

Fifteen minutes later, they were sitting in the diner with Maisey and Ben eating the best grilled cheese sandwich of his life with passable tomato soup. In a perfect world, this would be his forever. Sadly, the world was imperfect, but not in that moment.

Once the kitchen was cleaned, they piled into his truck. They didn't return home right away because going back to the cabin meant ruining this perfect moment, so they headed to the other side of the lake to visit Sam and eat ice cream.

Today's flavors were Bee's Knees, with honeycomb chunks and mini chocolate chips; Bloody Sundae, with vanilla ice cream and raspberry sauce; and Monkey in the Middle, with chocolate ice cream with bananas. Sam sprinkled them all with his 'ants'.

Samantha sat on Dalton's right side, afraid she'd bump into his left and hurt him. He loved the way she looked out for him even though all thoughts of his injuries were gone the second they hit the sheets.

They finished their ice cream, and he helped her into the truck when his phone buzzed. Cannon messaged him and told him to pull between their cabins and park on the lakeside of his property.

"I think the press is back in full force." He handed his phone to Samantha.

She read the text and groaned. "I'm so sorry. Maybe I should leave."

Before he started the truck, he turned in her direction. "You are not leaving me. We'll figure it all out. Eventually, they'll get bored and leave us alone."

She raised her perfectly plucked brow like she didn't believe him. He had to get her to believe because he wanted her to stay.

"I didn't come to Aspen Cove to ruin the town."

He unbuckled her seat belt and pulled her to his side. "How have you ruined anything?" She straddled his lap, and he bit back a groan when her shoe scraped along the deepest part of his injured leg. "You make everything sweeter." He kissed her passionately and pulled back. "You are the Bee's Knees."

She touched her forehead to his. "That's the ice cream you're tasting."

"Doubtful. I've tasted you and the ice cream. You are infinitely more satisfying."

"Remember that when something else goes wrong."

He cupped her frowning face. "Samantha, life will never be easy. I knew that before I met you, but you make whatever we have to face worthwhile. We are better together." They sat in the truck for another five minutes and held each other. They were enjoying their time together or maybe getting the courage to face what was to come.

When they arrived back in Aspen Cove, things weren't as he expected. Gone was the word 'Killers'. In front of his cabin was Wes Covington, the town's resident contractor. He stood in front of the newly sandblasted cabin, winding up the cord to his equipment. Dalton waved as he passed.

Samantha turned her head and watched the reporters run for cover.

"Are those bees?"

In front of his cabin was Abby Garrett in full beekeeping gear, setting up her hives.

One thing he loved about the town was how the locals circled the wagons around their own.

CHAPTER TWENTY-FOUR

"Bees?" Deanna said. "Your security system is bees?"

"That's right," Samantha replied. She took a diet soda from the refrigerator and walked to the front door, where she watched Abby shake bees from the hive. Swarms of them flew in every direction. The last of the diehard photographers took off running. "It's quite effective."

"Are you doing okay? I know it's been crazy."

Samantha popped the top of the can and listened to the hiss of carbonation escape. 'Crazy' didn't begin to describe the past week.

Whirlwind.

Fabulous.

Terrifying.

Heartbreaking.

There were a hundred words that could describe the past week. 'Crazy' was not the one she'd choose. "I don't know. It's been hard to watch Dalton get dragged through the court of public opinion. He's been great through it all. Keeps telling me that what we have is bigger than what anyone can throw at us, but I'm worried he'll change his mind."

"He sounds like a good man. Seems to have a handle on it. Don't worry. He'll let you know if it's too much."

Samantha walked away from the front door to the back of the house, where the windows faced the lake. She wished she could open the blinds and enjoy the view. The ice on the lake was melting, and the water had lapped up onto the shore. It made a soft, comforting swish she wished she could hear, but she'd seen more than one reporter ignore the sheriff's warning and sneak behind the cabin on the unlikely chance they'd get a sellable shot. Maybe they simply avoided the sting of Abby's bees.

"I'm not sure he would tell me. Look at what he's been through. Compared to prison, I'm sure everything is bearable. I don't want to be someone he has to bear."

"Believe me, there are days when you are unbearable." Deanna's laughter filled the phone. "Show me a day when I can't sneak you a piece of chocolate, and I'll show you unbearable."

"Now you're being mean."

Deanna sighed. "No ... mean is trying to cancel the benefit concert because the sponsor is stupid."

Samantha sank into the soft leather of her couch. "No. Tell me they're not trying to cancel it." She couldn't believe the Domestic Abuse Co-op would give up the hundreds of thousands of dollars the concert would pull in.

The silence on Deanna's end said it all. "It's not a firm no. We're talking about the potential to lose lots of money here. As you know, money talks, but they aren't happy with Mr. Black's background. Something about a pop star who's in love with a violent man can't be the poster child against domestic abuse."

"He's not that guy. If they could only meet him. He's kind and loving and—"

"I know, a good kisser among other things. Where is the hottie now?" Deanna had been sending Samantha all the pictures the press had taken and posted. She couldn't argue with her. Dalton

Black was one handsome man. He even looked good in prison orange. Like Indigo, he had that bad-boy image, but inside he was as sweet as Sam's Scoops ice cream.

"He worked all morning, so he went home to shower and change. He's coming back later to binge watch *Supernatural* with me."

"You're killing me. You have the hottest man I've ever seen in your cabin, and you're going to watch television?"

"We can't stay in bed all day."

"Why not?"

"Because people have to work." She picked up her notepad and looked at the pages of lyrics she'd written since she arrived in Aspen Cove. She had a whole album penned, from a song of hope called 'One Hundred Wishes' to a love song called 'In the Gray'.

"Speaking of work, all we need is a studio and a bass player to fill out your crew."

"Seriously? Dave has fired everyone else?" The thought of Dave Belton made Samantha's blood boil. She'd fantasized several times a day about seeing him face to face. Each time in her imagination, she fisted up and let him have it.

In reality, that wouldn't happen because the one thing Samantha knew about Dave was, he'd never let her win. She might get the first word in, maybe even get a hit, but he'd come out the victor.

"Yep, everyone but the bass player."

She set her soda can on the table and rolled up to a standing position. Samantha paced the room in front of the fireplace. "I haven't heard from him in days. I don't get what his end game is. If I don't have a crew, I can't make the music he wants. Where is this going?"

"You know him. He's killing you by a thousand tiny cuts. He doesn't know you've hired everyone. I've told them not to say anything. I'm pretty sure he thinks once your soft heart bleeds for a while, you'll give in. He knows you too well."

Deanna was right. She'd do anything for her crew. She'd sacrifice herself for them if she had to, but over the last two weeks, she realized she didn't have to. She held all the cards. She could move forward without Dave, but he'd never survive without her. She liked the power that position gave her.

"That was the old Samantha. That girl is gone, and in her place is me. I'll still bleed for my crew, but I can no longer fear Dave. It gives him too much power. Too much control."

"Rahrrr," Deanna growled. "Who let you out of your cage?"

"Me. I broke out. I'm tired of living in captivity. Tired of letting life live me instead of the other way around." A light knock sounded at the door. "Gotta go. Dalton's here."

"Skip *Supernatural* and go for the sheets," Deanna said before Samantha hung up. She had to agree. The sheets sounded appealing.

She rushed to the door. "You could have walked inside," she said as she swung it wide open, but it wasn't Dalton standing in front of her. It was Dave Belton, and he was pissed.

Her inner lion roared and then whimpered.

"You need to leave."

He flicked the stub of his filterless cigarette onto the deck and stepped forward.

She stepped back, her eyes on the hot ember and the wood.

"I don't need to do anything." He leaned against the rail of her back porch like he belonged there. "You need to do a lot. You can start by apologizing and packing."

She stepped forward and closed the door behind her. With the rubber sole of her tennis shoe, she ground the ash into the wood surface until it was extinguished. "You can burn down my house, but you won't get your way." All Dave thought about was Dave. It showed in every action from what he said to the careless tossing of his ember. "I'm not coming with you. You need to leave," she repeated. She hated the way her voice shook. What would Deanna think now that her roar had turned into a meow?

He shifted back and forth like a boxer. *Definitely high.* Dave always got jittery when he was coked out. "You need to come with me." He reached forward and gripped her left wrist, squeezing it hard.

"Don't touch me," she yelled. She pulled back, breaking his iron-fisted hold.

He raised his hands as if in surrender, but she knew better. Dave wasn't one to throw in the towel. "Look at you." He scanned her body from head to toe. "Two weeks, and you've gone to shit. You're fat and out of shape. Your hair ..." He shook his head. "It's a good thing I'm here. You've had your fun, now it's time to get back to work." He shriveled his nose in the way people did when they smelled something bad. "We have so much work to do."

"No." She had no idea where the word came from or where she got the strength to shout it. No one said no to Dave.

He pushed forward, taking a threatening step in her direction. "You owe me."

That statement was laughable. She pressed herself to the door. "I don't owe you anything. You've made a fortune on my talents. Without me, you have nothing." Gone was any semblance of calm. Her voice hit a decibel level that shook the windows behind her.

"I made you," he yelled.

"Wrong. *I* made *you*. No more. I don't need you to manage me. I'm a twenty-nine-year-old woman."

"Then act like it." He reached for her again and clamped his hand over her already sore wrist.

There was a flurry of motion. Several reporters stood by the lake, watching the action unfold. To Samantha's left, she watched Dalton come out of his cabin and take in the scene. A murderous look fell over his face when he saw Dave's hand on her. He hopped over the rail of his deck and raced forward. She knew in her heart if Dalton got to her before she took control of the situation, he'd be in jail for another murder.

Instead of allowing that to happen, Samantha pulled her right fist back and swung with all the might a hundred-and-ten-pound woman could throw. One hundred and ten because she knew she'd gained some weight. Her pants were tight, and the asshole told her she was fat. That was reason enough for her to strike. Add to that ten years of abuse, and she had her justification. When she connected with his nose, she heard the crunch of cartilage or bone.

Dave let her go. Both of his hands went to his face, where blood dripped between his fingers to her deck. He staggered back and stumbled down the stairs to the pine covered ground.

Dalton bolted past Dave and straight to Samantha, who cradled her right hand to her chest. She'd never hit anyone before. Inside, she felt amazing. She'd finally stuck up for herself. She'd shut a bully down. She didn't believe in fighting violence with violence, but with Dalton rushing to her aid, she had little choice but to get Dave's hands off of her before Dalton put his on the asshole.

"Are you okay?" Dalton placed himself between Samantha and Dave.

"You stupid bitch," Dave yelled from his place on the ground. "You've done it now." He stumbled to his feet and came forward. He was high, and high never meant smart.

Samantha tried to move in front of Dalton, but he kept her pinned behind him.

"You need to back away." Dalton's voice was low and deadly.

"Or what? Are you going to kill me too?" Dave pulled his phone out of his pocket.

"Dalton, stop. I'm hurt, and Dave Belton isn't worth it." She knew if she distracted him, he'd come to her rescue. It wasn't a lie. She was hurt. The crunch she heard was more than Dave's nose if the pain shooting through her hand was any hint. "I think I broke my hand."

By this time, the waterfront was full of paparazzi. They didn't care if they were breaking the law by trespassing on private property. All they cared about was getting the shot.

"I'm calling the police," Dave said.

Samantha peeked around Dalton's big body and said, "Good, you're going to need them when I press charges."

Her heart sank when she heard the asshole talk into his phone, "I want to press charges against Dalton Black. He assaulted me."

Samantha's world turned dark. "You liar. I hit you."

Dave hung up the phone. "Who will believe that? This only ends one way, Samantha. You come back to California, and it'll all go away. Stay here, and I'll make sure everything you have goes up in flames."

Minutes later, Sheriff Cooper arrived. He took statements from everyone, then turned to Dalton. "Dave Belton accused you of hitting him."

Dalton looked at Samantha and back to Sheriff Cooper. "He's a liar."

"I'm taking you both in until this is all cleared up," the sheriff said.

A gut-wrenching cry left Samantha. "He didn't do it." She raced toward Dalton, throwing her arms around him. Ignoring the pain in her hand because it came nowhere close to the pain in her heart. "I'm so sorry. This is my fault. I'll fix it."

Dalton cupped her face and kissed her. "No, sweetheart." He looked at the idiot. "This is his fault."

While Sheriff Cooper placed Dalton in his cruiser, Deputy Sheriff Bancroft took custody of Dave. It was a bittersweet moment to see him being placed in the police car. A heartbreaking moment to watch Dalton being driven away.

Standing alone on the back porch of her cabin, she turned to the press. "You wanted a story?" she yelled. "This is your story. Will you tell the truth? I challenge you to report the damn truth for a change."

Cannon came running up the beach. "What the hell happened?"

Samantha broke down and cried. "I've ruined Dalton's life."

Cannon hung his arm over her shoulders and walked her to his truck. "Let's get you to Doc's, then we'll figure out what the hell we're going to do about Dalton."

Samantha explained the situation to Cannon on their way into town. "He didn't do anything. He raced to help me. I'm the one who hit Dave."

"Any witnesses?"

"Yes, many. But will they come forward?" Samantha wasn't sure. It was his word against hers. Dave Belton's accusation turned everything upside down.

CHAPTER TWENTY-FIVE

Sitting in a jail cell wasn't the worst thing. Sitting in a jail cell and knowing Samantha was hurt and alone was insufferable. Having Dave Belton in the cell next to him was like throwing salt on an open wound.

"She'll be gone by the time you get out of here. That's her MO. She grew up running from trouble," Dave taunted Dalton from his cell.

It was a good thing he couldn't see him or get to him. All he wanted right now was to shut the asshole up. "You don't know what you're talking about."

"Ten years. I've had her for ten years. She's almost like a daughter."

Dalton sat on the cement bench and leaned against the wall. "That's irony for you. Her father was an abusive asshole too. If she wasn't contractually bound, you'd already be in her rearview mirror."

"Unlike you, she'll never leave me. I hold all the cards. You may have your dick inside of her, but my influence is wrapped around her so tightly, she can't breathe unless I say so. She's weak and scared. Always has been. Always will be."

"How's that nose?" Dalton hated that Samantha hurt her hand, but loved that she stood her ground and defended herself. "Scratch that. How does it feel to know someone you consider weak and scared kicked your ass?"

"Probably better than knowing you're going back to jail because they think you did it."

Dalton laughed. "You have no idea who you're dealing with. If I had been the one to hit you, you wouldn't have gotten up. They don't call my right hand the fist of death for nothing." It wasn't something he liked to brag about, but Dave Belton needed to know he got off easy. If Dalton had made it to Samantha before she threw that punch, Dave would be in the hospital or the morgue instead of jail.

"I'd gladly do time for Samantha. I can understand your need to lie. I mean, she's a hundred pounds soaking wet. Not sure my ego could take that beating either. I get why you have to invent a story. Tall tales compensate for your little wiener."

"You're lucky there's a wall separating us."

"Trembling over here." Dalton shook with a silent chuckle. The problem with guys like Dave was they were all talk and no action. They hid behind words and women. "Too bad I can still hear you. Makes me want to give you that smack down you're telling everyone about. Do you need a doctor? There's one across the street. He'll even give you a Life Saver if you don't cry."

"You two done?" Sheriff Cooper walked around the corner with keys jingling in his hands.

Dalton heard Dave shuffle and walk to the bars. "It's about time you came to let me out."

"About that." Sheriff Cooper stood between the two cells so both men could see him. "Seems to be a discrepancy with your story."

"Is this some small town, favoritism bullshit going on?" Dalton couldn't see Dave's face, but he could hear the rage in his voice. "I'll sue the hell out of you and this town if you don't let me go right now."

"There's a problem. I thought maybe you'd like to tell me what happened one more time."

Sheriff Cooper looked at Dalton. He wasn't exactly wearing a smile on his face, more of a pay-attention expression that Dalton found interesting.

"I told you already. I was talking to Indigo ... I mean Samantha, and out of nowhere Dalton Black attacked me."

"From which direction did he approach?" Sheriff Cooper jotted some things in his notepad as Dave recited his lie.

"He's so big, he was everywhere at once."

"Did you try to defend yourself?"

"I didn't have time. He punched me, and I fell down the stairs."

"Hmm." The sheriff walked towards Dalton's cell and unlocked the door. "You're free to go."

He exited and stood in front of Dave's cell. The man had his red face pressed to the bars. "You've got to be kidding me? He's a felon."

Sheriff shook his head. "Ex-felon. He did his time."

"He hit me."

"Deputy Bancroft? Please bring the evidence back here."

Seconds later, Mark Bancroft walked back, carrying an expensive looking camera. "Hold this button." The sheriff called Dalton over, and they stood in front of Dave's cell. He was far enough away that Dave couldn't touch anything or anyone, but he had a great view of the entire event captured pixel by pixel. The sheriff held the button down and displayed the pictures in rapid succession like a video.

"Seems to me that you assaulted Ms. White and she defended

herself. She's across the street getting a cast put on, and may press charges. You have the right to do likewise, but the evidence is pretty damning. Would you like to call your lawyer?"

Dalton didn't wait to hear Dave's answer. He bolted from the back room and raced across the street to Doc Parker's clinic.

Doc was putting the last layer of plaster in place when he walked inside. As he did for every patient, he unwrapped a cherry Life Saver and popped it into Samantha's mouth when she opened it to say something.

"Mmm," she moaned. "That's almost worth breaking my hand."

Doc turned to Dalton. "Might as well look at you while you're here. Take off your pants."

Dalton stared at the Doc and then at Samantha. "Now?"

"Don't be shy. I'm sure she's seen it all already."

Samantha laughed and waggled her perfectly plucked brows. "Yeah, Dalton, take off your pants."

"In a second." He walked to her and cradled her newly cast hand in his. "Does it hurt?"

She shook her head. "Less now than it did when it was pressed against Dave's nose."

Doc walked to the door. "I'll get her some pain meds. When I get back, only one of you better be naked."

He shut the door behind him, giving them some privacy.

"Answer me truthfully. Are you in pain?"

She lifted the black cast. Her choice of color wasn't lost on him. "It's not that bad. Doc says it's a hairline fracture. Should heal fine."

He cupped her face. "You were a badass."

She smiled and sat taller. "I kind of was. I feel good about it all." She lifted her good hand and pulled him down for a kiss. "I'm glad Jake got those pictures."

"You know him?"

"Yes, he's around a lot. I told him I'd give him an exclusive interview a few days ago. I guess that went a long way in his book. He chased me down here and showed me the footage he recorded. I sent him straight to the sheriff's office."

"Dave is furious."

Her smile lit up the room. "Dave is fired. I put in a call to my agent, and he's agreed to end the contract. I was so stupid to sign such a long deal with both of them. Talk about young and dumb. I didn't know any better."

"That's the thing: When you know better, you do better."

She narrowed her eyes at him. "Oprah said that a long time ago."

He'd never admit his love for Oprah to anyone but her. "Her show was my guilty pleasure for six years. It was all reruns because she went off the air in 2011, but I watched and learned."

She pressed her lips to his. "You are always a surprise to me."

"One of you better be undressed, and it better be Dalton," Doc's voice sounded from the end of the hallway.

"That's my cue." He unbuttoned his jeans and let them fall to the floor.

She hopped off the table to get a good look at his leg. "It still looks so painful."

"You have the most amazing way of making me forget the discomfort."

Samantha hummed, which made it near impossible for Dalton to not get hard. Her voice did things to his heart, but when she hummed in that low throaty way, it vibrated through his body and settled between his legs.

"You ready?"

Dalton hopped onto the cold table and eyed Samantha. "Behave yourself."

"What? I'm working on a melody." She went back to humming

the low tones that made him stiff. He kept his eyes on Doc's bulbous nose and overgrown eyebrows. That worked well to kill his desire.

Doc gave him a quick once-over and applied some antibiotic ointment to the deepest wounds. "You'll live." He walked to the door. "I don't normally tell my patients to spend more time inside, but I'm thinking you two are dangerous when left in the wild. Go home and climb into bed."

Dalton's eyes grew wide. "You heard him, he said we have to get into bed."

Samantha tossed him his jeans. "I heard him. Hurry up."

Dalton caught Doc before he walked out the door. "No Life Saver for me?"

Doc nodded toward Samantha. "She got the last one. You'll have to see if she'll share."

Samantha bolted past Doc toward the pharmacy. "Not sharing. You'll have to get your own."

"Kids," Doc grumbled.

Because they'd both been driven to town, they walked back home. Dalton wrapped his arm around Samantha's shoulders. He couldn't help hearing Dave's words in his head. "She'll be gone by the time you get out of here."

"I know your instinct to leave is strong ... but don't."

She slowed her walk to a crawl. "Tell me something good that's happened since my arrival?"

It twisted his gut that she didn't see them as being something good. "*We're* good. Don't forget, we're stronger together."

She held up her cast. "I don't know. I'm pretty strong on my own." She threaded her left arm through his right and leaned against him. "I'm pretty sure Aspen Cove will breathe a sigh of relief when I'm gone."

"If you leave, I may never breathe again." Dalton hated that he'd let her get so deeply imbedded inside his heart. Weeks ago, he teased his friends about catching a love virus. Apparently, he had been exposed and had no immunity to Samantha White. He was head-over-heels in love with her, and that scared him more than anything.

CHAPTER TWENTY-SIX

They'd almost made it to her cabin when the sheriff pulled his cruiser beside them.

He rolled down his window. "You didn't stop by to fill out the paperwork to press charges."

Samantha bit her lip. "Sorry." She had glanced at the sheriff's office when they walked through town. She'd taken care of the Dave problem when she called the Shepherd Agency. To do anything more would be like poking a bear with a sharp stick.

"I can't hold him without charges." Sheriff Cooper exited the cruiser and stood against the door. A few bees flew by to investigate and then left.

Samantha looked past the boxed hives to where a few reporters covered in netting held their cameras at the ready. She'd always hated how the press invaded her privacy, but her thoughts on that changed the minute Jake offered pictures to exonerate Dalton.

"I'm not sure that's wise."

Dalton stepped in front of her. "Press charges, or he'll come back for round two like Todd."

She knew they were looking out for her, but that was part of the problem. No one hesitated to tell her what they wanted her to do. No one asked her what she wanted, and right now that was peace and time alone with Dalton.

"I don't have to press charges, and I don't want to." She hated that she sounded so snippy, but pressing charges kept Dave in her life. She wanted him gone. She looked at Dalton. "It's the week of second chances. Todd got one. You got one. Dave gets one."

"So, no charges?" Sheriff Cooper frowned.

"Not unless he's charging me."

"Nope."

Samantha shrugged. "No charges, then."

"Can't say I'm on the same page as you. He seems like an unpredictable man."

Understatement. "I want this to be over. Charging him keeps him in my life."

"Your call." He opened the door and climbed back into his cruiser. "I'll take him to his car and escort him to the town line. Keep your eyes open." He rolled up his window and headed back toward town.

"It's a mistake to let him off. He broke your hand." Dalton glanced down at the black cast.

"I broke my hand on his nose. Really, he could press charges. He's not. Let it go." She walked past him, taking a circuitous route around the buzzing hives toward the remaining reporters. She had to give Abby Garrett credit. Everyone was afraid of bees.

She looked behind her and waved for Dalton to follow. He looked at the hives and frowned. Even Mr. Big and Brawny feared the buzz.

She approached Jake and gave him a hug. "Thanks for coming to our rescue."

Dalton advanced with caution. She knew his experience with

the press had been less than favorable. Hers had too, but maybe it was the way she thought of the press. She'd done a lot of swatting at them and avoiding them. Like the bees, they stung when they weren't happy.

"Dalton? Do you have time for a few questions?"

The grimace on his face screamed no, but he walked forward and stood next to Samantha. His body was tense until she leaned into him and rested her head on his chest.

"Can we get a shot of you two?" Jake asked. He didn't have his camera pointed and focused like the others. He held it up and lifted his shoulders in question.

She turned to Dalton. "You okay with that?"

"Sure." He wrapped his arm around her. She settled her cast against his stomach. "Anyone have a Sharpie that would show up on black?"

A young photographer in the back held up a pack of metallic, felt-tip pens. "These should work, they're good for proofs."

Dalton took out the silver Sharpie and drew a heart on Samantha's cast. In the center he wrote, "It's all about love."

Ray asked how they'd met, and Dalton told him that Samantha almost burned down her cabin the first night she was here.

"Cooking?" he asked.

"No, trying not to freeze," she replied.

"Do you love her?" Jake asked Dalton.

He looked at her and didn't deny it. "How could I not? Look at her." He smiled. "And have you heard her sing?"

"What about you, Indigo?" a girl off to the side called. "Are you in love with Dalton Black?" Samantha waited for her to say *convicted killer* as if it were his last name, but she didn't.

Samantha looked into Dalton's eyes. She'd never said the words to him. She wanted it to be a private moment, but to say anything less than the truth would be wrong.

"How could I not be? Look at him." She squeezed her arms around his waist. "Have you tasted anything he cooks?" She implied that love was there, but the words were for him alone.

There was collective conversation about the diner and his blue-plate specials. Turns out they had put two and two together, but as long as he was cooking, they didn't care.

Ray stepped forward. "What's next for you?"

She honestly couldn't say. "I was supposed to do a benefit concert for women and children suffering from domestic violence, but the misrepresentation of Dalton in the press has put that in jeopardy."

"It has?" Dalton stepped away. "They canceled the concert because of me?" He ran his hand through his hair. "That's ridiculous. Those families need support." He paced in front of the hives. It was said that animals and insects could sense tension and fear. The hive buzzed louder. Samantha and the press moved farther away. "It's never going to end, is it? I did something six years ago, and it changed my life. I did my time. When will it go away? Hundreds of abused women and children will suffer because I protected Bethany Waters. It hardly seems fair. And you know what?" He turned toward the small gathering. "I'd do it again." Dalton turned and walked toward his cabin.

Samantha stood in the center of the group. She pointed toward Dalton's retreating figure. "That right there is your story. *He's* not a monster. He *killed* a monster. He knew exactly what that looked like growing up. He was the son of one. I knew what that looked like too. When I was nine, my mother and I went on the run. We looked over our shoulders until I was sixteen. That's when we found out he'd died in a single-car accident. The scariest thing about that day was, he died in the town where we lived. He'd found us and had gone to a bar to celebrate."

"Did he say Bethany Waters?" Jake asked as he jotted down the name.

"Yes. It's public record. His entire story is public record if anyone wanted to know the truth. The problem is, the truth doesn't always sell the story." She handed the silver pen back to its owner and looked down at her cast. *"It's all about love."* That was a wise thing to remember.

Samantha found Dalton at his place. He was in the kitchen doing what he did best. "Hey." He continued to season the roast he had on the counter. "Look at me." She stepped in front of him and pressed her head to his chest. "It's all right."

"No, it's not. Look at what my presence has done to you—to others."

She sighed. Not the sigh of surrender, but a sigh of heart-warming goodness. "Yes, look what you did to me. You cared for me. You protected me. You loved me. Despite everything that's happened over the last couple of weeks, I'd do it all over again because I'm a better person when I'm with you."

"It's a good thing Dave never let you out of his sight, or you might know what a good man looks like, and I'd never have had a chance with you."

"Don't bring up Dave when I'm feeling all warm and fuzzy and romantic."

He pulled a bag of baby carrots out of the refrigerator and spread them around the roast. "Is your agent really going to let him go?" Next came the new potatoes.

"Dalton, you're shriveling my libido with talk about work." She plucked a stray carrot from the bag. "That's what he said. He told me he put in a call and will wait until Dave calls back."

"You think he'll do it?" He turned and slid the pan into the preheated oven.

"If he wants to work with me, he'll follow through. My contract is up after the next album and the benefit concert."

She reached around him for a glass, filled it with water, and popped two of the pain pills Doc Parker gave her. "Do you want to talk about Dave and Oliver, or do you want to take my mind off how much my hand hurts? I'll take your mind off how unfair the world can be."

He set the timer. "We have a couple of hours. Let's go to bed."

"Now, that's the best thing I've heard all day."

CHAPTER TWENTY-SEVEN

There was nothing more comforting than comfort food. Pot roast with carrots and potatoes topped that list with honors. They sat in front of his big screen television, ate, and binged *Supernatural* like it was crack and they were addicts.

A fire crackled in the fireplace. Samantha curled into Dalton's side. It was hard to think this wasn't ideal, but their relationship was complicated. In bed, they were perfection. In the bubble of their world, they were ideal, but they hadn't talked about tomorrow or next week or next year.

"This is perfect," he said. He moved them both so they were lying on the couch with her back to his front.

"It's too bad it isn't real." She melted against him like her body no longer had bones.

They'd loved the tension out of each other for an hour earlier, and she put tension back in him with those words.

"What part isn't real?"

She turned around to face him. "The part we don't talk about. The part where I have to go back to my life and leave you to yours."

"We can work it out." He had to stay positive, or the feelings of loss could swallow him whole. The thought of a day without Samantha would be as bad as the day the door closed and locked him in prison. That might have been better because he had a definitive date when things would go back to normal—his new normal.

Samantha lived states away. She spent months on the road. Her lifestyle didn't lend itself to normal. He remembered Doc's words. Samantha didn't come here to be Indigo. She came here to figure out who she was.

"You want a long-distance relationship?"

He rose up on one elbow and pushed the hair that had fallen into her face behind her ear so he could see her eyes. All truth was in Samantha's dark eyes. Looking into hers, he saw that she loved him as much as he loved her.

"Love looks different for everyone." He kissed her forehead. "I thought my life was pretty good before you came along. You showed up, and *bam*—I realized I was lying to myself. I'd be lying to you if I said long distance is what I want. It's not. I want you in my life and my bed every night, but I'll take what I can get. Some of you is infinitely better than none of you."

"You really should set your standards higher." She snuggled into his side and inhaled. She breathed him in like she was collecting his scent for a future he wouldn't be in.

"Higher than a hot-as-hell pop star who rocks my world and makes me feel like I can conquer anything when she's near?"

She laughed, and the vibration felt good against his chest. "When you put it that way, I guess I'm quite a catch."

"Have I caught you?"

"Dalton Black, I fell for you the day you left flowers and milk on my porch."

"Don't forget the bread and eggs," he said. "I only bring eggs to girls I'm sure to fall in love with." He pulled her against him and held her tight.

Her muffled voice asked, "Are there a lot of girls you've loved?"

"Three in my whole life."

She narrowed her eyes. He loved the way she couldn't help her jealousy.

"Were they pretty?"

"Stunning."

"Hmm. Do you see them around?"

He thumbed her chin so she was forced to look at him. "One is my mother. I see her regularly. One was Bea. It was a sad day when she left us, but she left a legacy of love. The last girl ... lately I've seen her a lot, but who knows what the future holds. All I know is I want one with her. I love you, Samantha. I don't care that you're a pop star. I don't care if you have a hundred houses dotted around the world or a million dollars in the bank. None of that matters to me. All I care about is making you happy and making you fall in love with me."

She swallowed hard like she was eating sand. "I've never said these words to anyone, but I love you, Dalton. Not because you're sex on a stick or because you have the most talented tongue in the universe or because you cook better than Bobby Flay. All I want is to care for you and love you so you don't regret the day you left me flowers and milk and bread and eggs."

She kissed him tenderly and passionately, and although she said the words for the first time, his heart felt like she'd told him a thousand times. When the kiss ended, he rose to a seated position. "Bobby Flay has cooked for you?"

She shook from a full belly laugh. "Yes. So have Wolfgang Puck, Gordon Ramsay, and Mario Batali, but they've got nothing on you." She curled into the corner of his leather couch and propped her feet on his lap. "You think I have a hundred houses?"

"No, but it sounded good. I imagine if we're going to try to make a go of this thing, and since we both let the L-word out, we should be transparent about our lives."

"You want transparency?"

"No, all I want is to be honest with you. Our relationship started on a mound of omissions. I'm an ex-felon. I killed a man. I'm a cook. Actually, I'm a cook at a diner. My employment potential is limited. I'll never be able to give you what you're used to, but I'll love you deeply. I don't care if your hair is blue, brown, or gray. I'll love you anyway." He reached over and laid his hand on her heart. "I love you here, and that's all that matters."

She pressed her left hand over his and pinned it to her chest.

"I'm a pop star. I love the music, but hate the fame. I have brown hair and plan to keep it that way. I own two properties. One is a house outside Los Angeles. One is a tiny cabin in Aspen Cove. I prefer Aspen Cove. I have a million dollars. Not on me but invested or in the bank. In fact, I have several, but it doesn't have the value that your love does. I don't know where all this will lead, but I'd like to find out."

She crawled across his body and straddled his lap. What they didn't finish on the couch, they completed in the bedroom. Exhausted, Samantha fell asleep naked in his arms. He wondered how he'd gotten so lucky. It was funny how luck came packaged as trouble. Samantha was that, but she was so much more.

He'd dozed off when the acrid smell of smoke filled the air. He was certain he'd banked the fire. His confidence faltered when the fire alarm rang through the silence.

He jumped out of his bed and into his jeans. He tugged on his boots and shook Samantha awake.

"Sweetheart, you need to get up. Get dressed."

She groaned and buried her head under the pillow.

"Samantha," he roared. "Get up. There's a fire."

That was one word that could wake anyone from a deep sleep.

She stumbled out of bed and struggled to get her clothes on. Dalton ran through his house but saw nothing. The fire alarms wailed in the distance.

When he stepped onto his porch, he saw Samantha's cabin engulfed in flames. He called it in. They had a phone tree for the volunteer firefighters, which included every able-bodied man in Aspen Cove.

Minutes later, while the wood of her cabin crackled and splintered under the heat, dozens of men donned whatever protective gear they had and went to work dousing the flames. Sage and Katie ran to get to Samantha, while Cannon and Bowie jumped into the melee. Even Doc Parker was there, beating back the fire so it didn't spread. In minutes, Samantha's car was set ablaze. As Bobby Williams raced with the hose to douse the new flames, it exploded, sending him back a dozen feet.

Dalton wanted to race to his friend, but Doc was already headed in that direction. The flames were out of control in the house. If they didn't get them under control, everyone nearby would lose their homes, including him.

The fire was already licking at the siding of his cabin. The freshly sandblasted section didn't stand a chance. Phillip Butler showed up with a case of bottled water from his Corner Store, and his wife carried boxes of snacks. It was a welcome gift for the firefighters.

The Dawson's only son and Lawyer Frank Arden showed up minutes later. They took charge of a hose and kept a steady stream of water where Dalton's siding had turned black.

He looked around for Samantha. He found her standing near Bowie and Katie's cabin with a look of horror on her face. He followed her line of sight to where Bobby laid on the ground with flames licking at his already burned skin. Dalton raced toward his friend to get him as far away from the smoke and flames as possible.

CHAPTER TWENTY-EIGHT

Samantha screamed. The scene was pure chaos as Doc rushed forward to provide care to Bobby, who only moments ago was on fire. Were it not for his quick actions, he would now be engulfed in flames.

Bowie rushed over and told Katie to pack up Sahara and go to Ben and Maisey's. Sage went straight into nurse mode. Samantha stood out of the way and knew this was all her fault. Dave Belton's words would haunt her for the rest of her life. *"Stay here, and I'll make sure everything you have goes up in flames."*

Doc asked Sage to call for an ambulance. He stood up and looked through the fog of black smoke. His hand went to his chest, and he hit the floor like a felled tree. Samantha raced over to help. She and Sage pulled Doc across the street. When he came to, he wasn't the same cantankerous old man she knew him to be. He was pale and quiet, and his breath wheezed from his chest.

Dalton carried Bobby Williams across the street and laid him down. "Call Louise and tell her he's hurt."

"I'll be okay," Bobby said. "Louise needs to be with the kids. I don't want her anywhere near this." Samantha recognized the man as the guy in the diner with the pregnant wife and seven children. Her heart broke. Holes burned through his jeans to show blistering and charred skin.

A loud crash drew their attention. The roof of Samantha's cabin gave way, collapsing into the house. Hot embers floated through the air.

"Go to my place and get as much ice and cold water as you can. There are baggies in the pantry. We need to stop the heat," Sage said.

Samantha took off like a sprinter toward the bed and breakfast. Because Sage often had guests, she was stocked with bags of ice. Samantha made quick work of gathering supplies and carried half her body weight in ice back to Sage.

"Get Doc to drink some water." Sage filled bags with ice and water and laid the cold packs on Bobby's legs.

Five minutes later, a hysterical Louise arrived. She dropped to her knees in front of her husband. "Don't you leave me, Bobby Williams. I can't raise eight kids by myself."

He raised a burned hand to her cheek. "Louise, I'm not going anywhere. We still have babies to make." The shrill of the sirens broke through the noise of the fire. Who would have thought a blaze could be so loud? It was almost deafening.

When the paramedics arrived, they praised Sage for her quick thinking by placing the ice packs on Bobby's burns and keeping Doc calm and quiet. He had a reputation for being a fighter, so to see him in such a sorry state shocked everyone.

Forty minutes later, two fire engines from Copper Creek came to put out what the volunteer force couldn't with their limited equipment.

Samantha couldn't believe that the town of Aspen Cove didn't have its own fire department. Then again, Aspen Cove didn't have much.

The sun was rising when the last of the volunteers left.

Cannon opened the bar for drinks, and Dalton told everyone he'd cook them breakfast if they gave him an hour.

Samantha sat across the street and looked at the utter devastation. Even Abby's bees had suffered. The ones that couldn't escape were devoured by the flames.

Her cabin had been reduced to a pile of smoke and ashes. Dalton's place stood, but the charred siding was sooty and black.

Sheriff Cooper took off, lights flashing and sirens wailing. She overheard Mark Bancroft tell everyone the arson case in Copper Creek had been solved. Turns out it wasn't arson after all. The house around the lake had burned down because of faulty wiring. Only Samantha's house was burned to the ground on purpose.

Dave Belton was caught racing out of town with enough accelerant to burn down the state of Colorado. He was always a man of his word. He'd made sure that she had only one option left, and that was to leave.

"Sweetheart?"

"I'm okay." She looked at what was left of her cabin. Among the ashes stood the fireplace. How funny that Dalton had accused her of trying to burn down the house, and it burned down anyway.

"I'm sure your insurance will rebuild the cabin. It will be better than before." Dalton squatted in front of her. His face was covered in soot and grime, but he was as sexy as ever. "It will turn out okay. It's all over."

He was right. It was over, but it would never be okay. She had to leave before another person suffered because of her. The problem was, Dalton would never let her go. He didn't blame her, despite the news of Dave's setting the fire spreading faster than the flames themselves. She blamed herself.

"This is all my fault."

"No. It's not. You didn't light the match, he did."

"I lit the match by pissing him off. I turned an ember into a blaze. You were right, I should have pressed charges. Had I done that, Bobby and Doc wouldn't be hurt. Bobby has seven kids and one on the way. I could have orphaned them all." Tears raced down her cheeks.

Dalton pulled her to standing and wrapped his strong arms around her. He smelled so good, like pine trees and pure man.

"Bobby will be fine. His burns will heal. Louise will take care of him. Doc has smoke inhalation. Some burning in his lungs. He's too ornery to stay down long. I'm worried about you. You look exhausted. Let's get you home and to bed."

She breathed him in, trying to save the smell and feel of him into her memory. There was only one thing left to do, and that was to leave. She'd make sure Aspen Cove and its people were cared for. When she first arrived, Katie told her that Aspen Cove took care of its own. Part of taking care of the ones you loved was protecting them. She was a liability.

Dave would no longer be a threat, but what about the next crazy person like Todd, or an overzealous paparazzo who would do anything to get the next sale-worthy photo? She couldn't risk it. She couldn't risk them.

"I am tired." Exhausted didn't begin to describe how she felt. She was devastated and hollowed out. Conflicted about what she wanted and what was best. Her heart told her to go to the diner and help Dalton serve the men who helped save the neighborhood. Without them, Samantha's house wouldn't have been the only one to burn. It would have spread down the line to Dalton's, Katie's, and Sage's. She owed them. Her payment would be her absence. She'd set up a fund to pay for Bobby's and Doc's medical bills. She'd make sure the town had the equipment they needed even if she had to build a firehouse. She'd ensure any lost wages were replaced. It was the least she could do. It was the easy thing to do. The hardest thing would be kissing Dalton goodbye and knowing it was for forever.

While Dalton took a shower, she gathered the few belongings

she had and raced to the bed when she heard the shower turn off. Dalton appeared with droplets of water running down his chest and a towel tied around his waist. All she wanted to do was pull him into bed and ask him to hold her, but that would make it harder to leave, so she closed her eyes when he entered the room and pretended she was asleep. After he dressed, he kissed her and said, "I love you."

She fought the urge to respond. The minute the front door closed, she jumped from the bed, called a car service in Copper Creek, and arranged for transportation.

An hour later, Samantha slipped out of Dalton's cabin and into a black town car. She made a quick stop at the bakery to tack her wishes onto the board. Only one was for her, the rest were for those she cared about.

She wished for Doc's quick recovery.

That Bobby Williams would be home soon with his family.

For Sage and Cannon to have the perfect wedding.

That Katie would have the boy she dreamed of having.

For Lydia to find a job.

That Cannon and Bowie would be there for Dalton.

And that Dalton would forgive her for everything.

Finally, it looked like luck was on her side because only Ben was present when she tacked the notes to the board. She bought a muffin for her driver. It was Thursday, and the poppy seed muffins couldn't be ignored. When she climbed into the back of the car, she curled into a tight ball and cried for the entire three-hour drive to Denver.

CHAPTER TWENTY-NINE

Dalton's ass was dragging when he entered the cabin. All he wanted to do was crawl into bed next to Samantha and hold her in his arms.

Though during the fire he appeared to be in control the whole time, he hadn't been. That asshole Dave could have killed them both. If they'd been in her cabin, who knows what could have happened? The dried wood and log siding burned like a grassfire. It went up so fast, there might not have been time to escape. It twisted his insides to see how close he came to losing his newfound love and happiness.

Samantha felt responsible, but she wasn't. Not once during breakfast did anyone say anything negative about her. They talked about the age of the house. That no one knew she was famous. That went a long way in her favor because weren't they all just people? Mostly the townsfolk talked about the idiot who thought bullying her could drive her away.

He toed off his boots at the door and took a deep breath. The air smelled like her under the lingering scent of smoke and fire. She was flowers and happiness and sunshine. He hurried down the hallway, and turned into the bedroom, only to find it dark, gloomy and empty.

He knew right away that she'd left him. Dave had won. There wasn't a trace of her around. Her phone was gone. She always tossed her bag and shoes in the corner, but the space was vacant. The only thing that remained was a note left on his pillow.

Dalton,

These are the hardest words I'll ever write. How do I tell the person I'm in love with goodbye? It would be impossible unless I knew that leaving was the right thing to do. I'm so sorry that I brought so much hurt to you and Aspen Cove. I will always love this town and the people who made it feel like home. I will always love you.

No matter where our lives lead us, please know that your name will be tattooed on my heart forever.

I am Samantha White.

You are Dalton Black.

The beauty of us will always lie in the gray.

Love

Samantha

Watermarks from her fallen tears marred the paper.

"She free-birded me and never intends to come back." He crumbled the page and tossed it across the room. "That's bullshit, and it's not going to happen."

Dalton started a pot of coffee. Outside of her new cell number, he had no way of contacting her. No way of knowing where she'd gone.

He dialed her number and was crushed when it went directly to voicemail.

A week later, he was still reaching out to her fan site. Sending letters to her record label and leaving messages with her assistant. He followed her on social media. Bought every one of her albums. Listening to her sing brought both joy and sorrow. He loved and hated the videos he found online where she talked to her fans about never giving up and finding your purpose.

He wanted to call her a liar. She'd given up on them. Then again, she'd sacrificed her own happiness out of some misplaced need to protect him.

When the demolition company arrived to remove the debris, Dalton felt a glimmer of hope. Maybe she would rebuild her cabin and return to rebuild their relationship. That dream was dashed when the following week, a for sale sign went up on the land.

He sat in front of the Wishing Wall one day, eating carrot cake muffins. Katie came out of the back with a stack of notes in her hand. Every few weeks, she'd sit down at a table and grant wishes.

"You need anything?"

"Yes. I need Samantha to come back to me."

She tossed a baggie of notes on the table and went to get a cup of decaf coffee. It was always decaf. She joked about Bowie being the only stimulation her heart needed.

"You love her?"

"Yes. Isn't it obvious?"

She sat down and placed the wishes into piles. He knew the routine. Had seen it many times. Knew that she put them into piles of yes, no, and maybe. This time, she had a fourth pile.

"Why are you here? If you love her that much, go and get her."

"Like that's so easy. I don't even know where she is. She won't answer my calls. I've sent dozens of flowers to every Samantha White I can find in the Greater Los Angeles Area. I've got quite a fan club of my own now."

Katie laughed. "You know where she'll be next week."

He knew. She'd be at the concert to benefit victims of domestic violence. "I'm glad they didn't cancel the concert." Maybe her leaving him was good after all. At least the venue would be full and the money would go to a good cause.

She slid a pile of sticky notes to him. "I think these fall in your lane."

Dalton raised his brow in confusion. "I'm not the wish granter."

"Today you are, and if you decide you want to go after what's important, I can help. I used to be a Middleton, and that still holds some influence."

Dalton leaned back in his seat. The metal design cut into his back. He opened the first note in the pile. It was dated the day after Samantha arrived. *A kiss from Dalton Black would be nice.* In his mind, he said, *Granted.* The second note written in her precise tiny handwriting said, *Is it silly to wish for love?*

"No."

Katie looked up from her pile. "Excuse me?"

Dalton shook his head. "Nothing, I was thinking out loud."

She sipped her coffee. "Then say, yes."

"But it's not silly for her to wish for love."

"No, but it's silly for her to think she doesn't deserve it."

He agreed, but how could he convince her that she was worthy if he couldn't get in the same time zone as her?

He opened the other notes that had wishes from the press leaving him alone to her wish for him to forgive her.

He pulled out his phone and dialed his parole officer.

"You better not be in jail," she said. He could hear the whinny of a horse in the background.

"Hell, no." Thankfully, there was no paper trail of him getting detained weeks ago. If Lucy thought he'd been in trouble, she'd never allow him to leave the state. "I'm leaving the state for a short period. Thought I'd check in."

"You asking permission?"

Was he? The truth was, no. He'd be leaving whether or not she said it was okay.

"I'm not asking for your permission. I'm following your advice. I fell in love, and I'm making sure she knows it. She can run and hide, but I'll find her, and I'll bring her back. We've got memories and babies to make."

"Hmm, I didn't hear you right. Sounded like you were going to stalk and kidnap someone, but what I think you really meant was, you were going to travel somewhere to tell your woman you love her. That's what I heard, right?"

He laughed. "Yes, that's what I said."

She cleared her throat but still sounded like she'd smoked a pack that day. "Call me when you get back."

"Will do." Dalton ended the call and picked up the notes. He opened his wallet and slid them inside. "Now all I need is a way into the concert and a ticket to California."

Katie held up a finger. She dialed her phone. "Daddy, this is Katie. I need a favor."

Turns out that once a Middleton meant always a Middleton. And being a Middleton came with perks.

CHAPTER THIRTY

"Call him." Deanna flopped onto the sofa across from Samantha.

They sat in her Malibu Canyon house and looked out the wall of glass. The sky was blue and crystal clear, but her mood was black. Not even chocolate made her smile. What seemed like a reasonable choice a few weeks ago was clouded with uncertainty now.

She'd done what she could for Aspen Cove and followed up on the recovery of Doc and Bobby. She'd even taken measures to build the town a firehouse so they could have their own truck. If they couldn't afford to pay for firemen, she was prepared to cover that expense as well. No person should have to depend on volunteers to save their life.

Samantha thought she'd done the right thing by leaving, but her broken heart told her differently. She ached for Dalton. There wasn't a second of any day where she didn't think of him, feel the ghost of his love hold her, kiss her, and love her.

"I can't call him. I left him. He probably hates me." She'd recited the letter she'd written him over and over in her mind. "I'm a coward."

"Why do you keep saying that?"

"Because I couldn't face him. I left him a Dear John letter. Who does that? I write lyrics that every woman feels, but I couldn't talk to the man I love. I should have told him face to face, but I knew ... I knew he'd tell me to stay, and I knew I wouldn't say no."

"You need to fix this." Deanna kicked her feet up on the coffee table.

"I have. Everyone is okay. Workers will start on Dalton's house next week. He'll show up, and it will be done. I've set up funds for the injured. Planned for the future. It's fixed."

"For being such a smart woman, you are so stupid." Deanna turned her laptop toward Samantha. "Do you see this folder?" She pressed her computer across the space between them. "Over a hundred messages asking for you to call him. You think he wants to tell you he hates you? This *isn't* fixed."

"What was I supposed to do?" Her voice wavered. She thought she'd cried herself dry, but there seemed to be an endless supply of tears for Dalton.

"You were supposed to stay. You didn't, so the next best thing is to go home and make it right."

Samantha covered her face with her hands. "I don't have a home."

Deanna moved to the space beside her. "Home isn't always a place. It can be a feeling. It can be as simple as knowing someone loves you, no matter what." She pressed her finger against the computer screen. "Dalton Black is your home."

* * *

THREE DAYS LATER, SAMANTHA STOOD BACKSTAGE WHILE THE crowd chanted, "In-di-go, In-di-go, In-di-go". She couldn't believe that not too long ago a different crowd chanted the same. That night she'd walked into the mass of fans and disappeared, hoping to find clarity, only to come back more confused.

She adjusted the blue wig and applied her watermelon lip gloss. It reminded her of Dalton. Everything reminded her of Dalton. Since her return, all she ate was grilled cheese and tomato soup because it made her feel closer to him.

She gave Jake his exclusive interview, which was more about Dalton than about her. She asked him to send it to print the day before the concert. If people were going to talk about him, she wanted them to know the truth. Jake had found Bethany Waters and interviewed her as well. She told the world her story about the man who saved her life.

Samantha asked Jake to send a copy directly to Dalton because at the end of the interview when Jake asked her if she had any regrets, she told him yes. Her biggest regret was abusing herself. By leaving Dalton, she'd eviscerated her heart and soul. The longer she was separated from him, the more battered she felt. She'd given him her heart and left it behind. The last line of the story said, "I gave away my heart to the most deserving of men. I abandoned him in the most cowardly way. I only hope that he'll forgive me and tell me to come home."

Ray asked where home was for Samantha White, and she pressed her hand over her heart. The place where she'd tattooed his name. "Home is where Dalton is."

"Indigo, you're on in five," Oliver Shepherd called from the door of her dressing room. They'd had several meetings concerning their future together. He'd released her from her last album, hoping to sign her for three more. He wasn't the enemy. She'd been her own enemy. She'd allowed her fears to paralyze her. She'd allowed Dave to take over because it was easier. One thing she learned along the way was, easy wasn't always best. Some things were worth fighting for.

Freedom.

Family.

The truth.

Her reputation.

Friendship.

Change.

Love.

Those were the things worth battling for. The hardest fight should always be for love.

Samantha looked down at her cast. In faded silver letters, she saw Dalton's inscription. "It's all about love."

Yes, it is. She put on her headset and made her way to the side of the stage. Deanna stood by with a bottle of water.

"Everything you want is out there."

Samantha gave her a weak smile. "Not everything."

Deanna gave her a push. "Yes. Everything," she said and winked.

The only thing Samantha wanted was a second chance. She put on her game face and rushed out to please the crowd. "Hello, Los Angeles!" Her voice didn't reveal her brokenness. Dave had been right about one thing. The fans looked to her for hope and inspiration. She'd give it to them.

She looked into the crowd of thousands and wondered how many of them had ever felt a love as profound as she felt for Dalton. "I'm so happy to be here tonight."

She looked at the signs people held that said, "I love you."

"I love you, too, but I want to start off by saying that you have to love yourself first. Allow yourself to be loved. Many of you are the victims of abuse. Love doesn't come easy, but open your hearts because love is worth it."

She walked to the edge of the stage and shook a few hands. The band played one of the songs she wrote while in Aspen Cove. "This is a song I wrote for a very special man. I want Dalton Black to know that I love him. It's called 'One Hundred Wishes'. My wishes begin and end with him." She took a deep breath. Saying his name made her heart race. "A woman told me that wishes cost nothing; that thoughts were important. Let's hear everyone scream out a wish." She held out her microphone while the crowd screamed their wishes.

Her headset crackled and hissed. She adjusted the volume, hoping the interference would disappear. She tapped on the earpiece, but it didn't help. In a low voice she recognized, she heard, "My wish is for you to come home. Come home to me." It played over and over and over until it was no longer in her headset but echoing through the stadium. The electronic displays flashed the words *come home, come home, come home to me.*

Confused, she turned to stage left where she'd left Deanna and found she was no longer there. She turned to stage right, which was also empty. The beat of the song got louder. Dalton's voice was modulated to fill in the backbeat. She moved to center stage, confused. She lifted the microphone to sing. The crowd parted, and up the steps walked Dalton Black, dressed to kill. He was a man of simple tastes, but he made jeans and a black T-shirt look better than an Armani suit.

Samantha stopped dead still. She blinked several times to make sure he was there. The crowd went wild. Many held signs that read, "Dalton is my hero." Her heart nearly seized.

"See ... wishes do come true." She threw herself into his arms. After he twirled her around and kissed her stupid, he set her down. "You've got a concert to perform."

She looked into his blue eyes. How she ever thought they looked like cold steel, she didn't know. They were filled with molten blue love. "Don't leave me."

He shook his head. "Never."

"What happens next?" Afraid that he'd disappear, she didn't want to let him go.

"I'm taking you home."

"You're here. I'm home already."

For the next hour and fifty-two minutes, Samantha sang about love and hope, and she believed every word that came out of her mouth because clarity wasn't always found in the messiness of life. It was found in the eyes of love.

CHAPTER THIRTY-ONE

Samantha had been back in Aspen Cove for a week, but no one would have known it because she and Dalton barely left the bed. They got up only to shower, eat, and binge-watch *Supernatural*.

"You're really buying the paper mill?" Dalton's hand rubbed her bare stomach, which was no longer concave. His skills in the kitchen came second only to his skills in the bedroom. His fingers trailed up her stomach to her chest, where she'd tattooed the word 'Dalton's' over her heart.

"Yes, I'm investing in some much-needed improvements here in Aspen Cove."

"What are you going to do here?"

She rolled her naked body on top of him. She knew he wouldn't have much to say because he couldn't think when they were naked.

"I'm building a recording studio. It's a bit selfish, but I never want to leave home again."

"Sometimes we have to be selfish." Several times, their friends had come to the door to say hello and Dalton growled at them that he wasn't ready to share her, but tonight was karaoke night, and he had no choice. "What else is going in the paper mill?"

She ran her hands down his chest. Goosebumps rose beneath her fingertips. "It will be the Guild Creative Center. I want it to be a place where artistic people can thrive. Wes is putting put a culinary center next to a recording studio because I like to eat. I hope this sexy chef I know will be willing to work there on the days he's not working at Maisey's. I'm thinking maybe you can sell ready-made meals. You know, like take-and-bake. That would be a community service. No one would have to eat Sage's frozen lasagna again."

Dalton laughed. "I think we can negotiate on that."

"Now you want to negotiate?" She leaned down and bit his lip.

"No, right now I want to make love to my girlfriend. Who will be my fiancée, and then my wife, and the mother of my perfect children."

"Confident, are you?" She felt his confidence firm and long between her thighs.

"Would you have me any other way?" He lifted her hips and set her on top of him.

"I'll have you any way I can get you." She loved the way his eyes rolled back when she sank onto his length. The way he moaned her name when she rocked against him. The way loved flowed through his kisses.

"I'm all yours, baby." Dalton turned them over so he was on top. He found the perfect rhythm that made her body sing. How lucky was she to make love to a man who proved to be as yummy on the inside as he looked on the outside?

They made love right up until they had to shower and leave.

At six o'clock, they were the first to arrive for karaoke night. Cannon and Sage stood behind the bar.

"Did you come up for air?" Cannon asked.

"No, we came up for wine." Dalton slid onto a barstool and pulled Samantha into his lap.

"Are you hungry?" Sage wore a smile. In her hands were a spatula and a pan of frozen lasagna.

"No!" they said together.

"You're being mean. It's perfectly fine lasagna."

Everyone including Cannon shook their heads.

Next came Doc, followed by a white-haired woman everyone greeted as Agatha. Samantha's heart broke when Doc turned and she saw the oxygen tank and tubes. He wouldn't be singing "Hound Dog" tonight.

Dalton wrapped his arms around her. "Not your fault. No one blames you."

The door opened, and in walked Bobby and Louise Williams. She proudly displayed her baby bump and walked straight for Samantha.

"Thank you."

Samantha sucked in a big breath.

"For what?"

"I know you thought what happened was a bad thing. It wasn't a good thing, but it wasn't your fault. I'm thanking you because I got to have Bobby home for several weeks. We claimed some quality time together. It was like when we dated. When he was my boyfriend and I was his girlfriend."

"Doc has a girlfriend," Sage sang.

"Come here, you." Doc flagged her over. As soon as she got within range, he cuffed her lightly on the side of the head. "Get my Agatha a glass of wine. I'll have a cup of joe. Tell me again when that sister of yours is coming to take over? Louise is bound to have her last baby before then if she doesn't hurry."

Samantha looked to Dalton. "Doc and Agatha?"

He shrugged. "I told you love was like a virus. I got it. You caught it, and Doc caught it. Never too old to give love a chance."

A lot had happened while she was gone. "Lydia is coming?" she asked.

"That's the rumor, but that's all it is until she shows up." Dalton caught the pint of beer Cannon slid down the bar.

Next in the door were Katie and Bowie. Katie ran up to Samantha. "Did Daddy's jet work out okay?"

Samantha blushed. They had the plane to themselves and hit the mile high club twice on the short trip home. "It was amazing." She turned to Dalton. "Do you think we should get a plane like that?"

His eyes grew wide. "Can you afford a plane like that?"

She could see the list of possibilities running through his imagination.

"Probably."

Dalton tucked her close to his body and set his chin on top of her head. "No ... but maybe we can get a dock and a Jet Ski."

She picked up the glass of wine Cannon had poured her and smiled over the rim. "You're cheap," she told him.

"I may be cheap, but I'm not easy."

She made a *pfft* sound and rolled her eyes. "You are *so* easy." She turned in his lap and kissed him. Her voice softened. "Easy to love."

Katie kicked off karaoke night with another oldie but goodie. When she finished, she brought the mic to Samantha, who was happy to get up and sing for her friends, but Dalton took it and walked her to the stage. He set her on a stool in the center and looked into her eyes.

"This is a onetime deal. I'd hate to subject the town to this more than once in a lifetime." He picked his music and turned to Samantha. "This is for you." When he sang 'Amazed' by Lonestar, she nearly fell off her seat. Though Dalton's cooking skills and bedroom skills outshined his singing skills, the song was pitch-perfect because he sang to the deepest part of her heart. The part that belonged only to him.

When he finished, she was more in love with him than she thought possible.

When Samantha had walked off that stage in Denver months ago, there were three things she wanted more than money.

She wanted a life.

She wanted to love.

She wanted the freedom that came with being invisible.

Aspen Cove gave her life.

Dalton gave her love.

And Samantha realized she'd never be invisible. Not to her fans. Not to her friends. Not to the one man who hadn't known her and saw who she was anyway.

As she looked around Bishop's Brewhouse, she knew without a doubt she was home.

GET A FREE BOOK.

Go to www.authorkellycollins.com

ABOUT THE AUTHOR

International bestselling author of more than thirty novels, Kelly Collins writes with the intention of keeping the love alive. Always a romantic, she blends real-life events with her vivid imagination to create characters and stories that lovers of contemporary romance, new adult, and romantic suspense will return to again and again.

For More Information
www.authorkellycollins.com
kelly@authorkellycollins.com

OTHER BOOKS BY KELLY COLLINS

An Aspen Cove Romance Series

One Hundred Reasons

One Hundred Heartbeats

One Hundred Wishes

One Hundred Promises

One Hundred Excuses

One Hundred Christmas Kisses

One Hundred Lifetimes

One Hundred Ways

One Hundred Goodbyes

One Hundred Secrets

One Hundred Regrets

One Hundred Choices

One Hundred Decisions

One Hundred Glances

One Hundred Lessons

One Hundred Mistakes

Cross Creek Novels

Broken Hart

Fearless Hart

Guarded Hart

Recipes for Love

A Tablespoon of Temptation

A Pinch of Passion

A Dash of Desire

A Cup of Compassion

A Dollop of Delight

The Second Chance Series

Set Free

Set Aside

Set in Stone

Set Up

Set on You

The Second Chance Series Box Set

Holiday Novels

The Trouble with Tinsel

Wrapped around My Heart

Cole for Christmas

Christmas Inn Love

Mistletoe and Millionaires

Up to Snow Good

Wilde Love Series

Betting On Him

Betting On Her

Betting On Us

A Wilde Love Collection

The Boys of Fury Series

Redeeming Ryker

Saving Silas

Delivering Decker

The Boys of Fury Boxset

A Beloved Duet

Still the One

Always the One

Beloved Duet

Small Town Big Love

What If

Imagine That

No Regrets

Small Town Big Love Boxset

Frazier Falls

Rescue Me

Shelter Me

Defend Me

The Frazier Falls Collection

Stand Along Billionaire Novels (Steamy)

Risk Taker

Dream Maker

ACKNOWLEDGMENTS

I started out with book one of the Aspen Cove Series with the goal of writing a heartwarming small town romance. I had a series in mind but didn't know if readers would love my small town full of quirky people.

Boy was I glad you do because I love writing about this town.

None of this would be as good without an editor. Thanks to Brooke for her work on this manuscript.

Thanks to the ladies who proofread this book. Judy, Sabrina, Melissa and Tammy, what would I do without your keen eyes?

Thank you to Victoria Cooper for the amazing cover which is photographed by Darren Birks of Darren Birks Photography. He made the perfect Dalton and Catherine made the perfect Samantha.

Last, but never least, I thank you the reader for being loyal fans. I hope you enjoy your time in Aspen Cove. There's so much more to come.

Printed in Great Britain
by Amazon

62633036R00271